EXPRESS ELEVATOR TO HELL

Instead of being smashed flat at the bottom of an elevator shaft, Sandy found himself in a shadowy room being stared at by a scraggly-bearded old geezer. Whatever the old man may have been, he was no fever dream—his saffron yellow robe was marred with acid stains, he stank of sweat and old cabbage, and he was mad as hell about something.

Not exactly the stuff of fantasy, thought Sandy.

"What manner of demon are you?" screeched the old man. "And how dare you interfere with the sorcery of Zhadnoboth the Great!"

"SOARS INTO NEW DIMENSIONS
OF IMAGINATION . . .
I AM IMPATIENT FOR THE SEQUEL!"
Marvin Kaye,
author of *A Cold Blue Light*

Worlds of Fantasy from Avon Books

BLOOD OF THE COLYN MUIR
*by Paul Edwin Zimmer &
Jon DeCles*

THE CRYSTAL WARRIORS
*by William R. Forstchen &
Greg Morrison*

THE DRAGON WAITING
by John M. Ford

THE GRYPHON KING
by Tom Deitz

THE PIG, THE PRINCE & THE UNICORN
by Karen A. Brush

TALKING MAN
by Terry Bisson

THE XANTH SERIES
by Piers Anthony
VALE OF THE VOLE
HEAVEN CENT

Coming Soon in the Xanth Series
MAN FROM MUNDANIA

A NAME TO CONJURE WITH

Donald Aamodt

AVON BOOKS · NEW YORK

AVON BOOKS
A division of
The Hearst Corporation
105 Madison Avenue
New York, New York 10016

Copyright © 1989 by Donald Aamodt
Front cover illustration by Tim Jacobus
Published by arrangement with the author
Library of Congress Catalog Card Number: 88-92973
ISBN: 0-380-75137-2

First Avon Books Printing: August 1989

AVON TRADEMARK REG. U.S. PAT. OFF. AND IN OTHER COUNTRIES, MARCA REGISTRADA, HECHO EN U.S.A.

Printed in the U.S.A.

K–R 10 9 8 7 6 5 4 3 2 1

To Marvin Kaye for discovering I was a writer and then making me become serious about it.

To my editor Chris Miller for whipping my manuscript into shape and forcing me to become a better writer.

To my daughters Jennifer and Britt without whose help I would have finished this book much sooner.

To my wife Karen for her invaluable help as first reader and stubborn critic.

And to Olsen and Johnson who once were kind to a twelve-year-old boy.

1

SANDY stared dumbfounded at his bowl of wonton soup—or what should have been a bowl of wonton soup: the bowl was empty and as dry as a bone. A moment before it had been brimming full. He'd taken a spoonful and dipped for another and found there was no more.

Hesitantly he reached forward and touched the bowl. It was real and as dry as it looked. Sandy shivered involuntarily. He poked at it again and got the same result. With a shaking hand Sandy wiped his brow and briefly wondered whether he was losing his mind. Then his innate tough-mindedness took over and he glared at the bowl as though he held it personally responsible for the situation. The bowl was there, it was empty, and that was that. Therefore the world was crazy, not Sandy.

This effort in positive thinking should have made him feel better. Instead, Sandy felt worse. The situation wasn't logical, and his subconscious knew it and was scared stiff. Disappearing soup is a small thing, but at the same time it is impossible. With a cold shudder, Sandy began wondering how real the world under his feet was.

He grabbed the soup bowl and hefted it. The weighty feel of it in his hand shocked him, its stark reality clashing with what had happened. Sandy glanced down at the paper place mat, colorfully decorated with the twelve beasts which symbolize the Chinese cycle of years, and hopefully searched for some hidden trapdoor or other explanation just as unreasonable. But he saw nothing except solid paper unmarred even by a spot, as he feared he would.

He remembered certain minor and yet unexplainable events from his past and shivered. They hadn't meant much to him when they occurred, but in light of what had just happened, he wondered. One of the burdens of his life was a talent for losing things. He had always assumed there was a logical explanation for the disappearances, but now he was unsure. Certainly the steel chisel he'd lost in the middle of a bare basement floor and the book he'd lost while reading in bed were hard to explain.

A wild thought popped into his head: Maybe he had some weird psychic power to make things disappear. Immediately he began to feel better. A lame explanation, but for now it soothed him.

Just then the Chinese waiter, third son of the restaurant owner and a philosophy student at Johns Hopkins, came with the rest of Sandy's order, and hunger drove all thoughts of uncanny happenings from his head. Once or twice Sandy did glance uneasily at his food, but the barbecued ribs and fried rice were remarkable only for how delicious they tasted and for nothing else.

Afterward, while Sandy sipped on some oolong tea and glanced idly at the ribs he had chewed down to nubbins, he experienced a momentary qualm. *How real is the world?*

He shrugged it off, telling himself the soup *could* have vanished because of some psychic talent he had, but more likely because of some quirk in his memory. His belly was pleasantly full and he felt at peace with the world. He was in no mood to believe in unexplainable events.

After his waiter had cleared away the dirty dishes and left behind a fortune cookie, Sandy poured himself another cup of oolong and relaxed. Lazily he picked up the fortune cookie, broke it open, and pulled out the slip of paper from inside. It was a small pleasure which went with Chinese restaurants, learning what destiny had in store for you. Unfolding the paper, he read, "An unexpected journey awaits you." Sandy sighed. He wished the fortune might come true, but as it was he could barely scare up enough money to get out of town.

He felt a twinge of envy for his parents, who had just left for a two-month trip to Scandinavia. He should really save his cash instead of spending it on fine food, good books, and fast women. Still, it was fun.

With a pang of foreboding, he thought of the soup and wondered whether its message might be a warning. No, he decided with some regret. This world was too stodgy for anything so magical to be true.

Feeling full and content with the world and Saturday afternoon, Sandy stepped out of the pleasant dimness of the restaurant and blinked as the bright afternoon sun hit his eyes. He paused while his pupils adjusted to the light and then began walking jauntily down the street, whistling a merry tune as he did so. It was three blocks to his apartment and he enjoyed walking, especially on such a good day.

Barely half a block from the restaurant, he was engulfed in a sudden downpour. He cursed and dashed to a nearby doorway. "Damn those weathermen," he muttered, shaking the rain off himself. "They always predict a week of sunshine just before the sky decides to fall in."

Sandy peeked out of the doorway to check on the storm and his jaw dropped open in disbelief. The downpour wasn't there. Instead, the sun blazed goldenly in a bright blue and absolutely cloudless sky. The street and the sidewalk were dry and coated with many days accumulation of dust. Nowhere was there even a faintly damp spot. Sandy looked down at his soaking clothes and then at the dry sidewalk. He leaned against the doorway as his knees became weak. He shook his head and wondered if he, the world, or both were becoming unglued.

A voice cackled from behind Sandy, "Do you want your fortune told, good sir? Do you want to see what wonders lie ahead of you?" The words had an old, used feel to them, but there was also an undertone of mystery and power.

Sandy started and whirled about. In the open door behind him stood an old crone.

Her ivory teeth formed into a sharkish smile and she reached forward, grabbing his arm with a hand of iron. Too bewildered to resist, Sandy allowed her to pull him into her dusty lair. The room was dark, with the very air seemingly made of shadows, and furnished only with a battered table and two rickety chairs. The chairs were bare wood, but the table made claims to grandeur: it was covered by a shabby cloth of black velvet, spangled with tarnished silver images of stars and moons.

Despite its down-at-the-heels look, the room felt weird and disquieting; and the woman was a fit occupant for it. She was inches shorter than five feet tall, wrinkled, bent—and for all of that he could feel a quiet power smoldering within her. The piercing black eyes framing her Roman nose were filled with hard-won wisdom, and undimmed by age. She dressed the part of a gypsy, but seemed more an ancient and proud queen.

"Five dollars is all I charge, fine sir. A small price to pay for a true glimpse of what lies ahead." The words were spoken as though she was playing at being an illiterate old biddy and yet there was a force in them belying their shabby disguise. Halfheartedly, Sandy started to protest. She held up a finger for silence and croaked, "Old Betty sees the truth. She is not like those Romany cheats who sham their foresight."

She maneuvered him to a chair and pushed his unwilling body onto it, despite the fact that he was a husky six-footer and she was a scrawny little stick. Somehow, a moment later, Sandy found himself handing over the last five in his wallet.

Her sharp white teeth glittered wolfishly as she shoved the money into her many-colored sash, blew the dust off her crystal ball, and sat in the chair across the table from him. Sandy blinked; he didn't remember the crystal ball being there before. The witch made a great show of going into a trance; her weird glass-eyed stare might have been enough to convince most normal fools she was in another world. Sandy was not so sure. He thought that for one instant he had caught a glimpse of a canny and most calculating look from one of those supposedly entranced eyes.

For long moments Old Betty stared intently into the crystal ball. Restless, Sandy wished she would get the charade over with so he could get out of there and feel less like a fool easily parted from his money.

Suddenly she began cackling words—much like the mumbojumbo he had expected. "Watch them well: man of sorcery, man of vengeance, and she who rules them all. Fortune, adventure, and love await."

There was a pause and then her voice rose in a shriek. "Beware! Beware! The black one from beyond comes. There is victory—there is death." Old Betty gave a convulsive shudder and came out of her trance.

Despite his doubts, Sandy had to hand it to her, she certainly made the performance seem real. Sweat was on her brow, terror in her eyes, and there was a dead-white pallor to her skin. The only thing marring her act was the gibberish she had spouted, the same unimaginative junk you'd expect from any other third-rate fortune teller.

Unsteadily she got to her feet and gave him a strange look filled with surprise, a little respect, and something almost like kinship. It was a look which shook his faith in her as a charlatan; there was too much belief in it.

The old woman turned and called in a soft and urgent voice. "Katya! Come to granny, child." There was a moment of quiet. Then the black velveteen curtain which covered the back wall of the room rustled and a young girl appeared.

Her dark hair was neatly braided and she was smartly dressed in a frock of pale orange and white gingham. What Sandy most noticed, however, was her wide-eyed stare and shy air. She seemed fey, and timid.

"Come to me, child," said the crone in a tender voice. Sandy watched silently, noticing how her cackle had sweetened when she spoke to the child and how her words were no longer those of an uneducated person. The girl hesitated for a moment, then darted shyly to Old Betty's side. The crone placed loving hands on the girl's shoulders and turned her to face Sandy.

"This is my granddaughter's youngest. Only she, of all my kin, has inherited any of my gift." There was quiet pride in her voice as she smiled fondly on the girl. A faraway look came into her eyes and she said, "When she is grown, I shall go, and leave one who is greater behind."

The old woman turned her eyes back to Sandy and he felt his skin prickle. It was as though she looked into his soul.

"Would you do an old woman a favor?" she asked in a grave, quiet voice. "The ways of my people may seem strange to you, but they have served us well through the ages. Place your hand on her head and bless her. It is our custom to seek such gifts from those we deem touched by destiny."

Her words troubled him, but he reached forward and placed his hand on the little girl's head. Silently he wished her blessed, calling on who or whatever would answer the prayers of a skeptic like himself. Sandy wondered if he did it because it seemed so right or if deep down he truly believed. Although he knew he was in the same dull old world as ever, the moment seemed magical. Maybe it was the utter faith of the old woman and the girl in what he was doing, but he thought he felt something pass through him and into the girl.

Sandy lifted his hand from her head and realized he felt a great satisfaction—the feeling you get when you give something only because your heart tells you to. Sandy smiled wryly to himself and wondered what he was coming to, giving nothing and feeling good about it. Still, he felt refreshed and slightly different.

"Thank you, good sir," said the old woman formally, almost ritually. Sandy started to protest, but she waved his interruption aside. "Perhaps we shall never see each other again in this life, but we will have memories and a new taste to our souls."

Sandy nodded dazedly at her odd words and turned to leave.

"Wait," called the old woman. "You must hear the foretelling you paid for." She closed her eyes and in a crooning voice began to speak. "You will have a long, long life filled with hardship and danger, but also filled with your share of its joys. The time of destiny is almost upon you; accept it and be glad. Though your way will often be hard, it is the price of such a gift as will be yours. For you, as well as for me, the ordinary is out of reach. We are touched by the strange and can only be walkers of the less traveled roads."

Sandy doubted the foretelling, but there was a poetry in the words which moved him.

The old woman sighed and opened her eyes. Her hand reached up and touched his forehead in a gesture of blessing and she said, "Go now. My thanks and my thoughts go with you."

Out on the sidewalk, Sandy found himself ambling toward his apartment. He shook his head to clear out the mental cobwebs and wondered whether any of it had really happened.

Then Sandy laughed at his brooding thoughts and pushed them out of his mind. Whatever his day had been, it had certainly been a change from his usual routine. Lately, finding a new restaurant or reading a good book was as adventurous as his life got.

For a moment he daydreamed, thinking how nice it would be if some adventure came along to spice up his life. Maybe he should have done some wandering after he had served his hitch in the army instead of settling down with a good solid government job as unexciting as it was secure. The only interesting part was the names of some of the people making claims for benefits from the government. He couldn't believe that some people had the names they had; names that would never be believed in novels—like the seventy-year-old man named Pretty Baby.

Still, he decided, he was a stick-in-the-mud and preferred it that way. He'd had a few wild adventures when he was younger and less sensible and found them more bother than they were worth: adventures weren't comfortable and you didn't always get your meals on time. He rubbed the scar on the side of his head and smiled at old memories.

When Sandy got out of the elevator, he first blinked in surprise and then beamed with pleasure. The gorgeous red-head—and he had a fatal weakness for redheads—who lived down the hall was knocking at his door. Maybe Old Betty hadn't been so far wrong. It was a day for miracles.

Sandy started toward his door. The redhead turned around, flashing an incandescent smile that swept him off his feet. He was a pushover, especially for women with eyes the color of new grass and long, billowing hair which glowed like a hazy sunset. "Hi," she said, and her voice was soft velvet. "My name is Chris—we've met in the halls several times. My roommates and I are giving a party tonight for people living in the building, it'll give us a chance to get acquainted. We wondered if you would come."

Sandy blushed very faintly—he'd had some success with women, but still was a bit shy. "Sure," he answered in what he hoped was a normal-sounding voice, "I'd love to come." He paused briefly, at a loss for words, and then bumbled out, "Can I bring anything?"

"Some munchies and something to drink would be nice. Thanks!" she replied. She gave him a cheery wave and hurried toward her own door, suddenly skittish for some reason. At the door she halted and called back over her shoulder, "Be there about eight." Then like a wisp of smoke she was gone.

Sandy stood for a moment in the hall, filled with a rosy glow. He'd liked her from the first time he had seen her, and had wondered how to make her acquaintance. Once he knew somebody he got along well; he just had trouble getting a relationship started. Now she had done the asking and Sandy felt he was on his way. Thank God for bold women.

Whistling happily, Sandy unlocked his door and stepped into his apartment. Once inside, he began sorting through the mail he'd picked up on his way into the building. The two bills he threw into the cream-colored stoneware bowl sitting on a dropleaf table by the door. The letter from his brother in Brazil he guiltily laid aside to be read later. He was the

most forgetful correspondent possible; Bob was lucky if he
got two letters a year from him. The one remaining letter
looked interesting. On the ivory-tinted envelope was his address written in a fine feminine hand, but the return address
named someone Sandy had never heard of.

Impatiently he tore the letter open and began to read it.
Then he gave a snort of disgust, crumpled the letter up into a
ball, and threw it into the wastebasket. *Why do I get all these
nut letters?* he asked himself. Somehow he wasn't too worried about the doom of the lord striking him down unless he
sent ten dollars and forwarded copies of the letter to five
other people.

Still grumbling about dotty con artists who thought him a
fool, Sandy ambled to his kitchen. He hadn't shopped lately,
so except for some cereal, several cans of soup, and half a
quart of milk he had nothing resembling "munchies." And
checking his wallet, he realized he had barely enough money
to buy a bottle of cheap wine. Cursing himself for being
softheaded and the old lady for bamboozling him, Sandy
began scrounging through his apartment for spare cash and
found a quarter, two pennies, and four nickels.

Sandy looked at his loose change and frowned. No help
for it. He hurried over to his battered rolltop desk and sorted
through the junk crammed into it until he found his bank
card. Once he could get to the automatic teller he'd have
enough money to get the necessaries.

Sandy started to leave, stopped in his tracks and swore,
and then hurriedly rummaged through his desk again. He
gave a great sigh of relief when he found the secret number
to go with his bank card. The last time he had tried to use the
machine he'd punched in the wrong number several times
and the damned machine had refused to give him back his
card. It had taken more than a week to get it back from the
bank and then they had made him feel like a criminal. It
wasn't his fault that machines instinctively disliked him.

Still whistling, Sandy headed down the hall toward the
elevator. Fantasies about the redheaded Chris floated pleasantly through his mind while he waited for the elevator to
creak all the way up to his floor. There was a good feel to
her, and he wanted to know her better. The doors opened
and he stepped into the elevator, oblivious to the world
around him.

That was a fatal mistake.

Sandy's foot came down on nothing and he tumbled forward into a pit of blackness. The shock of plunging into an abyss yanked him from his rosy dreams and he stared wildly about. A scream of pure horror came from him as he felt and saw himself falling to a sure doom at the bottom of this lightless dark. Sheer terror overloaded his brain's circuits and he passed out. Oddly, his last conscious thought was about Chris, her red hair, and an aching pain at the opportunity lost forever.

2

GLOWING with many shades of blue and white, a comet flashed through the night sky and into the constellation called the House of the Goddess. Below, inside her citadel of jade and crystal, the shadow which was the Goddess watched and rejoiced. Through seemingly endless centuries she had awaited the moment when she could begin to redeem what she had lost and gain vengeance for what she had suffered. Still, despite the fierce joy in her heart, she felt a kind of dread. Everything had its price. To gain something, something else must be given up, and the reckoning could be dear. The Goddess brooded, wondering whether the results would be worth the cost. Yet such a small price to unleash her full hatred upon its source: Kels Zalkri.

The shadow of the Goddess flowed through the halls of white marble to her throne. The shadow went to the obsidian throne, sat on it, and thought back over the long eons of her life. Long ago, in times so ancient even the Goddess could hardly recall them, she had left her homeworld, Earth, and passed through endless parallel universes until she came to Zarathandra. Somehow in the coming she was transformed from what she had been into a goddess; and was instantly plunged into the intrigues of this world. Those had been great days—a time of mighty deeds, fierce battles, and strange alliances, as the gods and other immortals fought for supremacy. She outlasted them all and her victory was overwhelming: she had become the supreme and unchallenged deity ruling this world. Only minor gods and goddesses shared her divinity. Some few of her old enemies still skulked in out-of-the-way corners, but they were powerless and could do little more than gnash their teeth when they thought of her domination. For a thousand years and then for a few

thousand more she reigned supreme over her world of Zarathandra. She had ruled well, she thought, being a proper
goddess, and letting humanity and the other races order their
own affairs—only now and then reminding them who was
the chief power in this world and therefore should be the
most worshipped. There were troubles and bloodshed
aplenty, mortals being what they were, but it was a golden
age both for them and the Goddess.

Then a thousand years ago, almost to this day, Kels Zalkri
had come raging out of the blackness which lay beyond space
and time. The gate was opened for him by a god who had
once been the overlord of Zarathandra, embittered by centuries of brooding over his defeats. He paid for his folly most
terribly, but the whirlwind had been unleashed. Kels Zalkri
and his minions swept through Zarathandra like an all-devouring fire, overwhelming empires and nations, murdering
her followers, and poisoning the earth and air of her realms.

Then, when the dark lord's victory was almost certain, she
struck back with fire, sword, and soul; she tore into Kels
Zalkri and his allies. It had been a near thing, as she and
Kels Zalkri rocked the cosmos with the might and savagery
of their striving, but in the end she prevailed.

The gate through which the dark one drew power and
soldiery was destroyed. However, her victory had one flaw.
She had been unable to destroy Kels Zalkri or even to force
him from her world. He was confined to his mountain, but
she could not keep him from using his human followers and
immortal allies to intrigue against her and the kind of world
she desired. Kels Zalkri had hovered by his mountain for
near a thousand years, taunting her with thoughts about the
unholy rites with which his worshippers profaned her Zarathandra, and the revenge he would take for his defeat when
the time came. Lately these thoughts had often sought her
out, gloating that soon it would be exactly a thousand years
from the day of his defeat and that again he would tear open
a gate to the realms of hell. The dark lord strutted his contempt confidently, for he knew his own immense strength
and could only despise an enemy who was among her many
aspects a goddess of love. But she was also a goddess of war,
and because she could love, her hate made his seem pale.

The Goddess had lost much in her battle with Kels Zalkri.
Lands she loved and helped form were devastated, nations
she'd nurtured had been destroyed, and many of her most

loyal followers and ablest lieutenants were slain. Moreover, her earthly body had been torn asunder and destroyed at the closing of the gate, and with it had gone many of her powers. However, her greatest loss had been the complete faith of the people of Zarathandra in her omnipotence. For a thousand years the Goddess had brooded over these losses.

Kels Zalkri was utterly sure that the final victory would be his. The strength of the outer darkness was his, and he had gained control of the deep secrets of the world he had chosen as his own. He knew nothing could withstand him.

The Goddess let him have his dreams, and planned her revenge. She had known Zarathandra from its beginning and understood its deepest secrets; mysteries too profound for a vainglorious interloper like Kels Zalkri to know. There was Earth and its hidden connection to Zarathandra and her. Though they existed in different universes, yet their fates were strangely intertwined. Such a world was beyond the ken of Kels Zalkri—and from it could come a threat he could not prepare for; from it could come a source of strength which belonged only to one born to that world.

The time Kels Zalkri was waiting for was almost here; the time the Goddess had been planning for had already come. One of her agents had thrown the first die in the game of death. Let that poor fool, Kels Zalkri, gloat. His doom had come.

3

WITH a bone-jarring thud, Sandy hit a hard and unyielding surface. The shock jerked him back to consciousness. Groggily he lifted his head, knowing only that he was alive, and feeling sore as hell. Finally, the scene before him registered and he got unsteadily to his feet, staring in disbelief.

Instead of being smashed at the bottom of an elevator shaft, he was in a shadowy room being glared at by a scraggly bearded old geezer. Whatever the old man may have been, he was certainly no fever dream: his rich saffron-yellow robe was marred by acid stains, he stank of sweat and old cabbage, and he was mad as hell about something. Not exactly the stuff of fantasy.

"What manner of demon are you?" screeched the old man, "and how dare you interfere with the sorcery of Zhadnoboth the Great? I called for a demon of power, not some minor devil who is only a power at the dinner table." The old sorcerer gnashed his teeth and tore at his hair in frustration.

Sandy stared at him like a slack-jawed idiot, wondering if the old man was a raving maniac and at the same time feeling strangely put out about the uncomplimentary remark regarding his waistline.

"Answer me, you damned halfwit!" snarled Zhadnoboth. "I haven't shed sweat by the bucket and endured the pains of hell just to be defied by a tongue-tied demon. By the Goddess, I yanked you from some hell and I'll get some use of you—if only to feed you to a being more useful. Who are you and what use can you be to me?"

Zhadnoboth's words had finally started getting through to Sandy—it's hard to ignore a human tornado. He shook his head, trying to get the cobwebs out, and started to answer, but his reply wasn't fast enough.

The sorcerer, never the most patient of men, raised his right hand and muttered a short incantation. Then he snapped his fingers, pointed, and from out of nowhere a small bolt of lightning came sizzling to zap Sandy. He lit up like a bright blue Christmas tree, howled in surprise, and jumped into the air.

When Sandy came down he was madder than a grizzly bear with a sore tooth. "You son of a bitch!" he yelled as he stomped forward and shoved his face into the sorcerer's.

That was a mistake: Sandy plowed nose-first into an invisible barrier. He bounced back from it, blood starting to leak from his nostrils, and stared dazedly at Zhadnoboth.

"As you see," Zhadnoboth said in an oily, self-satisfied voice, "you are hemmed in by a most potent spell." He pointed toward the floor.

Inscribed in red chalk on the dusty cobbles was a five-sided figure, surrounded by an untidy raft of mystic symbols sketched in blue and yellow chalk. Sandy remembered his readings in the so-called arcane arts and knew that he was standing inside a pentacle.

"You've had a taste of my sorcery," Zhadnoboth said in a menacing tone. "Now, cooperate, or I may show you how terrible my magic can be. Better yet, I just might give you over to the tender mercies of my associates." Smiling wickedly, he motioned toward the back of the room.

Sandy peered through the gloom. This place looked like the laboratory of a mad scientist: the walls were lined with dusty cabinets crammed with everything imaginable. Regiments of odd-colored and even odder-shaped bottles joined brigades of old books—bound in leathers ranging from horny alligator hide to the soft textures of human skin—and a motley army of magical paraphernalia, a row of shrunken heads, a pile of dirty crockery shoved into a corner, two skulls crowned with large black candles, a small stuffed manticore, a glass jar of eyes which stared at Sandy and the sorcerer, a pair of moth-eaten felt slippers keeping company with unicorn horns—this and much more were on those shelves.

Helter skelter around the room stood numerous worktables, all the worse for wear—their wood stained, splintered, and often charred. Most held weird arrays of glass utensils filled with strange-colored liquids that bubbled and smoked evilly. These fumes did nothing to sweeten the room's unholy stench—an awful combination of brimstone, rotting flesh, incense, and myriad unidentified reeks.

Two figures stepped out of the gloom at the back of the room. Sandy took one look at them and decided he did not like the old geezer's associates one bit. The sorcerer was bad enough, but these two looked hard-bitten and mean-assed, Sandy thought.

The small dark one was not much taller than a dwarf, but looked deadly for all his lack of height. His muscles rippled like corded steel and he moved with the liquid grace of a panther. But what riveted Sandy's attention were his eyes: pools of black fury flecked with hellfire. Looking into those eyes, Sandy realized the little man was utterly mad—not daft or merely crazy, but rabidly insane. Sullen hate radiated from him with an almost physical force.

In some ways his companion was worse. He was a hulking brute of a man, nearer seven feet that six and with thews which bulged from beneath every inch of skin. Volcanic malevolence seemed to boil within him.

"Uskban and Pognak have a way with those who displease us," the sorcerer said maliciously. Before he could say more he was interrupted by the little man.

"Cut the talk and get on with it," he snarled impatiently. "Kill this thing and get us a real demon—one with horns and a nasty temper."

The sorcerer plucked angrily at his scruffy beard. "You stick to killing, Uskban, and leave the decisions to me. True, this demon might not look like much, but my spellwork was too precise to allow a mistake. He's what we need."

Uskban's chill savagery sent a shiver down Sandy's spine —that, and the way his brutish companion licked his lips at the mention of possible bloodshed. Still, despite his terror, a corner of Sandy's mind noticed much which was unsaid. The sorcerer was as unhappy with the results of his spell as Uskban, but now that he'd been challenged, he refused to admit it. Moreover, despite his words, Zhadnoboth was not in as full command of his magic as he made out. Nor was the little madman without some wits. Almost hidden by his madness was a cunning the sorcerer seemed unaware of. Sandy felt Uskban's eyes measuring him even as they blazed. He was playing some deep game and Sandy was one of the pieces— an expendable one.

Sandy had a moment of blind panic when he realized that

these men were not speaking English: yet he understood them perfectly. Sandy wondered wildly whether he was crazy or merely caught in a nightmare, but he knew neither was true. The reeks, sights, and sounds of this place were too real and too bizarre to be mere phantasms.

Zhadnoboth's rebuke convinced Uskban as little as it had Sandy. "Big words, sorcerer, but what do they mean? That you have no idea of what use he actually is?"

"Er—not exactly," mumbled a flustered Zhadnoboth. But, though a catch-as-catch-can sort of sorcerer, he had an agile, devious mind combined with a glib tongue, and in a moment had regained his footing. "I set my incantations to fetch a demon who would best help us," he said grandly. "It is best not to be too specific when using magic, as we mere mortals often don't know what we really need, while sorcery goes to the root and achieves what is truly required." His voice became stronger and more confident as he spoke, his own words convincing him of his wisdom.

As Sandy listened to the old fraud's prattle he discovered that in some strange way he could see the truth which lay behind it. This new talent from out of nowhere was not te-lepathy, but a feeling for the rightness of things: somehow he knew the sorcerer improvised his incantations as he went along and never came out with the exact same result twice in a row. His hooking of Sandy was as much a surprise to him as it had been to Sandy—who began to glower. To be caught by such an inept angler added insult to injury. His mind hurled an obscene curse at whatever powers were playing with his destiny.

Uskban said sourly, "Those be fine words, especially for one some call a charlatan and a cheat." Zhadnoboth's face purpled at these words, but Uskban paid him no heed. "I think they are only half right. You do get results with your magic—that's why Pognak and I threw in with you."

Sandy looked at Uskban with new respect. He might be a bloodthirsty maniac, but he had wits as sharp as any sane person. Sandy could sense the feelings behind Uskban's words—he considered the sorcerer a bumbling cheat, but blessed with an almost divine luck. Sandy wondered about this sixth sense he now seemed to have, his feeling for the true meanings of things. It must have something to do with the way he understood the local language perfectly. Could it be a side effect of the spell which had brought him here? This raised another question: Where was here?

Zhadnoboth, somewhat mollified by Uskban's last words, replied, "I am a great sorcerer, despite what some small-minded idiots think." Then, as though a new thought had just entered his mind, he swung toward Sandy and asked sharply, "Who are you and what is your name?"

Sandy, by this time too exasperated to be sensible, retorted, "Send me back to where I belong. I'm no demon and therefore no use to you. I am simply a man, and worth nothing to a sorcerer."

Zhadnoboth bristled angrily for a moment—until all at once his eyes lit up. "Name," he muttered. "Why didn't I think of that before?" He turned to Uskban and cackled, "I knew my sorcery hadn't failed. He has a name of power. Of all magics, that is one of the most potent."

Uskban rubbed his chin thoughtfully as if sizing up a steer to be slaughtered. The fear which Uskban's look inspired also fueled Sandy's anger. "What's this hogwash about names? A name is a name and that's that. Nor is my name anything special, except for being too long."

Zhadnoboth fixed a beady eye on him. "A name is never just a convenient tag. Not even in the most benighted worlds is this so. A name has meaning. It tells who and what you are. There is magic in all names; and some few have great power."

The sorcerer was a shade more civil to this strange demon than he had been before, though what he considered polite might be interpreted as surliness by some. Zhadnoboth liked to hedge his bets, and the bearer of a name of power was not to be trifled with, even if he was a no-account minor demon from some far corner of hell who had no idea of the importance of his name. Sandy noticed this change in manner and wondered immediately what the old conniver was up to.

Zhadnoboth began to tell Sandy a smidgen of the truth—that part which would do no harm for him to know. "A name might not have any magical power in the world of its origin, but move its bearer to another world and his name might be able to rock the universe. Such a name, of a minor sort, you have. Wonders can be done with such a name when it is first made real in its new world. Destiny can be rewoven under the right circumstances. It takes skill to do so, the skill a sorcerer like myself possesses. Place yourself in my care and together we will do great things, and line our pockets with gold in the doing."

Sandy was not taken in by Zhadnoboth's blarney. Most of what the sorcerer said was true, but Sandy could sense that all Zhadnoboth really had in mind was to help himself and then let the devil take the hindmost. *Well, so be it.* Sandy would have to play for time and wait for any chance to get out from under the sorcerer's thumb. His new and rather odd sixth sense should help. Sandy couldn't read minds or foretell the future, but he could sense how things really were and how people felt and that was a big help. Moreover, the sorcerer apparently wasn't aware of this sixth sense and that gave Sandy a hidden edge.

Sandy spoke, making himself sound eager and at the same time trying to fish for information. "It sounds good, but why me? Wouldn't it be easier for you to use someone from this world who already has such a name?"

Zhadnoboth frowned sourly at the question. This oafish demon was turning out to be less half-witted than he appeared: he'd have to be watched and stepped on when the opportunity presented itself.

"Those with such names of power are not always available when one would want them," Zhadnoboth said ruefully, implying that he had tried to find somebody with a name of power and failed.

Sandy sensed the sorcerer was actually saying, *I wouldn't be idiot enough to tangle with anybody who had a name of power and knew it.*

"Also," Zhadnoboth continued, "those names are old and known to this world—what they can do is rigidly set and unchangeable. While a new name, one which has not yet become part of the fabric of Zarathandra, has the potential to become almost anything. Moreover, for the brief instant when it is first made real, a name of power is unstoppable by anything in this world."

Zhadnoboth spouted out his words with more and more enthusiasm as he became drunk with the grandeur of his vision. Sandy got carried away too, but for a different reason: here was his chance to get out of this damned mess with a whole skin. If his name was so powerful it should be able to blast him out of this damned magical world and back to the nice prosaic one in which he belonged. There was going to be one very surprised sorcerer when he skedaddled. "What's in this for me?" Sandy asked boldly, figuring that showing a little greed would be just the thing to make the sorcerer think he was taken in and could be persuaded to join up.

Despite the secret glee Zhadnoboth felt when he thought Sandy was falling for his line, he still frowned peevishly. The way his thought came across to Sandy was, *This worm of a demon is getting too bold and should be taught a lesson.* Zhadnoboth muttered a very short incantation, opened a tiny gate into another universe, reached in and pulled forth a bolt of red lightning, and flung it at Sandy.

Spitting and crackling evilly it shot by his head and smashed into the rough stone wall behind Sandy. There was a small explosion and, when the dust cleared, a jagged hole in the wall. Sandy turned to stare at the smoking hole. "Hare-brained sorcerers," muttered Sandy under his breath as he tried to appear suitably impressed.

"What you need to know you will learn in due time," the sorcerer said in a high-handed tone. "For now be satisfied with knowing that you will become wealthy beyond your wildest dreams."

These words did not daunt Sandy. By now he knew the sorcerer needed him and wasn't about to cut his throat until he had got what he wanted. There was a question of whether he'd ever get to spend this mythical fortune, or even see it. Besides, Sandy had a stubborn streak which tended to come out at inopportune moments.

"That's a damned poor deal, sorcerer," Sandy said in a tough voice. "I need more than vague promises of wealth. Tell me what I'm getting involved in, exactly what I stand to gain, and how to get back home. You most likely can force me to do what you want, but remember: A willing jackass is easier to move than one with his heels dug in."

Now Zhadnoboth's temper really blackened. His glare and the aura surrounding him told Sandy that he thought the demands outrageous, something no decent sorcerer should have to accept from a demon he'd called up. Sandy sensed that what vexed him most was that he'd have to put up with this damned impertinence until he got what he wanted. Sandy made a vow to run like hell if the sorcerer ever got a chance for revenge.

"Tell him," Uskban muttered. "He isn't much of a demon. He's got a bit of height and has some muscle under the fat, but he couldn't scare a five-year-old girl, let alone fight a Zalkring. Still, if he is in this venture with us, he should know."

The sorcerer glowered at his compatriot, but his mood brightened as he spoke. "We are after treasure, a hoard so huge that even an army couldn't walk away with more than a small part of it. Not only gold and jewels, but rare and magical relics which are beyond price. If rumor doesn't lie, things like the cloak of invisibility, which Wingalad of the Seven Sorrows used to steal the crown of the Dimberlings, are rotting away in this hoard."

Sandy realized the old scoundrel was really pouring on the snake oil, but he listened with all ears nevertheless. Something about the mention of treasure kindled a fire in him that he couldn't put out. It wasn't exactly greed, but something greater—though greed was inextricably mixed in. It was the kind of golden dream which moves more mountains than the cold-blooded calculation of how many pennies there are to be gained.

"A fourth of what we gain should be yours," the sorcerer said, casting a furtive glance at his cohorts. Apparently this was a different splitting of the treasure than what they'd previously agreed to. Pognak scowled and moved forward menacingly. His small companion touched him on the arm and the huge cutthroat reluctantly settled down. Uskban looked impassively at the sorcerer for a moment that seemed an hour and then nodded assent. Zhadnoboth now looked at Sandy to see if he would agree to the split, not that he expected him to know enough to turn the deal down.

Sandy's newfound sixth sense warned him that Zhadnoboth had no intention of keeping the bargain, neither with him nor the other two. That was all right with Sandy, who had no intention of keeping it either. He would play for time just to keep body and soul together until the magic associated with his name gave him a chance to set himself free. However, if some treasure should stick to his fingers, Sandy had no objection to that, either.

He had only one nagging worry, one the sorcerer seemed unaware of: Uskban didn't care a damn about the treasure. Sandy intuitively knew the little madman was in this for some darker purpose, pretending interest in the treasure to lull any suspicions Zhadnoboth might have—the sorcerer instinctively trusted the motives of greedy men. That could be big trouble. But Sandy planned to be long gone before the madman screwed up the works.

"Your offer sounds tempting," Sandy said. "But who decides what are fair shares? And, more importantly, what must I do to earn my share of the treasure?"

Zhadnoboth looked slightly pained, as if he were an honest man whose word had been doubted. "After we have obtained the treasure, you and Uskban can do the splitting. You can keep most of the gold and jewels for yourselves. I would rather take my share in certain old books and magical instruments we may pick up: they are objects of use only to a trained scholar of magical lore. If the Zalkring hoard is only a hundredth of what is rumored, we should have so much loot there will be no need to quibble over it."

By now Sandy was beginning to trust and rely on the sixth sense he seemed to have acquired when he had been yanked so unceremoniously into this world, and he didn't like the vibrations he was getting from the sorcerer. Sandy wished he had true telepathy. Instead he could only feel the mood coloring a person's thoughts; and sometimes he'd get a flash of insight and know what the true situation was, despite what anyone said it was. It was a very confusing talent, especially since it seemed to fade in and out, but it was useful. Right now he knew Zhadnoboth was lying about splitting the treasure—he wanted it all for himself. Besides, if he read the sorcerer correctly, any division which gave him all the books and magical devices could be considered outright robbery.

Sandy could have put up with the sorcerer's greed and lying, but the shudder which went through Zhadnoboth's mind when he mentioned the Zalkrings was something else. Anybody who could scare a hard-boiled egg like the sorcerer had to be pretty mean.

Zhadnoboth's mention of the Zalkrings also aroused Uskban who snarled their name and spat on the ground. An involuntary shiver shook Sandy as the madman's emotions washed over him: a swirling mixture of loathing, fear, and bitter hatred.

"Who are the Zalkrings?" Sandy demanded, beginning to fear the worst.

Zhadnoboth hesitated a moment. Choosing his words carefully, he said, "The Zalkrings are a religious sect. Its members, both mortals and demons like you, serve a black and deadly god who gives them power in both the seen and unseen realms. Only someone with access to sorcery of the most powerful sort has a chance to loot their treasure and anger their god, Kels Zalkri, with impunity. Your name gives us such sorcerous power."

"What more should I know about them?" Sandy asked sharply. He could sense that the sorcerer had left much unsaid, and had a sinking feeling that he wasn't going to like the answer.

Zhadnoboth answered with an almost bloodthirsty relish. "They are a most pious folk, and are fanatically faithful to their god. Few know of them since they are a secretive people, but those who do, fear them. They are ruthless in the practice of their religion, and their adepts in the black arts have such power that few sorcerers or other practitioners of the arts magical can stand against them. They are utterly true to their god, Kels Zalkri, and worship him with robbery, torture, and murder."

The sorcerer paused and then went on in slightly different voice, one whose tones were meant to excite Sandy's greed. "Most of what they rob they hoard to honor their god. They are very discriminating thieves, stealing only the most rare and beautiful objects. They have done this for unknown centuries—some say their sect dates from before the Time of Troubles a thousand years ago. The treasure they have amassed is immense." Zhadnoboth shook his head and added provocatively, "It's a shame such a great treasure is wasted on zealots. It would be better in the hands of those who could enjoy it."

"Haven't others tried to rob them of their treasure?" Sandy asked shrewdly.

"Till now no one has done it successfully," replied Zhadnoboth. "Those rabid fanatics guard their treasure well, both by earthly means and by powerful magics. And, if all other defenses fail, they can call on Kels Zalkri to aid them. On his own ground nothing can stand against him—except maybe the Veiled Goddess. No would-be thief has ever come back from the Zalkrings' mountain. There are whispers that they suffered fates which would make the gods of hell shudder."

"Those whispers are true," Uskban interrupted in a harsh, cracked voice. There was a red gleam in his eyes and his hands clutched convulsively. "I have seen their work. They do not kill cleanly. Their prisoners die slowly and with their souls defiled and damned. Pognak and I survived, and we know."

Uskban's voice had risen to a half shout and was filled with loathing. By his side the huge Pognak grunted and hammered at the air with a massive fist, as if smashing invisible enemies into a pulp.

The little man went on, "They celebrate each quarter of the year with a sacred festival; with blood, torture, and the damnation of innocent souls they hallow the seasons. I have seen such things as would make a demon from the deepest hell blanch."

Uskban's voice broke, and a choked sob came from his lips. "Afterward," he moaned, "afterward those maggots gorge themselves on the flesh of their victims."

He shuddered convulsively and fell into a deep brooding silence. His agonized eyes stared blankly as he again saw horrors long past. Sandy felt the madman's dark mood fill the room with an intangible cloud of emotion, and oppressive shadows forced their way into his soul. Pognak growled inarticulately, his ugly face filled with frustrated rage, and he moved to hover protectively over Uskban.

Angrily Zhadnoboth shook himself, turned to Sandy, and, in a tone purposefully unfeeling, said, "He returned from a journey to find his father's house a smoldering ruin. In it he found what remained of his parents and brothers, after the Zalkrings got through playing."

Uskban interrupted in a hollow, otherworldly tone, "I gathered the pieces and burned them to ashes. Those who are purified by fire and buried on the wind rest easy in the grave. None can rob them or defile their bones."

The sorcerer gave a disgusted snort and went on with his tale. "His two sisters were missing. So like a fool he set off after the murderers, hoping to rescue his sisters and avenge his kin. He followed them to the inner parts of the desert, to the black mountain called Tham Og Zalkri—the stronghold and place most sacred to the Zalkrings. He was a fool and so was captured. For weeks he was tormented, but the worst came last and left no scar on his body. They dragged him to their chief temple and made him watch their midsummer ceremonies. He saw his sisters scream their lives away on the altars of the Zalkrings. He went berserk and somehow managed to escape. Since then he has been as he is now, living only to take vengeance and exact retribution on the Zalkrings."

Uskban looked up, his eyes shining with madness, yet also with cunning. "Three of those whoresons I slew that day, and Pognak four more," he croaked. "And forty and more I have sent to roast in hell since." He yanked a braided rawhide cord from within his robes and held it up. "See!"

Sandy saw and shivered. Attached to the cord were at least forty shriveled ears and three corroded copper coins.

Zhadnoboth wrinkled his face in disgust. "I searched far and wide for Uskban and his companion. They're the only outsiders ever to return from the black mountain. Besides, they're the only partners I would dare to trust to have in this venture with me. Hatred holds them true as nothing else would. Not that a bit of gold to go along with vengeance doesn't help."

"Aye, it helps," Uskban said. "Sometimes it can buy vengeance. And it can always buy some forgetfulness."

Sandy looked at Zhadnoboth and then at his two partners and felt uneasy. The sorcerer might be a hotshot at magic and he was certainly a conniver of real ability, but he was sure as hell no judge of character. He spoke glibly of Uskban's desire for revenge, but had no understanding of the searing hatred in the madman's heart. Sandy sensed he relied more on Uskban because he thought he had bought him with a share of the treasure than because of his hatred for the Zalkrings. Sandy wouldn't trust either Uskban or Pognak as far as he could throw an elephant.

Figuring the more he knew, the better his chances for survival, Sandy got the ball rolling again. "What use are you going to make of me and my name?" he asked the sorcerer.

Zhadnoboth frowned at the question. "Your name is only a potential name of power now. Just a possibility—but a possibility with enormous latent power. With you by my side I can draw on this potential energy and give great substance and strength to my sorcery. Your name could be made real to this world, but there are dangers to all of us if that happens. It would be better for the name to remain a potential thing of power instead of letting it become an actuality."

Sandy kept a bland face and nodded. His sixth sense gave confused readings, but told him that Zhadnoboth left much unsaid. He felt the sorcerer would do everything he could to keep Sandy's name from being made real to this world—

there was a fear that uncontrollable power would be unleashed. Sandy resolved to jump in with both feet if any chance to make his name real appeared—however such a thing was done.

The sorcerer now shifted tack. "Enough of this dreary fussing over minor details. Let's find what I have to work with. Speak your name, demon. The pentacle surrounding you keeps you just beyond the bounds of this world, so for now there will be no unwanted consequences."

Sandy shrugged and casually spoke his name, giving the sorcerer what he had asked for. Neither he nor Zhadnoboth was aware the sorcerer was speaking through his hat. Luckily, Sandy did not bother to give the full set of names his parents had saddled him with. He only said, "Sandy MacGregor." It was almost more than enough.

The syllables of his name tripped easily from Sandy's tongue. For a moment his softly spoken tones hung innocently in the still air. Then those tones started to resound and echo as his name tried to force itself through the barriers which prevented it from becoming real to this world of Zarathandra.

Strained beyond its limits, the spell binding Sandy ruptured, although the pentacle managed to absorb and mute much of the released power. Even so, Zhadnoboth, Uskban, and the mammoth Pognak were knocked rolling head over heels. Tables did wild dances and overturned. Bottles, books, and manuscripts went flying from shelves. Glass shattered into millions of jagged fragments which sprayed the room with shrapnel. Cabinets flew open and spewed forth all kinds of strange objects, powders, and liquids. Finally there was one convulsive jolt like an earthquake and the carnage was over.

Sandy stared about in amazement, for the first time beginning to believe that magic was real and to understand what a name of power meant. A shell-shocked Zhadnoboth hugged the floor and cursed obscenely, afraid to lift his head until he was sure nothing was going to come flying through the air at him. A pile of debris shuddered, then a broken table atop it suddenly flew through the air and crashed into a wall, and a man-mountain came staggering out. He saw Sandy and started toward him with blood in his eye. Out of the dust behind him stepped Uskban. He put a hand on Pognak's shoulder and said, "No!" The big man stopped in his tracks, but sent a look at Sandy which said, *Sometime.*

The room was a shambles. Broken glass, splintered wood, and puddles of evil-looking and even viler-smelling messes covered the floor. Cabinet doors hung half off their hinges and the whole room seemed subtly bent out of shape. Every so often the building would groan and tremble, sending down a fine rain of dust from the cracked ceiling.

Zhadnoboth, battered and so mad he could spit tacks, picked himself off the floor. He glared at Sandy, quite obviously placing the entire blame for the fiasco on his shoulders, until he noticed that the spell which had bound Sandy within the pentacle had been destroyed. Reacting more from panic than good sense, he instantly muttered a quick incantation, snapped his fingers, and pointed at Sandy.

A pile of broken crockery on the floor began to move and a streak of silver slithered menacingly from beneath it. It was a chain of pure silver fashioned to resemble a snake. Serpentlike, it wound itself quickly into a coil—and launched like a missile through the air, striking Sandy in the throat and sending him staggering backward. In a moment it had wound itself three times around his neck.

Sandy gagged and tried to talk. The chain of silver just drew tighter about his neck. Desperately he tore at the links with his hands. It wouldn't budge. Soon he was red in the face and near collapse.

Zhadnoboth watched, a self-satisfied smirk on his face. When he thought he had driven home a point, he snapped his fingers. The chain loosened enough for Sandy to breathe, which he did gratefully.

"Keep a tight leash on your tongue, demon, and you will survive," Zhadnoboth snapped in a malicious voice. "Choose your words well and be civil and you will have no problem—try to speak your name or be impertinent and the chain will strangle you—and good riddance if it does."

Sandy said in a careful, though sullen, voice, "I am no demon. I am as human as you are." The chain tightened warningly at his almost uncivil words, but refrained from choking him.

Zhadnoboth gave a derisive snort and replied, "My inner nose smells the rank odor of demon; no sorcerer can mistake that spiritual stink. You are a demon, no matter how human you look and how small your hellish powers."

Sandy silently glowered, knowing he'd never convince

this hardheaded dunce he wasn't a devil, let alone get him to remove the choke chain. Still, in a way he felt better about the situation. Zhadnoboth had made a mistake, asking for his name. It had almost become real to this world. It had been a close call for the old scoundrel, but there would be other times—there were bound to be, with such a careless bungler. Sandy could wait for his next chance at freedom.

"Some sorcerer," snarled Uskban as he dusted himself off. "I need no enemies with a friend like you."

"It was just a very slight miscalculation," protested the sorcerer. "My spell held, and so the damage was only minor."

"Minor!" Uskban screeched, waving at the half-destroyed room. "I've seen no-quarter barroom brawls cause less damage! I joined you to get revenge on the Zalkrings, not to be murdered by your incompetence." Pognak growled menacingly, seconding the madman's words.

A murderous grin flashed across Uskban's face. "Still, this soft-looking outlander, be he man or demon, does have a name of some power. Maybe my vengeance will be greater than ever I hoped for."

"Both vengeance and treasure," Zhadnoboth said soothingly. He appeared worried by the uncertain temper of the little madman.

Uskban's rage wasn't stilled—only death could do that—but Sandy could see it burned less hot. A faraway look came into Uskban's eyes and in a voice both croaking and chuckling he said, "We'll hurt those soulless bastards—and their abominable god too."

The madman's mood suddenly changed. "What hell does the dark one come from?" he moaned. "I still feel the cold of him, the terrible cold. Black—oh, so black. The sight of him freezes the soul." He huddled against a wall like a cornered rat, terrified and yet ready to attack with murderous rage.

"Yes, yes," Zhadnoboth said in an easy tone. "But we'll not attract his attention to us. We'll sneak in like shadows in the night and rob the Zalkrings while they are occupied with their midsummer ceremonies. By the time they notice that the treasure is missing, we'll be long gone." The sorcerer gave a nasty smile and added, "And we'll leave behind some unpleasant surprises for our friends."

Sandy could see that the sorcerer was stringing Uskban along, keeping him calm and useful until he could be discarded.

He also noticed that while the words did brighten Uskban's mood, the mad, cunning look in his eyes said very plainly that he wasn't taken in by Zhadnoboth's words. Sandy wondered who was fooling who. Either way he was going to have to look out for himself: both Zhadnoboth and Uskban would throw him to the Zalkrings as a choice tidbit, if it was expedient.

And Pognak would do it for laughs.

4

THE Goddess made a sign and the air in front of her misted and became a mirror of true seeing. In it she watched the first encounter between Sandy and his chosen companions. When she had seen enough, she made a sign of dismissal and the mirror dissolved back into nothingness.

Then, for long minutes, the Goddess sat on her obsidian throne and brooded over the workings of destiny. Not even she, for all her power, could command the fates to do her bidding. By diligence and great persistence she could seemingly influence the workings of destiny, but she sometimes wondered whether fate manipulated her more than she did it.

Zhadnoboth, Uskban, Pognak, and Sandy were all vital cogs in the machinery she had set up to regain what was hers, but not one of them had been chosen for his role by her beforehand. She had known there would be four and what roles they would play, but she had not known whom they would be. Each had been sucked into the quicksands of destiny and then spewed forth to be pieces in her deadly game with Kels Zalkri. They were only mortals, but she felt a deep guilt at the way they had been manipulated by fate, especially the way Uskban and Pognak had suffered and been warped. Destiny had decided she would have a chance for vengeance, but it had exacted a bitter price.

Pognak had been born ugly and with a dark temperament, but he had a rare talent for music and a family he loved and who had loved him. Destiny had thrown him to the Zalkrings and he had lost his voice and his family. Now he was a sullen brute suitable for her purpose, but so much less than he could have been. Somewhere deep inside the maimed animal an artist and a human being still existed, but even she could hardly sense them.

The ache in her heart was even heavier when she thought of Uskban. There was a very deep and personal relationship between her and his family which went back many centuries. They were special to her both because their destiny was intertwined with hers and for an abiding love she had felt for the founder of the lineage. Uskban had been the golden child of fortune, secretly groomed by her to restore his family's fortunes and unify the Kri Shandri tribes once again, but fate had delivered him and his family into the hands of the Zalkrings. Now he was a warped loner, no longer sane and no longer a leader of men. She had gained an instrument of vengeance and lost what might have been the greatest king the Kri Shandri would ever have. There would be another to fill his role, if she survived in her struggle with Kels Zalkri, but never one who would have as great a hold on her heart.

Midnight came and a beam of moonlight filtered through a clear crystal window in the vaulted ceiling of the chamber, illuminating the dark throne and its occupant with a soft silvery light. The Goddess gave a sigh which echoed with a poignant sadness and then arose to glance again at what the future might hold. Her shadowy form moved gracefully across the room toward a table of jet-black wood, leaving behind swirls of iridescence in the moonlit air. Her fingers caressed the designs inlaid into the abakiwood table, an outer ring of alternating stars and lunes shaped from the lustrous greenish cream ivory of Tartegian seadragon and an inner ring of intertwined serpents made from dwarf-hammered silver.

The Goddess picked up an oiled leather cup with her shadowy fingers, its substance black with age and long use. She rattled the eight-sided dice within the cup and then with a supple flick of her wrist threw them on the table. An ironic smile played about her lips as she studied her throw. One die had the raven uppermost, one showed the snake who eats his tail, and the last two had turned up as grinning skulls. It was the throw she had expected; still, she'd hoped for a better outcome.

The destiny foreshadowed was not one she would have freely chosen, but it did promise a mostly favorable future. This future had one irritating drawback, but one she would have to challenge fate to change. After she had settled with

Kels Zalkri, then she could think deeply and long about finding a way to remove this hindrance to her complete freedom.

The Goddess let her thoughts drift to other matters and she smiled tolerantly as Zhadnoboth came to mind. She was rather fond of the old scoundrel, liking him more because of his faults than despite them. He had been a good choice to bring Sandy into this world. No one, least of all Zhadnoboth, knew the sorcerer was one of her agents and so the dark one would never bother to watch him, especially since he was such an incurable bumbler. But Zhadnoboth was more than he seemed and in his haphazard way was an effective if unconscious servant and a very good sorcerer. He had a strange aptitude for lucking out of his mistakes, sometimes getting unexpected results impossible for greater and more dedicated sorcerers. This was one of those times. In his own unique style, he'd brought Sandy into Zarathandra, and had done it in such a way that Kels Zalkri would have no forewarning. She'd made sure the right spell fell into his hands. Instead he'd used the wrong one—and got better results than if he had done everything correctly.

Idly the Goddess tossed the dice again—and got the same result. She had halfheartedly hoped the casting would change. Still, she couldn't expect to get something for nothing. She was lucky the price was small.

She traced a sign of calling in the air and Sandy's image appeared before her. The Goddess looked him over carefully and was satisfied in the main. He had gone a little soft, but that would soon be corrected. Otherwise he seemed quite presentable, even handsome. Hair brown and curly, eyes pearl gray, features regular, and temperament easy—none of these things set him much apart from his fellow men. She should be able to command him, though he was a bit too intelligent and the stubborn set to his mouth might bode trouble. But, for being pulled out of his world sight unseen, Sandy wasn't too bad a bargain.

The Goddess waved a hand and Sandy's image dissolved into nothingness. She turned her thoughts to Kels Zalkri and what she fervently hoped was his future doom. While she schemed and plotted, she tossed the dice again. No harm in seeing whether destiny could be cajoled into making the future a little more to her liking.

5

SANDY stood in a meager patch of shade and glowered at the sorcerer. Being utterly miserable, he wished everybody else would join him in his suffering—especially Zhadnoboth. Instead the sorcerer was enjoying himself as he haggled with a livestock merchant— it gave him a chance to use his natural propensity for irascibility and pettiness, which he was doing with zest. Uskban had apparently got tired of listening to his pettifogging and had stalked off to inspect the merchant's stock.

It was high noon in a godforsaken desert town, and as bad as that could be: the ground was a hot skillet under your feet and the air so dry that spit evaporated in midair. And to make it worse—it stank. The town itself was distinguished by a stench which would do justice to a pigsty, but the reek from the livestock pens overpowered it. Moreover, Sandy's robe was an instrument of torture. It had been woven of a wool which had to be more steel than fiber. Every time he moved it seemed to scrape another piece of skin off. And on top of everything else, his body clock had to be eight to ten hours out of sync with local time. The locals were their noonday selves, while he was his bedtime self.

Sandy's temper would have been less foul if his personal circumstances had been better. It was bad enough being stuck in a world that must be an afterthought of God's creation. Even worse was being dragooned into a crazy treasure hunt, a quest which seemed more harebrained the more he thought of it. The worst was having the damned silver chain wrapped tightly around his neck.

The choking feeling he could tolerate, but not being able to give full vent to his feelings was pure hell.

The livestock merchant was a fat and oily sinner with a

32

cast in his left eye. He had the feel of being an accomplished crook, but he was barely holding his own against Zhadnoboth. What the sorcerer lacked in knowledge he more than made up for with an obstinate nature and a sharp tongue. The merchant was slowly wilting under the sorcerer's assault, but he was fighting back valiantly.

"May the Goddess be my witness," hollered the merchant in false agony. "These are the finest riding beasts in my pens." He pointed to some rudhars, beasts obviously related to camels, who were staring evilly at them from behind a dilapidated post fence. "So gentle are they that my youngest daughter could ride them. And so strong that they can travel for weeks and hardly be winded."

Sandy cast a jaundiced eye toward the rudhars in question. They looked like a slightly shorter and more streamlined version of the dromedary camel—and with a temperament which promised to be even worse. These animals in particular looked mean, mangy, and ill-cared-for.

Zhadnoboth was of the same opinion. He wasn't the greatest judge of riding beasts, but he knew scoundrels and trusted nobody. "Pah!" he snorted. "These pieces of crowbait couldn't make it out of the city."

"Do you call me a thief?" the merchant asked in an aggrieved tone. "I sell only the best. Give me thirty silver axepennies each and you can have them, even if the whole city will be babbling about how you swindled me."

"Thirty!" shouted the sorcerer. "You'd have to pay me to take such carrion off your hands."

Uskban interrupted, "These beasts are garbage. Sell us the rudhars in your rear pens."

Uskban's sudden reappearance and his fiercely spoken words unnerved the merchant—that, and an uneasy conscience. He whirled to face the little man. What he saw came close to stopping his heart.

Behind the madman towered Pognak, huge and silent, who looked like something out of a nightmare. Especially when he was glowering with rage—as now.

Uskban nodded brusquely to the giant. Pognak stepped forward and grabbed the merchant by the front of his robe, lifting him easily despite his great bulk, and shook him till his teeth rattled. Pognak showed his enormous fangs to the merchant in a menacing grin as if he were aching to start chomping on soft city-bred flesh.

"Put him down," Uskban said in a quiet, no-nonsense voice. Pognak gave a guttural snarl of protest—having no tongue he could not say more—and abruptly dropped the merchant. The fat man landed heavily and staggered.

Uskban steadied the merchant with one hand and stabbed him in the chest with a finger from the other hand. "You'll sell us the rudhars you have hidden in the back pens."

The merchant was sweating profusely, but another fear warred with his fear of Uskban. "I—I can't sell them to you; they're not mine to sell." As he spoke the fat scoundrel regained some of his courage. "You don't dare do anything. Everyone in town will know you were my last customers if something happens to me. I have important friends who would avenge me. Within two days there would not be a town in the land where you would be safe from their justice." There was a desperate tone in the merchant's voice, as though he was trying more to convince himself than Uskban.

He gave the merchant a cold bleak smile far worse than any threat. "I would not bother to dirty my hands with you, fat one. I would just send word to Khalek the Knife as to where he might find his stolen herd. Word is that he has already captured two of those who took part in the raid. He skinned them alive and nailed their hides to his front door. And" —there was a sinister pause before he resumed speaking—"he has some very powerful friends, friends even the twelve kings would hesitate about offending."

The merchant's face went dead white. "Damn those accursed rudhars," he swore. "I never wanted anything to do with them." He glanced around nervously, ready to bolt at the slightest hint that retribution was stalking him.

Uskban shook him to get his attention and said, "We'll pay you fifty axepennies total for the beasts we need and keep our mouths shut. All you have to do is give us the beasts without a whimper and forget we were here." He looked straight into the merchant's eyes and asked coldly, "Do you think the price is fair?"

For one moment the fat merchant started to protest. Then thought again and halfheartedly nodded.

Uskban turned to the sorcerer. "Pay him."

Zhadnoboth scowled; he hated to part with his money, especially when it looked like the merchant would have given them the beasts just so they'd go. The sorcerer opened his mouth to say something.

Uskban silenced Zhadnoboth with a fierce stare. "We are not thieves. We pay our way." Grumbling, the sorcerer reluctantly counted the silver coins into the merchant's trembling hand.

Sandy watched and wondered what they were if not thieves. Very likely the Zalkrings more than deserved to be robbed. Still, that did not make saints of those who planned to rob them.

Dragging his feet, the fat merchant led them to the rear pens. Uskban nodded to Pognak, who crawled through the fence into one of the pens and started rounding up the beasts Uskban indicated he wanted to look at. The rudhars were not very tractable, but neither was the big mute—after a few cuffs from his stonelike fists they more or less behaved.

The rudhars were gray- and dun-colored beasts, looking much like a dromedary, though with less of a hump and a slimmer neck. Their breath was sour and their bodies had a stench redolent of a barnyard which had been visited by a skunk. Their piggy eyes were agleam with malice, and they had sneering lips which exposed scum-covered teeth. All in all they were ill-favored beasts, though they did move with a certain elegant grace.

As Pognak led a hissing and very reluctant rudhar over to be inspected at close range, the merchant whined to Uskban, "My partner will take their price out of my hide. He's utterly unreasonable. He'd as soon kill somebody as to look at them. I only agreed to take the beasts because I was too terrified not to."

Uskban stared back at him and said, "Kill him first. If you do that and get rid of the remaining beasts you might live—there might not be any link for Khalek to trace them to you when he gets here."

"Gets here," the merchant said shakily.

"Khalek is a relentless bastard. He'll be here. Maybe sooner, maybe later, but he'll be here. Those two he caught are bound to have babbled a lot before he let them die."

The fat merchant went green under his dark skin and protested, "I'm no cutthroat. I get sick every time I see blood."

Uskban shrugged and replied, "Then either run or wait around to die. Not that running will do much good. Khalek never gives up when he is tracking someone who has wronged him."

Sandy leaned back against a fence and thought what a

cold-blooded bastard the madman was, full of sense and with no heart. This was going to be a great adventure: the sorcerer was as crooked as a corkscrew, Uskban was a murderous maniac, and Pognak was just plain murderous.

Suddenly a big slobbery tongue, deep purple and as long as a fair-sized python, came from behind Sandy and lovingly caressed his face. Sandy jumped and gave a surprised screech which was immediately choked off by a convulsive contraction of the silver chain around his neck—almost as immediately, the chain relaxed when it decided his yowl was harmless. Coughing as he tried to get his breath back, Sandy whirled to see what had attacked him. On the other side of the fence was one of the ugliest creatures Sandy had ever seen. Huge and spiky-skinned, it looked something like a horned toad grown to nightmare proportions—six feet tall at the shoulder, six wide, and at least twelve long not counting the short, barb-covered tail. It was sandy gray in color, but with a multitude of orange speckles spattering its loose and baggy hide. The head was stove-sized, with the largest and widest mouth Sandy could remember seeing. Its eyes, though, were beautiful in a way—they bulged out and were the size of baseballs, but were colored a rich and sublime shade of emerald green.

The creature looked with adoring eyes at Sandy, and he felt an immense wave of love surge from it and envelop him. It opened its enormous mouth again and the purple and very wet tongue came snaking out from behind a forest of yellow teeth to take an affectionate swipe at Sandy. He stepped back to avoid it and then stared in bewilderment at the creature; he knew animals cottoned to him, but he had never made such a quick and complete conquest before.

Since Sandy refused to stand still and be licked affectionately, the creature gave a sad, rumbling sigh, reached down and bit off a huge clump of yellow-flowered thistles, and began chewing away. As it enjoyed its thorny snack, it stared with woebegone eyes at Sandy.

"Don't look at me like that," muttered Sandy, "I don't have time for a stray monster right now." He stared a little longer at those sad eyes and then, cursing himself inwardly for being a soft-hearted fool, reached over and scratched the big beast behind its left ear. It gave a sigh of pleasure and shoved its head through the fence—the stout wooden posts disintegrated like so much kindling—and rubbed affectionately against Sandy's leg. Looking askance at the powerful creature, but unable to resist its begging, Sandy continued with his scratching.

Suddenly Sandy was roughly jostled aside by Pognak. Sandy made a pungent comment about the big mute's ancestry, but Pognak ignored it and bent down to examine the beast's feet. The beast gave him a disgruntled look, then belched right in his face—a belch which smelled like a mixture of rotten eggs and musty hay. Pognak staggered back, gasping and choking. Sandy suppressed a chortle with difficulty, especially as the creature seemed to wink one huge eye as it reached down to chew on some more thistles.

"Will he do?" asked Uskban as he put a hand on the mute's arm to cool him down. Pognak looked the beast over with a vindictive eye and then spoke to Uskban using sign language.

Uskban nodded and turned to the merchant. "We'll take this grundzar to finish off our bargain."

The merchant complained bitterly, "I thought the price was only for the rudhars. Do you want to rob me blind? Glupp here is worth all of them and more. There is not one beast of burden in the city that can carry as much cargo half as far as he can. Besides, what of my fence?"

Uskban said coldly, "We made a bargain to take the beasts we need, and we need him. Four riding rudhars and a grundzar to carry our gear is not a high price, especially since all are stolen. As for your fence, you should have built it out of less shoddy materials."

The merchant wilted and reluctantly nodded agreement.

While Uskban saw to the rudhars, Pognak went into the pen to get Glupp. He got the beast's halter on and tried to lead him away. One powerful backward jerk on the halter almost yanked Pognak's massive arm from its socket. Glupp was as large as a small mountain and as stubbornly unmoving. Pognak gave an inarticulate snarl and grabbed the halter with two hands, but he still couldn't budge the beast. Furious, Pognak stepped back and shook his fist at the creature.

"He—he—he's a good beast," stammered the merchant. "He just gets a little stubborn once in a while. You have to get on the good side of him—that's all." But these words did not pacify Pognak, whose temper got blacker by the moment.

Sandy, surprising even himself, saved the day. Stepping forward, he grabbed the halter from the mute's hand, scratched Glupp behind the ears, and gave a gentle tug on the halter.

With a contented groan, Glupp trundled forward. Pognak snorted and stalked off to help Uskban with the rudhars. Glupp watched him go with what looked very much like a toothy grin covering his face.

Half an hour later they got the beasts to the house Zhadnoboth had rented in one of the more disreputable parts of town. Several questionable characters had cast calculating eyes on the beasts as they passed, but none was brave enough to do anything. One look at Pognak's enormous size and Uskban's murderous eyes was enough to discourage most of them—especially since two characters who might have been them had achieved a fearsome reputation throughout the desert and its borderlands. Local gossip about Zhadnoboth being a very nasty-tempered sorcerer scared off the rest.

They placed the beasts in the courtyard of the dilapidated ruin. The previous night's near disaster hadn't helped its state. The rudhars glared at the weedy wilderness about them with regal disdain and Glupp slobbered in anticipation at the feast awaiting him.

The grundzar's hungry look reminded Sandy that he hadn't eaten for a long time. "When are we going to eat?" he complained. "My belly is so empty it's rubbing against my backbone."

"Quiet, demon, we have more important matters to take care of," Uskban said in an unfeeling voice. He turned to Zhadnoboth and said, "Somebody followed us from the stockpens. It could be a Zalkring spy, though he moved like a tribesman. Most likely he's one of Khalek's men. Whoever he is, he's bad news. We better load up our gear and get out before there is any trouble." He sidled up to the courtyard gate, looked out cautiously, and started to slink through it.

"Where are you going?" Zhadnoboth asked.

Uskban snarled back over his shoulder. "Out to save your worthless neck. Get our gear packed and be ready to leave fast when I return."

Hurriedly Sandy and the other two began carting up gear and supplies from the cellars. Sandy did his share and more with a minimum of complaint, but the sorcerer was almost useless. He fussed about inconsequential things, dithered around not making up his mind, and carried out with each trip about as much as a ten-year-old child could tote. Luckily

Pognak more than made up for him. The giant was a sullen bastard, but he could carry enormous loads.

They loaded Glupp with magical paraphernalia, food, clothes, and all sorts of miscellaneous gear. Much too much for Sandy's taste, as the heat and prolonged use of flabby muscles soon made each trip like a walk through hell.

Glupp stood contentedly through it all, unbothered by weight or the haste the silly humans felt was so necessary. While they wore themselves to a frazzle, he enjoyed the bounty of the courtyard. It was filled with a very delicious assortment of weeds; nice thorny, chewy ones.

They were still hurriedly carting stuff up from the cellars when Uskban returned. "Hurry!" he snapped. "We have to go. The word in the street is that the mayor's next-to-eldest son has been knifed and that Uz-Kaldi-Baba the merchant claims that we did it." He paused and added wryly, "I didn't think that cock-eyed bowl of jelly had it in him."

"I haven't got half my gear loaded," Zhadnoboth complained.

Uskban retorted, "You can dally about and get your throat slit, but I have better places to shed my blood." Ignoring the sorcerer, he asked Pognak, "Do we have all the essential gear?"

The mute nodded.

"There are still things I need," Zhadnoboth snapped.

"Well, get them," replied Uskban. "We'll get the rudhars ready to go while you're rooting away. Be back within ten minutes or we'll leave without you."

The sorcerer seemed ready to howl out angrily about the deadline, but then held his peace. Instead he turned and stomped off toward the house. He was back in plenty of time, looking drawn and in no better mood.

"I cast a spell and got most of it in my hidey-hole or in my deeper pockets," he said. Then in a spiteful tone he added, "The cost of the gear I'm leaving behind is coming out of your share of the treasure. Not that it will do anyone else much good. Whoever enters the house next is going to get a most unpleasant surprise." A nasty smile crossed his face as he said these last words.

Uskban ignored his surliness. "Is there some sorcery you can use to get us out of the city undetected? I don't want to fight my way through half the town if I don't have to."

"You can't use sorcery to get out of every little scrape,"

Zhadnoboth said pettishly. "Magic is a wearing thing: too much can destroy a sorcerer."

Uskban perked up his head as though he heard something outside the gate. "Either use it or get ready to fight your way out."

Zhadnoboth snorted irritably and began to dig into the gear he'd already packed aboard Glupp. He came up with a long rope woven from some stiff black hair and a small bag of washed leather. The sorcerer handed Pognak the rope. "Tie all the beasts together in a string with this."

The big mute grunted in answer and began the task.

When Glupp and the rudhars were all tied together and each of them was mounted, Zhadnoboth rose up in his saddle and flipped the bag into the air. He pointed at it and said a word. The bag exploded with a small pop and sprinkled them with a fine orangish dust, the pollen of the beg-a-ride bush which had been slow-roasted over purified charcoal for six hours. The sorcerer turned his back to the others, mumbled his way through an incantation, and then leaned over in the saddle and smote the ground with the tip of his sorcerer's staff. For a moment nothing happened. Then the men and animals began to fade away from view in a herky-jerky fashion—an eye here, a leg there, half a face, or maybe part of a rump. Soon the last odd piece of anatomy disappeared and they were invisible to human eyes.

Sandy was confused for a second. He could feel himself here, but could not even see his hand when he held it up before his face. Nor could he see his companions or the animals. He wondered how they were going to coordinate their actions as they moved through the city.

Uskban wondered the same thing. "Damn you, Zhadnoboth," he shouted. "What good is it being invisible to others if we can't see one another?"

The sorcerer made a grumpy sound and hastily muttered another incantation. In less than a minute Sandy could see himself and his companions. They looked like wispy, colored shadows, but they could see one another.

"Sorcerer," Uskban said, "are we now invisible to all except ourselves?" sounding like he wasn't too sure Zhadnoboth had got the fine details of the spell right.

"Yes!" Zhadnoboth snapped. He turned to the gate, hit the ground three times with the steep tip of his staff, and spoke a word of power. There was a moment of tension; then the gate exploded outward off its hinges.

Sandy shook his head and wondered again about the old sorcerer's common sense—it was a hell of a way to sneak into the streets of the city.

As they rode out the gate, picking their way past the unconscious bodies of a group of men who had been ready to storm their way into the courtyard, Uskban leaned over and whispered to the sorcerer, "Khalek's men. Uz-Kaldi-Baba must have put them on our track to save his own hide."

Pognak's mount half stumbled over a fallen tribesman and the mute growled inarticulately at the beast. The tribesman, who had only been knocked down and not out, now looked up, screamed in terror, sprang to his feet, and took off down a winding street as if the legions of hell were at his heels.

"We're not going far if they can hear us," Uskban said acidly. "And even less if we step on their toes."

"You'd think I was a two-penny wizard who works small wonders for a mug of beer," muttered Zhadnoboth, rather illogically. Still grumbling, he pulled a shabby book from his robes and hurriedly looked up a couple of spells. When he had found what he wanted, he turned to Uskban and said, "I'll add a spell of avoidance and a spell of silence to the enchantment. But ask no more from me today. I barely have enough energy left to do even those simple spells."

Sandy thought the sorcerer did look a bit peaked. After Zhadnoboth spoke the proper incantations and made the right passes with his staff, he looked more like a limp rag than an old man, but the spells were working—at least Sandy assumed so. He did know his ears felt as if plugged with cotton and that he could barely hear words spoken by his companions.

They took the street leading to the north gate of the city. As they moved along, people unconsciously stepped out of their way and yet apparently didn't see or hear them. The only attention they got was from some chickens, odd-looking hens with purplish feathers and magenta combs, scratching in the street for some particularly juicy grubs. They squawked bitterly as they were forced away from their feast.

Sandy and his companions came to a square and stood aside as a posse of townsfolk swept by on their way to the sorcerer's just abandoned lodgings. At their heels rode a bunch of hard-bitten tribesmen, led by Khalek the Knife himself. He was a burly, scar-faced man wearing rich multicolored robes and a mean look in his eyes. Beside him rode Uz-Kaldi-Baba the livestock merchant: white-faced, sweating, and rolling uneasily in his saddle. Two tribesmen rode near him as guards, ready to knife him if he bolted. He looked as if he thought he was on his way to his own execution, and maybe he was.

Sandy and his companions halted when they got to where their street opened out into the square in front of the north gate. The gate hung open and the square was almost deserted. It was a slow time of day for traffic in and out of town and most of the townsmen who usually loitered there had taken off to see the excitement near the sorcerer's house. Several bored-looking guards stood about and wished sundown would hurry up and come. Also three of Kahlek's tribesmen were keeping hawklike eyes on the gate, but neither they nor the guards saw anything pass a few moments later.

A couple miles north of the city, the road went over a ridge and then down to a well where it forked. The left fork, the most traveled, led to Timzardin and the main caravan road leading to the Rithian Empire, far away to the north of the desert. The right fork was overgrown and little used. Once, long ago, it had been the main road leading north over the desert to the middle seas and their trading cities. But a terror had come and men now avoided it, though few remembered why.

As Sandy and his companions, still invisible, rode toward the well they saw that some travelers had stopped there. One group was a man, his very pregnant wife, two small children, and a couple of tired-looking rudhars. Sitting around the well were four mendicant priests in threadbare brown robes.

Sandy looked at the innocent scene and shivered involuntarily. Something was wrong, he could feel it.

As the father went over to the well to draw some water, one of the priests began a friendly conversation with him while the other three priests went over to help his family. The man started pulling the bucket out of the well, the priest made a joke, and the man laughed.

Sandy shuddered violently and shrieked, "Stop!"

His three companions started at his words and then looked with horror at the well.

6

THE Goddess stared bleakly at the mirror of seeing as brief scenes from out of the past appeared.

There was a young Pognak sitting at a low table with his young pregnant wife, their two-year-old boy Zizim, Uskban, and Uskban's two young sisters. They were eating and having a merry time, even sober-faced Pognak. Most of the merriment was due to Pognak's wife, a small stocky woman as plain as a board fence but with twinkling eyes and a joke ever on her lips. Pognak adored her and his son, seemingly hugging one or the other every five minutes. One of Uskban's sisters was much like her, except for being prettier and slimmer. The other sister was a quiet girl with a sly smile and a beauty which hinted it would be spectacular when she was older. Pognak joshed Uskban about having such ugly sisters, and the little man laughed and looked fondly at them.

The scene shifted: A bloody Pognak, his hands bound behind his back, shouted obscenities at a cloaked Zalkring and struggled to get at him—the three men who held him barely held their own against his struggles. At their feet lay the body of Pognak's son and wife. The boy's throat had been cut to the backbone. The woman's belly and the baby within had been run through with a spear and then her throat cut. Pognak suddenly stopped his struggle to get at the cloaked figure. Instead, with contempt on his face, he said something to his enemy. The words enraged his foe and the Zalkring screamed something and then, with several men aiding him, wrestled the giant to the ground. They forced Pognak's mouth open and the Zalkring slashed out the tongue. He held it in front of Pognak's eyes, threw it to the ground, and ground it into the dirt with his boot while he laughed. Pognak screamed his hate and spat blood at his

43

tormenter, who only laughed some more at this futile gesture.

Another shift: And Uskban sat in a bed with a naked hoyden, both for the moment sated, but still kissing and caressing each other. She shook her dark-nippled tits, patted her belly, and cracked a bawdy joke about what went in taking nine months to come out. For a moment they were dead serious and hugged each other tightly. Then she made another bawdy comment and they were laughing uproariously.

It was the next day and a washed-out Uskban was riding his rudhar around a bend in a mountain road. Suddenly he yanked his mount to a halt and stood up in the stirrups to stare ahead. In the near distance, from behind a jagged, rusty-red ridge, a column of smoke drifted toward the heavens.

A large sprawling residence of blue-gray stone and red brick lay in shattered ruins. The stink of smoke was heavy in the air and the ground in places was knee-deep in ashes, fallen rubble, and still glowing embers. Here and there small fires were burning themselves out. Scattered about were dozens of bodies, most burnt and some mangled and dismembered. Uskban knelt in an inner courtyard, his clothes and face streaked with soot, and sobbed. Nailed to the courtyard wall were five bodies: three young men, a gray-haired woman, and a scar-faced older man. Their bodies were almost cinders, but he could see that they had been tortured and maimed before they had died.

A grim Uskban, his face dirty and tear-streaked, followed alone some tracks through the desert. Sunset streaked the sky red behind him and ahead a black mountain loomed ominously against the gathering darkness. Out of the night a dozen figures came and attacked Uskban. There was a short struggle: one man fell dead to the ground, blood gushing from his ripped belly. An unconscious Uskban toppled a moment later.

Uskban was bound to a pole, his head tied so he had to look straight ahead. In front of him his two sisters were tied down by iron hooks embedded in their flesh, their bodies burnt and torn by torture, but both still alive and conscious —and both crying for death and moaning in agony. A naked Zalkring priest sliced at the inner thigh of one of the girls with an obsidian knife and her piercing scream split Uskban's eardrums. The priest carved off a piece of flesh, and began

chewing on the warm and bloody morsel—a look of divine
bliss on his face and of horror on that of his still-living victim.
Uskban went berserk, screaming in rage and insanely trying
to rip free from his bonds. Blood flowed over the rawhide
ropes binding the madly struggling Uskban; the priest with
the obsidian knife watched and sneered at the little man, and
behind the priest a giant mute slave had just slit the throats
of the girls and was advancing murderously toward him.

A shudder shook the Goddess and with an angry wave of
the hand she banished the mirror and its agonizing memories
from her view. She shook her fist in the darkness and yelled,
"Damn you! You bastard god. You'll pay, dark one, this I
swear."

She heard no answer except the mocking silence of her
throne room.

7

SMILING jovially, the priest by the well moved behind the father and drove a wide-bladed poniard into his right kidney. One of the other priests quickly slit the throats of the two children he had been showing a game akin to mumblety peg. The other two priests grabbed the pregnant woman. While one held her arms behind her back, the other made a couple of quick slashes with his dagger and then tore what remained of her clothes away. As she screamed in horror, the priest slashed upward, ripping open her belly from groin to breastbone. The priest reached in, tore out the unborn baby, held it up toward the sky, and then plunged his blade through its belly. The priest contemptuously tossed the tiny body to the ground, down beside its mother who was screaming incoherently through blood-choked lips as she thrashed convulsively amid her own entrails and gore—then she too was dead.

The priest who had killed the woman and her unborn babe lifted his bloody dagger to the heavens and roared joyfully, "My lord, Kels Zalkri, accept these sacrifices from your followers."

"Zalkrings!" screamed Uskban. He yanked a javelin from a sheath by his knee and threw it in one motion, impaling the Zalkring by the well through his lower gut. Then he was off his rudhar, sword in hand and sprinting full speed toward the remaining three Zalkrings.

As he got within ten feet of the Zalkrings, he left the area where Zhadnoboth's enchantments could still hide him and suddenly became visible. The nearest Zalkring, the one who had ripped open the woman's belly, stared in stupefied horror at this wild-eyed apparition who had appeared from out of nowhere.

Uskban's sword lashed out, first shearing off the Zalkr-

46

ing's right hand at the wrist; then his left. Shocked by the swiftness of the attack, the Zalkring stared uncomprehendingly at the bright red blood spurting from his wrists.

Uskban sneered at him. "How does it feel to be the sacrifice?"

Just as comprehension started to appear in the Zalkring's eyes, Uskban slashed forward, ripping his sword upward through the Zalkring's groin. The fanatic screamed and fell. Coldly Uskban watched him whimper and sob his life away.

Meanwhile, Pognak had taken care of the other two Zalkrings. One head went flying even before its owner knew he was being attacked. The other man managed to get his dagger up to face this huge monster who had suddenly appeared out of thin air, but in almost the same instant was disabled by a savage kick to the balls. Pognak dropped his sword and finished off the Zalkring slowly: first twisting one arm from its socket and then twisting the other in a complete circle before it tore lose from the Zalkring's body. Sandy could see by the unholy look of glee on his face that the mute relished the agonized screams of his victim.

While Pognak played with his Zalkring, Uskban reached down and sliced an ear off the Zalkring he had maimed, not bothering to wait until the fanatic was dead. The Zalkring shrieked and then took the easy way out by dying. Uskban now sauntered over to the Zalkring he had impaled with his javelin. This man had crawled to the well and was sitting with his back to it, holding onto the javelin where it entered his body. He saw Uskban stalking toward him and his eyes opened wide in horror. "Mercy," the fanatic gasped through the blood starting to leak from his mouth.

"As much mercy as you give others," Uskban said in a tight controlled voice. His sword flicked out and the Zalkring's left ear fell into the dust. Uskban leaned forward and grabbed the javelin, yanking it from the Zalkring's body with a gut-ripping twist. His victim screamed in agony and collapsed into the dust.

Uskban spat on the body with contempt. To Pognak he said, "These bastards can slay and torture without turning a hair, but when their turn comes all they can do is snivel."

The giant nodded a bloody head.

Out of thin air came Zhadnoboth's voice. "You idiot, what did you think you were doing? We're trying to sneak up on the Zalkrings, not have every one south of the desert after us to avenge their brethren." He paused and seemed to change thoughts in mid-stream. "And you almost disrupted my enchantments when you leaped off your rudhars and jumped into the fray."

Uskban calmly slit holes in the two fresh ears and added them to his string before he answered. "I came to hurt the Zalkrings as much as I can, not to stand by and watch them slaughter innocents."

"You'll never get much revenge this way." Zhadnoboth was exasperated. "Why kill four, if it ruins your chances to do them much greater harm."

"It's done. There is no way around that fact, sorcerer," Uskban replied. "We must make the best of what is."

Sandy shivered and wondered which of the men scared him most. At least Uskban and Pognak killed in hot blood. Zhadnoboth coldly ignored slaughter if it suited his purpose.

"Wash the blood off before you remount and bring yourselves back under the influence of my spells," the sorcerer said. "The power of fresh-spilled blood can affect even the strongest of spells."

Pognak and Uskban dragged the Zalkrings' bodies out into the bush, a good distance from the well, where the vultures could feed, undisturbed by traffic on the road. The slain family they lined up by the well and covered over.

"Travelers should be along soon," Uskban said. "In another hour the heat of the day will be lessening and people will be on their way out of the city. They'll give these ill-starred wretches a proper burial, better than any we could give."

"Yes, yes," the sorcerer said impatiently. "Now mount up and let's get out of here. We have a long way to go, and we could have either Khalek's men or more Zalkrings breathing down our necks any moment."

As Uskban and Pognak remounted, the integrity of the sorcerer's spells was disrupted for a second. Wavering images of men and animals popped in and out of sight until the spells regained equilibrium and all were invisible again.

They set off down the right-hand fork, the little-used one. The dust raised by the animals settled down behind them and smoothed out their tracks as Zhadnoboth's spells worked overtime to hide their master and his companions.

Just before sunset they stopped for a rest in a scrub thicket to the east of the road. Sandy said a silent prayer of thanks when they halted. Never had it felt so good just to stand on his own two feet. He knew now he was not cut out to be a rider. His mount had a jouncing gait which bounced him from side to side and pounded at his tailbone, his legs were sore from having to wrap around the rudhar's body, and his stomach was trying to decide whether or not to be sea-sick. Sandy had a growing suspicion he was going to hate this adventure.

Pognak doled out food and water and they ate a light supper. Everyone except Sandy seemed satisfied with it, but to his way of thinking, dried sausage, followed by a bland dried fruit called chakiss, and washed down with lukewarm water, was not his idea of a good meal—especially when the portions were so skimpy. If he had to be drafted into an adventure, why couldn't one of his companions have been a trencherman who insisted the edibles be very edible?

Sandy had just laid down to rest sore bones and sorer muscles when Pognak roused him by gouging him in the ribs with the toe of his boot. Sandy sat up angrily, glared at the big mute, and said, "Watch your feet, you dumb ox."

Pognak paid him no mind. Instead he grunted and jerked his thumb toward Uskban and the sorcerer.

Sandy got the message, so damning the universe and this half-assed world in particular, he got to his feet. Walking gingerly, he followed Pognak to where the other two were conferring.

Uskban was telling the sorcerer, "We'll have to travel at night. The land is too open and watched for us to dare the day. We'll have to follow the old road through the Pass of the Five Temples, but once past that bottleneck we can leave it."

Zhadnoboth protested, "Why not travel along the old road as far as we can? You have my magic to protect you and hide you. We'll never get to our destination by wandering aimlessly through trackless desert."

"There will be Zalkrings on the road, especially with the ingathering caused by the upcoming midsummer ceremonies —and some of them are adepts in the blacker forms of magic. Nor is the desert trackless, not to one born and raised in its midst." Uskban looked up and squinted through the growing dusk. "We best be going now. There is hard travel-ing ahead if we want to be as far beyond the pass as possible by daybreak."

Sandy groaned to himself, knowing he'd get no sympathy

from his involuntary companions. He felt half dead already; any more traveling was liable to finish the job.

Soon Sandy was too miserable to worry about dying. His rudhar had managed to kick him as he mounted; and from there things had gone downhill. In a short time his inner thighs and rear end seemed like one enormous and very sore blister. Then the desert night had turned bitterly cold. Sandy wondered how it could be so hellishly hot during the day and then be like this. Only a pigheaded stubbornness—he'd be damned if he would let these bastards outlast him—and a growing numbness kept him going.

The road led through open country and the moon was nearly full, so Zhadnoboth, grumbling at how much the correctly processed pollen of the beg-a-ride bush had cost him and how sorcery was wearing him down to nothing, again cast a glamour over them. It was well he did.

Half an hour after they had set out again, they heard hoofbeats coming up fast behind them. Uskban brusquely pointed to the side of the road and they pulled off and awaited their pursuers—Pognak and Uskban loosening their swords in their scabbards, the sorcerer fingering his staff, and Sandy hoping he wouldn't have to fight for his life with bare hands.

Out of the darkness six riders came charging. Sandy's heart was in his throat, but the black-cloaked riders sped by, hell-for-leather.

Uskban stared after them with fierce and burning eyes. "Zalkrings," he spat, his voice thick with hate and contempt. "I can smell their sour stench."

Warily and keeping their eyes open for more trouble, they resumed their journey.

Sandy stared up at the night sky and was convinced beyond any doubt that he was no longer on Earth—not even an Earth of a different eon. The stars were different and there were more of them. The clincher, though, was the moon shining so brightly in the desert sky. It was larger than Earth's moon and surrounded by a faint blue haze of atmosphere. Sandy wondered what kind of place he was in. Was he in a universe parallel to his own in space and time or in some realm of faery connected to his homeworld by tenuous bonds? Maybe it was the same thing.

Just before midnight they halted. Ahead of them loomed

an immense ridge, appearing to run on forever both to the right and to the left.

Zhadnoboth whispered to Sandy, "That is the Break of the Land, demon. It separates the true desert from the softer lands to the south." He pointed to a black gash in the moon-lit ridge. "There lies the Pass of the Five Temples. Once through it we'll be safe."

Uskban muttered, "Only safer."

Cautiously they headed for the Break. As they got near it, Sandy noticed a ruined town spread on the east side of the pass. Soon they were moving by the crumbling walls of the town. The dilapidated remains of buildings seemed more like ghosts than real things of stone and brick. They glowed eerily in the moonlight, radiating a cold menace which sent a shiver down Sandy's back.

Whatever lurked in the ruin, Zhadnoboth felt it too. He halted and began to mumble additional protective spells. When he was satisfied with his spellcasting, he urged his rud-har forward and motioned for the others to follow him.

"What is this place?" Sandy asked. "It seems dead and yet it watches."

"A thousand years ago, demon," Zhadnoboth said, "there was a time of troubles. The ruler of this city sold his soul to Kels Zalkri and rebelled against the Goddess and those who served her. After the dark god had been defeated, an army loyal to the Goddess put the city to sword, slaying all they found. The ruler they drew and quartered, then bur-ied his body at the four points of the compass. Since that day, the spirit of that ruler has roamed the ruins searching for the parts of his body, especially the head and the heart which were put in a silver casket and buried where no one would look for it. Until he regains his name, which was taken from him, no one shall remember who he was nor will he find what he seeks. The ruins now are an unhallowed place. Only Zalkrings, some of whose ancestors came from here, still fre-quent them."

It took forever to get past the ruins. The sorcerer's magic seemed to be working fine, but Sandy still had an uneasy feeling that eyes were staring out from the city looking for them. Somehow they got past without arousing whatever ma-levolence lay in wait inside the ruins. Sandy felt as though a thousand centuries had rolled off his back, once they were beyond it.

The pass itself was easily crossed. The slope was gradual, the road surprisingly good, and the travelers saw no enemies. At the far end, however, lay a final barrier.

Here, where the way plunged down from the ridge and into the desert, were two gigantic rocks, one on each side of the road. Atop the left-hand boulder, impaled upon a pole, was a skeleton glowing with a green phosphorescent light. Burning red sparks inside its bony eyeholes stared malevolently down at the road. Atop the right-hand boulder Sandy could see two dark-cloaked figures sitting and watching.

Fortunately Zhadnoboth's magic held and the group passed unseen. As they went by, they heard a soft laugh as if someone had just caught the point of a raunchy joke. Then they were out of the pass and into the open desert.

For the best part of an hour they followed the old road, now hardly more than a trail, but eventually Uskban called a halt. Pointing ahead he said, "There is a well just beyond that hill. The water is sweet and cold, but it is a place best avoided since the Zalkrings often stop there. We should leave this road now."

"Let's do it, then," the sorcerer snapped. "We don't have the time to spend here dithering."

Uskban said nothing, just brusquely turned his rudhar and started east.

Zhadnoboth grumbled, "Should we not go west and hide in the hills?"

Uskban snapped his head around and hissed, "You mind your wizardry and I'll take care of the pathfinding. The country to the west is too broken to travel easily in. Besides, there is an ancient and almost forgotten trail to the east which we can follow."

"Won't the Zalkrings have a watch on it also?"

Uskban gave a contemptuous smile and shook his head. "Those pieces of garbage don't bother with it. There is no water they know of along the way so they think no one can survive that trail. Though their stronghold lies in the middle of the desert, they have never bothered to become true desert men. They are interlopers; they know not the true soul of the land and how to love its bleak beauty. Their carrion crows fly as spies over the whole desert, but they hardly ever bother to send them to look at the forest road, since it is the driest and most fierce part of the desert."

"Then how can there be a trail in that direction, especially a forested one?" Zhadnoboth was feeling quite cantankerous after so many hours without sleep. "No one makes a road through the desert unless water is somewhere along it."

"The road is there, sorcerer, it is there. The trail is ancient, from a time when this land was green and fertile—a time, men say, when even the Goddess had not yet come. The rain has fled, but the trail is still there and still called the forest road. It is a way: a way that can be used by those who know how to claw out life from the desert."

Again Uskban started east. The sorcerer gave an ill-tempered snort and followed. Sandy, as he went with them, hoped Uskban, though mad, was competent.

Just before dawn they reached the ancient trail Uskban had spoken of—at least, he said it was the trail. Sandy could only see trackless desert lying at the foot of a time-worn ridge of black stone.

While the others set up camp, Zhadnoboth puttered about renewing and strengthening the spells which still hid them from prying eyes. His continuous grumbling made Sandy wonder if the sorcerer was ever in a good mood. But it wasn't long until exhaustion took over and everyone, animals and all, fell into a well-earned rest.

Sandy was laboriously struggling through a dream where he walked forever and never got anywhere, when he was rudely awakened by something jabbing him in the ribs. He opened his eyes and stared blurrily about. It was still daylight, though the sun had fallen low in the western sky.

"Well, my fine demon, are you going to lay there like a log or get up?" snapped the sorcerer.

Sandy stared mulishly at Zhadnoboth for a moment and then said sullenly, "I am not a demon. I am a human."

The sorcerer gave him a left-handed look and sniffed. "That depends on whether you come from one of the hells or from a parallel world in time—though some hold that any being not from this world is a demon. You are human enough looking, but for my purposes you are a demon and you will remain one."

Sandy started to protest more vehemently, but the chain around his neck gave a warning squeeze and he choked back his words. He got to his feet and then groaned. He'd been saddle sore once before, but never like this.

Zhadnoboth paid no mind to Sandy's misery. "Follow me," he ordered. "There are some things we should talk over before the others awake." He turned and stalked off to the north, not bothering to see whether Sandy followed. Gritting his teeth and damning the sorcerer in words too faint to rouse the chain's anger, Sandy started after him.

Zhadnoboth led the way into a small ravine carved into the ancient ridge which paralleled the trail. A short way in it opened up into a tiny oasis, one of those surprising edens you sometimes find in the desert. With only a trickle of water the hardy desert plants will survive and even flourish. Tufts of a sharp-leaved, greenish gold grass were scattered about, mixed in with a colorful array of desert flowers: tiny blossoms the hue of a morning lake intermingled with strings of bell-shaped flowers the color of a maiden's cheek. To one side grew a clump of spiky flowers the intense blue of lapis lazuli, and next to them, a large pearly-white blossom sprinkled with flecks of gold.

Sandy sniffed appreciatively of the faint aromas, pungent and exciting, coming from the desert plants surrounding them: a curious mixture reminding him of spice, smokiness, aged wine, and musk.

Zhadnoboth found a comfortable-looking rock and sat down. He motioned Sandy to sit on another. The sorcerer started to speak, caught a whiff of the subtle perfumes permeating the air in this secluded eden, forgot Sandy for a moment, and gave a wistful smile as though recalling other and better times. Then Zhadnoboth made a face, shook his head as though to clear unwanted memories, and snapped back to the here and now.

"Let's be to our business," he said to Sandy. "Cooperate with me and you will be rich beyond your wildest dreams. I don't trust Uskban. He is a madman; who knows what goes on in his mind? But with my sorcery and the power inherent in your name we can come out of this adventure unharmed and fabulously wealthy." He gave Sandy a sharp look and asked, "Will you stick with me if I have a falling out with Uskban?"

Sandy thought furiously. He didn't relish teaming up with a twister like the sorcerer, but Uskban wasn't much of a bargain either. The only ally he felt sure of was himself, but in a pinch his own company would be small comfort. He tried to gain time and motioned to the silver chain around his neck, implying he could speak more freely without that encumbrance.

Zhadnoboth's eyes glittered wickedly and he said, "Oh no, my fine demon, the chain stays on. I didn't become an old sorcerer by frittering away what advantages I have. The chain lets you say what you want right now—except if the words be threatening. Now enough of this shilly-shallying. Where do you stand?"

A heavy clomping interrupted them. Startled, they turned and saw Glupp trundling up the ravine toward them. The grundzar spotted the flowers and snorted happily, then hurried over and began gulping down great mouthfuls.

"What is that stupid beast doing here?" howled Zhadnoboth, forgetting his devious plans as he saw Glupp reducing the small oasis to a devastated wasteland. He whacked at the huge creature with his staff and yelled at him to go away. Glupp was too thick-skinned to care. He calmly went on eating the delicious-tasting flowers, only pausing to give a satisfied belch.

The sorcerer turned on Sandy and shook his finger at him. "Take that misbegotten brute away," he yelled.

Nodding, Sandy grabbed hold of Glupp, glad to have any excuse to leave. It took a bit of yanking and a lot more swearing to get the beast's attention, but at last Glupp heaved a thunderous sigh of regret and trotted away at Sandy's heels.

As they wandered back to camp, Sandy thought about Zhadnoboth's reaction to Glupp chomping away at the flowers, and shook his head in a kind of disbelief. The sorcerer could care less about somebody else's blood being shed, but he seemed to have a thing for flowers. Sandy reluctantly admitted to himself that the old scoundrel just might not be all bad.

A suspicion insinuated itself into his head and Sandy turned and looked quizzically at Glupp. The big beast kept plodding along, an air of angelic innocence surrounding him. "You interrupted us at a very opportune time for me," Sandy said in a musing voice. "I wonder if you are as thick-skulled as you put on?"

Glupp gave him an enormous toothy grin and Sandy felt a rosy feeling of affection emanate from the grundzar. Sandy gave him the fish-eye but said no more.

As Sandy and Glupp came into camp, Uskban looked up and saw them. For a very brief moment a smile flickered over his lips as he noticed the painful way Sandy was walking. The little man gave an annoyed grunt and rummaged through a pile of gear until he came up with a small earthenware jar. Stomping over to Sandy, he said, "Take this and rub it into your hind end. It's an ointment concocted from ground tharus root that will make the pain bearable. Doctor yourself quickly and then help Pognak get the animals ready." Then he turned and abruptly stalked off.

Sandy stared after the little man for a moment, shrugged, and began digging the pungent dirty-gray salve out of the jar. Reaching under his robe, he spread the ointment over his saddle-chaffed thighs and backside. It felt good—for about five seconds. Then, suddenly, his whole bottom felt as if on fire. He tried to yell, but his words were too charged with emotion and the chain around his neck tightened ominously. Speechless with pain and frustration, Sandy danced around and shook his fists at everyone and everything. Only Pognak took notice of his plight—and the mute only grinned and gave a soundless chortle.

After a while the pain subsided to a dull glow, and Sandy had to reluctantly admit that Uskban's remedy seemed to be working. It was still painful to walk, but the heat from the tharus root ointment had eased the stiffness in his muscles and it was much easier than it had been. Sandy turned an evil eye in Uskban's direction and thought, *The little bastard owes me for this experience.*

Pognak stomped over, grunted at Sandy, and pointed toward the gear piled on the ground. Sandy nodded and began to load the stuff on Glupp. The mute watched sullenly as Sandy botched things up; distributing the load wrong, not lashing the ropes tightly, and myriad other small but important things. Finally, Pognak got disgusted, roughly elbowed Sandy aside, and began doing the job himself. But he made Sandy pay close heed to what he was doing and growled threateningly anytime the demon's attention wandered.

When Glupp was loaded and the rudhars saddled, they paused for a brief moment to have a bite to eat—none too soon for Sandy.

It was a miserable meal, the food no different or better than before and the company a lot worse. Zhadnoboth had wandered back to camp in a foul mood, snapping at everybody. Uskban kept a black moody silence, occasionally eyeing the sorcerer as if he were measuring him for a coffin. Only Pognak was unchanged, being only his ordinary nasty self. Sandy smiled ruefully to himself, glad Glupp had kept him from putting his foot in his mouth. He didn't want to antagonize Uskban, and he had a feeling that if he committed himself to the sorcerer, the madman would know it. Uskban might be insane, but that hadn't dulled his wits—and he knew Zhadnoboth was up to something.

As the sun started to slip behind the horizon, they broke camp. Zhadnoboth thumbed through his spellbook, found what he was looking for, then muttered an incantation and thumped the ground three times with his staff.

Sandy felt an invigorating jolt of energy followed by the dissipation of an oppressive closed-in feeling he'd had ever since the sorcerer had placed his protective spells over them. He looked toward Zhadnoboth and saw that the sorcerer was dumbfounded. Apparently something had gone very wrong.

A flicker of motion caught Sandy's eye. Turning, he saw a large black crow with a white-topped head flying toward the north like a bat out of hell. Uskban saw it too, and gave a hoarse yell.

Zhadnoboth spat out an obscene curse and quickly tried a variation of his lightning spell. A sizzling white bolt shot out of the heavens to blast the bird. There was a brilliant burst of light—then nothing, except for a few black feathers and charred bones floating to the ground.

Uskban whirled to face the sorcerer. "Why did you remove your protective spells? It almost cost us our lives! Don't be so damned miserly with your magic."

Zhadnoboth retorted, "If you were as good a desert man as you boast, you would have seen that carrion crow sitting on the cliff. I took the spells off because my power is limited —I can't drain myself dry in order to take care of every small need which comes up. You'll need me at full strength when we get to the Zalkrings' stronghold. Night and your piddling skill at concealment will have to hide us until then. I will only use my magic if it is absolutely necessary."

Listening, Sandy knew the sorcerer was making up a lot of gabble about the limits of his magic. The truth was he'd blown the gaff and didn't want to admit it. Sandy's new sixth sense was suddenly sharp and he could sense that under Zhadnoboth's anger was blatant dishonesty.

Uskban didn't have the benefit of a sixth sense, but he had an ear for a lie. "Don't give me that, sorcerer. I know somewhat of magic—sorcery, by the use of spells and incantations, taps the energy of the universe. Once established, a sorcery is self-sustaining and need not drain more power from a sorcerer."

By the stormy aura he could sense surrounding the sorcerer, Sandy saw that Uskban's words hit close to the truth. But Zhadnoboth was never going to let a mere ruffian question his wisdom and ability, even if what he said was true, and he counterattacked.

"Like all generalizations made by misinformed amateurs, that is only half true." The sorcerer put as much high-toned dignity in these words as he could, at the same time shading his voice to subtly show his disdain for a layman who'd dare comment on something that was beyond his comprehension. "It's true, in theory, that a sorcery once established never need be renewed. But conditions are almost never perfect, so most sorcerers must use energy to correct aberrations which would destroy their spells. I'm no wizard who must maintain a constant flow of energy in order to work magic, but initiating and monitoring my spells does tax my strength."

Sandy thought it was grand-sounding garbage, most of it true, but still garbage.

Uskban had a like opinion. "Maybe so," he grunted skeptically, "but it also could be that you were unwise." Then he turned on his heel, strode over to his rudhar, and mounted it.

As they headed north into the night, the madman and the sorcerer shared a sullen silence. Sandy hoped things would get better. If this kept up, they'd be cutting one another's throats in a couple of days. Though that might be to his advantage . . . If he kept out of harm's way it could give him a chance to escape back to his own world—or it could leave him stranded in this back corner of the universe forever.

Sandy felt a sudden homesickness for Earth, not realizing until now how much he loved it, even Baltimore and its blue-collar rowdiness. He wondered if anyone would miss him. Probably not right away. His brother and parents were out of the country and it would be a couple of months before they noticed his absence. In the meantime nobody else would. His boss would be glad to be rid of him and his landlord would only bitch about him skipping out on the rent. Well, maybe that redhead, Chris, might have regrets and then again maybe not.

Sandy's mind wandered back to the last spell the sorcerer

had tried. He still felt full of energy and more alive than he'd ever been. Was it possible that the magic inherent in his name had short-circuited the sorcerer's spell? In any case he was going to keep quiet about it—he needed any edge he could get.

8

In a different place, another shared the black moodiness felt by Zhadnoboth and Uskban. The shadow of the Goddess sat by a black pool made from close-fitting blocks of basalt. The water within was the hue of ink. The surface of the water glittered and glimmered with the trapped glow of moon and stars. Absentmindedly she ran her shadowy fingers through the chill water, catching the shimmering slivers of light and weaving them into meaningless patterns.

Uncertainty and discontent plagued the Goddess's thoughts. Events were going much as she had planned them, but she was uneasy about the changes boded by her shaping of destiny.

Her intense hatred of Kels Zalkri helped the Goddess shake off any qualms. Anything was worthwhile if she could destroy this being who jeered at her and denied her godhead.

She began plotting the future of her four unlikely champions. Already they were a formidable combination, but needed two things more to make them into a force that could bring the dark one to his knees and then rip him forever asunder. One was an ancient talisman, long hidden, which must now reenter the world, to be wielded once again by a descendent of Idman of a Thousand Battles. The other was a harder thing, a oneness of spirit to give them the strength to persist when all odds were against them—this she could abet, but only they could create.

Her thoughts brought back memories of Idman and she smiled. A hero and a statesman, but more importantly one of the few mortals who had touched her heart. He had been honorable and straightforward when it counted and a conniving scoundrel when he had to be—and a magnificent lecher. Would she ever see his like again?

The Goddess turned her thoughts back to how she could influence her champions to choose rightly. She could often get Zhadnoboth to do her will by giving his mind unobtrusive nudges. But it was a chancy business because she could never be sure how the sorcerer would react. He was such an odd combination of eccentric, romantic, and scheming realist that in any given situation he could go any of a hundred different ways.

If Zhadnoboth failed her, thought the Goddess, she could always fall back on her spy. He was a superb agent and already had done yeoman service. Deep-thinking, resourceful, and devious: he'd find some way to get her will done. In the meantime, she had a pair of eyes which saw all and which no one would suspect.

Again the Goddess rippled her fingers through the water. It swirled darkly; in its crystalline depths she saw four riders and a lumbering beast of burden trudging through the night toward their destiny.

Her plots thought out, the Goddess went back to musing about the future. Every step that Sandy and his companions took brought closer her time of destiny—either destruction or a deeper and more profound authority. But even winning had its price. She must become less lofty in order to be more; wallow in earthy humanity in order to become more divine.

She laughed at her own grandiose thoughts. Truth to tell, it was really simple. She had to share some of her power to be greater and had to be more human in order to become a greater goddess. Still, it irked her that she had to give up her total independence and rely on another, but she would gain a more profound understanding of what it was to be human. She sighed; what would be, would be, but it need not be forever.

9

INTENSE heat and a flash of sunlight woke Sandy. Grumbling
sleepily, he sat up and looked for a shadier spot. He saw a
well-shadowed nook at the foot of the ginger-colored mesa
they were camped near. Groggily Sandy headed for it, leaving behind Glupp who'd been acting as his pillow and bed-
warmer. The grundzar half raised an eyelid and looked at
him, his thought seeming to say, *Why can't these crazy
humans ever be satisfied with where they are?*

Sandy threw his blanket down in the chosen spot, but
couldn't get back to sleep. Either a stone was in his back or
his position wasn't quite right or the wind was in his face—it
was always something. After tossing for a while, he gave it
up.

Sandy thought about his companions and smiled sourly.
They were the worst company he had ever had, bar none. If
he had picked any three people out of a crowd, he doubted
he could have found more uncongenial companions. If he
ever got out of this alive, he'd appreciate good-natured people a lot more.

The only saving grace to the journey was Glupp. The
grundzar and Sandy had developed a real friendship. The big
beast didn't talk, but Sandy could sense his warm feelings,
and in many ways that was better. Sandy could talk to Glupp
and intuitively feel the beast understood and sympathized
even if he might disagree. In many ways Glupp seemed wiser
than his human companions—he took life as it was and enjoyed it.

Sandy arose and walked about to get the kinks out of his
muscles. He was still sore—five nights of constant riding
hadn't helped much—but much less so than when he had
started on this adventure. Smiling wryly to himself, he sup-

posed that he must be getting toughened up. One look at his flatter belly and he was sure of it.

He noticed that Uskban's blankets were empty. Mildly curious, Sandy looked around for the little man. A faint path leading toward the top of the mesa seemed to show signs of recent use. Bored and feeling snoopy, Sandy decided to climb the path and see what Uskban was up to.

Several minutes later, Sandy was cursing under his breath at himself for being so damned curious. The path seemed more suited to a goat than a human, sometimes going almost straight up. Sandy stubborned it out and made it to the top, breathless but not exhausted.

Uskban was sitting on the edge of a cliff and staring off moodily toward the west. Through the clear desert air Sandy saw a distant range of mountains, mostly colored in harsh tones of brown and gray, but here and there touched with a muted green. Sandy thought they might prove useful in case he needed a place to run to, the green strongly suggesting he'd at least find water there.

"Sit here beside me," Uskban said brusquely. His voice was moody and brooding and in it Sandy sensed softer emotions than he had seen in him up to now. Surprised and curious at this change in the hate-filled madman, Sandy sat down beside him.

Uskban pointed to the mountains and said, "For years beyond number, men and women of my lineage have dwelt on the east flank of those mountains. My family was great in that land and once we ruled it. With the passing of centuries we lost our overlordship—there were rebellions and kings who knew not how to rule—but the lineage held true and the family persisted. Until I was a young man we were still a force to be reckoned with among the clans. We were first among them and led the council when it met—even our enemies among the Kri Shandri respected our ancestry and ancient kingship. Then we were betrayed, and all were slain except me. When I die the Naz Idmani will be no more."

There was a moment of black silence and then he spoke again, giving voice to some of his anguish. "One of our enemies among the clans sold us out to the Zalkrings, not daring to do the bloody slaughter themselves—else there would have been a blood feud which the rest of the Kri Shandri clans would have carried on until not one of that accursed clan was left alive. Some few I have made pay the price of their betrayal; only Zalkrings do I enjoy killing more."

This speech surprised Sandy. Up to now Uskban had been about as talkative as a doorpost, speaking only if something had to be said. The sight of the mountains had awakened a part of him Sandy hadn't thought existed. He kept quiet, partly to learn something which might be useful, but more because Uskban's words had touched something inside him.

"My ancestor, Idman of a Thousand Battles, is still the greatest hero of the Kri Shandri—even among those clans who were by tradition enemies to my family. He made the Kri Shandri one and thus became father to all the clans. He took a hundred warring clans and forged them into a nation. Warrior, poet, statesman, whoremonger, father, and rogue —he was all these and more."

Uskban stared moodily at the mountains. In a quiet voice he went on, "Idman died, and soon the golden age passed. Now only the clans and their blood feuds rule in the land of the Kri Shandri. It is prophesied that another will come to reunite my people. A tradition handed down for unknown generations in my family says that from the loins of Uskban the Lame, eldest son of Idman and our ancestor, this hero will come. When my time comes to walk in the land of the dead, my lineage will be at an end. A hero will come, but he will know us not, and the Naz Idmani will be forgotten."

Uskban stared westward, eyes filled with black despair and an intense longing. "When I die there will be no one to mourn me, no one to sing of my deeds, no one to torch my pyre, and no one to light a candle for me on the Day of Souls. I will have been as nothing."

Despite himself, Sandy felt pity for the bloody madman. His soul might be twisted and damaged, but something grand still lurked in the wreckage.

"All I have," Uskban said, "is revenge. Give me that and I can die in peace." He paused and added, "Maybe a certain shamed woman would cry for me, but she is not of my kith or kin."

For several minutes Uskban brooded silently. Sandy sat beside him and kept his quiet company. Suddenly the madman raised his hand and pointed to a faint light snaking through the desert toward the distant mountains. "That is Idman's Way—a fabled road. As a scared youngster Idman fled east on it, a nobody with no future and an inglorious past. He came back along the road a man and a warrior, and with him came the Key of Arimithos, a talisman of great power and a sign of the Goddess's favor."

Uskban spoke in a voice filled with mystery and reverence. Sandy shivered; he could feel some of the wonder that belonged to this world. He was also intrigued by mention of the Goddess. He'd heard snippets of information about her before and was beginning to suspect she was a deity he needed to know about. "Who is this goddess?" he asked.

Uskban gave him a shocked look. "You should know her, demon. She is a power in Zarathandra and in the invisible worlds. Demons tremble at the mere mention of her. She is the greatest of the gods and ruler of this world. She is mother, child, maiden, and crone. She is wisdom, love, justice, chance, and destruction. She is a comfort to the weak and a sword the strong fear. You know her, you must."

Sandy wanted to know a lot more about her, but never got the chance. Uskban sprang to his feet and then listened. "Come," he snapped, scrambling headlong down the sheer path. Sandy followed more slowly.

Back at camp Sandy found the sorcerer and Uskban arguing violently. Looking on and glowering ferociously at the sorcerer was Pognak, at whose feet lay a pile of empty waterskins.

"What did you do with our water?" Uskban asked in a quiet and very deadly voice.

Zhadnoboth, red-faced and looking very aggrieved, replied, "I needed it for a spell—a very important spell." He paused, glaring at Pognak, and shook his finger angrily at the mute. "And I had nearly completed the spell when this big oaf came blundering into the middle of everything and ruined the spell. The water went up in steam and it would have served him right to have done so also. Now there is no more water to recast the spell with."

"Damn your spell!" yelled Uskban. "What are we going to drink?"

"Find some more," the sorcerer said imperiously. "You're the one who knows the desert and its secrets. Do your job—find water. I only take care of the magic, and I have more than held up my end of the bargain."

Uskban grabbed Zhadnoboth by his scrawny throat, knocked the staff from his hands, and shook him like a terrier does a rat. "I can survive in the desert easily, but not if those with me are idiots! You don't waste water in the desert,

not when the next well might be two or three days away.
Even an evil old bastard like yourself would shrivel up and
die without water. I swear by the Goddess, I'll slit your
throat and drink your blood before I die because of your
carelessness!"

Uskban gave the sorcerer one last shake and shoved him
away. Zhadnoboth staggered backward for a few steps before
he caught himself. Then he stood and rubbed his neck, staring daggers at Uskban. But the sorcerer had only time for a
sly glance at his staff before Uskban put his foot on it and
fingered the hilt of his poniard.

"Don't do it, sorcerer. I can kill you faster than you can
bespell me. Besides, you and I need each other. After this is
over, there'll be time to settle grudges."

Zhadnoboth thought for a moment, nodded, and snapped
ungraciously, "Give me back my staff. I'll not use it on you,
not that I would need it—there are many dangerous magics
which require only ill will. As you say, we need one another
—for now."

Uskban handed the staff back to the sorcerer with a kind
of disdain. Zhadnoboth snatched it from his hand and spat
out, "I still need to do the water divination spell. It may be
the only way to learn vital information."

Uskban shook his head savagely, enraged that the sorcerer still didn't understand the situation, and retorted,
"What's vital right now is surviving. We have no water. We
will die if we don't get some."

"Surely," said the sorcerer in a tone implying he was hu-
moring a fool, "you know where to get some."

Uskban gave a sour laugh. "I know, but getting it is another matter. No well or spring lies nearby."

"Is there no water at all along this road?"

"From here to our destination there is no water. Only if
we leave this ancient trail and make for the road the Zalkrings use will we find water. That road is only an hour or so to
the west. Where Idman's Way crosses the old desert road
there's a well, but the water is barely drinkable and the
Zalkrings are often about."

"There's no water nearby?" asked Zhadnoboth.

"The nearest other water is almost a day's journey farther
along Idman's Way. The place is not much visited and the
water is sweet. But we lose a lot of time; a day to get there
and a day to get back. If you are the sorcerer you say you

are, you should be able to conjure up water for us. You can do that, can't you?"

Zhadnoboth gave Uskban a withering look. "I can't do it without attracting the Zalkrings' attention. Water magic is a type of witchery, not sorcery: it does not draw its energy from the universe, but instead taps the power inherent in the world close to it. Witchery sets up vibrations in the fabric of the world which can be detected, especially if it is close to a center of power like the Zalkrings' mountain." He paused and then added, "Besides, a sorcerer of my abilities should not be bothered to work such a small magic."

What Zhadnoboth said was half true—or so Sandy's on-and-off sixth sense told him. It was nice to have, but it was a strange ability which seemed to sense different things at different times. Sometimes he could only sense feelings; at other times he could see the deep truth underlying whatever was the present situation. Right now his sixth sense saw things as colors. When Zhadnoboth said water magic would be dangerous, his thoughts colored danger-red with his words. However, when he said water magic was a small magic, his thoughts seemed a shifty muddle of yellow and blue, signaling his words were less than the whole truth.

Uskban wasn't fooled, either. "Save your lies for idiots like yourself: Admit that water magic is too much for you, and stop wasting my time." He looked to Sandy and Pognak and snapped, "Get the beasts ready. It might be a long trip west and there is not much time until sundown."

While Zhadnoboth sulked, the others got ready. Uskban found one waterskin that the sorcerer had missed. There was enough in it for one cupful apiece. "Drink it all now," he said to them. "Don't be fools and take it a sip at a time—that's a sure way to get your brains fried."

They traveled west for a little over an hour, until Uskban rose in his saddle and motioned them to stop. He sniffed the wind, made an obscene remark, and then growled, "Zalkrings. Their religion requires that they eat certain herbs and spices each day; it gives them an unholy stink like no other I know."

Sandy took a sniff of the wind but couldn't smell anything. *The little bastard must have the nose of a bloodhound.*

Uskban turned to Sandy and the sorcerer. "You two wait here with the beasts. Pognak and I will scout ahead." He clearly didn't have much confidence in Sandy or the sorcerer being able to sneak around quietly. He gave them a hard look and added, "Don't move unless we uncork the demons of hell."

Sandy and Zhadnoboth waited silently, neither speaking to the other. After a few fretful moments Zhadnoboth muttered something about the chill and began rummaging through the packs on Glupp's back. He came up with a bottle of wine and began to sip on it, not bothering to offer a drop to Sandy.

Sandy ignored the sorcerer, leaned against Glupp, and began scratching the grundzar behind his wrinkled ears and on the neck. He'd found that the big beast adored this kind of attention. Glupp's thoughts became rosy with happiness and he pressed up against Sandy. "You big baby," Sandy murmured.

About fifteen minutes later Zhadnoboth sidled up to Sandy and whispered right into his face, "Have you been thinking over my offer?" His eyes had acquired a slight glaze and his winy breath gave Sandy a momentary high.

Suddenly Uskban stepped out of the night. Zhadnoboth choked on a swig of wine and stumbled backward with a guilty look on his face, muttering darkly about sneaking murderers. Sandy knew what he meant; his heart nearly jumped into his throat when the little man had so suddenly appeared.

The sorcerer's half-heard comments and guilty look didn't bother Uskban, who had more important things on his mind. "Lead the beasts and follow me. We have to circle south of the waterhole; the place is crawling with Zalkrings. And there's a mage with them—I nearly stumbled into a protective spell he'd placed around their encampment. Pognak has gone ahead to check out Idman's Way; if nothing lies in wait for us we should see him again about sunrise."

There was a fierce tension in the madman's voice which put Sandy on edge. Uskban seemed only a hairbreadth away from exploding into a killing frenzy. Zhadnoboth, despite his slight intoxication, also noticed it and casually took a crumpled handkerchief from his robe. Sandy wondered what the old shyster was up to.

With Uskban leading the way, they started to circle south of the Zalkrings. Trying to move quietly was nerve-racking, with every pebble grinding under his foot sounding like thunder to Sandy. However, all went well until they had almost worked their way to the west of the Zalkrings. Then a dark figure appeared from behind a rise in front of them.

Uskban had for the last few minutes been shaking with suppressed hate and casting wild eyes toward the Zalkring camp as his lust for vengeance threatened to overwhelm good sense. The sudden appearance of the Zalkring broke his control. He whipped out his wide-bladed poniard and silently began to charge. The sorcerer, with a speed and accuracy surprising for such a scrawny old coot, sprang forward and flicked his handkerchief in Uskban's face. A gray cloud engulfed the madman's head, and he stopped and soundlessly collapsed into a limp heap.

For a frozen instant, Sandy and the sorcerer waited in breathless anticipation as the Zalkring seemed to turn his head and listen. Then the Zalkring fumbled at his clothes and in a moment was relieving his bladder.

Finally he turned and went back toward the encampment, having noticed nothing. Zhadnoboth pointed to Uskban and whispered, "Pick him up." Sandy knelt by the body, silently cursing when his knee ground into the hilt of Uskban's poniard. Then, smiling crookedly, he unobtrusively picked it up and slipped it into the top of his left boot. Later on, it might be useful to have a weapon.

After a bit of fumbling around, Sandy got the little man over his shoulder, and managed to stagger to his feet. "How the hell can such a sawed-off runt weigh so much?" he whispered.

"Quiet!" the sorcerer hissed as he glanced nervously toward the Zalkring camp.

Sandy stumbled awkwardly over to Uskban's rudhar, the body harder to manage and as unbalanced as a plastered elephant, and dumped it across the saddle. The little man's body began to slide off the beast as soon as Sandy let go of it. "Son of a bitch," Sandy said as he grabbed hold of Uskban and kept him on the saddle. "Get some rope," he hissed between gritted teeth at the sorcerer. For once Zhadnoboth made himself useful, quickly bringing over a braided rawhide rope.

Once Uskban was lashed onto his mount, they headed northwest toward what they hoped was Idman's Way. They almost missed it in the dark, its surface hardly distinguishable from the rest of the desert floor. Only the moon, coming out from behind a cloud at a very opportune time, showed it to them. As the light struck the desert floor, Idman's Way appeared as a silvery white line wending its way through the desert.

"The Goddess favors us," Zhadnoboth whispered.

"At least something does," Sandy said in a sour voice.

"Watch your words," the sorcerer hissed angrily. "It's not wise to make light of the Goddess, she's got a long memory and takes insult easily. The moon is her minion and it aided us when we might have lost our way." Zhadnoboth turned his face toward the moon and said, "Forgive my companion, lady. He is new to this world and its ways. If you be watching us, smile on us and our quest."

Sandy held his tongue because the old heathen appeared to be a true believer, at least when it suited him, but mentally took the sorcerer's words with a pound of salt. Gods, in Sandy's experience, were never around when you needed them, if they were around at all. Besides, he wondered how favorably a goddess would look on a plundering expedition.

"Untie Uskban and put him down beside the road," Zhadnoboth said in a caution-muted voice. After Sandy had lowered Uskban's body to the ground, Zhadnoboth came over and knelt by it. "He's almost more trouble than he is worth," the sorcerer muttered. "The powdered root of the lesser bog lily, which I used on him, comes from the far north. A thimbleful costs a gold piece at the best of times."

Zhadnoboth patted his robes in a haphazard fashion until he found the right bump. He reached inside his robes and pulled forth a small glass vial, uncorked it, and held it under Uskban's nose. A faint but pungent odor filled the air. The sorcerer chanted a few words of binding and suddenly the nose-puckering smell was overpowering. "Elzarb's Elixir," he said to Sandy by way of explanation.

For a couple of seconds Uskban lay unmoving, then he sputtered and abruptly sat up. "Here, drink this." Zhadnoboth shoved a leather flask in his face.

Uskban took a swallow and shuddered. "By the balls of Behanus, where did you get that stuff? It could burn out the innards of a firedrake." But the rotgut did its job, reviving Uskban enough to go on.

Uskban sat on the ground rocking back and forth and holding his head. "What did you do to me?" he asked.

"I calmed you down so this venture wouldn't end before it's really begun," Zhadnoboth said in a caustic tone. "There is no aftereffect except for a slight headache."

Uskban gritted his teeth and rubbed his forehead. "Slight? My head is splitting down the middle."

"You deserve worse," Zhadnoboth said callously. "If I hadn't stopped you, we'd have been up to our necks in trouble. A killing this close to their stronghold would have brought out scores of Zalkrings looking for intruders. Most could be dealt with, but not their mages—when aroused even those second-raters can smell a well-hidden sorcerer."

"What about plain old hidden treasure hunters," Sandy said sarcastically. His boldness surprised both himself and the sorcerer, who eyed him askance.

Uskban looked bleakly at the ground. "I hate too much sometimes. I owe you for this, sorcerer."

Sandy started as a huge figure loomed up out of the darkness, but it was only Pognak. Sandy couldn't help wishing that this adventure was over. Sneaking around was starting to wear on his nerves.

Uskban conferred with the mute, Pognak talking sign language and Uskban replying in a near whisper. Sandy tried to catch what was going on, but darkness and the softness of Uskban's voice prevented him. After a few minutes the little man pointed off to the west and said something. Pognak grunted unhappily and shook his head. Uskban spoke a few crisp words and the giant reluctantly agreed. Rumbling unhappily, Pognak stalked over to his rudhar, mounted, threw a hard look toward Sandy and the sorcerer, and rode off toward the west.

Uskban turned to Zhadnoboth and Sandy and said, "Mount up. We have a long way to go before dawn. Two riders used this road today. Pognak is going ahead to spy out the land and make sure we are not surprised. If there is trouble laying in wait, he'll find it." The last words were spoken with utter confidence.

Sandy wished he had as much confidence. He was beginning to feel like a minnow surrounded by hungry sharks. He caught Uskban's eye and asked, "Why the glare he gave me and Zhadnoboth?"

Uskban gave a wolfish grin and replied, "He worries about me, but I told him you two have more to fear from me than I from you."

Uskban set a killing pace, but Sandy hardly noticed it. He'd done so much hard riding lately that he'd grown accustomed to it. The sorcerer was too wrapped up in his own thoughts to notice the pace either. Only Glupp complained, every now and then giving a disgusted *woof:* the tone of his thoughts telling Sandy he much preferred a slow steady pace to this ridiculous rush. Sandy reached over from his rudhar and patted the big beast on the top of his head, thinking, *I don't like it either.* Evidently Glupp caught the drift of Sandy's thoughts, for he gave a pleased rumble in reply.

Sandy was fond of the big lummox. They had hit it off from the first, each sensing in the other a kindred spirit. Sandy's newfound sixth sense had given them a means to communicate, not so much words as feelings, and they'd drifted into a solid friendship, enjoying each other's company and not minding any faults.

Sandy watched the desert as they swept by it. In the moonlight it was a weirdly beautiful place, filled with dim silvery shapes outlined in ebony. Here was a tall thorny bush shaped like a bent old man; there, white moths fluttering around a spiny plant the size and shape of a basketball. Randomly scattered through the desert were tiny plants with ash-white blossoms; flitting between them were insects with pulsing greenish lights.

During the day the desert was soundless except for the wind, but at night it came to life with sharp whistles, muted coos, eerie wailings, and occasionally a low rumbling croak. Listening, Sandy wondered what weird creatures made them. Were they much like the creatures he knew from Earth? Or like nothing he'd ever come across?

These thoughts got him thinking about Earth and this world called Zarathandra. The flora and fauna he'd seen seemed like a mixture of life definitely related to that of Earth and life that had no counterparts to anything he knew of. There had to be some connection between this world and Earth and he wondered what it was. Maybe some people and other things which disappeared from Earth ended up here. Maybe he wasn't so alone in being marooned in this backwater. He thought some more and shrugged, deciding to survive the best he could and to keep his eyes open for any evidence for his theories.

Uskban dropped back to ride beside Sandy and began talking to him, though it was more as if he were talking to himself. "Pognak is my mother's cousin's nephew. He's a Naz Gagmani, descended from a son Idman had by a Mahandak singer he seduced. We were of an age and as boys went through the Six Month Dying, learning together to be men. We both ran the death race the same night and became men together the next morning. Four of us drank of our blood mixed with summer wine and bitterwood sap. Of those four, only he and I now live." He paused and then added, "Now four of us go to a testing." Having said these enigmatic words, he spurred his rudhar and rode ahead into the darkness, as if what he had said explained everything.

Sandy followed him with his eyes and tried to puzzle out what his words had meant and why he had said them in the first place. Finally, he shivered and made a fervent wish that the madman's words were no omen of doom.

It was just before dawn, when the night is blackest, that Pognak reappeared. One moment he wasn't there and the next he was riding beside Uskban. Sandy could see him rapidly talking with his hands. Uskban's face was grim.

He turned to Sandy and Zhadnoboth, a faint gleam of hatred in his eyes, and said, "There is trouble ahead. Pognak says maybe a dozen people are at the well. Most are Naz Mathoni, descended from a bastard son Idman had by a one-eyed drunken whore, who are the hereditary enemies of my clan. There is a Zalkring with them, a mage if Pognak reads the signs right." He paused and then added, "There is also a woman, but she is not with the others."

"Now what are we going to do?" Zhadnoboth nagged. "I am already as dry as a year-old prune. I can't go much longer without water."

"Hold your peace, sorcerer," Uskban snapped. "I must think this over." For a moment he settled into a sullen silence as he mulled over the options.

Just when Zhadnoboth seemed ready to explode, Uskban spoke again. "There are too many to attack head on, especially if they have a Zalkring mage with them, and any major sorcery could draw unwelcome attention to us. Our only hope is for you and the demon to ride into their midst and pretend to be innocent travelers. Pognak and I will hide in the desert and do what we can to aid you."

Zhadnoboth did not take kindly to this suggestion. "What? You want me to ride into a nest of cutthroats? I'll be damned if I'll do it—they'd as soon slaughter us as look at us; I am not risking my hide."

Uskban shrugged and said, "No, it is not safe, but we haven't much choice. Besides, they'll think twice before trying to slay you—enraging sorcerers has never been a healthy practice. And they are still Kri Shandri, even if they be back-stabbing Naz Mathoni dogs. It has always been the custom of my people to show hospitality to visitors, even if we plan to kill them once they leave the protection of our campfires. Boldly stride into their midst, and they'll be forced to break bread and share water with you."

Sandy cocked his head and looked at Uskban as he said these last words. If he wasn't mistaken those last words had been spoken with deadpan humor. The madman had to be the oddest crazy he'd ever run across.

Zhadnoboth was too steamed up to notice Uskban's wry tones. "And how do I get close enough to get this hospitality?"

"You're a sorcerer; that should be easy. Haven't your spells been hiding us the last few days?" Uskban added sarcastically. "Besides, you have a way with words when you turn your mind to it, sorcerer."

"Easy!" Zhadnoboth screamed. "A lot you know. I'm worn down to nothing." Zhadnoboth paused for breath, and a crafty gleam came into his eyes. Sandy could almost see the wheels turning inside the sorcerer's head as he began thinking of ways to turn Uskban's idea to his advantage. "It can be done. Not that it will be easy."

Uskban replied swiftly, "Just establish yourself inside their camp and wait for sundown—then be ready to fight for your lives. You will be safe until then. The Naz Mathoni are great traditionalists: if they mean to slay you they won't do it until after sunset. Pognak and I will be ready to attack if they turn on you. We should dispose of them easily as they will be caught between us—especially if you fry a few with your lightning."

"You'll get us killed!" the sorcerer screamed louder than before. "I'm no warrior and this demon"—pointing a finger at Sandy—"has no claws. And what about the attention my sorcery would attract?"

Uskban gave a mad wink and said, "Don't worry. There are secrets to this place that only the Naz Idmani know, and those secrets will spell doom for our foes."

"I hope those secrets can keep my throat from being cut," Sandy cut in sourly. "Facing a pack of murderers with bare hands if things go to pot is not my idea of good planning—there has to be a better way."

Zhadnoboth and Uskban ignored him and haggled a bit more, the sorcerer plainly thinking the plan was lunatic, but resigned to going along with it. Sandy could sense that he had figured a way out for himself if things went completely awry. Sandy fingered the hilt of the poniard hidden in his boot and wished he had a bolthole.

"What about a sword for me?" Sandy asked. "I saw you pack a couple extra."

"Do you know how to use one?" Uskban asked.

"No. But it would make me look dangerous."

The madman gave a snort of disgust and stalked off.

After Uskban and Pognak faded away into the desert, the sorcerer began rummaging through his robe for a spellbook and other odds and ends needed for the enchantment he was going to do, all the while muttering about harebrained schemes.

Sandy agreed with him. Uskban's plan looked like a great chance to get their throats cut. He loosened the poniard hidden in his boot and decided to stick like a burr to the sorcerer just in case the Naz Mathoni decided to observe their rules of hospitality in the breech.

All this thinking and planning still didn't calm Sandy. His belly felt like it was full of cold lead and his heart kept climbing into his throat—he wished he had the option to run.

10

THE Goddess called her minion the moon, and its rays streamed down from above and focused to form a mirror of viewing on the floor in front of her throne. She saw again a place she loved well: the Kri Shandri called it Idman's Well, but of old it had been Talith Kumari. It was here that she had entered Idman's dreams and set the feet of a wayward shepherd boy on the road to greatness. The embers of an old sadness stirred within her at the memory.

Movement caught the eye of the Goddess and she frowned as she saw the Zalkring mage cutting the throat of a sand fox pup and letting the blood fall to the ground as an offering to his god. Enraged, she vowed that Kels Zalkri would pay dearly for allowing his follower to profane a place sacred to her. The black god was growing bold as he thought his time drew near. Despite reminding herself that she'd drawn the dark one's attention in order to pave the way to his downfall, the presence of a Zalkring at Idman's Well rankled.

The Goddess turned her attention to Sandy and his companions. She had got them to Idman's Well; now to make her next move in the deadly game she played with Kels Zalkri. If she didn't misplay she would accomplish two things: draw the black god's attention away from his mountain and deliver a powerful weapon into the hands of one who could use it.

Her priestess would be the catalyst. The priestess had known Uskban of old and her presence would turn his thoughts to the future destiny of the Naz Idmani. A new woof should be added to the weavings of fate, one which should not only help determine the outcome of this venture, but events still years ahead in the future she schemed for.

The Goddess turned her mind to Uskban and saw him

and his mute companion mashing up the fleshy roots of a bitterthorn bush. Watching them drink the peppery, life-sustaining fluid, she felt compassion. These mortals had been hard-used by fate, which had crippled their souls but shaped them into the type of men she needed. In turn their actions would help to shape her future and the future of everyone living in the world of Zarathandra. She murmured, "Serve me, my mortals, just for this short time, and I will give you ease."

The Goddess smiled her thanks to the moon and it withdrew its beams. She looked quietly into the darkness and nodded with satisfaction. The weavers of destiny—with a little help from her—would shape the present to create the future she wanted.

11

HAZ the Widow-Maker lumbered out of his tent and headed toward the campfire. The thin angular form of Igsban, The Old One Who Stalks in the Night, was already sitting by the fire. He was drinking a morning cup of hot barzi tea. Without a word, this old companion handed a cup of the steaming stuff to Haz.

Haz took a long sip and savored it. "Ah, that tastes good," he said. "It's almost as good as a woman in bed or the morning sun warming my old bones."

Igsban gave a short grunt in reply.

Haz ignored the customary brusqueness of his companion and took another long pull of the pungent red brew, twice steamed and heavily laced with ant honey, and sighed blissfully. He looked around the camp and shook his head. "They just don't make them like they did in the old days."

The sour-faced Igsban nodded and grunted agreement.

Haz went on, "They're a good enough bunch of ruffians, but they couldn't begin to fill the boots of some we've known. All the old ones now are gone, except for you and me. Not one of these pups can boast of bedding over a hundred women in the first year of his manhood like my brother Nathyogar. Or will there ever be another like Yil of the Red Hand? He slew his first man before he was thirteen and over a hundred before he was twenty." He winked at Igsban and added, "Not that you and I weren't as mean as any who have come down the road."

"No spunk," Igsban muttered.

"I was a war captain at twenty," said Haz. "But this bunch of witlings may reach eighty and never cut more than a dozen throats. I don't know what's going to become of the Naz

Mathoni when young warriors can't hope to win against old men like ourselves."

Igsban grunted in full agreement.

Haz took another sip of tea and nearly choked on it. From out of nowhere company had arrived: riding on a couple of rudhars well worth stealing were a scrawny old man and his servant, followed by an enormous grundzar loaded with a mountain of equipment—the big beast alone was worth twenty Rithian gold cartwheels, Haz almost absentmindedly figured.

Sandy could sense that for a moment the fat scoundrel wondered if he was still a fit leader for his cutthroats. Then a slow anger began to burn within him, quickly followed by thoughts which had a cool and calculating feel. The fat old bastard might be past his prime, but age hadn't dulled his wits. He knew neither he nor his men were inept enough to have let Sandy and Zhadnoboth slip unnoticed into camp.

"May the sun shine gently on you, may your pastures be green, and my your wells never run dry," said Zhadnoboth. This greeting common to the Kri Shandri clans came surprisingly easily from his mouth. "May I and my servant share your campfire and your hospitality for a while?"

Haz gritted his teeth and replied, "Welcome to my humble fire. Sit and share water and break bread with us." He was obviously much put out by their sudden appearance, but still seemed determined to uphold the laws of hospitality, even though it choked him to do so. "I am Hazgaryul n-Akab of the Naz Mathoni clan," he added with a strained politeness.

Zhadnoboth respectfully bowed his head as one would to an equal, further angering Haz (who felt only a fellow tribesman could be an equal), and said, "I am Zhadnoboth of Khoiyam, a sometime student of the arts sorcerous. Your offer is most welcome. I shall be glad to break bread with you and share of your water."

The old cutthroat brightened at the sorcerer's words, apparently relieved that it was no ordinary mortal who had so taken them by surprise. However, Sandy could see his eyes narrow and sense a hidden determination. Old lard guts wasn't scared off, he'd just try to be extra careful when it came around to killing them. Haz threw a wicked eye toward his sentries, and Sandy felt sorry for them. Not even a magically hidden sorcerer was an excuse for their carelessness, or at least not one that Haz would accept.

Sullenly Haz motioned to Zhadnoboth to sit beside him at the campfire. The silent Igsban handed a battered leather cup and a matching canteen to Haz. He poured some water into the cup, sipped from it, and handed it over to Zhadnoboth, who also took a sip, then poured the rest on the ground as custom demanded. Haz then took a piece of waybread, rye-brown and shaped like a thin silver dollar pancake, and sprinkled salt on it. This he broke in half, giving one piece to the sorcerer and keeping the other for himself. Haz first ate his piece and then waited while Zhadnoboth did the same.

The sorcerer completed the ritual by saying, "It is well for fellow travelers to share as brothers."

Hiding an aggrieved surliness—because Zhadnoboth had not muffed the ritual and therefore Haz must offer him the protection of custom—Haz answered, "When you share my fire, you are my brother."

Sandy noticed that the blubbery tribal elder settled down as he and Zhadnoboth began to breakfast together. The tone of the old man's thoughts showed that he thought himself in control of the situation again. There also seemed to be a grim determination to make his sentries pay heavily for their inattention; he wanted no repeat of this morning's fiasco.

Igsban looked up, started, and then stared with sour displeasure past Haz. His fellow villain saw the look and twisted around to see what had upset him. Sandy followed their eyes and saw a woman standing in front of a tent, surprisingly pretty for causing so much discontent.

Using his sixth sense, Sandy tried to read Haz. This talent was doing rather well right now, even though Sandy was only getting impressions, not clear thoughts. Haz seemed to consider the woman mule-stubborn and a wrongheaded troublemaker. He itched to use fire and iron on this obstinate female, but a superstitious fear held him back: This woman was sacred to the Goddess. Haz was too much of a survivor to anger such a deity unnecessarily. Sandy caught a dim picture of a dark and hooded figure, and the chill this image caused Haz also sent an icy ripple of fear through his soul.

The priestess saw Haz's eyes on her and she strode purposefully toward him, a hard and unsubmissive look carved into her face. Sandy could tell that the priestess knew Haz dared not harm her, and that she went out of her way to gall him. Casting an interested glance at the sorcerer and a too-fleeting one at Sandy, she said to Haz, "Ah, gorbellied one, I see you have new guests. I trust you didn't let your bastardly temper sour your hospitality."

Her words got to Haz, as they were meant to. Clutching his gut as though in sudden pain, he swallowed a gulp of the soothing tea. For a moment he tried to hold his anger within himself, but it broke free of his rein. "Some would wonder why one of the wildest hoydens ever to disgrace the Kri Shandri does not respect an elder of the Naz Mathoni—one who is renowned as a great warrior," he said in a venomous voice. "Though now she is a priestess, many have not forgotten her scandalous past."

The priestess laughed and retorted, "Why don't you say it right out, lard belly? I was a hot piece, as wanton as they come. No doubt you would have preferred me to become something respectable like a brothel madam—one who knows her place when she meets a whoremongering braggart."

Haz winced and turned white at her plain words and barefaced gall. He preferred his sluts to be less outspoken. "Your language has much improved from the days when you could make a shameless sinner blush, priestess, but there are many elders who think your words should be more temperate and more holy."

The priestess threw back her head and laughed derisively. "It makes no difference what the elders think of me, and they know it. What counts is that I have been chosen to speak for the Goddess. Do you wish to complain to her, you sanctimonious reprobate?"

Turning her back on the red-faced Haz, the priestess bluntly introduced herself to the sorcerer. "Good day, gray-beard, I am Izme-Lal, one-time strumpet and now the Veiled One's voice to the Kri Shandri." She cast a challenging look back over her shoulder at Haz, who was ready to explode at the way she'd breeched good manners and usurped his rights of introduction. Then she added, "As chief priestess I do the Goddess's work and say right out what needs to be said—except when certain misguided curs try to hinder me because their ears are offended by the truth."

Haz rose to his feet and opened his mouth to roar out a rebuke, but his rage made him speechless. He stood like that for a moment and then turned on his heel and stalked pon-

derously away. Igsban said nothing, but poured himself another cup of tea and waited to overhear what the priestess
would say to these unexpected guests.

Sandy surveyed the priestess with an appreciative eye.
She was slightly long in the tooth, but her looks could still
catch a man's attention. Her body was lithe and muscular,
taller than that of most men, and full-breasted. She'd be a
real handful in your arms and the way her eyes moved hinted
that she still appreciated a good man. What Sandy most noticed was a sparkle in her eye, a spring to her step, a bawdy
laugh in her voice, and a sense that she had a heart that
cared deeply. Hers was not classic beauty, but something
deeper and longer lasting.

And she was tough. Haz was a mean old buzzard, but
she'd talked to him as though to a troublesome brat. That
took guts. Sure, she had the power of her goddess backing
her, but to act that way took an inner strength which no deity
could confer. Somebody like her could be a very useful ally
—and Sandy was sure he needed every advantage he could
gain if he wanted to come out of this adventure with a whole
skin.

Zhadnoboth also looked at her with an approving eye:
despite his age he was not beyond indulging in a bit of
wenching. "I am called Zhadnoboth, my lady," he said in a
surprisingly urbane and pleasant voice.

Sandy rolled his eyebrows back and shook his head, wondering how long the old grouch could keep the oil flowing.

The sorcerer motioned to the ground beside him and said
courteously, "Why don't you join us for breakfast? My servant and I were just about to start."

The priestess smiled at Zhadnoboth and replied, "I would
be delighted, grandsire." As she gracefully sat her long body
down, Sandy could almost have sworn she slipped him a
wink over the head of the slightly put out Zhadnoboth. At
certain times the sorcerer did not want to be reminded of his
age.

Sandy enjoyed the meal. The food was better than he had
eaten in days: hot tea, stringy cheese with a pleasant tart
flavor, flat cakes freshly baked, and a long ropy sausage,
fried crisp and deliciously spicy.

While he ate, Sandy casually took count of the enemy.
The odds were not good, but they could have been worse.
Besides Haz and the sour-faced tribesman keeping them

company at breakfast, there appeared to be eleven others. All but one seemed to be Naz Mathoni clansmen. The odd man out was a dark, slinky individual who ate by himself and kept a beady eye trained in their direction. To Sandy's heightened senses this man had a cold venomous feel to him. The Naz Mathoni were vicious rogues, but he was of a different and worse sort. Uskban had mentioned a Zalkring and this had to be him.

As they were finishing breakfast, Haz came out of his tent. He spoke briefly to two of his men and then lumbered over to the campfire, sat down, and began chatting with Zhadnoboth. "It's not often there are travelers on this road; very few of even the Kri Shandri know of it." He paused and continued innocently, "Strange how some roads are all but forgotten and then suddenly everybody seems to be using them. Only chance whim, for instance, brought me and my clan brothers along it. No doubt other such happenstances brought both you and my lady here to it."

Izme-Lal sniffed and said acidly, "I go where the Goddess's business takes me. As for scavengers who follow in my tracks, who knows the whims of such beasts?"

Haz pointedly ignored her comments, though Sandy noticed his voice lost some of its oiliness and his left eye began to twitch. "There are probably important reasons a sorcerer would want to roam the desert, though it might be thought odd he shows up at this place just when other strangers stop here."

"Yes, it is strange we should all come together at the same moment," the sorcerer mused, playing the game with a skill Sandy didn't think the old geezer had in him. "Truly, the ways of fate cannot be fathomed, throwing an odd jumble like us together for a brief moment. I, for instance, am only here because I am searching the desert for certain herbs needed in an obscure spell I unearthed accidentally last year. Mere chance, what a potent force, brought me here at this time."

Sandy thought the old scoundrel made a remarkably convincing liar, mixing just the right touches of arrogance and bland unconcern. However, Haz thought so too. "Yes, chance is strange," he agreed, letting just a hint of suspicion show in his voice.

The priestess caught Sandy's eye, inclined her head slightly toward the two connivers, and lifted an eyebrow.

Sandy smiled at her silent comment, agreeing wholeheart-
edly: together they made as fine a pair of hypocrites as you
would ever want to see.

The priestess stiffened and her eyes flicked to the left.
Sandy casually turned his head in that direction, but at first
saw nothing important. Then he noticed that the two Naz
Mathoni who had been talking to Haz just a while before
were now gone. Sandy raised his eyes and looked at the low
ridge which bordered this oasis on the east. There was a faint
haze of dust above it, centered on where the road he and the
sorcerer had traveled on crossed it. That should make the
odds two better in their favor if Uskban and the mute were
as viciously efficient as they had been in the past. Sandy
turned his head back to the priestess and nodded slightly in
understanding.

In the meantime Haz and the sorcerer had continued their
verbal fencing. "What land is your servant from?" asked
Haz. "I have not seen his like before."

Zhadnoboth shrugged casually and answered, "I think
he's from the far north, but I really don't know. He's never
spoken a word; and the trader I got him from knew nothing
of his origins. What counts is that he is a passable servant. I
only have to beat him occasionally."

"You're lucky," Haz said heatedly. This subject was close
to his heart. "Hardly any of the servants you pick up nowa-
days are worth the salt. In my father's day it was different—
servants knew their place. You didn't have to beat them half
to death to get decent work out of them."

Bored with the verbal sparring, Sandy got up to stretch
his legs. This conversation could have been taking place on
Earth. He unobtrusively noted the positions of the eight foe-
men still around.

Sandy started strolling toward a ruined structure built into
a rocky cliff just to the south of the camp. He'd spotted it as
they had ridden in and had itched to investigate it. Antiqui-
ties had always interested him and he had irritated his parents by taking a lot of archaeology courses in college instead
of more practical subjects.

The place must have been grand in its heyday; its ruins
were immense and built on huge foundation stones—the
smallest being at least six feet in its shortest dimension. On
top of them rested the main part of the keep; it was made
from much smaller stones, irregular in shape but well fitted

in a crazy-quilt pattern. The whole ruined structure reeked of immense age, but the foundation stones seemed to date from the dawn of time itself.

A voice behind Sandy started him out of his reverie. "It is called Baraz Kul Idmani. Among these ruins Idman slept and had the dream which set him on the road to his destiny. In later days he rebuilt it and dwelt here at times. It is a sacred place to those Kri Shandri who hold true to the old loyalties."

Sandy turned to look at the priestess. Some distance away two Naz Mathoni were keeping an eye on them. Izme-Lal's words seemed innocent enough, but he sensed a deeper meaning in them. He nodded for her to go on, hoping to catch the drift of what she wanted to tell him.

"Legend tells of secret passages built into this ruin. Men have searched for them and the treasure rumored to lie below; but if they have been found, no one has heard of it. Still, legend says those ways exist and that they are open to those of Idman's true blood and to those the Goddess favors. Whatever the truth, it is still a good place to make a stand in time of trouble."

Sandy nodded slightly to indicate he was catching the drift of her conversation. He didn't dare speak, since Zhadnoboth had implied he was mute and the Naz Mathoni were watching.

Izme-Lal continued to talk casually, but she turned so her back was to the two Naz Mathoni. "Legend also says that Idman's tomb lies in a deep cavern beneath these ruins" were her spoken words. Her hands said other things in the sign language Sandy had seen Pognak communicate with. Now that Sandy could see the gestures clearly, he understood them perfectly. He briefly wondered if this gift of tongues was part of his new sixth sense, or something different.

The priestess's hands said a message he interpreted as, "Watch Haz. Be wary as sundown comes. If he should ritually wash his hands of you, be prepared to fight for your life."

Then, her message delivered, she casually turned and pointed to the stump of a tower on the eastern edge of the ruin. "That is Idman's Tower, where he slept when he had his dream." And for the next quarter of an hour she led Sandy around the ruin and prattled about its history.

After the tour they wandered back to the camp. They

split up, the priestess going to her tent, leaving Sandy standing by himself.

Sandy figured it was time to see to the animals, so he strolled over to where they were hobbled to do his work and to do some thinking. Izme-Lal's manner had bothered him: the way she appeared to know more about him than she possibly could. She served the Goddess and the Goddess was the deadly enemy of the Zalkrings' god. He stopped and considered this thought again. Had he heard that some place or did he somehow just know it? Whatever, the priestess was at least an enemy of an enemy. He began wondering about this quest they were on. It was aimed against the Zalkrings and it seemed awfully coincidental that the priestess of a goddess who hated the Zalkrings so fiercely should show up now. Was the Goddess directly involved in this adventure he'd been shanghaied into? Feuds between gods could be deadly for anyone caught in the middle—all Earth's mythology said so.

Sandy took care of the rudhars first, preferring to get the most unpleasant part of his job done first and as soon as possible. The rudhars were mean-tempered, picky beasts: They nipped at him, stepped on his toes if they could, complained noisily about their feed, and in general were low-down surly sneaks. This time Sandy got done with minimal trouble—one stepped-on toe and a bump in the back by a bony head.

After the rudhars it was a pleasure to care for Glupp, who was always good-natured, if not cooperative. The grundzar gave him a toothy smile and rubbed his huge head against Sandy's leg, nearly knocking him over.

Sandy gave him a playful cuff and whispered, not wanting the Naz Mathoni to know he wasn't a mute, "Mind your manners, you big lummox."

Glupp gave him a wide-eyed innocent stare, seeming to say, *I was just being friendly.* "Don't give me that saintly look," Sandy muttered. "You'd laugh yourself sick if you accidentally knocked me over."

Sandy pulled an ancient, round wooden box, the size and shape of a paint can, from out of their gear. It contained a mixture called water-dragon fat which was black as pitch and smelled like a combination of camphor and rancid butter. Glupp loved to have the stuff rubbed into his hide, snuffling happily at the reek and groaning in ecstasy as Sandy worked it into every crack and crevasse of his loose skin. The rudhars snorted in disgust and moved upwind when they caught a whiff of the foul stuff. Sandy smiled, glad to see the bitchy beasts discomforted.

While Sandy worked, the dark man came by and stopped to give them a venomous look, either on general principles or because he suspected something. Glupp saw him and rumbled angrily. Sandy gave him an understanding pat and then dug out a great lump of the tallowlike ointment. With it in his hand, Sandy walked casually around to the other side of Glupp, passing close to the Zalkring. Quite by accident the ointment fell out of Sandy's hand and onto the Zalkring's boot. The Zalkring swore, wrinkled his nose, violently kicked the glob off his boot, and stalked off. Sandy kept silent, but Glupp began to wheeze like a locomotive.

The dark man turned, let fly a few appropriate remarks about Glupp's probable ancestry, and stalked away even angrier than before.

Glupp controlled his chortles, gave a derisive snort, and settled down to enjoy Sandy's ministrations once again— plainly indicating he wasn't going to let one evil-minded pruneface spoil his day.

Sandy gave the grundzar a wall-eyed stare and muttered, "Damn animal doesn't know he's not human. Next thing you know, he'll want to ride instead of walk." A picture of the huge beast trying to ride a rudhar—and flattening it— formed in Sandy's mind. He chuckled at the ridiculous image and went back to his rubdown work in a very happy frame of mind.

Once he had taken care of Glupp, Sandy wandered over toward Zhadnoboth. The grundzar had given him a soul-wrenching look and a pleading rumble when he left, trying to coax more attention from him, but Sandy had hardened his heart and walked away.

Zhadnoboth was sitting with his back against the knobby trunk of a tanyaras tree. A small bronze brazier filled with burning charcoal was in front of him. Suspended over it by a bronze derrick attached to the brazier was a smallish copper pot filled with boiling water. Mumbling, the sorcerer began to add the long, thin silver-green leaves of the tanyaras tree to the pot. Soon blue-tinted puffs of steam were coming from the pot and the air was filled with a pleasant camphorlike aroma. Every so often Zhadnoboth would sip hot tea from a cup suspended in midair beside him. Sandy smiled at the sight, enjoying the sorcerer's showboating. Even Haz's crew of cutthroats seemed suitably impressed. If it came to a flight, their respect for Zhadnoboth's prowess might prove crucial.

Sandy sat down across from Zhadnoboth. The sorcerer raised an eyebrow almost imperceptibly. Sandy relayed the priestess's message using the sign language he'd learned, though not with the practiced skill Izme-Lal had shown. The sorcerer answered with an aimless-seeming hand flick, showing he understood. Sandy was pleased; he hadn't known for sure that the old coot understood the sign language.

The sorcerer fumbled about a little more, pulling various objects from his robes, then leaned forward and whispered, "I am going to try a spell or two—something to make these unlettered louts wary of me."

Seemingly unaware of the eyes locked on his every action, Zhadnoboth began his spell. First he spread a bright red silk handkerchief on the ground and smoothed it out carefully. Then he cautiously uncorked a small bottle of dark blue glass and shook a spoonful of white crystals onto the middle of the handkerchief. "Sea salt from the western ocean," he said in an undertone. "Blessed by a priestess who serves the Goddess in her aspect as the deity of wisdom and mystery." The sorcerer's careful motions made it seem like he was doing something dangerous, but to Sandy the crystals still looked like common salt.

"Now for some balm of Hagabah," the sorcerer said to himself. He picked up a small jar of plain brass, half the size of a teacup, dug out some yellow mush and mixed it with the salt. Next he added some grass seed, a boiled tanyaras leaf from the pot he had been fiddling with before, a pinch of charcoal ash, and a couple of splashes of his tea. Humming with satisfaction, he stirred the unappetizing mess.

The preliminary steps done, the sorcerer went into the rest of his charade. First he scratched his head as if trying to remember something, then his face lit up as though he'd suddenly snagged hold of an elusive memory, and he picked up the handkerchief by its four corners. He made it into a bag and ran his hand down it, squeezing the contents into a hard bulge at one end.

Now Zhadnoboth paused and stared about as if resting and not really seeing anything. (It didn't fool Sandy, who saw that the old geezer was checking to make sure his audience was hooked.) In one swift motion Zhadnoboth's hand slid down the handkerchief again, and this time squeezed the bulge into nonexistence. Looking puzzled, the sorcerer opened the handkerchief and there was nothing there.

Sandy glanced around surreptitiously to see how the Naz Mathoni took this simple parlor trick. The common clay were bug-eyed, but Hazgaryul looked disdainful.

Meanwhile, Zhadnoboth shook the handkerchief, frowned when nothing happened, and shook it again. Still nothing. He gave the red handkerchief a well-staged glare and scratched his chin in thought. Then, nodding as if he finally knew what he was doing, Zhadnoboth wadded the handkerchief into a ball and wrapped his left hand tightly about it. Muttering some words in a mysterious, indistinct manner, he made a few mystic passes with his right hand, then pulled the handkerchief from his left hand through the hole made by his thumb and forefinger.

He shook the handkerchief—now bright blue and spangled with stars—hard. With a muffled squawk, a large black buzzard exploded out of it. The mouths of the Naz Mathoni dropped open in astonishment—including Haz's. Their surprise was nothing to that of Zhadnoboth, who recoiled in shock from what he had wrought.

With powerful strokes of its huge wings, the buzzard quickly climbed high into the sky. It circled twice before folding its wings and coming down in a power dive. The bird missed Zhadnoboth's head by the width of an eyelash, and only that because the sorcerer threw himself to the ground.

The buzzard whizzed by close to Sandy and he caught a whiff of it. Whether bird or devil, the creature stank like something long dead. The thing, still poisonously angry at the sorcerer, started making another climb to dive-bombing altitude.

Zhadnoboth scrambled to his feet and hurriedly yanked out a large green glass flask from his robes. Sandy blinked; the flask was at least gallon-sized and much too big to fit into any normal pocket. Carelessly scrawled runes on the flask spelled out *essence of cockatrice,* or so Sandy's gift of tongues interpreted it. Zhadnoboth quickly chanted a spell while he made frantic mystic motions over the flask, and the sluggish liquid inside began to bubble and boil.

Meanwhile, the black bird had attained the altitude it wanted and began another hell-for-leather-dive at the sorcerer. Halfway down the thing met a spouting column of green foam erupting from Zhadnoboth's flask.

There was a thunderous explosion. Animals, tents, trees, people, and whatnot went flying every which way. Tethers and hobbles were torn asunder, setting the rudhars free. The riding beasts, squealing in terror, ran headlong into the desert as though pursued by devils.

Of those at the oasis, only Glupp seemed unaffected by the turmoil. He had hunkered down at the moment of the blast, and though the maelstrom had buffeted him, it could not move or shake him. Now he espied a bumbleweed drifting by and his long tongue shot out and snatched it. Placidly the great beast chewed on the weed's thorny husk, to get at the sweet and succulent interior, all the while staring in mild bafflement at the destruction and the humans picking themselves up out of the wreckage.

Sandy rubbed a bruised backside and looked around. The air was still dry and crystal clear and the sky above was still cloudless and a brilliant blue. A faint smudge overhead, rapidly being dispersed by the wind, was all that remained of Zhadnoboth's creature.

The sorcerer got up from the ground, brushed the dirt and debris from his robes, and looked about peevishly. He was angry that his spell had gone awry, and furious about the beating his dignity had taken. It did not occur to him that the others were in no shape to notice his embarrassment.

Zhadnoboth turned to Sandy. "May the swindler who sold me that spell roast in the deepest hell! Three times have I used it, and it hasn't worked quite right once!"

Just then Haz came stalking over, blood in his eye. "You damned incompetent! Look what you've done."

Zhadnoboth stared Haz right back in the eye. He was in no mood to be browbeaten. If the whole fiasco hadn't been his fault, he might have been more reasonable. "I am not to blame for an act of nature nor for a bunch of scruffy cutthroats who know nothing about how to pitch camp."

The sheer audacity of the sorcerer's words struck Haz speechless. The obese villain stared in red-faced fury at him, mouth open, but too stunned to release the steaming invective bottled within him. Then, realizing this was no time to get involved in a set-to with the sorcerer, he gritted his teeth, turned, and stalked off—his manner saying there would be another and safer time to deal with this doddering incompetent and then Haz would make him pay dearly.

In a quarter hour, Haz got things organized. Two of his men he sent out into the desert to locate and retrieve whatever beasts were still around. The others he set to cleaning up and keeping an eye on their unwelcome guests. But Haz was in a foul mood: his men were battered, and it would be a miracle if he could get where he was going on time—especially as he also had orders to keep an eye on the priestess.

Haz motioned to the dark-visaged Zalkring and they went off by themselves to confer. As he picked up the sorcerer's gear, Sandy noticed that the two were having a heated discussion—with Haz apparently trying to browbeat the Zalkring, and the Zalkring plainly reluctant to go along. From the venomous glances thrown their way by both Haz and the Zalkring, Sandy gathered both wanted to scrag them, but couldn't agree either on when or how.

It was a tense afternoon. Sandy, the sorcerer, and the priestess were gathered around a small campfire while grim-faced tribesmen watched them from all sides. It was an undeclared war, and both sides were waiting for the most favorable moment to attack. Sandy hoped the moment wouldn't come because as far as he could tell the odds were still against them. He kept a hand near the poniard concealed in his boot, and noticed that Zhadnoboth kept his staff in hand at all times.

As the afternoon wore on, Haz became more and more agitated. The non-return of the two tribesmen he'd sent to search for the rudhars especially made his temper fouler. Plainly he thought they might have run into trouble. Sandy could see that the lard-bellied cutthroat was spoiling for a fight, but feared the sorcerer's powers. Sandy could vaguely sense that Haz was waiting for something, something which would nullify any advantage the sorcerer had. When that something came about he'd make his move.

As evening came on, Sandy, the priestess, and the sorcerer drew closer to the fire and waited. Spread in strategic locations around them were six of the remaining Naz Mathoni. Haz and his old crony Igsban kept an eye on the desert while the Zalkring sat at another fire in what appeared to be a trance.

Zhadnoboth inclined his head toward the Zalkring and said, "He's keeping a spell of awareness encircling us. These Zalkring mages charge themselves with energy from their god and then do magic by brute force, just doing and not understanding what laws of magic underlay their spells. It's not like sorcery, which manipulates the magical energy permeating the universe by saying or doing the right thing at the right moment. A great sorcerer can thus work mighty enchantments with the use of minimum energy from himself, though he must take more time and know what he is doing. Now, that Zalkring mage is squandering most of his stored magical energy maintaining that spell—and he cannot recharge himself until he can form a union with his god again. In his weakened condition his magic should be no problem for me."

Sandy gave the sorcerer a sidelong glance. Considering the unreliability of Zhadnoboth's sorcery, there was room for doubt.

Looking in a polished bronze mirror and dabbing at bruises on her face, Izme-Lal whispered sarcastically, "You're a gifted sorcerer, old man. That spell this morning nearly finished us all, though our enemies seem to be in worse shape."

Despite the sarcasm, Sandy sensed that she was trying to calm his doubts about Zhadnoboth's sorcery—implying it was both erratic and powerful.

Zhadnoboth replied huffily, "My magic helped, didn't it? No doubt losing their rudhars ruined their plans." Then he threw in a brag: "It was a mere trifle, but something I thought might serve."

Sandy nearly choked on his tea. If the sorcerer had planned the whole thing, then pigs had wings and the sea was boiling hot. Zhadnoboth heard his sputterings and gave him a killing stare. Izme-Lal watched the interchange and smiled to herself.

Moments later she stiffened and her eyes glazed over for an instant. She came out of her trance and whispered, "We must be prepared for trouble at sundown. At first dark a messenger is expected, a being from the lower hells who is a minion of Kels Zalkri. When it arrives, our time of waiting will be over."

Zhadnoboth took her information matter-of-factly, but Sandy wondered where she got her information—having a very disquieting suspicion it might be her goddess.

Izme-Lal nodded almost imperceptibly toward the entranced Zalkring. "That is Iquetzal-Tigwar, a minor priest and mage of sorts. He serves his god by skulking about the desert towns, spying and plotting dirty deeds with certain unprincipled curs. He will have some manner of control over the messenger they expect. If I read their plans rightly, they mean to turn the thing loose on us. Only with such a thing from hell at their command would they dare attack a sorcerer and a priestess of the Veiled Goddess.

"You," she said to Zhadnoboth, "must deal with the messenger. I and your *servant* will do the best we can with the others—as will the two from the desert."

Sandy looked sharply at her, wondering again how she knew so much. The sorcerer, meanwhile, gave her a sour look. He didn't much care about her commands, or doing what she wanted. He started to protest, then, scowling furiously, pulled a spellbook bound in red leather from his robes and began to read it.

The priestess proved handy at other things besides giving orders. While they talked, she'd also been busy cooking a meal for the three of them. It was just a type of fried dumpling and more tea, but compared to the trail fare he'd been forced to put up with, Sandy found it delicious.

Izme-Lal talked to Sandy as they ate their spartan meal; Zhadnoboth was too engrossed in his spellbook to listen.

"There is a power still in these ruins which will be to our advantage: a deep creative power which comes from the Goddess, and opposes the dark forces commanded by Kels Zalkri and his worshippers. In time of need it can aid us."

Sandy nodded his understanding, but wished she had cheerier things to talk of. If it came to a fight he suspected he'd be as useful as a fifth wheel. His heart was willing, but his hands were untrained—in the army he'd found he was a good shot, but he never did learn much about knife fighting. If there was power in the ruins, he hoped it jumped in with all four feet before his shortcomings caught up to him.

As dusk came closer, Haz became increasingly fearful. They had no rudhars, the two tribesmen he sent to find them still hadn't returned, and no sign of the two he'd sent east for reinforcements. If he and his fellow clansmen had to flee, it would be on foot—and that could be suicide. Nor did he relish the idea of holding up here. The place had an unfriendly feel to it, as though the very earth knew that the Naz Mathoni were blood enemies to those who rightly belonged here. He still had a deadly piece held out of the game, but it gave him cold comfort.

As the sun began to slip beneath the horizon, Izme-Lal rose. "The time is close. Let's be nearer the ruins when things break loose." She sauntered toward the ruins, and Haz who stood near them.

Zhadnoboth got up and followed after, mumbling grouchily under his breath. Sandy topped off his cup with more hot tea and trotted after them—wishing now that the army sent him into combat instead of putting him behind a desk.

Haz gave a shark's grin when he saw them approach. It was nearly time to attack; the Zalkring had come out of his trance and was looking their way. Haz beckoned to him.

As Sandy and his companions drew close to Haz, two of the Naz Mathoni took positions on the ruined wall where they would have a good field of fire for their bows. The rest of Haz's clansmen hemmed them in from the other side. Sandy's mouth was dry with fear, but his mind was still keen enough to take count of the enemy. Nine, instead of the thirteen who'd been here this morning. Not impossible odds if you counted Pognak and Uskban and ignored the fact that the other three were a woman, a doddering old man, and a complete novice.

"I had been meaning to call you over," Haz said in his oiliest and most menacing voice. "It is time we said farewell."

He turned and motioned to the youngest of his clansmen, Igsban, grandson of his old crony. The youth nodded, picked up a wash basin of hammered brass, and brought it over to Haz who dipped his hands in the water and then dried them.

"As I bid you welcome to my fire, now I wash my hands and bid you farewell." The words seemed a simple phrase of parting, but were far more ominous. With this ritual washing, the old cutthroat had absolved himself of any responsibility to them. Haz put great store by the amenities: he had killed many men, but never a guest.

Izme-Lal smiled enigmatically at him and said in a searing tone, "What now, Widow-Maker?"

Haz snapped to Igsban, "Hold her," and the taciturn old man grabbed her arm and held a dagger to her throat.

A fuming Zhadnoboth stepped forward. "See here," he began, but was interrupted by a loud *whoosh* as a winged monstrosity plunged from the darkening sky. It came to roost atop a wall near the Zalkring.

Sandy could not quite catch the shape of the thing, maybe because of the dusk or maybe because the creature was not quite of this world. What he did see was frightening enough: eyes red with hellfire, talons the size of daggers, and fangs dripping with a green and luminescent saliva.

Iquetzal-Tigwar barked out something to the creature in a harsh language while he pointed to Sandy and the sorcerer. "Slay them" was how the words translated in Sandy's mind, though he had never heard this language before.

Then old Igsban screamed—the most he'd spoken all day —and fell to the ground with Izme-Lal's knife buried hilt-deep in his belly, and the camp was in chaos. One bowman died as a small shadowed figure reared up from beneath him and rammed a sword through his gizzard. At the same time the other bowman collapsed with an arrow through his neck.

Zhadnoboth chose that moment to lift his staff and point it at the creature. He spoke a word and blue flames shot from it to envelop the creature. There was a thunderous explosion and the thing was hurled back into the darkness.

There was a moment of stunned silence and then the battle was on in earnest. Uskban charged out of the gloom, with sword in hand and a bloodcurdling battle cry on his lips. He got to the Zalkring, who had just barely managed to unsheathe his saber. The madman's blade flicked up and then down, moving with the speed of a striking sidewinder, and Iquetzal-Tigwar's sword hand was sheered off and his left leg was hamstrung.

Swiftly turning away from the crippled Zalkring, Uskban was just barely able to meet the attack of the onrushing Haz. Sparks flew and metal screeched as the madman staved off the onslaught of his hereditary enemy. After the fury of their initial exchange, Uskban and Haz, both master swordsmen, settled down to a dogged no-quarter duel.

With a bone-chilling screech, the hell-creature came barreling back out of the night toward Zhadnoboth. The sorcerer let loose a blast of blue lightning—a bit weaker than the first, but enough to send the fiend rolling and tumbling backward through the air. "Take that, you misbegotten hell spawn," snarled Zhadnoboth.

Young Igsban came from somewhere and charged the sorcerer's unprotected back. Sandy reacted instinctively, flinging the earthenware teacup in his hand at the boy. It caught Young Igsban on the forehead and he tumbled to the ground. Still game, even with blood streaming into his eyes from a deep gash, the boy searched for the dagger he had dropped. Just as he found it, Sandy stepped forward and whipped his stolen poniard across the boy's throat. Igsban gurgled horribly and collapsed into the dirt. His hands clawed futilely at the ground for a moment and then he was still, his head surrounded by a crimson pool of blood.

Holding the poniard ready, Sandy searched for another enemy. Haz was still fighting, but his men all seemed to have fallen. He saw Izme-Lal reach down and daintily slit the throat of a wounded tribesman. Nearby another Naz Mathoni lay dead with an arrow in the eye. Sandy searched for the last Naz Mathoni and saw Pognak carrying his mangled body. With a triumphant scowl the mute giant tossed the body contemptuously atop the one Izme-Lal had finished off.

Again the creature from hell screamed its unearthly howl and dove at the sorcerer. Once more Zhadnoboth fended it off with bolt from his staff—but just barely. The blue flame had lost most of its zip, and the sorcerer was gray with fatigue.

The thing sheered off and began circling for another attack. It filled the night air with bloodthirsty howls, knowing that its next attack would finish the sorcerer. Shakily Zhadnoboth roused himself for a final effort.

When the hell spawn got enough distance and elevation, it swerved and charged full tilt at the sorcerer, passing over the broken tower which had been the heart and soul of the ruined structure. Here, some of the ancient power still lingered; and it pulsed with an eerie blue-silver light which rose to engulf the creature.

The devil-thing let out a terrible, agonized shriek that tore through the air and into the innermost nerves of those who heard it. Then its body erupted into flame, spewing thick clouds of black smoke mixed with orange fire as it plunged to the earth. The impact sparked an inferno—even the very dirt and stone started to burn.

There was one last terrible shriek—full of agony and deep despair—and the thing was dead. The blaze now exploded into a fast-rising column of blinding white flame mixed with great gouts of black and gray smoke. The fire writhed, spit, crackled, and danced wildly for a few moments, then was gone. Only specks of white ash and black soot were left, floating away on the wind or gently settling to the ground. On the desert floor a blackened pit remained, filled with cinders and cooling slag.

Sandy looked around for Uskban. The madman and Haz were resting, catching their breath for another go-round. Both were in rough shape, with bodies covered with sweat, and blood seeping from many small wounds each had. As they gasped for their second wind, they stared at each other with utter loathing. Theirs was an old and undying hatred.

"Look, Widow-Maker," snarled Uskban. "Look and despair. Your clansmen are dead and so is your pet from hell. Nor will help come from the east. The two you sent for aid are now feeding the gravedigger beetles. Soon you will be roasting with them in hell."

Haz looked around and saw death. Then he laughed and sneered, "Aye, I see, little man. But I don't give a damn. Perhaps I'll die, but you'll be dancing over the fires of hell alongside me tonight."

He sprang forward with a swiftness surprising for such a ponderous man and nearly skewered Uskban. But Uskban staved him off at the last second, and nearly spit the Naz Mathoni on his blade.

From then on the action was fast and furious, neither man paying much heed to his weariness or his wounds.

The battle surged back and forth with neither gaining an edge. Uskban had mad fury, speed, reflexes, and great skill going for him. Haz, though old and fat, had savage determination and skill gained during a lifetime of bloodletting. Gradually the killing pace got to both, but more to Uskban than Haz, the old cutthroat's great bulk proving more than a match for the little man's fierce will. Haz grinned with savage glee and pushed his attack.

The madman backed up, stubbornly contesting every inch, but inexorably losing ground. More and more he had trouble blocking Haz's strokes. He stumbled and fell backward to the ground. Haz grinned in savage anticipation.

An arrow shot out of the night to bury itself in Haz's belly.

The fat old cutthroat staggered in pain and shock, but with grim determination tried to renew his attack. Another arrow hit him, this time in the sword arm. The blade fell from his suddenly lax fingers. He glared at Uskban with impotent fury and sank to his knees.

Haz knelt there for a moment, his hand against his belly, his blood leaking out between his fingers. He looked his hate at Uskban and snarled, "Kill me, you son of a bitch. Are you man enough for that?" He gasped in pain, and added, "I'll wait for you in hell, you little bastard."

"May you roast your balls while you're waiting," growled Uskban as he lunged with his sword. With a superhuman effort, Haz ripped the arrow from his gut and tried to stab Uskban with it. The madman laughed, skipped aside, and laid open his good arm from wrist to elbow.

Haz gasped and dropped his improvised weapon. Alone, crippled, and slowly dying, he faced Uskban. After throwing the madman a defiant glare, he bent his head and deliberately spat to show his contempt for his foe and for death.

Uskban disdained mercy. Too much Naz Idmani blood had stained the fat villain's hands for that. The madman coldly rammed his blade into the cutthroat's neck, severing the spinal cord with the force of his thrust. Haz gave an involuntary gasp and collapsed.

For a moment Uskban stood and stared in hatred at his enemy. Then he stepped forward and ritually—and with surprising gentleness—touched his sword to each shoulder and to the forehead of his dead foe. "He was an evil bastard who got no better than he deserved; but he was a man for all of that," Uskban rasped. He bent his head and intoned a short prayer the Kri Shandri say for their dead. He had to: tribal honor and a grudging respect for the dead man forced him to lay this last blessing on a bitter enemy.

Pognak, bow in hand, stepped up beside the corpse and looked contemptuously down at it. With a sneer he spat upon the dead body: not for him any false pity or final compassion.

There was a scrabbling behind him. Uskban whirled about, blade ready. It was the Zalkring, grievously hurt, but determined to avenge himself before he died. He clutched at something in his belt with his remaining hand and tried to intone what might have been a spell. Uskban slashed out with his sword and the Zalkring choked on the blood from a slit throat. The mage's left hand flew open and a gray powder fell from it, flaring greenly as it touched the ground.

With an unearthly vitality the Zalkring sprang erect and

tried to flee on one leg. Pognak lashed out with his foot and caught the Zalkring in the knee with an audible crack. Iquetzal-Tigwar collapsed, but still tried to escape. As he tried to crawl away he came face to face with Uskban's boots, and burbled in terror through his ruined throat. He was a merciless killer in the service of his cult, but didn't have the grit to face death without a flinch.

Uskban reached down with his sword and coldly sliced off one of the Zalkring's ears. Carefully he untied the string of dried ears he kept on his belt, skewered the fresh one on the tip of his sword, and lovingly added it to his string—callously ignoring the whimpering Zalkring dying slowly and painfully at his feet. It sickened Sandy, who stepped forward and rammed his borrowed poniard deep into the mage's back, sundering his heart and ending his misery.

Uskban grabbed Sandy roughly and swung him about. His eyes were full of fury as he demanded, "Who gave you the right? That thing was *my* meat."

Izme-Lal stepped forward and laid hold of Uskban's sword arm with authority, "Let him be. He is right: we should slay our enemies, but not try to outdo them in evil."

"Have you seen what they do to those they take? *Have you? I* have, and I will never forget—or forgive!"

"I have," she said, and the pain of an old memory showed in her voice. "But it is not right to repay evil with greater evil. That will twist your soul, and soon it makes no difference whether you or they die or live."

"It makes a difference to me," growled Uskban. "They killed what I loved and now they must pay and pay. May they be damned forever."

"Enough of this!" Zhadnoboth was in a tack-spitting mood and making no effort to hide it. Spreading his arms wide, he continued, "See what you have done. Now the whole damned desert and most especially the Zalkrings know we are here—or at least that something is here. I'd have a better chance of going unnoticed if I were naked in a harem than I have with you."

Sandy smiled involuntarily at the image of the scrawny sorcerer naked in a harem. No doubt the ladies of the harem would die laughing.

Uskban snapped back at the sorcerer, "You did more than your share in attracting that attention."

Zhadnoboth snorted. "I wouldn't have had to do so if you hadn't dragged me into this mess."

Uskban didn't bother to reply to the accusation. Instead he said sharply, "We have much to do if we are to get out of here before the Zalkrings find us." Then he and Pognak strode off to break camp and retrieve the rudhars they had hidden. Zhadnoboth sent a *may-you-fry-in-hell* look after them and stomped off on business of his own.

Izme-Lal stared sadly after Uskban as he disappeared into the night and murmured, "Oh, Uskban, if you could only be as you once were. Damn those Zalkring whoresons. They killed your soul and left your body alive." A tear trickled down from her eye.

Sandy should have been surprised that the priestess knew Uskban, but he was too emotionally spent to feel anything. The evening's frenzied activity had drained him, and he stared listlessly about until he caught sight of the Naz Mathoni youth he had slain. Without warning Sandy retched. The need to survive had frozen his emotions; but he was beginning to thaw out, and to feel and think rationally again. The sights and smells of death plus the sudden realization he was a killer shook him to the core. He had always suspected that he *could* kill, but doing it, at least for the first time, was different. He threw up with great convulsive heaves until everything in his belly was gone. And still he tried to throw up more.

Finally it was over. He staggered to the embers of their campfire and sat down. The priestess came over to him and held out a cup. "Drink this," she said. "It will help."

Sandy took a sip and quickly spit it out. The liquid mixing with the bitter bile coating his mouth and throat tasted awful. He steeled himself, then gulped the contents down in one great swallow—and gave a convulsive shudder as it hit his stomach. His belly almost shot it back up, but it stayed down—barely. It wasn't until the next day that he realized it had been a rather good wine.

The priestess spoke softly and with understanding. "Dealing out death, especially for the first time, is terrible. It shocks one's soul. Some men get used to it; killing makes no more difference to them than grinding a worm under their heel. Others may do it many times and still suffer—and these are the most damned and the most human. Everyone must die; but to end life is to destroy what you cannot re-

make. There are those who forswear killing, and they may be
what is best in mortals, but neither you nor I are of that kind.
When the need arises, we are killers. We must know that and
live with it."

Sandy nodded, and looked bleakly into the starry sky. He
remembered how easy it was to kill. And how ungrand it
was.

12

THE Veiled Goddess walked in the desert, in the shadows between the moonlight, and her heart was filled with a fierce joy. The dark one had been stung by her power. He would ignore the warning and retaliate, but that was all to the good.

She finished her climb to the top of a hill and looked down at Talith Kumari. Once the border fortress of an ancient empire and now only a desert oasis, but now as then its ground stained with blood. She looked and she pondered over her plans. Kels Zalkri didn't bother her; he was predictable in his evil and efficient way. The vagaries of fate and the unpredictability of humans, those were the problems. The first, one could not do much about; but a skilled conniver could manipulate the second to advantage. Bringing Izme-Lal to this place at this time should cause several crucial choices to be made, choices which if made rightly would greatly further her plans both for now and for the future.

The Goddess turned her thoughts to Sandy and nodded in satisfaction. He was starting to shape up rather well. As he became more attuned to Zarathandra the powers inherent in one with his name should become stronger, though never predictable. She still had misgivings about him, but he had promise.

13

As rapidly as he could, Sandy cranked away at the mechanism which drew water from the well. It was hard work and soon his muscles ached from the effort. An endless chain of buckets descended into the well and then came back up filled with the precious water. When they reached the top they tipped over and dumped their burden into a large trough hollowed from a solid block of black basalt.

When the trough was full, Sandy paused to catch his breath and then got on with the next part of his job, filling their waterbags. Zhadnoboth had hidden himself away with these waterbags, either out of peevishness or for reasons of sorcery, and ensorceled them so they held four or five times more water than they did before. It also took them that much longer to fill up.

Finally, every waterbag was filled. Then, one by one, he loaded them on Glupp. Despite their great weight, the huge grundzar accepted them without complaint. Not so Sandy. He swore continuously and not so silently at the sorcerer for making the waterbags so heavy—if he could put five times as much water in a waterbag he should also be able to make the water weigh five times less.

The loading done, Sandy flopped down beside Glupp and took a breather. Despite his fatigue, he was surprised at what good physical shape he was in. It was one of the few good things about this adventure—he was getting into reasonably good trim very quickly.

After leaning against Glupp for a while, Sandy reluctantly got up and went looking for Zhadnoboth. He found the old sorcerer standing by the priestess's rudhar and trying to boss Pognak. The mute was pointedly ignoring him, saddling the beast like he wanted to and doing a much better job than a crabby old sorcerer could ever hope to do.

Exasperated beyond endurance by Pognak's suddenly acquired deafness, Zhadnoboth really laid into the mute giant. He had an amazing command of invective when he wanted to use it, and now his words were hot enough to blister a dragon's hide.

He might have been talking to a wall. Pognak went about his job as if nothing was happening.

The sorcerer turned red in the face and was lifting his staff as if to cast a spell, when he stiffened. He held his head cocked, listening, then looked toward the northeast, staring intently into the blackness of the night.

Zhadnoboth turned to Sandy and snapped, "Get Uskban quickly. There's trouble brewing and we have little time."

Sandy looked around, wondering where the little man had disappeared to. A fuming Zhadnoboth pointed to the ruined tower and said, "Look there. He took that back-country priestess that way only a few moments ago. No doubt that stupid madman is snogging her while we sit on the edge of disaster."

Sandy hurriedly trotted over to the ruined tower. As he approached he could hear them talking; some trick of the night air made their soft words clearly audible. "It was long ago, woman. The past is gone. You have a son, but he is none of mine—at least not one I can give a name to."

"Or to a loose woman, either," she replied bitingly. "That would not do for one of the high and mighty Naz Idmani." She paused and said in a softer voice, "But enough of that. The past is dead, but I don't ask for the past. I ask for now and the future."

There was silence for a moment and then Uskban spoke. "No! You ask what I cannot give. The Naz Idmani are true to their heritage. We do not disobey ancient law." He spoke the words reluctantly.

"Idman was the bastard son of a man outlawed for killing his older brother. How true to the ancient law was he?"

Her words rankled Uskban and he replied hotly, "I say again, woman, *no!* The thing cannot be."

Sandy was closer now and could see them standing in the doorway of the ruined tower. The priestess gave a soft sigh, but her back stiffened with resolve. She looked to that part of the heavens called the House of the Goddess and said as if in prayer, "My lady, give a sign. Show what is nearest to my heart. Let this stiff-necked Naz Idmani see what is the truth."

A profound silence fell upon their part of the night. A shimmering curtain of moon-silver mist formed in the night air beside the ruined tower. Soon it became crystal-clear, a window to another place.

It showed a room, a child's room, not grand but comfortable and well lived in. It was night and the darkness was lit only by the gentle flow from a brass oil lamp hanging near the door. In a far corner was a bed. A young boy slept in it, peacefully curled up beneath a quilt embroidered with dancing unicorns. He had dark curly hair like the priestess and strong features inherited from his father. A child now, but someday a man to be reckoned with.

On the wall above the boy's head hung a straight sword in a sheath of green leather wrapped with silver wire. The crosspiece of the sword was of blue steel chased in silver and the hilt was of blue-tinged ivory. Inset into the ivory hilt was the design in silver of a key. Moonlight shone through from their side of the magical window and touched the silver key. The design glowed gently and threw a beam upon a small hand poking out from beneath the quilt—as though the hand held a key.

For a timeless moment the vision hung there, then it quickly faded and was gone, leaving behind only the night air.

"That is my son, Dajnan," Izme-Lal said, a softness in her voice. "He is fatherless and without a clan name. It would be good if he had both." There was an almost imperceptible pause and she added, "And the Goddess placed the key the Naz Idmani call their own into his hand."

"No!" spat Uskban. "Naz Idmani do not give their names to fatherless waifs. Not even if the mother *is* a priestess to the Veiled One. We do not lessen the honor of our names. We do not humble ourselves before the other clans."

"No one need know except the boy and she who bore him. It would be a great gift—one worth more than gold, and which cannot be stolen. It would mean much to him."

"No!"

The priestess bowed her head in defeat and said, "Then so be it. The dead, even if they still breathe, can give nothing."

Uskban stared stony-faced at her, but his voice trembled. "Woman, let me be. I may be on my way to damnation, but I go to it true to the traditions of my ancestors."

"Aye, with a backbone of cold steel and a steel heart even colder."

Sandy had been brooding about himself as a man and a killer; but those thoughts quickly paled by comparison to the searing emotions within Izme-Lal and Uskban. Sandy's new sixth sense became a kind of curse as their intense anguish battered at him: a raw ache in the gut, a bitter sadness in the heart, a wailing in the soul. The priestess's emotions were a smoldering agony and Uskban's a searing misery. Sandy knew he'd never forget the pain, a pain which had darkened and yet strengthened his soul.

A tense and awkward silence now raged between Uskban and the priestess, impalpable but so intense it had the force of iron. Neither knew how to break it. There was too much pain and human feeling to be expressed, especially by Uskban. It disquieted his soul and challenged his madness.

Sandy broke the mood. He stepped forward, scuffling his feet to warn off his approach. They impaled him with fierce stares, silently demanding to know why he had dared to break in on them. "Big trouble," he blurted out. "Zhadnoboth says to hurry."

Uskban swung his head around and looked apprehensively toward the east. He gave an angry grunt and hurriedly trotted off. Sandy and Izme-Lal fell in together and raced after him.

Zhadnoboth was standing by the well, stewing, and stamping his feet with impatience. He saw them coming and snapped, "It's time you got back. Hell is on its way."

He pointed to the northeast. At first Sandy saw nothing, but gradually became aware of a great darkness, a swirling nothingness occasionally lit by flashes of a faint flickering orange light. Huge it was, so huge it blotted out the stars. And it was coming toward them at what seemed a furious rate.

Uskban stared madly at the approaching whirlwind and fell into a fighting crouch, unconsciously ready to take on whatever was coming.

"None of that, you damned loon," screeched the sorcerer. "That isn't something you can knife in the ribs."

The sorcerer looked at the priestess. She was standing in a

rigid trance, a rapt expression on her face, as though her mind were in another world. Then, as suddenly as it had happened, she was back with them.

Izme-Lal swung toward Zhadnoboth and began to bark orders. "The Goddess has spoken. Go with Uskban. He will know where to hide you, a place where the dark one can't reach. I will flee west, back to my temple in the heart of the Kri Shandri lands. The doom which is coming toward us will follow me—and the power of the Goddess which goes with me." She smiled grimly and added, "It will catch up with me, and then it will know the folly of challenging the might of the Goddess."

"What about you, priestess?" Uskban snapped, his voice harsh to hide the worry in it. "I'll have no woman sacrifice herself for me."

Izme-Lal touched him on his shoulder to reassure him. "Peace, my madman," she said calmly. "I do this for you all, for everyone. I am my goddess's servant; this is a task I must do. She will look after me. I will be as safe as if I were in my own house."

Uskban gave a brief snort. "How many have died soldiering for her? Aye, and how many have died in what they thought was the safety of their own homes?"

"If my death lies ahead, so be it. I did not enter her service to live on cream and honey and then to slink away when I am needed. You do what must be done, whatever the cost. How can you fault anyone who does the same?"

Uskban nodded in resignation. Somberly he said, "Go, then, and take my blessing with you. May destiny be with you and with the Goddess."

Silently, madman and priestess looked at each other, wanting to say more, but each too bound by the past and pride to speak. Then Izme-Lal gave the grim-faced Uskban a quick smile, turned and hurried over to her rudhar. With practiced ease she mounted and rode off quickly toward the west. She paused atop a small rise, waved, and then was gone into the gloom of the night.

Uskban watched her go and murmured, "Farewell, my priestess, until we meet again—though I doubt it will be in this world."

"Cut the damned mooning," Zhadnoboth said. "We have no time for it. Not with that doom rushing at us. Where's the place of safety your priestess mentioned?" He glanced worriedly toward the west and asked, "She won't betray us, will she?"

"She is no sniveling sorcerer," Uskban said in a biting tone. "That hard-assed hoyden gives nothing unless she wants to. Kels Zalkri might as well try to force the rocks to talk as to try and open her up."

The rebuke bounced, unnoticed, off Zhadnoboth's hide. He was too preoccupied with saving that hide, for the onrushing darkness was getting ominously close. "Yes, yes," he said abstractedly, "whatever you say. Just let's get away from here."

Sandy agreed heartily. The sorcerer, for all his faults, at least knew what came first. Once they were safe from this maelstrom they could get back to their squabbling.

Uskban nodded sullenly and began leading them toward the ruined tower. Zhadnoboth hurried after him. Sandy and Pognak followed, leading the animals.

Uskban took them through what had been the main entrance to the tower. Once it had been closed by gigantic doors made of gilded steel. Now it was a large hole flanked by decaying walls, but still impressive in its ruined vastness.

Beyond the entrance was a wide, empty space—once the grand hall of the tower. The broken pieces of alabaster and marble lying about its rim spoke of the days when it had been magnificent. Now all that remained of its grandeur was the floor: huge slabs of black marble closely fitted together. Each slab measured about thirty feet long by about half as wide.

Something about the place nagged at Sandy's mind. He looked again and still couldn't put a finger on it. Then it struck him: Although the structure was a total ruin, the floor was remarkably clean and unlittered. It was odd, very odd.

Uskban went over to the left side of the entrance and pulled a dagger from his belt. He searched the wall carefully and then inserted his blade into a crack in the stone. With a sharp movement, he jerked the blade to the left. There was a click as if something had fallen in place, and a stone block gave and sank into the wall.

For a moment nothing more happened. Then, without warning, the floor shook and groaned, and the largest slab began to sink at one end. Slowly it dropped, creaking and protesting all the way, until, with a grinding crash, it came to a halt—

—And formed a ramp leading down into the gloomy depths beneath the tower.

Grimly silent, not bothering to see whether anyone followed, Uskban led the way into the tunnels below. Zhadnoboth scuttled right behind him. Next came Pognak and the rudhars, the beasts nervously crowding next to him. Sandy and Glupp brought up the rear. The choice of pace was Glupp's; not even fast-approaching doom was going to make him rush.

Sandy and the big beast had barely cleared the ramp when it gave a grinding roar and crashed back up to its original position. It had a mighty final sound to Sandy's ears.

They had just started moving down a corridor, lit every twenty feet by a large luminous sapphire in the ceiling, when the ground shook and heaved for a second. Momentarily the corridor went completely black, making Sandy realize that the rock glowed with a faint and eerie silver light. Several more times the blue light coming from the sapphires flickered out, dust trickled down through cracks in the rock, and the ground trembled as though an enormous beast were angrily stomping on the ruins overhead.

The sweat stood out on Sandy's brow. An irrational dread made him shudder; he moved closer to Glupp and his wholesome solidarity. Sandy's heightened senses felt a deep evil seeping down through the rock, like a million immaterial tendrils searching for life to suck dry. Sandy closed his eyes and in his mind could see the silver light that permeated the rock closing in about the evil to shrivel it into nothingness. In his mind he heard a shrill chittering scream of pain, seeming to come from millions of different *its* and yet from only one being.

There was a final jolt as the presence recoiled and fled. Sandy could feel it leaving, ravenously craving life and glad to flee this place which bit at its unearthly flesh. He could sense it had picked up the priestess's spoor and was following after her. He wished her luck, but was glad it wasn't trying to root them out.

Sandy couldn't help wondering what the maelstrom had been. It did not have the feel of real intelligence—it was more like a rampaging appetite ever seeking to be satisfied.

Uskban told the sorcerer, "It's gone. The Caves of Talith Kumari are sacred to the Goddess, and that thing likes this place none too well. It's gone to hunt easier prey, or so it thinks."

Sandy had thought he had only felt the evil above because of his enhanced senses; now he saw he had been wrong. Apparently the thing's alien and ravenous hunger was so powerful and so malevolent that all life near it felt its horror.

Uskban motioned with his head and said, "Follow me. We had best stay in these caves until this night and the day following are over."

"Another whole night wasted," Zhadnoboth said irascibly. "We'll barely get to Tham Og Zalkri on time."

"If you hadn't wasted our water we wouldn't have come here at all," Uskban said shortly. Without another comment, he stalked down the winding corridor. The sorcerer stared after him, then sulkily followed.

The tunnel wound downward for quite a way. The air got chillier as they went deeper, but stayed fresh. After a while they were all wrapping their robes tighter about themselves in order to save as much heat as possible.

Eventually the corridor took an abrupt turn and opened out into a large cavern. The silver coming from the rock was brighter here, but Sandy had difficulty seeing to the other side of the vast cavern. The walls were full of nooks and crannies and were so shadowed that it was hard to tell how huge the cavern was.

Sandy looked about the place with interest. It appeared to be a natural cave which in ages past had been reworked by human hands. The floor was covered with well-fitted stone blocks. Parts of the cavern walls had been smoothed down and some of the natural columns carved to more graceful shapes. And the stonework was ancient, most of it covered by a thin translucent layer of dripstone which must have taken centuries or more to form.

They stabled the beasts in a small grotto to one side of the main cavern. It had rough stalls and obviously had at some time in the past served the same purpose as it did now. Sandy wondered idly why they had needed beasts so far below ground.

At one end of the grotto were several shallow pools of water, and Glupp woofed happily when he saw them. Immediately he waddled over and splashed about in one happily for a while before laying down to luxuriate in the tingling coolness of the water.

The rudhars went to another pool and with haughty elegance began lapping up the water. Every now and then they lifted their heads and looked disdainfully at Glupp, seeming to comment that only a boorish clown could enjoy himself so. Glupp was too wrapped up in his joyful wallowings to notice—not that he would have cared anyway.

While Zhadnoboth took Uskban off in a corner to doctor his wounds with a spell, Sandy found a comfortable nook near a pool of slowly boiling water and settled down to catch up on his sleep. He was a day behind on the rest he needed and now even a hard rock bed looked good. Sandy wrapped a wool blanket about himself and soon was dead to the world.

Sandy woke once or maybe he dreamed: he saw the blanket-shrouded form of Uskban sitting nearby and staring sightlessly into the depths of the cave. The little man spoke in a dreamlike voice, as though his mind were seeing events far away, "Make that hell-thing howl, my goddess, for it is music to me." Sandy listened and then slumbered once again.

Just when Sandy was in the middle of a wonderful dream, gorging himself on hamburgers, french fries, and raspberry yogurt, he was rudely interrupted by a hand shaking him so hard his teeth rattled. He snarled, sat up, and glared about. Pognak's ugly face was glowering malignantly back at him. Sandy growled, "I love you too, bastard."

The giant mute gave a contemptuous grunt, then motioned for Sandy to get up and follow him.

Sandy obstinately refused to move for a moment. Then he got to his feet and followed after Pognak, wobbling a bit until his muscles unstiffened. He had a sudden and very strong hunch that something important was going to happen.

Pognak led him down a crooked passage to a small cave. The builder's hand had barely touched this cavern: opalescent stalagmites and stalactites, looking like drippings from a gigantic candle, festooned the place. Small pools of lime-whitened water were scattered across the floor of the cave. At the far end a niche had been chiseled out of the stone as if for a shrine, but whatever might once have been there had long ago disappeared. Still, some handiwork remained: the walls were carved with a pattern of interlacing branches and the floor of the niche inlaid with black marble blocks.

Uskban was nervously pacing back and forth, waiting for

them. "You took enough time," he said, then walked to one wall of the niche and pressed on a carving. A small door in the wall popped open and Uskban pulled two objects out of it. He handed one to Pognak and kept the other for himself. Sandy saw a couple of oddly shaped steel hooks, long and narrow and with cross-mounted handles of a dark wood.

Uskban motioned Sandy to his side and Pognak to the opposite end of one of the long, narrow marble blocks composing the floor of the niche. Then he and the giant mute inserted the hooks into slots in the ends of the block. "Grab hold," he said to Sandy, indicating the hook he held.

On Uskban's signal they began heaving at the block. Pognak lifted his end easily, but Sandy and Uskban together had to struggle and fight with theirs. When they had set the block down to one side, Sandy flexed his arms, marveling that they hadn't been pulled from their sockets.

"Let's lift the next one," barked Uskban. Sandy groaned inwardly but stepped forward to do his share.

They rested a moment after the second block had been taken out. Sandy and Uskban needed it, though Pognak hardly seemed winded. Sandy wondered sourly if this was what adventure was all about: hard work and never enough sleep.

"Come," Uskban said finally, and climbed into the hole they had opened. Pognak followed immediately, though he was barely able to scrape through the opening. Sandy hesitated. The stone below had none of the faint light which lit the upper caverns, but seemed to have a watchful sentience. Sandy got the impression that anyone who went this way uninvited would feel the slow wrath of the stone. Steps hewn from this living rock led into absolute blackness. A cold mustiness drifted out of the hole, not unpleasant, but reeking of unimaginable age.

From below came a harsh grating noise and a shower of red sparks; then utter blackness followed by another shower of sparks. This time they caught hold and the darkness was soon lit by flickering torchlight. Sandy could see Uskban and the big mute hunkering down by the torch at the bottom of the steps.

"Get your dead butt down here, demon," hissed Uskban. "We haven't much time."

Wondering what he was getting himself into, Sandy reluctantly climbed down the stairs.

Uskban led them through an ever-descending corridor into an irregularly shaped room. Once it had been a small cave, but someone had reshaped it—sheathing the walls in rose marble and placing benches of a cloudy gray marble at their base. In the gloom beyond the torchlight, Sandy could see several corridors leading out.

Uskban stopped and began to mumble something that sounded to Sandy like a nonsense rhyme. But the little madman nodded in satisfaction and decisively headed for one of the corridors.

The corridor split three times; each time Uskban murmured a nonsense rhyme before choosing his path. Sandy hoped nothing happened to the madman; only he seemed to have the key to this maze.

Gradually as they traveled through the corridors, Sandy became aware that the rock in its slow way had taken a liking to him. It had decided he belonged here and was beaming fuzzy, pleasant thoughts his way. More surprisingly, the rock seemed softer under his feet, as though it was making the way easier for him. Sandy smiled wryly to himself and thought, *That's all I need, a pet rock.*

The corridor made a hairpin turn, and they were at the head of a broad and steep stairs. With difficulty they descended the worn and slippery treads. Ahead Sandy could hear the sound of running water.

At the bottom was a low corridor. Tiny beads of water dripped from its ceiling. As he walked, half stooped over, Sandy realized the running water was overhead. He shivered, wishing they were through the tunnel. Eventually the corridor began to slant up and the ceiling again got high enough for him to walk upright. Sandy breathed a heartfelt sigh of relief when he felt he was beyond the reach of the underground river.

The corridor kept ascending and soon was bone dry. It turned a corner and opened into a broad natural cave. In the torchlight its walls and stalactites glimmered with shifting hues: earth arrayed in all its splendor.

At the far end of the cave another broad stairs led up to a huge door. Each white marble step was inset with jade, beryl, onyx, rose quartz, opal, and other precious and semi-precious stones arranged in a circular arabesque around a key of sapphire.

The door at the top of the stairs was enormous, twenty-five to thirty feet high and nearly as wide. It was made of solid bronze, the surface covered with a faint green patina which enhanced the beauty of the metal and gave it an aura of immense antiquity. Each half of the door was decorated with twelve panels, three feet wide by four high, sculpted in high relief out of the bronze. The twelve panels on the right part of the door showed scenes of battle, apparently following a man's life from youth to old age: the panel in the upper left showed him in the first flush of youth, celebrating a great victory; the panel at the lower right showed him as a wounded old man surrounded by dead enemies and being attended by his followers. The twelve panels on the left-hand side showed scenes of everyday life: from birth through marriage and harvest, and ending with a funeral scene.

Uskban went to the right half of the door and took hold of a great bronze ring in the shape of a snake eating its tail, then motioned Sandy to grab a similar ring on the left. "When I have said the needed words, twist the ring to the left and push," he ordered.

Uskban looked toward the top of the door and in his most majestic voice croaked, "Open! I command you: Open, by the right given to the heirs of Idman's flesh." He gave a brusque nod to Sandy and they both twisted and pushed on their rings.

Sandy was surprised at how easily the ring moved: it had looked too corroded to ever budge. A surge of energy shot through him as the doors swung inward smoothly and silently.

Before them was a huge room, ceilinged with a ribbed dome like that of a gothic cathedral. The walls were of misted blue jade alternating with jade the color of a new moss. Into each blue section of the wall was set a panel of white alabaster, seven feet high by five feet wide. Each panel bore a scene from what could have been history or myth; there an army of men battling trolls, here a minstrel singing to the king and queen of some winged folk—and over there a bridegroom, drunk at his wedding feast, and an assassin with drawn knife sidling up behind him.

Uskban put aside his torch and Sandy noticed for the first time that the room was lit with a faintly blue glow, very gentle to the eyes and not seeming to come from any particular source.

At the far end of the room stood another set of huge

doors, of gold-studded black wood. Just in front of them rose a five-stepped dais of black marble, flanked by two torches carved from milk-white quartz that glowed with a soft pearly brilliance. Atop the dais was a sarcophagus shaped from a single block of translucent crystal. Dimly through its side could be seen the body of a man.

Uskban, trailed by Pognak and Sandy, walked in a somber and formal manner toward the dais. Sandy felt as though he were taking part in some profound ritual.

Uskban knelt at the foot of the dais, said a silent prayer, and mounted one step. He did the same for each step until he got to the top of the dais—there he positioned himself facing the sarcophagus, with his back to the great wooden doors. He motioned Sandy and Pognak to mount the stairs, place themselves at the head and the foot of the sarcophagus, and then to face it. He began chanting a dirge which lamented the death of Idman and sang of his deeds. The solemn chanting moved Sandy deeply, despite the fact he knew almost nothing of the man the dirge commemorated or of the turbulent world he lived in. Maybe it was the somber tone and archaic language or maybe there was a kind of magic in the words. Either way, Sandy felt an immense sadness.

The ritual done, Uskban carefully studied the sarcophagus. The top of the sarcophagus was fastened to the main body by twelve golden bolts, six to each side. Uskban recited something under his breath, nodded to himself, and then began pushing the four middle bolts on his side in a complex and repetitive pattern. Suddenly an audible click came from the sarcophagus.

Sandy looked down through the translucent lid. Inside lay the body of an old man—old but not feeble. Idman's scarred features still showed the strength and purpose of a man who had been forged by adversity. In his day he had been somebody to reckon with.

The body was dressed in a simple robe of white silk. Around the neck was a fine silver chain with an iron key attached to it. The key was smooth and unadorned. It reminded Sandy of a skeleton key he had seen his grandmother use, except the end of this key had a three-notched ward both on the top and the bottom of the barrel.

Uskban looked at the body with reverence and said, "Forgive me, my ancestor, for disturbing your rest, but the need is great. Once again the key must come into the world and help shape its destiny." Then he lifted his eyes to the faraway heavens and said, "My lady, I ask that you look with favor on me. Fulfill now your promise of so long ago, that one of Idman's seed would reclaim this talisman to fight the dark one."

The crystal torches dimmed almost to darkness, then blazed back to their former brightness. Uskban took this as a favorable sign. "Thank you, my lady." To Pognak and Sandy, he said in a matter-of-fact voice, "Lift the lid."

For Pognak the six-inch-thick crystal might have been cork, but Sandy had to struggle mightily to just barely get his end up. The sweat popped out in great beads on his forehead.

Reverently Uskban reached in and removed the silver chain and the iron key from his ancestor's body. Sandy wished fervently that he would hurry—the strain of holding up his end of the lid had become sheer agony. Finally, the madman drew his precious burden out, and Pognak and Sandy were able to slowly and carefully lower the sarcophagus lid back on. There was a locking click when it settled into position.

For a moment Uskban looked with dark triumphant eyes at the talisman, then put the silver chain around his neck. "I will use it well, my lord Idman.

"Come." The madman started toward the door they had entered by, Sandy and Pognak at his heels. They were barely over the doorsill when the doors closed with a mighty *whoosh* behind them—yet silently, with no hint of a closing smash.

As they hurried back the way they had come, Sandy wondered what it had all been about. The talisman had enormous power, of that he was sure. His sixth sense could feel its latent energy waiting to be unleashed. He had an uneasy foreboding that he was going to learn a lot more about the key than he cared to.

By the time they were up in the main caverns and closing off the secret stairway with the black marble blocks, Sandy was so numb with fatigue that he barely noticed the great effort it took. All he could think about was getting back to bed—even if it was hard stone.

His hopes were dashed when they got back to where they had sacked out.

"I haven't slept this soundly since I was a lad," Zhadnoboth said, yawning. For the first time since Sandy had known him he sounded happy—but the mood didn't last long: "Just don't stand there like clods. I feel night coming on; let's eat and get going. Maybe you feel we have time to waste, but I don't."

14

THE Goddess slumped wearily in her chair of state. Her trial of strength with the dark one had been close, but she had taught him a lesson he'd remember. She had destroyed one of his mightiest weapons. The Shurva were tiny bits of demonic energy which Kels Zalkri had recruited from some far hell. They were billions of separated pieces of evil acting as one. By themselves they were mostly unreasoning hate and voracious appetite, but with the dark one giving them purpose they had been terrible. In the black days when Kels Zalkri first invaded Zarathandra they had ravaged and destroyed whole lands and peoples. In his pride Kels Zalkri had unleashed the Shurva on her priestess as she crossed the white sand dunes the Kri Shandri called the Moonsilver Sea. At the moment of the Shurva's attack, a mighty army of moonbeams had poured from her ally the moon and then rebounded from the dunes to annihilate the Shurva in a crossfire of silver.

She smiled grimly. The dark one would be a little more hesitant from now on to attack her servants and violate those places she called her own. More importantly, his rage and attention would be focused on her priestess and on the temple to which she had fled, not on the real danger creeping close to the heart of his power on Zarathandra.

Let the dark one be arrogant in his power for a while longer, she thought. It would make the doom she planned for him just that much sweeter. Kels Zalkri was wise and knew many things—but not half of what he thought he did, especially about her world. "The Oldest" and "The Deathless" his followers called him. But she was older, and there were magics in Zarathandra which could slay even the mightiest of gods.

118

15

THEY emerged from the ruined tower just as the last sliver of sun fell below the horizon. Sandy looked about and gave a shudder. The oasis lying about the well had been devastated: nothing remained of the sparse vegetation except blackened scraps and scatterings of soot and crumbling bone. Only the ruined fortress seemed unaffected by the destruction, maybe because of the power which lingered in it.

Uskban started to lead them back the way they had come —to the east.

"Why this way?" Zhadnoboth grumbled. "We're far enough behind as it is. Why not save time and distance by cutting straight to the northeast?"

Uskban turned in his saddle and said, "As the bird flies it is shorter—but we are not birds. On foot or riding that way is well nigh impassable. If you have some magical way to get us across we'll go that way. Otherwise we'll follow the roads I know and get where we are going faster than if we followed the advice of certain misinformed fools."

The little man, having done his best to keep a feud going, turned and set off doggedly toward the east. The sorcerer fumed for a moment and then set off after him. The sulky glances he gave Uskban now and then suggested there would be a reckoning someday—like barbecued madman, for starters.

They rounded a turn in the trail and came upon two bodies lying beside it.

Uskban gave a grunt of satisfaction. "These are the two cutthroats Haz sent to rouse the Zalkrings. We slew them, and the other two sent after the rudhars. I thank the Goddess for making that old villain into a doddering fool—if he had not split his forces, it might be our bones."

119

Moments later, after Uskban had sent Pognak ahead to scout out the Zalkring camp at the crossroads, Sandy edged his mount up beside that of the madman. He wanted to ask some questions about this world and the Goddess, partly because of an itching curiosity but mostly because he'd need the information in order to survive. The Goddess, especially, seemed to be getting too involved in their affairs to ignore. "Who is the Goddess?" he asked.

Uskban turned and gave him an odd look. "You should know, demon. You are both from the immortal realms."

I wish it were the immortal realms, Sandy thought sourly. Aloud he said, "My home is far from this world and is much like it. I never heard of the Goddess before I came to Zarathandra. Perhaps I knew of her under a different name. Tell me more about her and maybe then I will be able to place her."

Uskban shook his head in disgust. "You're a poor excuse for a demon. You're just as frail and uninformed as any human. I'd say Zhadnoboth made a mistake in bringing you here, except my heart knows different. My family has ancient ties to the Goddess and we can feel her touch—and I can feel it in you. Now that I have the Key of Arimithos I can sense even more the workings of her power. You are destined for this quest."

Sandy gave an uninterested nod. *Hogwash.* Aloud, he asked, "Has she always ruled this world?"

"Just because you are part of a miracle don't doubt its existence," Uskban snapped. Then his tone changed and in a sober voice he spoke of his goddess. "Our legends say that long ago there were many gods and goddesses and that they shared the rule of Zarathandra. Together they ruled for ages, until they had a falling out. Then war raged among the gods until only the Goddess remained of the great ones. Since that time she has ruled supreme in Zarathandra, sharing her rule only with a few minor gods and goddesses who acknowledge her sway."

He fell silent and Sandy took the opportunity to ask, "What is she like?"

"No one knows," replied Uskban. "When she appears in visions her face is veiled or covered by shadows. Some say to see her face is to die. She is called the Seven-In-One. Certain old dunces waste their time arguing endlessly whether she is seven beings with one soul or one being with seven aspects to her nature—they cannot see that it is enough to know that she is. It makes no difference if you worship her as the Great Mother or the Mistress of Beasts, just so you worship her."

Uskban paused and then went on in a darker tone. "A thousand years ago Kels Zalkri arose to challenge her. Though he was defeated, his poison still lurks here. The dark one says, *Worship and obey me or else*—and some small-souled worms fall down and kiss his feet. To worship the Goddess is to expand your self by worshipping her. She belongs to those who want to know the true meaning of religion."

Sandy nodded and thought cynically, *She sounds great.* He knew he didn't care for Kels Zalkri, but he wondered how much more of a bargain the Goddess was. He had the impression she could be quite ruthless when it suited her.

Toward morning they found Pognak waiting for them just to the west of the Zalkring camp. The mute astride his rudhar was an eerie sight: He was surrounded by large moths, pale white and the size of doves, which fluttered about him in a cloud. Pognak didn't seem to mind; he acted as if it were a kind of blessing.

Zhadnoboth saw the questioning look on Sandy's face and leaned over and whispered in his ear, "It's a superstition among some of the desert tribes that if moon moths surround you it's a sign of the Goddess's favor. I doubt, though, that she'd look with favor on anything as ugly as our friend."

Pognak rode up to Uskban and spoke rapidly to him in sign language. The madman told Zhadnoboth, "He says the Zalkrings have struck camp and are headed north. Is it safe to cut straight through their camp or would it be better to circle around?"

Zhadnoboth sniffed the night air. Then he spoke a minor word of power and moved his staff above his head in a circle. The staff glowed a faint green, then faded out when he was done. Zhadnoboth grunted in satisfaction and said, "There's no spell left behind to guard their leavings. It should be safe to go through."

Uskban nodded and carefully led the way. As they approached the well at the crossroads, Uskban stopped, looked at the remnants of a campfire, and gave an enraged curse.

Sandy spurred his rudhar forward to see what was wrong. Scattered through the ashes of the campfire were some blackened bones. The skull was small, belonging either to a child or maybe a woman. It had been smashed in at the base and the brain extracted. The thigh bones had been split down the middle and the marrow scraped out. The Zalkrings apparently had a taste for the delicacies.

Sandy stared at the campfire with horror and then mounting revulsion. Pognak gave an inarticulate scream and shook a giant fist at the northern sky. Even hard-boiled old Zhadnoboth was sickened and he hastily turned his eyes away.

Uskban muttered in a voice thick with hate, "This is one more deviltry those bastards must pay for. They say they eat their victims as a way of honoring Kels Zalkri. I say they do it because they like the taste of tortured meat."

Just before dawn they were back where they'd been three nights before. Everyone except Zhadnoboth settled down to sleep as soon as possible—they'd had a hard day and night. The sorcerer, however, dug two dictionary-sized books out of the seemingly endless spaces concealed within his robes and settled down to do some hard reading. Time was short and he needed to refamiliarize himself with certain spells.

A sudden tearing pain from the top of his head woke Sandy. It felt like some critter had crept from under a rock and had taken a bite out of his scalp. He sat up and looked about angrily. Out of the corner of his eye, Sandy caught sight of the sorcerer walking away with several hairs dangling from between his thumb and forefinger. Fuming, Sandy thought, *Someday I'll give that cantankerous old fossil a taste of his own medicine.*

Still seething, Sandy laid down again, but couldn't get back to sleep. The sorcerer's offhanded treatment of him had put him in a foul mood which wouldn't go away. Finally he arose and stomped over to see what the sorcerer was up to.

Zhadnoboth carefully put one hair into a small iron pot, sealed the lid with beeswax, and hung the pot from a small brass tripod. He fumbled with a lizard-skin bag, finally shaking out several pieces of red sandstone. These he placed under the pot. "Now some essence of true salamander," he mumbled to himself and dug a small black-glass vial from his robes. Carefully he put three drops on the red sandstone, chanted a short incantation, and touched the stones with his staff. There was a crackling sound and the stones began to glow with a ruddy light.

The sorcerer frowned and furiously began paging through

one of his spellbooks. He found the passage he wanted, read it, and nodded his head in satisfaction. Confidently, he made a few mystic passes and hissed out a word of power. This time the stones burned with a furious crimson flame and in seconds the pot turned a bright cherry red.

Zhadnoboth smiled triumphantly...

Until the pot turned white-hot and began to melt. With a roar the lid shot off into the sky, and the sorcerer was engulfed in the cloud of steam spewing from the pot. Then, as fast as it had appeared, the steam dissipated, leaving behind a rather disheveled sorcerer.

Zhadnoboth glared at the heap of melted slag—all that remained of the pot—and screamed, "May that old harridan be eternally damned. I *told* her it had to be made of virgin iron!" He stewed for a moment and then the venom spewed out again. "I'll teach her to cheat me. I swear on the bones of my ancestors I'll hunt her down and cook her in one of her own pots. Maybe then that old witch will learn the value of honesty."

Sandy smiled wryly. It warmed the cockles of his heart to see the sorcerer defrauded. Knowing Zhadnoboth, he probably had only got his just desserts. He was a fine one to rant about dishonesty.

Still grumbling, Zhadnoboth consulted his spellbook again. This time he pulled from his robe a copper ring, green with age and half eaten away with corrosion. Next he reached into the air and grabbed at nothing. His hand came away filled with a black oily goo. Disgusted, he flung most away. The rest he rubbed into the ring until it shone like a new-minted coin.

Zhadnoboth inspected the ring and then, satisfied, started into a new spell. He slowly ran his forefinger around the outer edge of the ring, chanting what seemed a child's nonsense verse about porridge and pie with each complete rotation. Then he would start over again with the same motion and the same verse. It seemed like complete garbage—and maddening, repetitious garbage, at that—but it worked. Each time his finger made a complete circle the ring got larger. It was an eye-catching piece of magic, though Sandy wondered why he didn't forgo the rigmarole and start with a hoop of the right size.

When Zhadnoboth had the ring enlarged to about two feet in diameter, he blew gently on it and said in an oddly accented voice, "Be what you should be." Like a piece of down, the ring floated up into the air. Placing his hands underneath, but not touching it, Zhadnoboth maneuvered the ring into position. When it was in front of his face he said "stay" with the same odd accent and the ring froze in place.

Now he began the last part of the enchantment. First he tossed various ingredients into the middle of the ring: two blue feathers weighted with lead, a drop of salamander essence, a thumbnail-sized green egg covered with brown specks, a gray marble with red stripes, half a dried sausage, and a thimbleful of a light blue ink. Instead of falling through on the other side they disappeared, but with each ingredient the hole grew darker, until it was jet-black.

Lastly, he carefully put another of Sandy's hairs on the palm of his hand and blew it into the ring. As it passed through, the blackness tightened like a drumhead, and a shrill piercing screech much like that of chalk scraped over a blackboard came from the hole. Sandy gritted his teeth in agony and clapped his hands over his ears to keep his eardrums from cracking.

Ignoring or maybe unaware of the terrible sound, the sorcerer raised his staff and commanded: "Write, oracle. From the realms beyond this mortal coil come and write his name." Then Zhadnoboth goosed the blackness with a bolt of blue lightning from his staff.

This time the spell worked—in a way. A taloned finger appeared and wrote on the blackness, a white line appearing where it touched it. Sandy's full name was written in a beautiful and elegant Gothic script, every "i" dotted and not even the least of his names left out. Zhadnoboth looked at it for a moment and then started to turn purple with rage. He knew uncounted alphabets and scripts, but all were native to Zarathandra. Such outlandish gibberish as Gothic script was beyond his ken.

"You fool," he yelled as he shook a scrawny fist at the writing. "Write his name in a language I know." There was a dry sound, almost like a chuckle, and the script crumbled into a fine dust and was gone.

With a crack, the ring broke into three pieces and fell to the ground, each fragment now back to its original size.

Zhadnoboth stomped his foot and turned to Sandy. "It's disgraceful—that's what it is. You call an otherworldly being and nine times out of ten he turns out to be a blithering idiot."

Still grumbling, Zhadnoboth turned a watchful eye toward Uskban. Seeing that the madman was still asleep, he sidled over to the waterbags. Sandy could see he was itching to use the water in his next spell, but his previous set-to with Uskban had made him leery of using it—even though their supply of water was now more than ample.

The sorcerer tried to lift one of the waterbags, but his scrawny muscles couldn't even budge the magically over-loaded container. He gave an angry snort and turned to Sandy. Before he could say a word, Sandy walked over and heaved the bag up onto his shoulder. Zhadnoboth nodded with satisfaction, said, "Come," then scuttled off to find a more secluded spot. Puffing a bit and trying not to show it, Sandy trudged doggedly after him. He was getting intrigued by the sorcerer's magic and hoped what was coming would be worth watching.

They rounded a corner of the mesa at whose foot they camped and found the spot Zhadnoboth was looking for. Sandy thought it was about time. He dropped the weighty waterbag to the ground and sat down to watch the sorcerer and regain his breath.

Zhadnoboth began smoothing out a place at the foot of a large standing stone. Sandy looked at the stone casually and then with more interest. It was rough and almost shapeless, but it had the look of something that had been deliberately carved. Sandy could only assume it had magical properties.

Zhadnoboth finished with his puttering and began to work on his spell. He drew a large circle in the dirt in front of the stone, then drew thirteen symbols equally spaced around the outer edge. Zhadnoboth pulled back and inspected his handiwork while he rubbed his scruffy beard thoughtfully. Then he stepped forward and drew several more symbols just to the upper left of the circle.

Content with that part of the spell framework, Zhadnoboth got some fine white sand from a nearby dune and covered the inside of the circle until it was smooth and white. "Now some ink of the ghost squid," he told Sandy. He pulled a cut glass flask from his robes and poured a blue-black fluid on the white sand. "And some extract of emberdrake eggs." He added three drops of a pale amber liquid to the sand.

Smiling complacently, Zhadnoboth stepped back and

pointed his staff at the circle. At his word of command, a blue flame shot from the end of his staff and the circle ignited with a *whoosh*.

Sandy was caught unawares by the ball of fire which exploded from the circle. He jumped back, but not before he got his eyebrows singed. *Damn that idiot!*

Zhadnoboth, unconcerned and untouched by the fireball, went calmly on about his business. Carefully he traced over the circle's outline with the tip of his staff which left behind a ring of pale blue electricity that sputtered and cracked angrily.

"Pour on the water," the sorcerer said over his shoulder.

Sandy hurriedly picked up the waterbag and walked to the now mirrorlike circle. Stage magic had always fascinated him; now he was finding real magic to be even better. Flimflam just could not curl your toes and make your hair stand on end like the real stuff could.

He tipped the waterbag upside down and let its contents gush into the circle. Every drop was absorbed by the mirror-bright surface. The only change Sandy could see was that the mirrored surface now had a wet sheen. And one thing more: the inside of the circle still shone, but now reflected nothing.

Zhadnoboth, feeling feisty and proud of himself, stepped forward to begin the next part of the enchantment. He spoke the ancient cadences of Kythornak's Twelfth Chant with exuberant confidence: the words rolled off his lips with a full flourish and all the frills. The air throbbed with the power released by the chant. As the last syllable went its way, there was an instant of sheer rightness as the perfectly invoked pattern took hold.

"Watch closely, demon, and see my mastery," Zhadnoboth said proudly. Sandy thought the sorcerer was going overboard with self-congratulation, but he was still impressed. Something great and wonderful had been done—he knew not exactly what, but his sixth sense had every atom of his being tingling. Grudgingly he gave Zhadnoboth a little more respect. The scrawny old man might not always know what he was doing, but he could still throw a mean spell.

Sandy looked hard at the mirrored ground, then looked again. He could almost see something in it. Its shadowy depths hinted at a wild, weird world beyond. Maybe he truly saw a windswept land peopled by entities of constantly changing shape and hue, or maybe his mind put them there.

Sandy glanced up from the shiny circle and his heart jumped. For a moment the standing stone had looked like a huge malevolent being crouched and ready to spring. Then he saw it as it was, just a huge stone, and relaxed.

The sorcerer took the final and crucial step in his enchantment. He placed another hair he had stolen from Sandy's head on his palm, said a minor word of power, and blew on it. The hair wafted gently off his palm and floated down to land at the midpoint of the mirrored surface. Then he went into a trance, his smoldering eyes fixed on the hair. After a few moments, the hair began to smoke. It broke into flame, and in another instant was only ashes.

In the circle images began to form, vividly clear for only an instant, then gone. There was Sandy as a teenager singing in the church choir, enjoying himself and totally unaware of the pained expressions on the faces of his fellow choir members. Another image showed him kissing his first girl, her hair golden and intricately braided in a Scandinavian manner. He saw himself chinning himself by the door of the mess hall during army boot camp and then as an eleven-year-old catching his first walleye pike. If there was an order to the images, he couldn't figure it out—Zhadnoboth's magic seemed to be retrieving them on a catch-as-catch-can basis. Eagerly he waited to see what else would show up.

It was a familiar scene—a high school classroom. He smiled ruefully when he saw who was teaching. Old Pruneface had taken an instinctive dislike to him and he'd had to struggle to get a passing grade in English. Still, in spite of her, he had a fondness for that year: that was when he got to know poetry and the varied glories of Shelley, Andrew Marvell, Edward Lear, and Robert Service. In the scrying circle, Old Pruneface had fixed one of her fish eyes on Sandy and was getting ready to call on him. Zhadnoboth leaded forward eagerly, waiting to hear what name she would say. . .

And a deafening roar shook the desert air. Both heads snapped up and both mouths dropped open in shocked disbelief. Where the stone had been, there now stood a giant troll-like creature. The huge blocky body—twelve feet at the shoulder—had skin like flaking shale and a mouth which seemed big enough to swallow an ox whole. Slavering with hate and hunger, the thing roared again, and charged thunderously at them.

The old sorcerer gave a squawk and took off. Sandy took

off in the opposite direction but stopped when he realized the creature wasn't chasing him. He looked around and saw it tearing after Zhadnoboth, who showed a remarkable turn of speed despite his age. The thing moved surprisingly fast for its huge size and bulk. On the straightaway it could easily outrace Zhadnoboth, but had trouble dealing with his scuttling and dodging tactics. Still, it looked like the creature had had it; the creature kept getting closer and Zhadnoboth was wearing out. Then the sorcerer made a sudden dart and ran pell-mell at Sandy.

Sandy hesitated for a vital moment as he saw the sorcerer and the monster coming right at him. When he moved, it was too late: Zhadnoboth had rushed by and disappeared in a puff of smoke.

The simpleminded creature gave a howl of disappointment and looked around in bewilderment for a second, saw Sandy, and decided to gobble him up.

Cursing, Sandy sprinted into the desert, the thing close behind him. As he ran and dodged, Sandy tried to figure a way out of this pickle. He certainly wasn't going to outrun it forever. He cast a hopeful eye around for the sorcerer, wanting to return the favor. No such luck.

Sandy darted to the right, feeling a breeze as the creature just missed him. He got an idea and ran headlong for the magic mirror. It might not work, but it was worth trying.

He got to the mirror, running full tilt. He took a long leap over it and kept going. Then he spun on his heel and watched to see what the creature would do.

The thing had the luck of the damned. Its long strides took it over the mirror without touching it.

Swearing to himself in frustration, Sandy took off again. A straight dash and a sudden swerve kept him from being caught—until an unlucky step to avoid a bush which looked like a thorny upside down ice cream cone sent him sprawling. He was on his feet in an instant and didn't realize he had severely injured his ankle until he stepped on it. An excruciating pain almost made him collapse; only fear and an ornery determination kept him going.

Sandy hobbled clumsily aside as the thing made another rush. Then he gritted his teeth and took off again for the mirror, hopping and hobbling as best he could.

He felt the creature's thunderous stride at his heels and threw himself to one side. A swipe of the monster's flailing hand almost got him and he fell half stunned to the red desert soil. The creature braked to a stop, sending chunks of the rocklike dirt flying, then charged back at Sandy. Only a savage burst of white-hot lightning at the last moment saved him.

Seconds later a dazed Sandy regained full consciousness and looked around. The first thing he saw was the rock creature advancing stubbornly on Zhadnoboth. The sorcerer kept blasting the thing with lightning from his staff. With each strike the beast howled with pain, but it was too stupid and evil-tempered to give up. Slowly it advanced on Zhadnoboth.

For a moment Sandy watched unbelieving. This wasn't Zhadnoboth's style. The sorcerer generally preferred knife-in-the-back tactics. Then he saw the look in the sorcerer's eye and understood: it was pure greed. Zhadnoboth was not going to lose his investment in Sandy without a fight. The cantankerous old cuss moved up a couple notches in Sandy's estimation. He was an underhanded conniver, but he had grit to go along with it—if he wanted to, and if something he considered precious, like treasure, was involved.

Zhadnoboth frowned at the monster slowly advancing on him, clearly wondering what kept the damned thing going, then he screwed himself up to a supreme effort. Howling a great chant, Zhadnoboth let loose the granddaddy of all lightning bolts.

When Sandy's sight cleared, both the sorcerer and the creature were on the ground. Zhadnoboth picked himself up and turned a tetchy eye toward the creature, now a blackened pile of smoking flesh.

Then, incredibly, it stirred, mewing with agony, and staggered to its feet. Again it started to advance on the sorcerer.

This was too much for Zhadnoboth. He stomped his foot bad-temperedly and vanished again in a puff of smoke.

The thing howled in angry frustration. Befuddled, it looked around wildly for the man who had hurt it so, saw Sandy, and again settled on him as prey. At least he was available. Its cracked and blackened lips curled with a hungry smile. Then, like hell on wheels, it charged him.

Not again, thought Sandy as he hobbled quickly to one side. Painfully he ran as best he could for the mirror, cursing himself for not getting away while the thing had its attention focused on Zhadnoboth.

This time when Sandy got to where the magic mirror was, he hobbled around it, the creature almost on top of him. With a cry of bestial joy the thing grabbed at Sandy with its massive hands—and stomped one mighty foot squarely in the middle of the magic mirror.

What happened then, Sandy was never sure of. There was an explosion and Sandy felt his flesh sizzling, his body slammed to the ground, and his soul shredded into infinitesimal pieces. There was agonizing pain so terrible he had to scream—and couldn't. Finally, a merciful blackness overwhelmed him and he was nothing.

When he regained consciousness, strange visions and fragments of memory floated through his mind: drinking a fiery liquor cup for cup with a crew of rotting skeletons in some feast hall in hell, racing on a steed of fire across a waste filled with molten rock and hot bubbling sulfur, and playing chess on a board made from human bones with an ancient king who held his severed head in the crook of his left arm. These and other fleeting images bedeviled his mind. The last and most chilling was seeing his dead body laid out on a funeral bier and the great lady cloaked in shadows standing beside it. She bent over and kissed his cold lips, life burning like fire surged through his dead veins, and he opened his eyes and saw the sorcerer looking down on him.

Zhadnoboth poked him in the ribs with his staff and commanded, "Get your carcass off the ground. We still have things to do."

Sandy got to his feet gingerly and was pleasantly surprised by how good he felt. By some freak of luck or magic, the blast had flung him free without hurting him; and his twisted ankle had miraculously healed. Nor did he feel any discomfort from the singeing the sorcerer had inadvertently given him. The pain had been so real when the explosion had caught him.

Sandy looked around and saw where the magic mirror had been. Now there was only a blackened hole blasted into the orange-red desert soil. Of the creature he saw nothing, unless scattered fragments of gray rock were its remains.

"What kind of idiot are you?" the sorcerer said, giving Sandy the sharp edge of his tongue. "You could have gotten yourself killed and spoiled years of effort by me! Then where would I have been? What's more, I had to risk *my* life to save your worthless hide. Do you think sorcerers of my skill are as common as trees in a forest?"

Sandy was seething. Who did the sorcerer think he was, God's perfect creation? It certainly hadn't been *Sandy* who'd roused the monster. At least they were both still alive, which was a miracle considering the way the sorcerer had screwed things up.

Sandy's anger erupted into words—and immediately the silver chain tightened into a stranglehold, as the fierceness of his anger activated the spell Zhadnoboth had placed on it. Sandy fell to his knees, purple-faced. After what seemed an eternity the chain loosened, and he drew great breaths into his aching lungs.

"Let that be a lesson to you," Zhadnoboth said self-right-eously. "Hold your tongue and know your place."

Sandy got up and looked with cold fury at the sorcerer. He spoke in the only way he dared: he gave Zhadnoboth the finger and spat contemptuously on the ground.

At that, the sorcerer looked like he was going to go into a conniption fit.

"What of the Zalkrings and their god?" Uskban's harsh voice surprised them. "Has your damn fool sorcery roused them? If you have spoiled our chances, I swear I'll cut out your liver, sorcerer, before they can get to us. And from what hell did that creature come? Is it one of the dark one's minions?"

Uskban's interruption threw Zhadnoboth off stride and by the time he got his mental gears remeshed he realized the little madman had to be placated. Uskban's uncertain temper could be the ruin of their whole venture. Hurriedly he said, "Those things are ancient—so old that even Kels Zalkri seems young compared to them. They are no friends to him —or to anyone."

"Quit the doubletalk," spat out Uskban. "Tell me some-thing I need to know. Are Kels Zalkri and some legions from hell likely to come charging in here?"

Zhadnoboth smiled sourly. "I think not. There is a pecu-liarity to this area you've led us to. Magical energies are damped out if they go beyond the limits of this place. An enchantment so old that even I cannot tell when it began lies upon this place." He stopped and thought for a moment. "It is odd, though, that the creature should appear; most of its kind have long been only dust and memories." He rubbed his chin and added, "It seems to me I have read about this place in one of my books of lore, about a battle between the gods here. Perhaps my sorcery somehow interacted with the ancient enchantments which still permeate this place."

What else could the old scoundrel expect, Sandy thought, building his magic mirror right at the foot of an enchanted stone? If he was such a hotshot sorcerer, he should have known that.

Uskban was thinking much the same thoughts. "You and your rash blunderings will get us all killed yet. But enough of this. Can you be sure the Zalkrings and their god do not know of us?"

"I would know if the dark one turned his eye this way," Zhadnoboth said in a cold, clipped tone. "I am a sorcerer, a sorcerer whose like will not be seen again."

Thank God for that, thought Sandy.

"Prove it," said Uskban.

"There is a way," Zhadnoboth said, "one even a knownothing like you could understand. I could cast a spell of perception."

"Then do it."

Casting a sulking glance at Uskban, Zhadnoboth turned sharply on his heel and stalked toward their camp. For an old man he had a lot of spring in his step, slamming each foot down angrily as he walked.

Quickly the old sorcerer gathered together the necessary gear. Then he made them stand close while he made a circle of twine about them. When this was done he chanted a spell over a small silver knife, cut the twine from the rest of the ball, and tied the ends together with an intricately braided knot. Next he rubbed into the twine a mixture of tallow and an herb which smelled like wintergreen. Placing his hands on each side of the knot he gave a yank, simultaneously speaking one of Kythornak's words of power. The knot slid apart, leaving an unbroken piece of twine. Now there was a tension in the air—an aliveness—a sense of otherness.

Zhadnoboth placed an earthenware bowl on the ground and filled it with a silvery liquid he called essence of pearl from one of the innumerable flasks and bottles he seemed to carry on his person. Next he pulled from his robes a peculiarly shaped iron needle that had a double hook on one end and a split point on the other. This he carefully floated in the essence of pearl. Three times the sorcerer touched the needle with the tip of his staff, each time saying the same word of power he'd used on the knot. With the third repetition, the needle quivered and then slowly began to spin clockwise.

Sandy noticed that almost invisible lines of vapor were streaming in from the perimeter of the circle toward the needle, which had lazily spun two full circles. Then it caught one of the vaporous lines on its hooked end. Instantly it changed directions and swiftly spun widdershins. Only when the line of vapor was taut did it stop. It gave a jerk and the line snapped. For an instant they could see a small orange and brown lizard hiding under a rock and staring lazily at them with three eyes.

Again the needle started spinning clockwise. This time it only went about once before it snagged a line. This time they saw Glupp's large placid eyes looking bemusedly at them.

For a third time the needle began turning clockwise. This time it kept spinning until the sorcerer gave Uskban an *I-told-you-so* sniff and cut the twine with the silver knife. Instantly the spell was broken. Again it was only the dust and the heat of the everyday world which surrounded them.

"No one watches us," the sorcerer said as he gathered up his gear. "At least no one who counts for much. Now let me be. I have more important things to do than calm your piddling worries."

Zhadnoboth stalked off in what he thought was a grand manner and at the same time absentmindedly stuffed his equipment back into his robes—not even leaving a lump to show where they had gone. Uskban gave him a snakelike stare, then nodded to Pognak, and the two of them went off to check their gear and prepare for that night's journey. Sandy watched them go, shrugged, and followed after, wondering whether anyone had noticed he'd almost gotten killed.

16

THE Goddess wrapped a mantle of gossamerlike black silk about her shadowy form and walked the moonstone path to the Pool of Gygongarian. She sat on the low wall surrounding the pool, a wall of dark-green jade inset with serpentine patterns in silver, and looked into the water.

Here was stored what had been, from just the last instant to the beginnings of creation. The Goddess pictured Sandy and Zhadnoboth in her mind and called for a re-creation of the events just past. The pool responded to her will and began by showing the sorcerer plucking three hairs from Sandy's head. Then at a slow dreamlike pace events unfolded, up to the moment Zhadnoboth *proved* they were not under observation. The images in the gently undulating medium were sharp but tiny, as though seen through a telescope located a million miles or more away.

The Goddess watched the explosion of the stone-souled one and its aftermath. Exultation and a kind of dread lay side by side in her inmost being as she watched. Before, only her mind had known Sandy was the one foretold. Now her soul also knew. When the magic mirror had shattered and death had come she had felt the jolt through her whole being. She had so much to gain, much more than even her cherished revenge, but there was a price to pay. Even so, the price was almost a gift to her.

The Goddess turned her thoughts to the adventure and the four who were undertaking it. Fate was rolling the dice, and she could feel destiny shifting. More in her favor all the time. Her plans were working out to near perfection, even mishaps like Zhadnoboth rousing the morzikkan-tam working in her favor. For a moment she worried—Was fate going

too much her way? Destiny could and had taken some surprise turns.

She mused about her champions. The chosen four were
nearly perfect. Zhadnoboth knew enough to get the cauldron
boiling, but not enough to be wise and back off. Pognak and
Uskban had the fury which would provide the spark. And,
most important, Sandy was becoming the sword she needed.

He had changed in the short time he had been in Zarathandra. At first he had been mostly unrealized potential—a
man with qualities, but one who didn't bother to use them.
He was harder now, both physically and mentally—and a
taste of death had made him subconsciously more aware of
the spiritual realm most mortals didn't know they were part
of. Someday, if he and she survived this venture, Sandy
might be quite formidable. He was like a late developing
wine, unremarkable tasted young—but tasted at full matur-
ity...

The Goddess laughed and turned to the faraway darkness
which was Kels Zalkri. "Watch your shadow, dark one.
Maybe your doom is stalking you and you know it not."

17

THE next three nights were steady hard traveling, each one bringing them closer to Tham Og Zalkri. The mental pressure of getting so close to such a dreaded place made everyone short-tempered and they hardly talked except to snap and bicker.

Sandy spent a lot of his time composing bawdy limericks and then telling them to Glupp. The grundzar was a great audience, beaming hearty appreciation at even the worst of them—probably because he didn't understand them. After trying out his latest creation on Glupp and getting a warm response, Sandy growled good-naturedly at the big beast, "You don't fool me, I know a bootlicker when I see one." Glupp gave him an enormous idiotic grin and his long purple tongue shot out and lovingly slavered over Sandy's boot. Sandy gave him a suspicious stare and said, "If you're a dumb beast then I really am a demon." Glupp proved him *wrong* by being very obviously deaf and dumb, not hearing or responding to these words.

The long nights with nobody to talk to except the unspeaking Glupp gave Sandy a lot of time to think. He began to wonder if Zarathandra was such a bad place to be. Both on Earth and here he had been dragooned into doing what he didn't want to do, but there was something grander about an adventure than a routine job shuffling paper for the government. At least he was getting fresh air and needed exercise. Still, if he had his druthers, he'd go back: this world was just too dangerous. If he ever got home, he'd somehow find a happy medium between his two lives—something interesting and well paying to do, but not full of constant danger and uncertainty.

Sandy woke during the late afternoon of the day following

their third night of hard travel; yawned, stretched, and looked around curiously. His sixth sense, which seemed stronger since his encounter with the stone beast, filled him with a vaguely pleasant anticipation. He looked around and saw Zhadnoboth pacing testily, every so often throwing an uneasy glance toward the northeast. They were less than a day's journey from the Zalkrings' stronghold and sanctuary, and the strain was wearing the sorcerer down. He had doubled his protection spells, but this only seemed to make him worry more. His soul did not have the faith in his sorcery that his conscious mind did.

Zhadnoboth caught Sandy watching him and snarled, "I hope you slept well, demon." Fear had honed his tongue to a diamond-edged sharpness. "Rouse those other two sluggards and we'll get on our way early."

From behind Sandy's back, Uskban snapped, "No!"

The sorcerer's head jerked up angrily and he yelled back, "Why not? Let's get this miserable traveling over with and find a place to settle down and plan our strategy. My magic will hide us from their sight, magical and otherwise, even when we are only a stone's throw from them."

Uskban shook his head and said, "Magic hides only so much. The Zalkrings might not be desert bred, but they still can hear and see. That close to Tham Og Zalkri, there'll be Zalkring stragglers streaming in toward their fane all day tomorrow. If even one notices something, we're dead before the next breath leaves our bodies. We'll go tomorrow night. By then they will all be safely within and too preoccupied with their midsummer ceremonies to pay much heed to anything outside their citadel. And the new moon that night will cloak us."

Zhadnoboth fumed for a moment, then reluctantly nodded. The madman was right; getting to their destination early might sorely tempt fate.

"Good," Uskban said with satisfaction. "Now we can prepare for a death feast."

"Death!" shouted the sorcerer. "Who said anything about death? This is no suicide mission—it's a secret raid to obtain treasure. We go in and get out before they know we've been there. There'll be no killing or violence unless we're forced into it."

Uskban turned cold eyes on the sorcerer, who was almost jumping up and down in his agitation. In a voice filled with suppressed emotion he said, "I am a Kri Shandri; I would go into great danger as a Kri Shandri should. When we knowingly go to war or set out on a dangerous venture we hold a death feast. It is our way of putting our souls right with this world and the world after. Thus, if fate is against us, our souls will be lightened and free to travel." After a pause he added, "It is not given for many outlanders to share a death feast with the Kri Shandri, especially with one who is the last of the Naz Idmani clan. Pognak and I would be honored if you and the demon would join us."

It was an invitation you couldn't refuse, not if you didn't want to mortally insult the two Kri Shandri. Zhadnoboth's mouth dropped open a couple of times, then he gulped and accepted. Uskban turned his eyes to Sandy, who quickly nodded.

The death feast began just after the last glimmer of twilight. Uskban sat on the north side of a small fire, the place of honor. Three black leather bottles studded with brass rivets were on the ground beside him. On the south side of the fire sat Pognak, holding on his lap a round brass tray stacked with wafers of unleavened bread. Zhadnoboth and Sandy sat to the west and east.

Sandy cast a sour eye toward the food and drink, knowing he was going to hate the death feast. What he wouldn't give to be home again sharing a Christmas feast with his parents and his brother. The table would be loaded with food that smelled so good you grew fat just sniffing it; turkey, mashed potatoes and gravy, hot rolls, roasted squash, pecan pie, hot mulled cider, butter beans, cranberry sauce, and innumerable other things to pleasantly fill the belly. That's what he missed most about being on his own, his mother's wonderful cooking and the warm sense of being part of a family. Would he ever see any of this family again?

Uskban began the ceremonies by lifting his eyes to the dark sky and chanting, "My lady, look with kindness on us. Hear our words, feel what is in our hearts, and heed the soft murmurs from our souls. Help us to find the strength we need. Set our souls at peace. Give us your blessing and your sublime understanding."

Uskban then bowed his head; Pognak did likewise. For the first time Sandy saw something akin to peace on the little man's face. Sandy and the sorcerer caught each other's eye, both looking for some clue as to what to do. Then, almost as one, they bowed their heads and went through the motions of silent prayer.

After a few minutes of quiet prayer, Uskban picked up one of the black leather bottles and pulled out the stopper with his teeth. He filled his cup to the brim. It was one of the frayed leather jacks they used every day and its battered appearance contrasted sharply with the bottle's rough elegance.

Uskban passed the bottle to the right—toward the west, and age. Zhadnoboth filled his cup, then Pognak, and finally Sandy as the bottle finished up in the east and the position of youth.

When Sandy had again stoppered the bottle, Uskban solemnly spilled three drops of the dark amber liquor on the ground. "For those of our kith who are one with the dust," he said. He raised his cup in a kind of salute to each of the others, again going from right to left, before taking a long slow swallow from it. Then he looked expectantly toward Zhadnoboth.

For a moment the sorcerer looked befuddled, then he boldly faked his way through the ritual, copying Uskban's motions. He even managed to do it with the proper amount of piety, though Sandy noticed a faint gleam of exasperation in his eyes.

Pognak went through the ritual and then it was Sandy's turn. He played his part with style, even though the liquor had a much fiercer kick than he had expected: the first mellow taste slid easily down his throat to become a pool of glowing lava in his belly. Soon rivers of liquid fire were racing breakneck through his veins and for one brief moment, his flesh seemed pure flame. Then the fire subsided and he was mere mortal flesh again, but deep down a lingering glow remained.

Uskban nodded to the big mute. Pognak picked up the brass tray and held it out in front of him, silently asking a blessing on the food. Then he took a piece of the unleavened bread from it and passed the tray on to Sandy. When the tray had made a full circle, he put the wafer in his mouth and washed it down with a swallow of the liquor. Each in turn, the others did the same. Now Sandy was glad to drink the liquor; the bread was like salty hardtack and had got stuck in his craw.

Several more rounds of the bragberry brandy and the unleavened bread followed. The hardtack got shoved to one side, but the liquor kept making the circuit as they got down to serious tippling. Soon the early ritual somberness was replaced by a half-rowdy, half-serious mood.

From a worn leather case lying beside him Pognak dragged out a musical instrument that slightly resembled a zither. It had about forty strings and its lemon-colored wood was inlaid with checkered panels of jet and ivory. The mute slipped some picks on his fingers and began to play.

As the first note of the music penetrated through the pearly fog Sandy had drifted into, he looked up with surprised pleasure: Pognak played his instrument with a magic and loving touch. Sandy listened, entranced. He loved music, but especially that produced by stringed instruments like the oud and the dulcimer.

The music's sad wailing tone struck deep into Sandy's heart. It spoke of fierce sorrow with an eerie beauty that made the soul soar and weep at the same time. He heard it with more than his ears—he felt it in his bones and rippling through the rivers of his mind. It seemed a kind of hymn which spoke of valor, death, and the grief of those left behind.

Pognak stopped playing; and Sandy looked at him in confused wonder. He was still the same ugly, silent giant he had always been, yet now his thick and clumsy fingers had a magic in them. He even looked like a different person as he played his music. His deep absorption in what he was creating produced a softening and a smoothing down of the hard lines of hate and malice engraved into his face. For the first time Sandy saw him as more than a bully.

Uskban spoke out in a quiet, moody voice, "A death feast is a time to speak out about what troubles your heart. It's a chance to brag of your prowess, slander your enemies, wonder about life and death, or maybe just a chance to babble about mere nothings if you so wish it. Each in his own way says what is right for himself. If one cannot speak for oneself, then a friend may speak for him. Tonight I will be Pognak's tongue and say what must be said."

The mute had listened intently to Uskban's words. Now the dour giant broke into a rare smile and gave him a nod, thanking and giving permission at the same time. Uskban started to speak again, but the mute held up his hand to stop him. Then Pognak ran his fingers once across the strings of his instrument and launched into another song: a wild lilting piece, full of wind, the stars, and a love to go with them.

Sandy and the others swigged their brandy and listened, carried by the music to another place and another time. When the song was over, it was as if they had lost something precious.

Uskban broke the silence. "Once he was a bard to the Kri Shandri clans. Men said he would be remembered with the great bards of old: with Kimmardzan the Spellsinger and Om-Pelisse of the Sorrows. Some sang sweeter and others with greater skill, but none with his force and feeling. All the songs of our heritage were his and to this he added much."

Uskban paused and then, in a deep brooding tone, added, "Then he was brought to Tham Og Zalkri by his enemies and a singer was slain. His fingers still have the skill, but now there is no voice to harmonize with. Nor has he the heart for something so loving and good. He lost much, but the Kri Shandri and Zarathandra lost more. The Zalkrings owe him a debt, a debt which not even blood can repay. Only reborn in death will he sing once more." Uskban took a shot of the fiery liquor and fell back into a black silence.

Uskban's words and then his silence irritated Zhadnoboth who complained tipsily, "Stop that. There you go speaking of death again. We're out to make our fortunes, not get killed. So let's enjoy our guzzling instead of throwing a dismal cloud over the party."

Uskban fixed him with a cold eye (which the sorcerer was too drunk to heed) and said, "At a death feast one has the right to say what is in the heart. No one can deny him this right, on pain of death. You can babble or cry, just as long as it comes true from the soul. Grief has as much right as joy at a death feast. If you like it not, hold your tongue or hold out your throat to get your weasand slit."

Zhadnoboth shrugged, gave a drunken belch, and replied, "So be it, though your dismal broodings make for a poor feast. Thank the Goddess for liquor worth the drinking." So saying, he swallowed another slug of the bragberry brandy and settled into a testy silence.

"There is more to a death feast than joy and drunkenness," Uskban said in a voice starting to get fuzzy with liquor. "And there are things in it more filling than food and drink."

"I can't think of any," quipped the sorcerer. Then he drained his cup in one angry gulp: a mistake. His eyes suddenly glazed over and his mouth fell open in a speechless croak. For a moment he was unable to breathe and he grew red as he gasped helplessly. Finally he was able to draw in a great lungful of air and so remained among the living—though what was left held little resemblance to the crotchety old schemer they were used to. Instead they saw a slack-jawed, glassy-eyed, and thoroughly soused sorcerer.

Uskban glared blurrily at him for a second and then remembered this was a death feast where anything was permitted. He nodded to Pognak and pointed to the flask. The giant picked it up and refilled the sorcerer's cup. Zhadnoboth automatically lifted his cup to his lips and began swilling the liquor down. Sandy looked at him and wondered how he managed to do that—he seemed too drunk to even remember his name.

For a long while there was hardly any talk as they did some serious guzzling. Sandy tried to hold up his end, but couldn't match the other three—drinking had never been his long suit. Even Zhadnoboth, who was pickled to the gills, kept putting the liquor away like he could go on forever.

"To die and leave no one or no accomplishment behind is the worst," Uskban suddenly said. He took a healthy slug of the brandy and stared moodily into the night. "None will mourn me when I die: I have no kin, no friends, and I have done nothing to be remembered by. I am the last of my lineage and the least. If I had done a great deed or left a child my name, death would be less fearsome."

Sandy looked at Uskban as he said these last words. There was an odd brooding tone in the madman's voice. Something was being said, but not in words.

"No it wouldn't," interrupted the sorcerer. He gave a hiccup and went on, "Children make no difference, except for the worse. You're better off without children. You give of yourself and earn heartbreak in return."

Unsteadily Zhadnoboth filled his cup to overflowing and took a great gulp. Tears streamed from his eyes.

"I have a daughter. She's like her mother, so lovely words cannot express it and so determined to have her own way that she'd flatten a mountain if it refused to move. When she was a child she was a joy; how she loved her *dada*. Then she became a woman and decided I was unworthy of her."

Zhadnoboth gave a deep sad sigh and took another swig of the bragberry brandy. Smiling sadly, he said, "I met her mother at Madame Tilza's—that was in my younger days, before I became a full-fledged sorcerer. Didn't have two coins to rub together in those days so I tried sneaking out without paying her. Damned if that brazen hussy didn't chase me down the street, barefoot and bare-assed, demanding her money. Caught me, too, but only because I turned into a dead-end alley by mistake. She was threatening to carve my privates into little pieces when the watch arrested us. A real hellion."

Zhadnoboth gave a wry smile and went on, "They brought us before the judge the next morning—he was scandalized. That prissy bastard tried to nail us with almost every count in the book: rioting, lewd behavior, blasphemy, whoremongering, assaulting the watch, and I forget what else—though there must have been at least twenty more charges. I thought I was going to rot my days away in a dungeon or working in some hellhole of a mine: the city fathers were as prim and pious a bunch of hypocrites as I've ever seen—even as they grew rich off the graft. On top of that the judge was a notorious puritan, so pure he only bedded his wife out of duty."

Zhadnoboth refilled his cup and went on. "That iron-nerved hoyden saved our skins. She was tight with the money and had saved almost enough to start her own whorehouse. She used it to bribe the judge—that and something she whispered to him about his son. Still, that sanctimonious old fraud, thank the Goddess, made her pay a price she hadn't expected: he set her free on the condition that she become an honest woman by marrying me, and that we get out of the city before nightfall."

Zhadnoboth sighed drunkenly and shook his head in a kind of admiration. "Damn her, that woman was tough. We had hardly shaken the dust of the town off our heels when she had a dagger at my throat. Told me that if I tried to skip out on her before she had her money back—and with interest—she'd flay me alive and roll me about in rock salt. There was no reasoning with her. She stuck to me for over twenty-five years. I thought she had her hooks into me forever, then she up and dies on me."

Zhadnoboth, tears streaming from his eyes, ceremoniously poured his brandy on the ground. "Here's to that damned bitch. As hard-assed a rig as I've ever known and ten times more the lady than most who boast of their fancy breeding." The sorcerer wiped his eyes on his robe.

"What of your daughter?" asked Uskban.

"She married well—a rich merchant with hordes of ancestors, everyone so proper they must have been embalmed at birth. Curse that ungrateful whelp. She marries into this family and becomes twice as virtuous as they are. She looks down her nose at me, saying I am a disreputable scoundrel." A tear came from his eye and he asked, "What does that count? I loved her and did the best I could for her. She calls the money my wife and I earned tainted, but it was that money and the schooling we gave her which got her her marriage."

"So what?" grunted Uskban. "Just because one well poisons you it doesn't mean all the water in the world is bad."

Zhadnoboth bristled at this. "Hold your tongue. What do you know of love? You can only hate."

Uskban's eyes narrowed to pinpricks and he clutched convulsively at his dagger. But he held his peace—he would not profane the sacred feast with blood. Instead he muttered sullenly, "Even I, old one, know of love."

Zhadnoboth was too befuddled to sustain anger. His mood shifted and he became maudlin. "She's a good child, just gone wrong a little. Still has a soft spot for her old dad, always slips me a bit of gold if I come by. Even if she calls me a bad influence and chases me away from her children, she still loves me."

The old sorcerer started to fill up his cup with more of the bragberry brandy but fell asleep in mid-motion. His head slumped to his chest and the cup slipped from his lax fingers, spilling good liquor on the thirsty desert floor. A soft wheezing snore started to come in short bursts from his mouth.

"That woman must have been blind or a fool to put up with him for twenty-five years," Uskban muttered sourly as he gazed disdainfully at the drunken sorcerer.

Sandy took a swig of his brandy and said, "Maybe that is what love is about. Even the worst of us can have someone who'll love us."

Uskban's mouth crooked in a smile. "You're right, demon. Though *why*, only the Goddess knows."

Sandy nodded. Some unlikely people had spouses and children who loved them. The thought rankled a bit. He didn't consider himself a bad sort, but he had no one who gave a damn whether he lived or died—except parents and a brother, and that was because he was family. Aloud he said, "I knew a man once. He was a back-stabbing sneak, yet he had a wife and children who adored him—I never understood it. Maybe he loved them and that made up for a lot of faults."

Uskban swigged on his brandy and smiled bitterly, then said, "Even a damned soul like me, demon, had a woman who loved him. She was a brazen wench who tried to mount every man who struck her fancy. Not that I was any less randy in my younger days—I'd spread the legs of half the wenches within a day's ride of my home. But there was much more than passion between us. Wild lad that I was I just might have married that jade if fate had been kinder."

He scowled and gulped down more of the brandy with savage determination. "Curse that strumpet," he swore. "Why can't I forget her?" He stared wildly into the night, toward the mountains of his homeland. "She has a son, a fine lad if I hear right. No doubt he'd be a pride to his father."

The little man lapsed into a sullen silence and Pognak began to play a slow, mournful lament: dark like a moonless night and as bleak as cold stone, but mixed with a deep sadness from the quick of the soul and fierce determination to go on with life. It was like the people who lived in this desert land—hard and realistic, but fiercely loving.

Maybe it was only the drink in him or maybe it was the sheer beauty of the music, but Sandy more than heard its terrible sorrow, he lived it. It wove a powerful spell, enriched by Pognak's deeply buried emotions. It touched and reawoke Sandy's sixth sense, which had been dormant since his brush with death, giving it a dimension it never had before.

Clear and distinct as though etched in crystal he saw a distant place: a desert valley, desolate and harsh except where a small stream quickened it into lushness. Sheer cliffs of rose sandstone walled the valley on three sides; the fourth opened out to a dry, stony plain. At the head of the valley were three cairns, one large and two small, with tops blackened and scorched by the fires of ceremonial offerings. Twined about them like green robes was a mass of vines bearing myriad white flowers the size of peas.

Uskban saw the rapt expression on Sandy's face as he listened to the song and spoke, yanking Sandy back to reality. "It is called 'Mardana's Lament.' It is an old song, so old that no one can say how long we of the Kri Shandri have sung it. It is a gift from the Goddess, giving visions to those who have been touched by death. It is Pognak's greatest treasure; he plays it and remembers his family. It gives him a voice to speak of his love and grief. It's a fell song, a dark song for a dark soul."

Sandy, touched by the mute's heartfelt anguish and mellowed by the bragberry brandy, spoke his sympathy. "I know what it is to lose one you love." Vivid in his memory was the image of a young girl impaled upon the hood ornament of a car and the black despair he had felt. He hadn't been able to comprehend how both could ride bicycles side by side and only she be hit—her death had left an emptiness he'd never quite filled.

Pognak looked up from his playing and looked hatefully at Sandy. He made an obscene gesture with his hands.

Sandy, his feelings of fellowship suddenly gone, glowered back and said, "The same to you, ugly face."

The giant gave him a silent sneer and turned his back.

Uskban opened the last flask of bragberry brandy and said, "Take some more, it'll cool your temper. Don't mind Pognak, he hates everybody, and lets no one feel sorry for him except himself."

Sandy sipped on the brandy and replied, "Some he hates more than others, especially me." He swirled the brandy around in his cup and stared moodily into it. "He and I are a lot alike; neither of us loves easily. But at least he had someone he loved and who loved him. Me, I'm afraid to give my heart and so people are cold to me."

Uskban shrugged and said, "So what? You can't be loved or even liked by everyone. There are those who like honey and those who like vinegar; who can say either is wrong in their preference. What counts is that you like yourself."

Sandy thought his words over slowly. With drunken grandeur he said, "But if you love yourself, then how can anyone else love you?"

Sandy's interpretation of his words perplexed Uskban and he tried to set him straight. They spent the next hour finishing off the flask of bragberry brandy and squabbling over the philosophy of love and hate, more often than not arguing over something the other wasn't talking about. At some point Pognak joined in, mostly to share the brandy and add an appropriate growl once in a while.

The end of the death feast was a vague jumbled mess to

Sandy. He remembered a few things but in no particular sequence or importance, strange tantalizing fragments: Uskban shouting something in his face, a something which seemed of earth-shattering importance. Pognak carrying the sorcerer's limp form draped across one huge arm, staggering in a drunken dance around the fire, the night sky turning silver and coming down to envelop them in an eerie mist. And the odd imagining that a woman veiled in shadow came and stood over him as he sat in a stupor on the ground. Sandy thought he felt her kneel down and lightly kiss his forehead —then he knew no more except dreams.

18

A bare sliver of sunlight glimmered on the horizon. The Goddess walked through the morning dew and out of the desert to stop beside Glupp. He lifted his ponderous head and looked at her through half-open eyes. She touched him gently on the brow and caressed his lumpy skin. The grund-zar gave a deep sigh and drifted off to those delicious mead-owlands you find in dreams.

The Goddess looked at the drunken forms sprawled about the dying fire and smiled, a fiercely possessive and strangely doting smile. These were her bravos. Rough, rowdy, and dis-reputable. Each man was flawed and twisted in his own way, but each was somehow greater because of his flaws. In them was the stuff that moves mountains and makes the thread from which songs are woven. They were the ones who could and would do what was needed—whatever the odds.

She moved quietly among them. As she came to each one, she laid a healing hand on his brow—until she came to Sandy. The Goddess paused and for a long moment stared at him with deep fathomless eyes. Then, instead of touching his forehead with her hand, she knelt down and kissed it with her shadowy lips. She looked bemused for a moment, then turned and walked off into other places.

19

Sandy awoke with the sun shining brightly into his eyes and with sand in his mouth. He spit out the sand and tottered feebly over to the shade, where he began snoring as soon as he touched the ground.

Toward evening, Pognak roused Sandy by digging his toe into his ribs. He struggled up out of a tangled mess of dreams and stared about with blurry eyes, too miserable to care about Pognak's mistreatment. The world seemed a hellish place, filled with the harsh glaring light of a dying sun and the earsplitting clamor of the evening breeze.

He'd had hangovers before, but none had ever come close to this one. He made a silent vow never to touch another drop of that hellbrew called bragberry brandy. He was lucky that he had survived the poisonous dose he had taken.

Somehow he struggled through his chores with Glupp and the rudhars. Glupp was his usual slow-moving but pleasant self, but the rudhars were even nastier than normal: they stepped on his feet, nipped at his backside, squealed angrily when he gave them each a fair share of the fodder, bumped against him, and in general made themselves as obnoxious as possible. His choice comments about their probable ancestry didn't improve relations any.

When he made it back to the campfire Sandy almost had to spew up his guts. The others were eating and—even worse—enjoying it. He hated them savagely; they should at least have been *half* as sick as he felt.

Thinking dark thoughts about his fellow boozers, Sandy sat down and sipped some cold tea. It was a struggle, as it tried to come up as fast as it went down. Eventually, though, the tea soothed his writhing innards.

At dusk they got underway. Zhadnoboth had some of his

best spells protecting them, but Sandy was too sick to worry about whether they'd hold. The swaying motion of his rudhar was sheer agony. They hadn't gone far when he leaned over the side of his beast and spewed up the contents of his guts. Then came the dry heaves as his empty innards tried to throw up what wasn't there. If there was a hell, he now knew this was part of it. Finally he stopped retching, feeling just barely alive. He looked up and saw the others had stopped and were looking at him, Uskban with blank, unreadable eyes, Pognak with contempt, and the sorcerer pettishly. Zhadnoboth fumbled in his robe and withdrew a small vial filled with a dark, oily liquid. He put five drops into half a cup of water and said, "I've put some tincture of bloatfish in the cup. Drink it slowly, and with your head turned from me. I didn't come on this journey just to have weak-stomached demons puke all over me."

Sandy croaked, "I'm no demon," and took the cup. He took a cautious sip—and gagged; it tasted like a mixture of sulphur, iodine, and rotten worms blended with less mentionable substances. For a moment he thought he was going to heave again, but his innards suddenly went numb and he was past the crisis. Steeling himself, he drained the cup. The initial shock made his eyes bulge out and his stomach give a slight quiver. Then he felt only an ice-cold numbness—a vast improvement over feeling he was going to die the next minute.

"Now that this idiot is taken care of, let's be on with our journey," Zhadnoboth snapped. He matched his words with his actions, abruptly yanking his rudhar's head around and cantering off into the darkness—toward the Zalkrings. His angry voice drifted back through the darkness, "Stop that, you blockheaded beast, or I'll set your bowels on fire!" Apparently the rudhar had retaliated for the rough treatment he'd been given.

Sandy and Glupp trailed along at the rear of the procession, pointedly ignored by the others. A demon who couldn't hold his liquor, even if he said he wasn't a demon, was at the very bottom of the totem pole. Glupp moved up beside Sandy and gently rubbed his head in commiseration against Sandy's leg, giving more comfort with this simple gesture than a barrelful of kind words could ever do. It cheered Sandy immensely and he reached down and scratched the grundzar on the top of his head.

Sandy's rudhar, however, did not take kindly to being bumped by the lummox. With a snarling hiss it bit savagely at Glupp, but its teeth couldn't make a dent in his tough hide and Glupp went on blissfully unconcerned about the other beast's bad temper. In frustration, Sandy's rudhar spat its cud at the big beast. The shot missed as Glupp clumsily—and seemingly inadvertently—stepped aside, in the process managing to step on the rudhar's right hind toes. The rudhar gave a squeal and then hobbled forward hurriedly, its nose in the air as it disdainfully ignored its uncouth companion. Glupp blissfully waddled alongside, at peace with himself and the world.

They had been traveling for a little over an hour when Zhadnoboth held up his hand and pulled his rudhar up short. "Hold," he whispered, "I smell hostile magic."

While the others waited impatiently, he moved slowly ahead, peering intently at the desert floor. Sandy craned his neck to see what was going on, but could barely make out the same sort of sand and rock they had been traveling through. Even Pognak and Uskban, sitting still and using their finely honed desert senses, couldn't see anything out of the ordinary.

Zhadnoboth stopped and chewed his lip, then pulled a small packet of glowfly dust from his robes. He mumbled a few words in a peckish tone and the packet began to glow with a faint green light. Suddenly he said Kythornak's second word of power and threw the packet into the air where it burst and spread a fine powder which hung together in mid-air as a gently undulating sphere the size of a basketball. Like a snake striking, the sorcerer lashed out with his staff. A spurt of blue fire shot from its tip and struck the ball of dust at its core. There was a small flash, a dull sizzling hiss, and the powder shot off in two different directions.

For a moment a thin greenish line stretched from horizon to horizon in front of them. Then, in a twinkling, the suspended powder fell straight down to the desert floor. The eerie green light waxed to an intense brightness before diminishing to a dimly glowing shadow: then repeated the cycle again and again, each time waxing just a little less and diminishing a little more.

"Come," Zhadnoboth snapped, "we must find a way across before my spell on the glowfly powder fades into oblivion." He licked his finger and held it up as if testing for a faint breeze. He must have received some sign for he kneed his rudhar toward the right. With a grumbling snort the beast moved that way and the others followed close at his heels.

Sandy noticed as they traveled beside the flickering green line that it was not solid. At irregular intervals were breaks in the glowing line, most very tiny, but some as wide as a handbreadth.

They went over a small hill and saw in front of them a wide gap in the glowing line. Deep furrows and claw marks showed where some huge beast had dragged itself across the line.

"Sand dragon," Uskban said brusquely. "I thought the last had been killed in my grandfather's day."

Sandy did not care to think too much about a creature which could make such tracks nor about the huge scorched area not far away on the other side of the line.

"The Zalkrings grow careless," the sorcerer said. "They've been unchallenged for too long. This type of spell is very effective, but it must be maintained, and the gaps closed. Let's get across while my spell still shows where the safe area is."

Much to Sandy's relief, they crossed the gap without incident. As they passed near the fringe of the scorched area, Sandy could see many pieces of charred bone scattered around the blackened area. Some of the fragments were large enough to put elephant bones to shame but what most impressed him was the remains of an enormous talon. It was dug deeply into the earth, as if driven in during a last convulsive death agony. Just the thought of dragons made Sandy uncomfortable—he wanted no part of such a beast nor what had destroyed it.

Half an hour later, Zhadnoboth halted once more and waved for the others to stand back. Then he dismounted and began pacing back and forth in front of his rudhar; every so often he cautiously probed with his staff into the night air in front of them.

Finally, the sorcerer picked up a rock and heaved it into the sand ahead. Pognak snorted derisively at the throw, but Zhadnoboth merely returned a second-rate scowl in reply.

In truth the scrawny sorcerer hadn't made much of a toss, but it was enough. The sand rippled—a faint and uncanny motion that didn't please Zhadnoboth. He glowered at the sand, as if demanding it do something more, then stalked angrily about until he found a much larger stone—one his age-withered muscles couldn't budge. From the corner of his eye, Zhadnoboth saw the giant silently laughing at him, so he crooked his finger in an arrogant beckoning gesture.

Pognak gave a disgusted grunt, dismounted, and walked over with a surly swagger. He reached down and with a mighty heave raised the stone to a position over his head. He acted as if the feat was an everyday sort of thing; Sandy noticed, however, that the way his muscles knotted told a different story. The mute looked at Zhadnoboth with a self-satisfied sneer and then heaved the stone. It was a mighty throw, one even a giant could be proud of, and the rock landed well out into the middle of the sandy stretch with a loud *thunk*.

For a split second nothing happened. Then, with a thunderous roar, an immense whirlpool churned through the sand. It sprang upon the stone, chewed it into fine splinters, and spat it out. Then, gnashing its sand together in satisfaction, it charged off to the northeast.

Zhadnoboth sniffed scornfully. "Stupid amateurs. They wouldn't know a good spell unless it bit them—and then they'd botch it up."

Sandy lifted an eyebrow. The display had looked awfully impressive.

Zhadnoboth knew how to counteract the spell. Confidently he had the party, animals and all, line up in a column behind him. He rummaged through Glupp's packs and came up with a thin rope made from braided hair. He had them tie the finger-thick rope around their waists, to the rudhar's saddles, and to Glupp's harness until they were linked in a long chain.

The sorcerer hastily thumbed through a tattered spellbook, found the passage he wanted, and then began to chant a spell. The rhythmic cadences of an ancient language, Middle Eskarganian, were accented at every fourth beat by the thump of Zhadnoboth's staff against the ground.

At first nothing seemed to happen except that with every thump of the staff the tension in the air increased by one iota. Sandy noticed that his rudhar's feet were resting very lightly on the ground and then barely off it. A glance around showed him that others were affected in the same way. Soon Zhadnoboth and all the animals were hovering just a fraction of an inch off the ground. Even the ponderous Glupp was as light of foot as the rest of them. Only the rudhars didn't take the levitation in stride. They skittered about nervously, coming close to unseating their riders, as they tried to plant their padded hooves solidly on the ground.

Zhadnoboth finished his chant and swung around to see the effects of his spell. He smiled, full of self-congratulation, when he saw how his handiwork had taken hold. He grabbed the rope looped about his rudhar's saddle, tied it around his waist, and then tried to stride off across the sand leading his rudhar and the rest of the procession.

Since he gave no warning of his intentions to the others, he fell flat on his butt when he jerked the rope taut. Squawking curses like an angry hen, Zhadnoboth tried to pick himself up—a struggle, since he couldn't get any traction. Several times he fell on his face or his rear end as he tried to scramble to his feet. Finally, by a supreme effort, he managed to stand, unhurt except for his pride.

Zhadnoboth turned to the others, the expression on his face changing what had been suppressed snickers into full-fledged chortles. "Quiet!" he yelled. "What do you lackwits think you are doing? How can I move forward with your dead asses holding me back? Now move with me!"

His angry words got them going—or at least trying: for a while all was confusion as everyone took nosedives and pratfalls, and feet and hooves shot in as many directions as there were. Glupp's four legs shot from under him and he came down with a resounding *plop* on his generously endowed belly. Sandy, Uskban, and Pognak did much worse as their rudhars flipped over and crashed to the ground with them in the saddles—it was a hectic few minutes as they fought to untangle themselves from their bawling and wildly thrashing mounts. Zhadnoboth managed to outdo them all in the number of times he hit the ground, once even turning a complete somersault in the air. The spell had made them so light that no one was seriously injured, but neither could they get much purchase on the ground.

After many falls, a lot of squealing and cursing, even more hard feelings, and a fine assortment of bruises, beasts and men finally all got back on their feet or hooves. The men remounted and got their nearly hysterical rudhars moving forward, but progress was painfully slow. If a rudhar started to get up to a respectable speed its feet would shoot from under it, and down would come beast and an obscenely cursing rider. They made headway, but even an average-fast turtle could have made them eat dust.

Pognak's rudhar lost its footing, its hooves shot forward, and it did a flip in midair. It landed on its back and on top of the giant mute. For a second Sandy thought he was dead. Then Pognak gave an inarticulate roar, heaved the stunned beast off himself, and staggered unsteadily to his feet. He looked slightly battered, but his innate toughness plus the magical lightness of his mount had saved his life.

Pognak's accident was the last straw for the sorcerer, who was getting more and more frustrated by their slow pace. Grumbling, he dug out his spellbook again.

After much paging and cursing, Zhadnoboth finally found the spell he was searching for, and started pulling things out of the bottomless depths of his robe: string, scraps of parchment, a piece of cheese, a chunk of red chalk, assorted vials and flasks, and various other odds and ends of junk. At last he located the small bottle filled with tincture of bloatfish, opened it, and wrinkled his nose—the stuff smelled like mackerel left out in the sun for a couple of days. With a grimace he began rubbing it into his staff.

Sandy watched and wondered ironically how many uses there were for the foul-smelling stuff. If the next step was to rub it on them he was going to squawk—choke chain notwithstanding. The tincture did a beautiful job on the sorcerer's staff, giving it a deep glistening sheen, but Sandy wondered how polishing a hunk of wood was going to help them.

Zhadnoboth held the staff out in front of him and carefully inspected it. He frowned and polished it again with grumpy agitation. Then he inspected it once more; this time he was satisfied. He pointed the staff at a distant boulder and chanted an incantation with great confidence and authority, plainly expecting this spell to be one of his more masterful achievements.

A bolt of crackling energy shot from the staff, the same dark amber-red color as the tincture he'd rubbed into the wood. It hit the boulder and clung to it, hissing and spitting. For a couple of moments nothing more happened, then slowly the whole string of men and animals began to inch forward. From then on the speed they moved at increased rapidly. Soon the whole kit and caboodle was sliding across the sand at breakneck speed toward the boulder, as the sizzling line of energy tried to shorten itself down to nothing.

Zhadnoboth, at the front of the whole mess, gaped in horror at the huge boulder that his version of the Nantucket sleighride would soon smash them into. In his haste to get going, he'd given the spell much too much *oomph*. Frantically, he screeched out Kythornak's seventh word of power, even though he hadn't done any of the preparation needed to use the word safely.

Instantly his spell became undone. A whirlwind of men, beasts, and gear rolled in a confused jumble across the desert floor—to end up in an enormous pile against the boulder. In a mass of dust and flailing limbs they began untangling themselves using barroom rules—every man and beast for himself.

With ill-tempered curses, kicks, and shoves they sorted themselves out. The rudhars were almost uncontrollable—the world as they knew it had been turned upside down and they wanted to run gibbering into the night. Fortunately Zhadnoboth's rope kept them together long enough for Pognak and Uskban to knock some sense into their heads and get them ready to be remounted.

As Uskban straightened the harness on a still shaking rudhar he said bitingly, "Maybe next time I'll take my chance with whatever trap the Zalkrings set. I might have a better chance of surviving."

Pognak grunted his approval of Uskban's words and added emphasis of his own by glowering blackly at the strangely quiet sorcerer—they hadn't heard a peep out of him since he had broken his spell. Apparently the hasty use of a word of power had taken a lot out of him.

"We got here," Sandy said. "That's what counts; not the hoof marks on our bellies and backs, or the living hell that was scared out of us. Let's get on with it and out of here."

The sorcerer paid no heed to Sandy's backhanded compliment, except to get on his uncooperative rudhar and head off into the night. Glupp plodded right after the determinedly unapologetic sorcerer, followed by the three glumly quiet men riding some very sulky and complaining rudhars.

An hour or so later they were making fair time—or so it seemed—when Uskban barked, "Halt." He vaulted down from his rudhar and examined the ground. Then he stalked over to the sorcerer.

"Where in seven hells are you taking us, old man? This is the third time we have come by this very same spot."

The sorcerer glanced at him, at the sky, and then at the ground. Then he snapped, "You must be mistaken. I follow the stars."

"Well, they're lying to you. Look down: these tracks are ours. As I read them, they say this is the third time we've passed here."

"You're the great tracker, why don't you lead us?"

"I'd do better than a fumbling old faker."

Uskban took the lead, guiding them with a quiet assurance. A quarter hour later they had returned to the same spot.

Uskban rode up beside the sorcerer and snarled, "This stinks of magic, old man. If you were any kind of wizard you should have known we were being enspelled."

Zhadnoboth bristled at the little man's insulting use of the word *wizard*. By now some of his energy and all of his crankiness had returned. "I'm a sorcerer, not some charlatan who doesn't know what he is doing," he hissed. "And it is your fault, yours and those two simpletons with you, that we are entangled in a simple confusion spell."

Uskban replied with beady-eyed coldness, "You are the sorcerer. If there is magic it is your job to deal with it." Then he added ironically, "Surely such a great one as yourself can free us from such a simple spell?"

"Simple does not mean easy. Even when I am in full possession of my powers those types of spells are devilishly hard to untangle. Now, thanks to you, my magical powers are temporarily gone. I had to use Kythornak's seventh word of power without the proper preparation in order to save your necks. The backlash rendered me powerless, besides nearly killing me. Only now are some of my magical abilities beginning to return. In a few hours, when I am fully recovered, I will be able to get us free from the spell."

Uskban looked at him with disgust. "It was *your* neck you were saving. Anyway, we can't wait. If we are caught in the open at daybreak, we're dead—or worse. You have to do something *now.*"

Zhadnoboth began to edge his rudhar away, but Uskban noticed and grabbed him by the front of his robe, shaking the sorcerer until his teeth rattled. "Hear me: If we are caught here I'll send you to hell in pieces before I join you."

Glupp watched the humans impatiently; he wanted to settle down and chew the thorny dainties he could smell ahead. When the humans started arguing again, Glupp gave a huffy rumble and trundled off toward the feast which awaited him.

Sandy had been watching the sorcerer and the madman with a sour eye, wishing they'd stop fighting and come to their senses. When he saw Glupp stomping off into the desert, he began to hope again. He spurred his rudhar forward, grabbed Uskban by the arm, pointed, and said, "Look."

Uskban quickly caught Sandy's meaning and sent his rudhar trotting after Glupp. Pognak and Sandy hurried after him, leaving the sorcerer alone. Zhadnoboth watched them go for a moment and then grudgingly followed.

Sandy rode along, surprised he'd had the nerve to interrupt the quarrel between Uskban and the sorcerer. Neither was wrapped all that tight and their argument had been turning ugly; getting between them could have been a quick way to get killed, yet he had somehow known it was the thing to do. His intuition had been right, and it had made the stupid bastards do the right thing. Besides, since he had come this far, he wanted a chance to look at some gold and jewels.

Dark rocks and shadowed crags suddenly loomed in the blackness surrounding them. Glupp gave a happy wheeze and plunged up a ravine, as though he had caught a whiff of paradise. But Uskban raised a hand and halted the rest of them. Curtly he asked the sorcerer, "How safe are we? Is there more Zalkring magic ahead?"

Zhadnoboth shook his head. "We are safe here. These hills are called Admith's Knuckles; they lie between the inner and the outer defenses of the Zalkrings. There were only three spells protecting the outer limits and we passed all three. Now we only have to penetrate their inner defenses." He gave a contemptuous sniff and added, "Not that they will be any better than those we have penetrated. The Zalkrings have been unchallenged too long; they grow careless."

"Like a certain sorcerer I know," Uskban said. Zhadnoboth gave him a withering look, but before he could say anything Uskban went on, "If these hills are Admith's Knuckles, we should be almost on their doorstep. They *must* keep a watch over the land in this direction."

Zhadnoboth brushed aside his warning. "They do, but not all the time. Remnants of an ancient power linger here and that makes them uncomfortable; they come here only when necessary. Nor can they use their magic here; it will not take hold. They send patrols every day, except when one of their great seasonal ceremonies is in progress. Then Kels Zalkri is very near and they feel nobody would be fool enough to come this close."

"Are you certain?" asked Uskban.

"As sure as one can be of anything. I have good sources. I should—I paid enough for them. These sources say that not for hundreds of years have the Zalkrings kept watch or visited these hills during the midsummer ceremonies—as I said before, they get careless." The sorcerer looked around and then, as if telling a great secret, lowered his voice and said, "This is an especially important ceremony. It marks the thousandth anniversary since the coming of Kels Zalkri. Every Zalkring will be expected to be at Tham Og Zalkri; it would be considered a sacrilege for a Zalkring to be outside the mountain at such a time."

"You be content with your faith, but I'd feel safer if you used some of your magic to hide us from their eyes—and that of their god. Has enough of your power returned to do that?"

"Yes, but I would not use it on such a futile thing. We are safe or we are not; my magic will not make a difference. The power which lingers here is no threat to Kels Zalkri, but it makes this area a place of blankness he cannot see into."

Uskban nodded fatalistically. "The hills are much better cover than the open desert, but I still don't like it." He turned and led the way up into the hills, following the path Glupp had taken. They found the grundzar in a perfect location for a campsite. He was a wise beast with a sure taste for such things: there was fresh spring water, protection from sun and wind, and plenty of thorny graze for him and the rudhars.

It was still three hours until dawn, so they settled down to get what rest they could. It would be hard and tricky work to penetrate the inner defenses of Tham Og Zalkri without being detected. And come daybreak, things could get hot and heavy, if Zhadnoboth had been wrong about the watch the Zalkrings kept on these hills.

Sandy was too wound up to get to sleep right away. He surprised himself when he realized that, despite being shanghaied and forced into this ridiculous situation, he was happy. Hard travel and fresh air agreed more with him than he had ever thought possible. And, most importantly, it looked like tomorrow would bring an end to this cockeyed adventure.

He was happy, yet a cold ball of fear that wouldn't go away chilled his innards. What they were going against could kill them, and quite horribly. He was scared stiff, but not about to back out now. He felt obligated to go through with it for the sake of his companions—though why he felt that way about people who'd forced him into this was beyond his understanding.

He thought about it a bit more and decided maybe it was because he had faith in them, though he would never have freely chosen any of them to go adventuring with. Pognak was a sullen bully. Zhadnoboth was trustworthy only if you didn't turn your back. And Uskban was plain crazy: wise and cunning in his way, but still a maniac—and a bloodthirsty one at that. Sandy hoped his feeling that in a crisis they'd be a greater bane to the enemy than one another was true.

Sandy's hair suddenly prickled as a dreaming thought brushed against his mind. It was utterly alien and full of strange images and concepts—and with an assurance of power which was terrifying. It was the thought of a god and he sensed it came from deep beneath the hills. By some means he knew this being would not awake until the end of time, yet he still shivered. What kind of world was this Zarathandra? he thought. And what terrible mysteries lay in its past? Were the Goddess and Kels Zalkri just two of many players?

He brooded for a while, wondering if this adventure was just their own or was a gambit in some greater game. He wished fervently he was back on Earth and didn't have to worry about such uncanny things as real magic and gods who might be around the next corner—and this strange sixth sense he had picked up somehow or other. Still brooding, he dropped off as sleep crept up on soft feet and caught him unawares.

20

THE Goddess cast an apprehensive yet satisfied eye over her adventurers. In them was the steel and guile needed to bring this venture to a successful conclusion. Still, even with the best of material—and not one of them was that—things could go wrong. The characteristics which could make them extremely effective against Kels Zalkri, idiosyncrasy and unpredictability, also made it hard to keep them within the bounds of her schemes. Even Sandy, the most stable, had his quirks—especially a stubbornness which could cause problems.

The Goddess flew through the narrow spaces between worlds and back to a place which was her own, a grassy arbor near the Pool of Grygon-Zymor. Her shadowy form sat on an ancient bench of grayed wood, its arms and back thickly inset with yellowed and worn ivory plaques. She composed herself, and began to sink into a trance. The ordeal ahead would wring from her every ounce of will she had and every iota of strength she could command. Now she needed rest and meditation in order to bring to hand her every power—both for herself and those who would fight her battles.

Just as her mind was drifting off to the realms beyond, a cold dark thought sidled into her consciousness:

Little feeble thing, my time comes. Soon all Zarathandra and its souls shall be mine—and yours shall be the first soul I feast on. For a thousand years I shall savor and taste it, until you are no more. I shall rule your world better than you ever could and make its mortal herds prosper, culling and selecting its beings so their souls can best spice my diet, forever.

Utter rage and loathing filled the Goddess and she hurled back the thought, *Never!*

The dark one cackled contemptuously and then sent his

mind flying back to his citadel, there to plan the final details of her defeat and torment—and to gloat.

The Goddess was white-hot with rage; her angry thoughts raced after the dark one—only to smash repeatedly and fruitlessly against his redoubt. Then she regained control of her temper and with much effort composed herself for meditation.

Just before she disappeared into the sublime depths, a thought crossed her mind: Tomorrow was another day. Before it was over Kels Zalkri should know how sharp her talons were. That bastard god would know a pain and humiliation he'd never felt before.

21

MOMENTS before daybreak they were looking toward the mountain called Tham Og Zalkri (the house of Zalkri in the language of Uskban's ancestors), the combined stronghold and holy of holies for the Zalkrings. It towered over the bleak desert of red and yellow stone, an immense chunk of dull black rock, far more forbidding than the wasteland into which it intruded. The place was ominous, the abode of shadow, a piece of hell on mortal earth.

"Once," Uskban muttered angrily, "this was empty desert. A harsh and dangerous land, but not hating life—just not caring. Then from some deep hell came Kels Zalkri. He lusted for Zarathandra and its life and tried to make it his; when he struck, there came night, bitter cold and long beyond understanding. But the Goddess fought for what was hers—she smote him with her anger and gave strength to the sun so it waxed hot again. Day and hope came back to this land, but where once had been unsullied desert lay this abomination. The dark one had lost, but was too strong and too evil to be hurled back into the void. Since that time he has waited and plotted within his mountain for the hour when he shall strike again and take Zarathandra for his own."

There was a kind of poetry in his words, as if the little man was chanting lines from an ancient song. The solemn majesty in his voice was disquieting to Sandy, hinting more of a crusade than a plundering foray.

The four of them stood atop a rocky hill, looking east toward the mountain. Between them and it lay only a small plain of scorched and pitted rock; blackened with hellfire, scarred by the hooves of demons, and bleeding with the blackly crimson rock which is the blood of the earth. As their

163

souls measured distance, however, the mountain was an eternity away.

Sandy shivered. It was the morn of midsummer's day, but the desert air was bitterly and unnaturally cold. He looked about, disgruntled and bone-weary. It hadn't helped to be awakened at an ungodly hour to take part in this fool's vigil —the sun would come up whether they watched for it or not. Nor had the sadistic pleasure Pognak had shown as he tumbled him out of his blankets improved his temper. Only the enchanted silver chain around his neck had kept him from fully expressing his anger loudly and vehemently. Despite his dread, adventure had seemed better in the night than it did this morning.

Suddenly there was a moment of utter blackness: the night became a lightless murk without a single star to break its darkness. There was a silence, immense and seemingly endless. The only smell was that of dust—ancient, dry, and lifeless. Then the spell was broken and a faint red glow broke above the horizon.

Like an immense giant clothed in black, the mountain was outlined by the first light of the sun. Sandy noticed that the summit's crown was cleft by a notch.

The sorcerer said quietly, "When the first rays of the sun come through the notch and hit the heart of the mountain, then do their midsummer ceremonies begin. And then do we also strike."

The others seemed to be in no hurry to get off the exposed hilltop, but Sandy's teeth were chattering. He went down to a small hollow on the reverse side of the hill, protected from the chill morning breeze but still within sight of the others. Glupp lay there, chewing leisurely on some brambles with bright yellow flowers. Sandy sat down beside the grundzar and absentmindedly began scratching his neck. Glupp loved the attention and heaved a contented rumble of pleasure.

Eventually Zhadnoboth noticed Sandy had left the group. He looked around frantically, spotted him, and barked an order to Pognak, who nodded and came trotting down the hill toward Sandy.

Pognak gave Sandy a sneering smile and without warning kicked him in the rump. With an insulting and rude eloquence he pointed to the top of the hill.

Sandy had had all the bullying he could take. His foot

shot out and caught Pognak across the ankles. The lumbering brute, taken unawares, windmilled his arms as he went crashing to the ground. Not giving him a chance to recover, Sandy sprang to his feet and gave him a savage kick to the gut.

Pognak bellowed like a wild bull and heaved himself to his feet, the iron-hard muscles of his belly undented by the force of Sandy's kick. Slowly and unrelentingly he began to stalk Sandy. Sandy circled to his left, waiting for some chance to strike without getting himself killed.

Suddenly, without even a twitch of the lip to give warning, the giant charged headlong. He was a horrifying sight—a wild-eyed and sneering personification of death. If he had gotten hold of Sandy, he could have torn him limb from limb. But he didn't. Sandy, his rage giving him extra speed, threw himself down and away. Again his feet lashed out, and again the mute went crashing to the ground.

Pognak landed near Glupp, who had gotten to his feet in order to watch the fight better. The berserk giant gave a garbled roar, staggered to his feet, and began to charge Sandy. As he did so, Glupp lowered his huge head and rammed it into Pognak's behind. The giant went flying through the air, landing with a slam on the other side of Sandy, and then tumbled head over heels like a rag doll until he smacked into a boulder and stopped.

Pognak lay stunned for a second, then showing unbelievable toughness, he staggered to his feet. He turned around looking for Sandy just in time to get Glupp's head in his gut. As the air rushed from Pognak's lungs in an agonized gasp, the grundzar tossed him up and over his back like a bag of penny candy.

Pognak lay where he had crashed to the ground for several moments as he frantically tried to get air back into his lungs. Finally he caught his breath and managed to get to his knees, where he sucked in air with great painful gasps.

He started looking around with blood in his eye, too much the son of a bitch to give up. He came eye to eye with Glupp, who'd ambled over while he'd been recovering. The beast nudged him hard, easily knocking the giant back to the ground. Then the grundzar with slow deliberation opened his mouth and let the prostrate Pognak have a close look at his huge teeth, silently daring him to move. Pognak glared back in wild-eyed anger, but wisely lay still.

At that moment a fuming Zhadnoboth came stomping over. "Move, you boneheaded beast," the wizened old sorcerer yelled, trying to push Glupp away from Pognak. He looked like an ant trying to move a mountain. The sorcerer uttered a few choice obscenities and began beating on Glupp with his staff. Both were useless: Glupp remained stubbornly hovering over Pognak.

Furious, Zhadnoboth turned to Sandy and shook a finger in his face. "It's all your fault, you idiot demon. Tell that block-headed thing to let Pognak up."

Sandy's first fury had cooled, but he was still mad clean through. He didn't give a damn that he had as much chance standing up to the sorcerer's magic as he had to beat up on the giant. "No!" he said quietly but emphatically. The enchanted silver choke chain around his neck remained quiescent, his tone too soft to activate the spell controlling it.

"Why not?" howled the sorcerer. Sandy jerked his thumb toward Pognak, who was looking at him with eyes full of bloodlust.

The sorcerer stared in frustration at the two of them for a second. He saw the iron set to Sandy's jaw and chose Pognak as the one more likely to be reasoned with. "Forget this senseless brawling!" he snapped. "We'll never get the treasure if you two are going to act like snot-nosed brats."

Pognak stared sullenly back at him and shook his head.

Uskban pushed the sorcerer aside and knelt by Pognak. "Forget this fight, old friend. We have far more important scores to settle—you know what they are. Don't let your hatred for this so-called demon keep us from revenge."

The two men were silent for a moment as they locked eyes, and an unspoken message passed between them. Pognak gave Sandy a withering look, then gave a nod to Uskban. The madman got up and walked over to Sandy. "Tell the beast to let him up," he said. Then he turned on his heel and stalked off.

Sandy went over to Glupp and beamed a mental message to the grundzar, *Let the bastard up*. Glupp looked pleadingly at Sandy for a moment, his manner saying, *Make him suffer a bit more*, then belched in the mute's face and in an unhasty fashion backed away.

Pognak got to his feet and looked long and hard at Sandy— silently promising that sometime there would be a reckoning for this. Sandy glowered right back. The bully scared him, but he wasn't going to back off—he'd had his fill and more of that. With a sneer Pognak turned and went after Uskban.

Sandy gave Glupp a heartfelt hug. "Thanks, you big galoot," he whispered. "He'd have beat me to a pulp if it hadn't been for you. I was too mad to think straight. At least there is one brain between the two of us." Glupp listened solemnly, then rubbed his head affectionately against Sandy.

"Now that you are done with that tomfoolery, are you ready to get on with our business?" Zhadnoboth asked sarcastically. "Follow me," he ordered, then strode purposefully toward the top of the hill.

At that vantage, the sorcerer said, "Look east and tell me what you see." Sandy saw nothing out of the ordinary, just a black mountain outlined by the light of the rising sun. He turned to the sorcerer and shrugged.

"Speak, you dolt," snarled Zhadnoboth. The nearness of Kels Zalkri and his terrible power had him on edge, especially since they were very soon going to try and sneak around that power. "The Goddess only knows," he muttered, "why I got stuck with such a bunch of numbskulls."

Sandy had had about all the old scoundrel's carping he could take and he was getting damned tired of the choke chain. He pointed to his neck and the silver chain, his silent insolent manner saying more than words ever could.

Zhadnoboth flushed angrily at the rebuke, mad at himself and even madder at Sandy for using his spell as an excuse for not talking. "You know very well, demon, that you can talk if you keep your tongue under control. The spell was never meant to keep you completely silent and you know it. By the Goddess, I've heard you talk many times. Now speak!"

Sandy obstinately kept his mouth shut and tapped on the silver chain with a forefinger.

Zhadnoboth stewed for a moment and then said sourly, "Hold still." He ran his fingers over the enchanted silver chain and crooned a short incantation. The snakelike grip of the chain seemed to ease a trifle. "The spell binding the chain has been lessened. It will let you say almost anything except your true name. *But,* speak your true name and in that instant you die."

Zhadnoboth's last warning did nothing to stem the spate of words coming from Sandy. His anger had been bottled up too long for him to contain it. "Why didn't you do this before—afraid an angry word from me would ruin your day?

You knew the full spell was unnecessary." The fierce anger in the words made the silver chain quiver, but it did not choke him.

He would have gone on, but the sorcerer interrupted him. "I did it because it was needful. Most men and demons speak too much and say too little anyway. Besides, I had no wish to hear you."

"You're one to talk, sorcerer. You sling around more garbage and hot air than anyone I've met."

Zhadnoboth flushed. "Mind your tongue, demon. I could turn you to ashes in a moment if I had a mind to."

His will stiffened by anger and a newfound confidence, Sandy refused to be overawed by the sorcerer. "Try it, old man!" he shouted back. "But only if you want to lose all chance to loot the Zalkrings of their treasures. You *need* me."

These harsh words quieted the sorcerer. He didn't like this new Sandy, but he could live with him until the treasure was in his pocket. Besides, he was beginning to be just a little worried about this stiff-necked idiot. He *did* have a name of power, and if Zhadnoboth's schemes went awry, he'd be nobody the sorcerer wanted as an enemy.

By now Sandy had calmed down; just being able to speak freely had drained off a lot of his anger. Nor did he want to push the sorcerer too far; the old bastard had shown he could be mean when crossed.

They came to an unspoken truce. The sorcerer turned to the mountain and said, "Look again. You should see more than just bare rock and empty air—if you possess the kind of name I think you have."

Sandy looked again. At first nothing seemed different. He looked harder; still nothing. Only when he started to give up, and relaxed, did he sense anything. Faint but clear—a kind of *otherness* came through. Sandy didn't perceive it with his sight, hearing, or any ordinary sense—he *felt* some otherness. The mountain before him was not quite where it seemed to be. And he sensed a foulness—not totally evil, but alien; and the more terrible for being so.

Sandy turned to Zhadnoboth and tried to explain what he felt, but there were no words to give a definite and true form to what was there. At least Zhadnoboth understood some of what he tried to say.

"Good," he grunted. "It's as I have read: The mountain is not of this world. What's better—Kels Zalkri is not there, except for the merest shadow of his being. I did not expect him to be fully materialized into Zarathandra yet, but it's best to be sure. My books and other sources say that only at midnight, and then only at the end of their four great yearly ceremonies, does he ever fully materialize in this world. If things go as I planned, we'll have our treasure and be far gone by that time."

"Shouldn't we get started?" asked Sandy. He was getting an itch to see some of this fabled treasure he had been dragged so far to steal. Even more, he wished the whole business was over. The feeling he got as he looked toward the mountain made him sick and uneasy. It was a feeling of ravishing hunger, an icy hate and incomprehension of life, and a bleak strangeness which made his soul shrivel.

The old sorcerer looked at the mountain and then gauged how far the sun had risen. "We've got an hour—maybe a little more—before their ceremonies start. When the first sunbeam shines through the notch at the top of the mountain and down to their main altar, they shall plunge fully into their midsummer ceremonies and be oblivious to the outside world. We have just enough time."

Zhadnoboth turned and started trotting down the hill. Thoughts of gold put a spring in his step. Sandy shook his head and offered a silent and fervent prayer for aid to any deity with a soft spot for fools and madmen. He had a hunch they were going to need all the help they could find. He took one last look at the fearsome mountain and hurried after the sorcerer.

When they reached their camp in the hidden valley, Zhadnoboth motioned Sandy to sit on the ground, took something from their gear, and sat down cross-legged facing him. He placed a board and a few arcane items on the ground between them.

The board, round and roughly the size of a chessboard, was made from a lustrous ruddy wood, divided into thirteen pie-shaped segments by inlaid silver wire. In the center of each segment was a distinctive symbol inlaid in ivory. Around the outer rim of the board was a solid ring of moss-green crystal.

Zhadnoboth pulled several spellbooks from his robes and thumbed through them rapidly, making hasty scribbles on a piece of parchment as he found items of interest. When he finished paging through the books the first time, he stopped and looked at his notes. He gave an angry grimace, uttered a curse, and began paging through the books again—obviously searching for something he'd missed.

Apparently he didn't find what he wanted the second time either because he threw the last spellbook to the ground in disgust. Muttering to himself he began pawing through his robes again. He gave a yelp of glee when he found what he was looking for, a small book with a mustard-yellow leather cover. Zhadnoboth gave an expert tap to the spine of the book and it fell open, apparently to the passage he wanted to read. He scanned the page rapidly and then scribbled away on his parchment.

Now Zhadnoboth read through his crib notes, pulling various needed items from his robes and setting them on the ground near his feet. He saw Sandy eyeing him and said, "Sorcery is the art of doing magic with the least effort. By saying the right words at the right time and doing the right things at the right time, one can channel the energy which flows through the universe and get it to work your will. Done correctly, such spells can give the barest nudge in the right place and unleash forces that can shake worlds."

Sandy nodded as if he understood.

Zhadnoboth began crooning a chant, and waving his hands in intricate patterns over the board. Abruptly he stopped singing and brought his hands together in a loud clap. The board blazed with a bright white light that gradually dimmed to a mellow glow.

"I've energized the board so that it is sensitive to the tides of destiny. If my sorcery can manipulate these forces correctly, we should be able to foreshadow what effect your name will have on destiny."

Zhadnoboth placed a small balance of plain silver in the center of the board. It was a simple device—merely an upright, a crossbar, and two pans suspended by fine silver chains from each ends of the crossbar.

The sorcerer tinkered with the balance, delicately adjusting it into perfect equilibrium. Then he picked up two bags made from a supple gray-toned leather. From one bag he poured thirteen pebbles of milk-white quartz into his hand, then placed them in the right-hand pan. From the other bag he poured thirteen obsidian pebbles. These, one by one, he placed in the left-hand pan, slowly bringing the balance back into perfect equilibrium. He gave a grunt of satisfaction at that feat, as though he had been worrying that it might not happen.

He bragged to Sandy, "Certain small-minded fools may question my ability, but only a great master could have accomplished what I have just done. In the centuries to come students of the arts sorcerous will read about this moment and know it as one of the great feats of magic."

Sandy wondered who the old fraud thought he was fooling.

"Bend your head this way," Zhadnoboth commanded. "Again I need some of your hairs to work my enchantments."

Sandy was not about to have the sorcerer do any more yanking. Instead, he quickly reached up and jerked out four hairs. He handed them to Zhadnoboth, then rubbed the spot they had come from, wondering why he couldn't use something like a fingernail—it probably would be just as effective and certainly less painful.

Zhadnoboth rubbed his beard thoughtfully, and looked at the scales. Then he carefully placed a hair on the side of the balance containing the white stones. Slowly the balance began to bob and rotate clockwise.

Sandy watched, fascinated, thinking that maybe the sorcerer knew what he was doing...mostly. Zhadnoboth was not altogether pleased with the balance's behavior. Frowning, he muttered, "How can this be? I have not yet unlocked the wards separating this world from the realms beyond. Nothing should happen yet."

The balance made thirteen full rotations and stopped abruptly. For a moment it hung absolutely still. Then the side holding the white stones shot down and hit the board with a clang. The stones should have gone flying in all directions, but they stuck to the metal of the pans as if magnetized. And the pan holding the white stones was also stuck—to the board.

Sandy wondered about the significance of the spot on the board where the pan had touched down, squarely atop a cabalistic sign that Sandy was able to translate as the "Veiled One." He asked Zhadnoboth, "What are the meanings of the signs?"

"They stand for several things. Each is the sign for one of the thirteen months. They can also be interpreted as representing the thirteen ages of Zarathandra, or they can be used

to signify the thirteen influences which most affect destiny."
He gave Sandy a cantankerous look and added, "Now keep
quiet and let me figure out what the board is trying to show
me."

Disgruntledly Zhadnoboth rubbed his chin and stared at
the balance: He'd half expected this kind of result, Sandy
could see, but would have been happier if his forebodings
had been wrong. Sandy had a sudden flash of insight into the
sorcerer's thoughts. *If the demon's name is tied to her, the
situation could get very touchy.* Sandy strained to catch more,
but his contact with the sorcerer's mind had faded as fast as it
had come.

Muttering some very colorful obscenities under his
breath, the sorcerer tried to pick Sandy's hair from the balance. He touched it, yelled, and yanked his fingers away;
blisters were forming. Sucking on his burnt fingers, he fumbled in his robe with the other hand and drew out a pair of
silver tweezers. Very delicately, he plucked up the hair—and
immediately the pan holding the white stones shot up from
the board.

Once the balance settled down and again was in perfect
equilibrium, Zhadnoboth stuck the hair on the side holding
the black stones. Immediately it began bobbing and spinning
widdershins—much faster than the time before. It made
thirteen full turns and then stopped. The pan holding the
black stones hit the board with a crash and stuck there,
squarely atop the same symbol as before.

Zhadnoboth showed the board his evil eye and scratched
his beard angrily. An idea struck him and he scrabbled in the
dirt with his right hand and came up with a grain of sand.
After a moment of hesitation he put it in the pan holding the
quartz stones.

What happened next startled them both, but Zhadnoboth
even more than Sandy—he knew what *should* have happened. The balance was spinning like a whirling dervish,
widdershins instead of clockwise, so fast it just became a
blur. It created a wind that beat against them with hurricane
force and sent dust swirling in great clouds. Then, abruptly, it
exploded: shards flew like shrapnel in all directions.

Dazed, Sandy picked himself up off the ground. He didn't
know if he had been flung there by the explosion or had
unconsciously dived for cover. But he seemed to have come
through intact—a miracle, since the ground all around him

looked like it had been raked with grapeshot. Through the dusty haze he saw that the sorcerer was also unhurt.

A frazzled and battered-looking Zhadnoboth stomped about looking at the damage. He shook a finger at Sandy. "Now see what you caused. That balance cost me dear." He paused for breath and added one of his standard threats, "When we split the loot its cost comes from your portion."

Suddenly Zhadnoboth's face lit up: his loss was not complete. The round board had been flung to one side but was undamaged. The sorcerer scurried over to pick it up but stopped: On the segment of the board bearing the symbol of the Veiled One, thirteen black pebbles were lined up in a row.

Zhadnoboth studied the board for several minutes, pulling at his beard and looking glum. Sandy could see that for a moment he considered backing out of the venture. Then greed blazed in the sorcerer's eyes and his resolve hardened; he thought for a while about how to best use Sandy's name without putting his neck on the line.

With the natural optimism of a con man bubbling happily inside him, Zhadnoboth started to map out his moves. Sandy watched him and worried—the sorcerer had too angelic a look on his face, like a holy terror plotting his next misdeed. Whatever Zhadnoboth's idea was, he seemed to consider himself a genius for thinking of it.

The sorcerer called over Uskban and Pognak. "It's time to make final preparations for our raid."

While he waited for the other two to get there, Zhadnoboth reached inside his robe and grabbed at something, missed, and then caught hold of it. He pulled out an ancient book, its parchment cover cracked and the title so faint it could not be read. He opened it up and showed his fellow conspirators a map, though it was hardly more than a few lines.

"This is Tham Og Zalkri. The straight line going to its heart is the pass they call the Durm Gad Zalkri. It is the only way into the vale which lies near the center of the mountain. These two red circles and the line connecting them are the two towers and the gate which seal the outer end of the pass."

"How do we get through it?" Uskban asked.

The sorcerer ran his finger along the line representing the gate. "We walk through."

Uskban snorted. "You're a fool if you think we can just toddle on through unnoticed. Your invisibility spell is good enough for ordinary occasions, but here you are challenging the full power of Kels Zalkri—if a bug goes through that gate and down the pass he knows it. The mountain is his stronghold on Zarathandra and no ordinary magic can withstand him here." He paused. "If you get beyond the gate there are things even worse—things which would freeze even your black soul, sorcerer."

Old memories flooded into Uskban's mind: flayed bodies twitching and screaming on live coals, a woman writhing on an altar as her intestines were slowly being wound around a spiked rod, men harnessed to rudhars and ridden like sleds down a roadway of broken glass—this and much worse he remembered. The madman shuddered, then went blank-eyed as he forcibly buried the intolerable memories.

Zhadnoboth replied crassly, "Have no worry. The magic I will work using the demon's name will get you through unscathed and undetected. Those true-believing idiots would not expect robbers to be so bold. You need not worry about being caught and tortured."

"You do not understand, sorcerer," Uskban said.

"Bah," replied Zhadnoboth. "With the magic I will use, there will be nothing to worry about." The sorcerer's mind was on treasure, not horror, so he couldn't comprehend what Uskban was trying to say, let alone know the madman was saying it.

Uskban stared at Zhadnoboth with sullen bafflement, shook his head at the sorcerer's blindness, and said in a wicked tone, "How certain are you, sorcerer? Can the power of even a true name stand against the full might of the dark one?" Madness was welling up strongly within him and glittered in his eyes.

"His name can. There is no mistaking the augury: He has a name which is linked to the Veiled One. Nor are we seeking to defy the dark god directly."

"The Veiled Goddess," Uskban half shouted. "That indeed is a fell omen. But tell us how we can enter the Zalkrings' stronghold unnoticed? There is a deadly enmity between the Goddess and Kels Zalkri. How can you control the magic inherent in his name? Her magic is uncontrollable—that is part of her nature. And what is this so-powerful name?"

Zhadnoboth snapped, "Can you think of a better plan? I am your only chance. Take it."

Uskban regarded the vainglorious old twister with bleak eyes. Sandy could sense his feelings: A terrible thirst for revenge gnawed at his vitals; he'd take any help as long as it gave him a chance to quench his hatred. Better an old charlatan who dared, than a mighty sorcerer who didn't have the courage to defy a being he thought mightier. Even if the old scoundrel botched things up in his usual manner, there was still a good chance to send a few more Zalkrings to burn in hell. "Aye, sorcerer, I'll take it," he said.

Sandy listened attentively to their conversation. He didn't particularly like what he heard, even if he was learning more about what was going on than ever before. From what he had learned today and before, the Veiled Goddess seemed as dangerous as Kels Zalkri, though she would probably kill you cleaner than the dark one would. He had a feeling that if the two deities clashed head on, he'd lose out, whoever won. Earth seemed an unreachable dream.

Behind them a shaft of sunlight burst through the notch at the top of the mountain. After a moment of unnaturally intense silence, the booms of a great bronze gong sounded from the heart of the mountain. Beat after thunderous beat resounded through the desert air, making it shimmer and shake before the terrible cadence: doom, doom, doom.

22

THE sound of the gong echoed through the desert, then through Zarathandra, and finally through the spaces which lay between the worlds. It struck the Goddess to the quick; she shuddered, and awoke from her trance with a start. Swiftly she swirled her hands through the air, making signs of power to ward off the avalanche of energy rushing out from the black mountain.

Just as she strengthened the barriers surrounding her citadel, a mocking thought slipped through. *My time comes, little worm. Soon I shall have your soul. For a million years I shall devour it little by little. How you will scream and beg for mercy.*

The Goddess was shaken for an instant by this latest invasion of Kels Zalkri, but it only made her anger burn more fiercely. "Watch yourself, black one," she said to herself. "You may find that this little worm has a bite that can destroy you."

The Goddess cleared her mind and began to marshal her thoughts and her forces. The hour of the first trial of strength was fast approaching. When it came she must be ready to throw herself and her power into the breech.

23

ZHADNOBOTH made his three companions, and Glupp, stand in the middle of a flat next to where they had set up camp. Then the sorcerer began to circle them, clockwise, while simultaneously drawing a line in the red dirt with the tip of his staff. When he had made a full circle, he joined the two ends of the line together carefully. Next he chanted a short spell over his staff and coaxed little bolts of pale yellow lightning from it. These he placed inside a pentagram inscribed on the palm of his left hand. Soon he had over a hundred collected there, sizzling and hissing as they tried to escape from confinement. The sorcerer said a word over his right hand and then reached with it to crumple the tiny lightning bolts into a ball. He kept kneading the ball of energy until its tiny components were fully integrated. Zhadnoboth placed the ball of energy on the line he had drawn in the dirt, at the exact spot where he had joined the ends. At his word the lightning ball, crackling fiercely, began to follow the circle in a clockwise direction. After one revolution it jumped into the air, shot back toward the tip of the sorcerer's staff, and disappeared into it.

Meanwhile, Sandy was wishing he were someplace else. Plunging headlong into danger, he wouldn't have minded so much, but having to wait was turning his stomach sour. He glowered at Zhadnoboth and wished the old bastard would hurry up and get his spellcasting done and the raid started.

The sorcerer, finished with the preliminaries, plunged into some real spellwork. Again walking clockwise, he scattered a fine green sand over the line he had drawn and intoned an interminable number of doggerel verses in a singsong voice. Sandy listened carefully for a while, but could make no sense of it.

Zhadnoboth pulled a leather bag from his robe and started to pace around the circle widdershins, still uttering his tuneless chant. From the bag a thin stream of orange sand flowed down to mix with the green. Now Zhadnoboth really got involved in his magic. He hopped excitedly about outside of the circle, furiously scribbling cabalistic signs in the dirt with the tip of his staff—one to the north, the west, the south, and finally to the east.

Sandy was all eyes, trying to understand how Zhadnoboth's sorcery worked, but couldn't figure out what was going on. He suspected a lot of it was just plain hooey and showmanship, but there was definitely *something* going on. Sandy could feel the tension building; his hair seemed filled with electricity and was starting to stand on end. Frowning, Sandy watched the sorcerer even more closely.

Zhadnoboth finished scribbling a last sign in the dirt. He straightened, stared hard at the symbols, and then thumped the ground hard three times with his staff. Instantly Sandy's hair lost its electrical charge and collapsed limply back onto his head. In the same moment, all sound muted, as if what they heard came from another world away. The sorcerer surveyed his work with satisfaction and gave a happy grunt. To those in the circle the sound was a whisper—faint but icy-clear.

Zhadnoboth pulled a crystal ball from his bottomless pockets. It was about the size of a grapefruit, unflawed, and limpidly clear. He held it up and blew gently. At first nothing happened, then it began to take on a faint orange glow, as if the crystal ball were an ember which the sorcerer was trying to kindle into flame. Zhadnoboth kept on blowing and the glow waxed stronger, eventually brightening to the smoldering ruddiness of full sunset.

Zhadnoboth put the crystal ball in his left hand and held it in front of him at eye level. With his right index finger he touched his right eye, then he touched the crystal ball with the same finger. As he did so there was a brief flare at the point of contact. In turn, he did the same thing with his right ear and the tip of his tongue. Then, holding the crystal ball in two hands and close to his mouth, he spoke a word of binding. The crystal ball blazed like a small sun for an instant, then subsided into a barely glowing ember.

The sorcerer took some sweat from his brow and rubbed it into the crystal, then did the same thing with a pinch of dust. The ball was still clear, but now its glow had dimmed to a nearly invisible glimmer. Zhadnoboth intoned a short enchantment over the crystal ball.

Sandy could not hear the words, but strangely he could see them: they looked like a blue-green mist which spewed from the sorcerer's mouth, swirled through the air, and wrapped itself about the surface of the crystal. When he had spoken the last word of the enchantment, the words were woven in an intricate mesh over the entire surface of the crystal ball. Zhadnoboth looked at the ball and nodded with satisfaction, then he tapped it once with his fingernail. The pattern of words began to flow sinuously about the surface of the crystal, gradually sinking into the depths of the ball and disappearing.

Triumphantly Zhadnoboth held the ball high. With a smile he tossed it to Uskban, somehow making the simple act into a grand gesture.

The crystal ball flew high, moving with an unnatural slowness. As it crossed above the line of the circle, it flared a bright orange for a split second, then dove like a hawk toward Uskban's outstretched hand.

"Now comes the final and greatest part of my enchantment," the sorcerer said. His voice was clear and distinct, but seemed to come from far away, like words across a lake at midnight.

Sandy jerked his head around and looked at Uskban. The sorcerer's voice was coming from the enchanted ball, not from where he stood. Sandy stared into the crystal and gave a shiver. Glaring at him from out of its depths was the bloodshot eye of the sorcerer.

"But first this warning," Zhadnoboth said. "Keep the crystal ball with you always. Once the final wards of my enchantment are in place, it will be the only way we can reach one another. Wherever you are you will be able to speak to me here."

"And why will you be here?" Uskban snarled.

"Why, to keep proper control of my enchantments," replied the sorcerer. Somehow he managed to appear surprised and hurt by the question.

"Why you good-for-nothing cheat," Uskban raged. "You want us to risk our necks for the treasure while you sit here in safety. If things go wrong, we'll get slaughtered and you'll sneak away unscathed. We agreed to risk equally and split the loot equally. You risk nothing. Why should you get anything?"

"You ungrateful cur," Zhadnoboth yelled as he shook his skinny fist at the madman. "Where would you be except for my magic? Dead, most likely. You certainly would not be here—only my magic enabled us to get so close. And only my magic can get you into the mountain and to the treasure. You need me. I have contributed way more than my share to this venture."

Uskban gave him a contemptuous stare. "So be it," he said. "We'll do your dirty work, but afterward we'll have a reckoning. You pledged yourself as well as your magic to this venture."

The sorcerer replied, surly, "I *cannot* go with you. If I get within the circle my enchantments will be disrupted. The final spell, especially, must be performed from without the circle. Either go without me or forget about the treasure."

Uskban stared back at him with expressionless eyes for a moment and then spoke. "You have ears, sorcerer. I said we would go."

"Good," Zhadnoboth snapped. "Now I can get on with the rest of my spellwork."

"Don't trust that old snake," whispered Sandy. "His words have a wrong feel to them: they say one thing, but his voice another. If he had to, he could come with us."

Uskban gave him a crooked half smile and whispered back, "I know, demon. I always figured he'd find a way to weasel out when it came to the crunch. He's that sort."

"And you came anyway," Sandy said in surprise.

"Why not? What counts is that he can get me into the mountain. That makes up for a lot of dirty dealing. Besides, not only sorcerers can be connivers—sometimes muddle-headed madmen can cozen others into doing their will." He threw Sandy a wink and gave a soft, crazy laugh.

Sandy felt icy fingers of fear creep up his back. He didn't know if the vindictive little bastard was completely crazy or not, but either way the future looked unpromising—between his maneuverings and those of the sorcerer, anything could happen.

Zhadnoboth commanded, "Now hand the crystal ball to the demon; he must hold it for the next part of the enchantment."

As the ball touched his palms, Sandy jerked and almost

dropped it. Despite its dim glowing fire, the crystal was cold and it bit into his flesh.

"Watch it, you fool!" screeched Zhadnoboth. "Do you want to destroy us all?"

"No more than you do," retorted Sandy.

The sorcerer shot him a steely glance, as much as saying, *Someday you'll pay for such impertinence to your betters.* Aloud he said, "Hold the ball with both hands and stare hard into its depths while I begin the most dangerous part of my enchantments. When this enspellment is done, not even the mightiest sorcerer or god will be able to pierce the veil surrounding you. Even Kels Zalkri, for all his terrible power, will not be able to destroy it or know that it exists—and he is the last and greatest barrier we must penetrate."

Sandy listened and wondered when the old windbag would get down to the action.

"Now stare deep into the crystal and concentrate," the sorcerer said as he closed his eyes and tuned his mind to the crystal.

Fretfully Sandy stared into the crystal ball. Stray doubts and thoughts floated through his mind. He wondered how reliable was the sorcerer's magic. The old bastard sounded sure of himself, but the more Sandy saw of him the more he was convinced that Zhadnoboth was a seat-of-the-pants sorcerer—sometimes getting great results, but not truly knowing what he was doing.

"Stop fighting my will," Zhadnoboth complained. "Blank your so-called mind and lay it open to my thoughts."

Some choice replies were on the tip of Sandy's tongue, but he kept quiet—with difficulty. Grudgingly he followed the sorcerer's orders and tried to make his mind a blank slate.

Zhadnoboth started to say something, then stopped and gave a peevish glance. In Sandy's mind a thought formed: Was it Kythornak's second or third chant he wanted to use? Then the unbidden question disappeared as the sorcerer's face lit up as he remembered.

The Veiled One smiled as she heard Zhadnoboth begin Kythornak's third chant. That chant had been created to enhance and bring to the fore inner realities. It was a most potent and subtle enchantment. An enchantment most suited to her needs, though not one Zhadnoboth would

*have chosen if his mind had not been clouded. It was close
enough in effect to serve the sorcerer's immediate needs,
but oh so different in the long run.*

In a droning, hypnotic voice, Zhadnoboth intoned the
great cadences of the third chant. A combination of the sorcerer's mesmerizing tones and the power inherent in the
chant lulled Sandy quickly into a trancelike state. His senses
became dulled, but at the same time his mind became fine-
tuned to the rhythms of the spell.

The sorcerer's chanting reached a crescendo as he spoke
the final and most potent word. For a bare second there was
an intense silence. Then something happened: a threshold
was crossed, an attunement attained, a possibility made real;
what it was, none of them could name—but all could feel the
difference.

Sandy was suddenly fully alert and wondering what had
jolted him back to consciousness. He felt different, as if what
was really him stretched to infinity in all directions, as if what
was within his skin was only a small part of himself. He
looked at the world and it seemed odd to him; yet still the
same—as if he saw another color in it but could not be sure
he saw it, yet which gave him a sick feeling in the pit of the
belly. He gave Zhadnoboth a dark look and hoped the old
twister hadn't screwed up.

The sorcerer's enchantments had honed Sandy's sixth
sense to a razor sharpness and Zhadnoboth's thoughts were
now like shifting mirages—every so often he caught a clear
glimpse of them. Right now the old fool was boasting to
himself, patting himself on the back for having the gestures,
words, and intuitive feel for magic just right. The queasy
feeling in Sandy's gut said different.

Zhadnoboth stared up from the crystal ball and he said in
a grand, faraway voice, "Repeat the words I say exactly as I
say them." Line by line he chanted out an incantation he had
found in a tattered manuscript he'd recovered from a ruined
temple. Line for line Sandy repeated the words in a voice
sonorous and resounding with the echoes of eternity.

It was an ancient tongue from the eighth age, so old that
not even the sorcerer knew what the words meant—only
what the spell could do. As Sandy heard and spoke the
words he knew their literal meaning, but was too unversed in

magic to have a true understanding of what he and Zhadnoboth were doing.

The words ceased. For a moment—a frozen instant of
time which lasted forever and had no beginning—Sandy felt
an attunement with Zarathandra and with every world of the
universe.

With something like panic on his face, Zhadnoboth
looked at Sandy, his thoughts demanding a response. *Oh,
no,* thought Sandy, *that ninny's flubbed again.* He could
sense that they were on the brink of doom, and knew it was
up to him to save their necks. Thinking rapidly, Sandy
hunted for an appropriate response—and a memory welled
up from a dark corner of his mind: A woman clad in shadows
was facing away from him and murmuring to herself some
words of binding. Not stopping to question his memory,
Sandy grabbed the words and used them.

"By sand, soul, and name let this spell be bound. By what
was, what is, and what shall be let this spell be bound." The
words came easily from within him, as if he had always
known them but had forgotten.

These simple words of binding rolled off his tongue with
darksome power: shook and reshaped the strands of reality
into a new pattern. Their last uncanny syllable forged the
spell into perfect unity; the fabric of the world throbbed with
suppressed power and for a moment all eternity hung in balance. Then the spell and Zarathandra locked into a perfect
and unbreakable harmony.

Sandy felt a sharp stomach-turning yank, like being pulled
through a too-small knothole. The preliminary enchantments
had made the world of Zarathandra seem dim and far away
but it was not gone totally. Now, Sandy found himself alone
in a place of gray nothingness—where he wasn't sure he was
right side up or even if he was breathing.

He received some welcome reassurance of his own existence when he heard an eloquent outburst from Uskban.
"What hell has that toad's bastard landed us in?" The next
moment Glupp's big head bumped him and he was completely sure he was alive—though where was another question, especially since he couldn't see the grundzar right
beside him.

The crystal ball in Sandy's hand throbbed painfully. He
brought it up to the level of his eyes and it began to glow
with a deep red color which made the swirling grayness sur-

rounding him seem dyed with blood. Despite the grisly color, Sandy's heart lightened: once again he could see his companions. In a place like this company meant a lot, especially since they didn't appear to be standing on anything more substantial than mist.

The sorcerer's voice crowed to them from out of the crystal, "What a masterpiece! These enchantments make the work of Wen-Tarlac the Spellmaster seem like child's play—nay, the fumbling of an infant. Zarathandra will long remember me for this feat of sorcery."

"Yeah, it's great," replied Uskban. "But where are we? And what good does it do to have us here? Here there is nothing and any way we go is nowhere."

Zhadnoboth, irritated because Uskban seemed so unimpressed with him and his great magic, retorted, "You're in a kind of shadow world, a place just a fraction away from everyday reality. To those in this world you don't seem to exist. Only the crystal ball links you to me and to Zarathandra. If the link should ever break, you would float forever in a nothingness between worlds."

Uskban scowled and craned his neck to look around. He bent down and tried to feel the ground, but his fingers went through it as if it were mere emptiness. Straightening, he asked, "What good is it to be here? We can't see the real world, and if we could we couldn't touch it. We can't steal what we can't grasp."

The sorcerer brushed off his objections with the wave of a hand. "Mere trifles. With my help you'll have no trouble finding the Zalkrings' treasure or being able to steal it."

"Quit the spouting and tell us how to do it," Uskban said shortly.

Zhadnoboth glowered but gave an almost civil answer. "Use the crystal ball. Do you think I gave it to you as a plaything? Why must I have idiots to serve me?"

Uskban spat back, "Because *you're* such an idiot: you explain nothing and expect us to know all."

Zhadnoboth swallowed his anger and explained, "The shadowland makes you invulnerable to anything from this world, nor can you be perceived from here. While in it, you can go through anything in Zarathandra as if it did not exist —be it air, water, solid rock, or boiling lava: it makes no difference."

Sandy spoke up before Uskban could stick his foot in it

again. "How do we find the treasure? And how do we steal it?"

"I was coming to that," Zhadnoboth snapped. "The crystal ball is a key. With it you can control the link between Zarathandra and your shadowland. Whoever holds it has but to want to know about that part of Zarathandra which corresponds to where you are in the shadowland and a window will open. You can look through it to guide your steps in the right direction."

Sandy held the crystal ball up in front of his eyes and turned his thoughts to Zarathandra. Rather surprisingly his first attempt worked. An area of grayness in front of him took on a faint blue glow. Then, abruptly, the murkiness cleared and he could see into the outside world. There was an eerie clarity to what he saw. Everything had sharp and distinct edges, with none of the softening usual in real life.

The most uncanny thing about what he saw was the absence of sound; but Sandy had no sooner wished for sound than he could hear it. The sounds seemed to come from a million miles away, but now the world seen through the magical window seemed real and alive.

"So we can see," rasped Uskban. "How do we lay hold of something so we can steal it?"

"When you get to the treasure chambers, you'll have to suspend the spell and return your bodies to the real world. You only have to hold the crystal ball in your hand and imagine a key unlocking the spell, and the spell will cease to be. Then you can loot to your heart's content."

"What will the Zalkrings do when we pop up in the middle of their treasures?" Sandy asked sourly. "It will be hard looting with one hand and fighting off a thousand bloodthirsty zealots with the other."

The sorcerer brushed off his objections. "That's the safest part of the whole venture. They guard the gates *to* their treasure chambers, but have no safeguards within. They'll not even know you are there."

"Still things could go wrong," Uskban said darkly. "And what do we do after we have gathered the treasure? Stagger out the doors of those treasure chambers carrying the ransom of kings and tell hordes of angry Zalkrings to step aside and let us through?"

"If things go wrong," Zhadnoboth said in exasperation, "you'll just reactivate the spell and they won't be able to touch you, let alone know where you are. As long as you keep the crystal ball in your hands you have no real worry: you can come back out the way you went in and with as little trouble, even if they know they have been robbed. Kels Zalkri himself cannot locate you or get to you while you are in the shadowland."

"But afterward, what then?" muttered Uskban.

"I can't look after you forever," Zhadnoboth said. "They and their god will have no clues to who robbed them. If you don't draw attention to yourselves, they will never find you."

"Zalkrings don't give up . . . *ever*."

Sandy interrupted, afraid the sorcerer and Uskban would go on bickering forever. "Stop the goddamn squabbling. Either we rob those bastards or we don't. If we do, I'd like to know where their treasure chambers are."

Uskban and the sorcerer abruptly stopped arguing to glare venomously at him.

Then, in a peevish tone, Zhadnoboth replied, "There is a great vale deep in the heart of the mountain—just follow the Durm Gad Zalkri to its end. Because you are in a shadowland you could go through solid rock to get there, but you'd have to do it by dead reckoning. While you are within stone you cannot see to guide your steps. It is much easier to follow what roads there are and use the light of the sun to see where you are going."

"Why not send us directly to the treasure chambers with your magic?" Uskban asked.

"There is a sorcery that can do that," replied Zhadnoboth. "But an item from the place where you are going or knowledge of the exact location you want is needed. Even if I could do it, the spell most likely couldn't penetrate the barriers Kels Zalkri has placed around his mountain. If by some miracle I transported you into the treasure chambers, it would be the same as screaming, 'Dark one, we are here.'"

"I thought we couldn't be detected while in this shadowland," Uskban said in a shrewd tone.

Zhadnoboth retorted, "You can't, but neither can I use a transportation spell while you are in the shadowland. It's the hard way, but you have to move a step in the shadowland for every step you wish to take in Zarathandra."

Sandy stepped in again. "Just tell us where these treasure chambers are and we'll get to them the best way we can."

After a moment of stubborn silence, Zhadnoboth replied:

"Opposite to where the Durm Gad Zalkri opens out into the inner vale is the Zalkrings' chief temple, and in front of it is a large square. Directly under the stones of that square are the treasure caves of the Zalkrings. Once you get there, you only have to think the right thoughts and you will sink down to the treasure chambers below."

"What if we pick a spot that is solid rock to the center of the world?" Sandy asked.

"A mere nothing," Zhadnoboth said. "Just get to the square and sink downward and you can't help but find the caves—the ground beneath the square is honeycombed with them, one layer after another. If by some impossible mischance you miss the caves, just rise up and start over again. Only if you lose your sense of direction would you have to worry."

Great, thought Sandy. He looked at his feet and doubt crept into his mind. He started to sink.

Uskban grabbed his arm and said harshly, "Hold, you fool. We are here. That is what counts. This mist is no less real than solid earth." Uskban's mad certainty gave Sandy the faith he needed and he stopped sinking.

Zhadnoboth went on talking, oblivious. "After you get into the treasuries, search for a room closed off by a door of bronze. You can't miss it. The Book of Askordas says it is green with age and completely covered with deeply incised runes. Here are kept the greatest treasures, mostly books of lore and certain objects of power. Do most of your looting here. Even the least of the treasures in this room is worth the price of a kingdom."

"Enough of this prattling," interrupted Uskban. "Let's get on with it." Sandy was disquieted by how fiercely the words were spoken and turned to look. He was shocked by how visible were the emotions raging within Uskban: the terrible hate and lust for revenge were still there, but mixed with them was something worse—an awful fear which threatened to overwhelm him. Anything that could chill Uskban's raging hate, even for a moment, must be too horrifying to even think about.

"Then go on and die," Zhadnoboth snapped. "But don't come crawling on your belly when you need my prattling."

Sandy stepped in to cool them down, figuring he needed both of these blockheads if he was going to come through this with a whole skin. "Let's go now," he said to Zhadnoboth's image in the crystal. "You can tell us what we need to know as we make our way to the mountain." Sandy hoped this suggestion of immediate action would keep Uskban from cracking up—he seemed near a breakdown. Sandy wished he had the option to back out.

Zhadnoboth nodded sullenly. Uskban also gave his nod; and Pognak followed Uskban's lead.

Sandy waited a moment for someone else to start moving, then struck out on his own for the mountain. Glupp, blissfully chewing on a cud, fell in at his heels. Uskban and Pognak hesitated a moment, then followed.

24

THE Goddess smiled grimly to herself. The last die had been cast: her champions were on their way to destiny—theirs, hers, and Zarathandra's. Much more importantly, Sandy was beginning to lead them. The others might balk a little, but they followed. At first she had despaired of him. This man fate had chosen for her seemed too soft, but he had grown. She still wasn't sure she completely approved of him, but she was developing a liking for him.

The Goddess brooded about the sacrificial atrocities going on in the mountain. If she could have hurried the dark one's doom by a second, she would have; the knowledge of what was going on sickened her soul. She did not believe in pampering mortals, but neither did she approve of drinking of their life and making their last moments an unimaginable torment. Not for her was the roasting of living babies over open fires, the impaling of women on fiery stakes, or having men devoured by hell spawn that slowly ate their way up from the toes.

In rage the Goddess looked to the black mountain and said in a soft, deadly voice, "You'll pay, you abomination, for the way you have befouled my world and wronged its creatures. When you are damned you shall suffer torment as will make the suffering of your victims seem nothing—and each who suffered will in turn be your judge and executioner from that moment to time's end."

25

SANDY found it unnerving to cross the open plain which separated Admith's Knuckles from the black mountain. He knew that they were hidden from prying eyes, yet he felt like a sacrificial victim marching into the jaws of some monster from hell. While his conscious mind told him he was invisible, his subconscious said an elephant in a tearoom couldn't be more conspicuous.

Aside from his dread, he found the rest of the trip easy. The plain was pitted with jagged craters and strewn with half-melted debris, but this was no problem. They just walked through or over any obstacle they came to, one big advantage to the shadowland they were in. Still, it was an odd sensation to know you were walking through boulders or to see a pit yawning blackly under your feet.

They set a blistering pace toward the mountain, traveling much faster than was possible in the real world. Despite their great exertion, they didn't even work up a sweat. Sandy, in fact, felt a bit chilled.

The closer they got to Tham Og Zalkri the more sinister and terrible it appeared. Nothing grew on it. Its surface was as bare as a death's-head, and colored an all-devouring black: more like a shadow lurking within the rock than its actual color. The very stone seemed alive and malevolent.

As they drew near, three huge creatures flew by just ahead of them. Sandy looked at them through the crystal and was glad to be in a place where they couldn't get to him. They were like a combination of bird and reptile: their triangular leather wings were covered with a sparse growth of black feathers, the short bodies were furred with a black fuzz and ended with a long barbed tail, the long scrawny necks were liberally endowed with dull red wattles, and the scaled

190

heads had a huge, curved beak filled with needlelike teeth. And that was not to mention the massive three-toed talons, each claw eight inches long. These formidable sentries flew past as if Sandy and his companions weren't there—and maybe they weren't.

After what seemed an eternity, they got to the black iron gates which barred access to the interior of the mountain. On each side of the gates were immense towers built from a lusterless black stone. Each black stone block was taller and wider than a man is high. To Sandy, the towers seemed like two gigantic vultures, hunched over and ready to tear apart any prey foolish enough to stray within their range.

He looked closely at the gates and a chill slithered like a snake up his spine. Each gate was of black iron forged into the shape of a hideous demon. The gates seemed unearthly, more like pieces of hell than things of metal. With the gates closed, the demons appeared to be engaged with talon and fang in mortal combat, the teeth and claws glistening bone-white against the blackness of their bodies. The black iron had a scaly surface fashioned with great cunning to look like true demon hide—even to the old scars and bleeding wounds. The demons had nightmare eyes carved from immense crystals of some cloudy green gemstone, each lit from within by demonic fires. Sandy could feel their glare raking across his flesh.

Intimidated by the awesome sight towering above him, Sandy whispered into the crystal ball, "We are at the gates. Now what do we do?"

Before the sorcerer could answer, Uskban croaked, "Just step forward and through them."

Sandy turned toward him, alarmed by the sound of his voice. What he saw was not reassuring: Uskban's face was dead white. Beads of sweat stood out on his brow, and his jaw muscles were rigid cables. Hate and fear raged against each other in his eyes. Uskban seemed ready to explode, either to charge ahead with berserk fury or to turn tail and flee in terror.

"Do as Uskban says," Zhadnoboth snapped. He was still too huffy, besides being occupied with certain schemes he was concocting, to notice how touchy the situation had become.

Sandy took charge and stepped forward just as Uskban

gave a scream of defiance and charged the gates. They touched the black iron simultaneously.

Uskban shrieked in agony, staggered back, and collapsed. Sandy too reeled backward, sick with shock and shaking in horror.

The gates were alive with a terrible and unbearable type of life. Zhadnoboth's spell had given them the ability to physically pass through the gates unharmed—but did not shield them from the mind-warping thoughts of the beings who comprised the gates. They almost destroyed the puny beings who invaded their madly alien minds, unaware they even did so. Sandy knew that the one faint touch he had experienced had left a scar forever on his soul.

With a convulsive croak, Pognak fell beside the body of his friend and master, cradling the little madman in his huge arms. Tears streamed from his eyes and down over his ugly and hard-bitten features.

Sandy shook the crystal ball and screamed, "You idiot, why didn't you tell us the gates were alive?" The silver chain about his neck quivered, but did not choke.

An ashen-faced Zhadnoboth, sick from the backwash of the encounter, answered shakily, "I never knew."

"Why didn't you?" Sandy yelled. "You're some hotshot sorcerer! I doubt you could find your backside unless someone told you where it was."

Sandy glanced down at Uskban's crumbled body. When he spoke, anger mixed with baffled concern filled his voice— he hadn't realized until now that he had developed a liking for the bloodthirsty little bastard. "What do we do about Uskban? We can't just leave him."

"Why not?" Zhadnoboth replied. "He's useless now, and he's as safe in the shadowland as anyplace else." As he spoke his voice grew testier and more commanding: the sorcerer was like crab grass, too mean and stubborn to be squelched for long.

Sandy looked in the crystal ball with disgust and snarled, "Don't be a blind ass: Pognak won't go anywhere without Uskban and neither will I. I may be the fool you take me for, but I'm not fool enough to enter this outpost of hell without any backup." He paused, then added, calmer, "Besides, you owe him—you owe us all. We can't just abandon one another when the going gets rough; if we do, we destroy ourselves. He served you well in his way, and now you should do what you can for him in return."

Zhadnoboth stared daggers through the crystal ball at Sandy; big-heartedness was not one of his noticeable traits. Then he relented—maybe a little stirred by Sandy's words, but more by the stubborn set of his jaw—and Uskban could increase their chances of walking away with a greater share of the treasure.

"There is a way to revive him," the sorcerer said in a sulky voice. "Place your right hand on his heart and hold the crystal ball tight in the other, and I will invoke a spell of healing."

Sandy bent down beside Uskban and tried to pry him loose from Pognak's grip. The giant snarled and shoved him away. With a lewd curse, Sandy stuck his face right into the big mute's and yelled, "Let go of him, you damned idiot! Hold on to him and he's dead meat. Give him to me and maybe he will live."

The maddened brute hesitated, then gently laid Uskban down and backed away. Sandy knelt and put his hand to Uskban's chest while Pognak watched, scowling, ready to rip Sandy apart if things went wrong.

Uskban was in a bad way: his heartbeat slow and irregular, his breath coming in convulsive gulps. "Do your thing, old man, he hasn't much time," Sandy shouted into the crystal ball. Under his breath he muttered a prayer that Uskban would recover, because he would truly miss the cunning madman if Zhadnoboth's spell failed.

Zhadnoboth quickly rattled off an incantation and then stabbed the air with his staff. A flash of lightning—a lapis lazuli bolt wrapped in strands of jade-green static—shot from his staff, into the crystal ball, out through Sandy, and finally into Uskban.

Uskban gave a convulsive jerk and for a moment his breath stopped. Zhadnoboth muttered an obscenity and hurriedly invoked another bolt of lightning. Sandy had inadvertently moved his hand and this time the jolt hit Uskban right where the Key of Arimithos hung down around his chest.

For a brief moment Uskban lit up with blue fire. He gave a convulsive shudder, screamed, and staggered to his feet. Weeping with joy, Pognak ran over and threw his arms around him.

In the meantime, Sandy was blistering the air with curses.

He had dropped the crystal ball and was shaking his hands, which felt as if they had been ripped apart by red-hot knives. He looked at them and saw that jagged blue scars had been branded into his palms.

A hand touched his shoulder and Sandy whirled to see Uskban, pallid and shaky, but alive. Just as important, the fear which had been threatening to tear him apart was gone.

"Thanks, *man*," Uskban croaked. "I owe you blood debt."

Sandy grimaced. "Thank Zhadnoboth. If it wasn't for his spell, you'd still be laying there like a cold fish. All I did was channel his magic—and damned near burned off my hands doing it." Then he looked sharply at Uskban as he realized the madman had called him *man* instead of *demon*.

Uskban's eyes glittered brightly and he gave a derisive snort. "Even frozen, I could still hear and see. There would have been no cure for me except for you. Someday, even if I be dead, I'll settle our debt."

"And then I will owe you," Sandy protested.

Uskban nodded and said, "The scales never balance, that's what life and friendship are about. We constantly incur debts and then repay them to create new debts."

Sandy looked at him in surprise, wondering once again if he was truly mad.

Uskban caught his look and a crooked smile lit his features for a moment. "Oh, I'm mad enough. But even mad-man are sane at times and wonder about the meaning of life. That just makes our madness worse."

Zhadnoboth's voice shrilled up from the crystal ball lying at their feet, "Dunderheads, pick up your crystal ball. I cannot see or hear you if it does not touch your hands."

Uskban bent over and picked it up. Zhadnoboth saw him then and cackled, "That was a mean spell I whipped up to revive you. I never used it before, but I got the wording and elements just right. It was your lucky day, Uskban, when you teamed up with me."

The madman and Sandy exchanged glances, silently expressing to each other how lucky they felt to have Zhadno-both as a fellow traveler.

Done with his self-congratulations, Zhadnoboth snapped, "Get moving! And watch where you are going from now on."

Sandy took the crystal ball from Uskban, almost choking

with indignation when he heard Zhadnoboth's last words. By a supreme effort of will, he held his tongue and turned to stomp off toward the tower to the right of the demon gates. Glupp and his two companions tromped after him, in silent accord with his opinions about Zhadnoboth.

They halted at the foot of the tower. Sandy was reluctant to test whatever sorcerous barriers lay ahead and barked into the crystal, "Old man, is there anything in front of us to be beware of?"

After a moment of silence, Zhadnoboth answered carefully, "There is magic and power within the tower, but nothing which can cause you trouble. The walls are just walls and not enslaved demons. All you have to do is step forward and be on your way. Now don't bother me for a while, I have other matters to attend to."

Because of their attunement to the crystal ball, they could sense his attention leave them—an opportunity Uskban used to settle other matters. "Hold!" he said harshly.

Sandy turned to see what the madman wanted and his heart stopped in shock. A foot-long poniard was an inch from his jugular. Seeing the bloodthirsty grin on the madman's face, Sandy knew he was dead.

Just as Sandy decided, *The hell with it*, and tensed his muscles to make a desperate try at the madman, Uskan held a finger to his lips and whispered, "Quiet." Then, with a sudden twisting motion which gave Sandy no time to react, he slashed forward and upward with his blade—slicing through the enchanted silver chain encircling Sandy's neck as if it were made of butter. The severed pieces of the chain fell to the ground, writhing like snakes, then they stiffened and in moments had crumbled into dust—just as a wobble-kneed Sandy felt like doing.

"The crooked one will not know until too late that his shackle no longer curbs your tongue. We control the crystal ball. He cannot see here unless we will it, nor can his magic touch us."

"Thanks," Sandy said in a shaky voice, a question in his eyes.

"I owe it to you," croaked Uskban. "Now the scales are more balanced." He gave a bleak grin and added, "Besides, we might need your name. Better damnation by it than by Kels Zalkri."

Sandy rubbed his neck, savoring his freedom from the

silver chain. He did wish, however, that the next time Usk-ban did him a favor he wouldn't do it in such a hair-raising fashion. "Now I owe you."

"Maybe so, maybe not." Uskban touched the crystal ball and the image of the mountains of his homeland appeared. He stared longingly at them with heart-burning sadness and then turned to Sandy. "Do one thing for me: When the time comes, find my son. I have wronged him, and his mother. My heart tells me I have not the time to set things right between us, so you must do it for me. Find his mother—you know who she is—and you will find him. Say that I leave him my name and my love, the only heritage I have to give. It is little enough if you measure in terms of gold, but its true worth is beyond price. Gold can be lost, but one's forefathers and their deeds are eternal. They can be forgotten, but never destroyed."

Uskban paused, then added bleakly, "Tell him I was one of the damned and had to go my own way. I ask no forgive-ness of him, just understanding." A sad, crooked smile flick-ered across his grim face. "And tell his holy strumpet of a mother that I loved her."

"If I live through this, I will," Sandy vowed. He felt a deep, piercing sorrow for the little man.

"You'll live," rasped Uskban. "The Goddess never lets those she has chosen die before they've given her full value."

Sandy wondered what he meant by those odd words, but was distracted by Pognak's inarticulate growl. The mute's face was twisted into a hateful scowl. Maybe Uskban had befriended a demon, he seemed to say, but he'd rather be damned before he would stoop so low.

Sandy shouted, "Hate my guts, you surly bastard, but I'll still call you friend!" He added sardonically, "Because the thought of it will gall you to hell and beyond."

Pognak sneered in reply and made an obscene gesture, telling Sandy what he could do to himself.

Sandy grabbed Glupp's harness. With a curt, "Follow me," he led Glupp toward the tower's wall. Uskban and Pognak followed almost on his heels. He hesitated one step from the wall for a moment, hoping Zhadnoboth knew what he was talking about and this time they would succeed in penetrating into Tham Og Zalkri. Then he stepped forward.

This time only ensorceled stone instead of ensorceled demon barred their way, and they passed through with ease.

Sandy felt slightly queasy when he found himself wading waist-deep through stone flooring after he passed the wall. Then, remembering the sorcerer's words, he thought himself *up* until he was apparently walking on the surface of the stone. Glupp and the other two men managed to do the same and with a lot less worry.

Sandy unconsciously wished to see more of the room and the crystal ball obeyed his unspoken command, giving them a rapid and panoramic view of the inside of the tower. The ground floor of the tower was one gigantic room. Along the wall a circular staircase spiraled its way to higher floors. There was only one occupant, a Zalkring priest.

He sat atop a dais of red-streaked black marble in the center of the room. His spare, angular body was naked except for a black leather loincloth and a string of burnished jet beads around his neck. His long black hair was tightly braided and wound in an elaborate coil atop his head.

"He's a priest of the second circle." Uskban's voice was coldly venomous. "The priests of the first circle wear their hair long and unbraided; those of the lower circles shave it all off."

The priest was in a trance. His muscles were rigid wires and his eyes stared fixedly into space. Only his head moved. First it swung as far in one direction as it could go, halted, and then swung slowly as far as it could go in the other. Then the whole cycle started over. Sandy felt a chill every time those blank eyes swung past him: like icicles lancing through the fabric of his soul.

Suddenly Zhadnoboth's voice piped up from the crystal ball. He, too, had felt the chill of the priest's eyes upon the crystal ball. "He searches beyond the gates with his inward eye. It is a simpleminded but effective way to guard the near borders against intruders. Without a great sorcerer you would have been detected long before now."

Sandy had held his breath when the sorcerer first started speaking, waiting for him to rage about the missing thrall collar. Now he let it out with relief. Either Uskban was right or the scoundrel was too wrapped up in his own schemings to notice.

Zhadnoboth went on, "Look at the priest's skin and notice how it glistens. That is a special Zalkring secret, a magical oil which they rub into their skins to bring on the trance. It is brewed from the sap of the traveler's-thorn and mixed with the squeezings from twenty-one different herbs—only the Zalkrings know which herbs, what proportions, and the proper ceremonies. The oil is worth more than its weight in gold to a sorcerer. It is stored in small pots carved from a light green alabaster. If you should come across any such pots, gather them up for me. I'll make it well worth your while."

From the greed which oozed from Zhadnoboth's voice, Sandy thought the oil had to have great worth, much more than the price the sorcerer set on it. More than a little put out by Zhadnoboth's continual connivings, Sandy retorted, "If you wanted it so much, you should have come yourself."

Then he led the way toward the rear wall of the watchtower. As he passed close to the entranced priest he noticed faint purple fumes rising from large copper braziers placed to each side of the Zalkring. When his attention focused on the fumes he could suddenly smell the incense: redolent of tropical spices laced with the oil of bitter almonds.

As Uskban passed the priest he stopped and looked at him, his body trembling with fury. Then he stepped forward and spat at this hated foe. The spit passed harmlessly through the body, but the gesture satisfied the madman.

They passed through the rear wall of the watchtower and into the outer precincts of the Zalkrings' domain. It was a rocky glen which stood between the gates and the entrance to the great ravine called the Durm Gad Zalkri. Here and there hardy thistles grew from cracks in the rock. Glupp tried to stick his head through the magical window the crystal ball had made in the shadowland and chomp on these luscious-looking plants. He gave a rumble of disgust as his teeth refused to grab hold of these tempting ghosts.

The entrance to the Durm Gad Zalkri was an enormous crack in the side of the mountain: dark, menacing, and awesome. A road of gray cobbles led up to and into it. They hesitated for a moment, unnerved by its fearsome appearance, before marching down the road.

Inside, the ravine was even more grim and horrific than it appeared from the outside. Sheer walls of black stone rose to terrifying heights on both sides. To Sandy they seemed like gigantic jaws, jaws ready to chomp down on them and spit out their bones.

The ravine was hardly wide enough for the road—the perfect place for an ambush and slaughter. If their raid went sour and they had to fight their way out, they'd never get through here alive. That thought Sandy quickly pushed to the back of his mind, reassuring himself they'd have the shadowland to retreat to.

There were thousands of niches carved into the rock walls, and within each niche was a grinning skull. Some were so new you could still see the dried blood on them, but most were yellow and crumbling with age.

It may have been the shadowland they were in, or perhaps Sandy's new sixth sense, but Sandy saw more: misty green-gray swirls of ether eddied about each skull. And the swirls seemed to have a kind of life; wispy tendrils were groping toward them. Soon he and his companions were enclosed in a great writhing cloud of green-gray mist.

For Sandy it was hell: like trying to wade through a ghostly sea whose breakers beat at the boundaries of his mind. He could sense faint wailings and feel phantom fingers plucking beseechingly at him. His companions must have felt something too. Uskban's eyes grew red and his face froze into a contorted grimace. Pognak glared more ferociously and stomped instead of walking. Only Glupp seemed unaware, placidly plodding along and blissfully dreaming of heavenly meadows filled with sweet thistles and tangy brambles.

Just as Sandy began to wonder if they would ever get to the end of the gorge, they were there, and a great weight was lifted from his shoulders. The ghostly things hadn't felt hostile or malevolent, but their uncanny presence had been wearing. As they stepped out of the gorge, Sandy sensed a terrible wail of despair and then an utter and hopeless silence.

Before them lay the rocky vale that was the heart of the mountain. Sheer walls of black rock towered on both sides and in front of them. The only approach was the narrow ravine they had just come through. The valley seemed like a monstrous hole torn in the side of the mountain by the talons of some leviathan from hell.

Carved into the stone walls were the homes and temples of the Zalkrings. Every building was covered with intricate carvings: of death, torture, and mortality, all mixed together. Dancing skeletons capered among flayed corpses, heedless of the vultures that scrabbled over bloody booty. Stone priests ripped hearts from living bodies while below their feet ghouls and demons diced with human bones. Captive women split apart as they were raped by horned apes built like elephants, whole families roasted in giant skillets while slavering Zalkrings waited for the meat to be done, goat-footed demons stuck victims with hot needles until they became human pincushions, and a girl decked in flowers rode a ritual sledge which passed over and crushed a road made of bound captives. Exquisite artistry and delicate shading of color had gone into the carvings, but they turned Sandy's stomach and he had to look away.

In the center of the small valley was a large square, paved with four-foot-wide white marble squares alternating with squares of dull black basalt. Each black square was inlaid with a symbol depicting a blood-red talon, eight-clawed and reaching as if to grab the world.

Here most of the Zalkrings were gathered, three thousand or more. The men were clustered to the right and the women and children to the left. All knelt on prayer rugs of black stitched with scarlet designs. Periodically a gong would boom, and the Zalkrings would bow their heads to the ground three times, rise, and let go a great wailing chant that echoed and rebounded through the canyon like muted thunder. It was eerie and horrifying but at the same time was profoundly religious: it moved Sandy even though he knew he wanted no part of them or what they worshipped.

Directly opposite and across from where the Durm Gad Zalkri opened into the vale was the Zalkrings' chief temple, the heart and center of their dark beliefs. All the worshippers faced it. The temple was enormous, stretching across the canyon from one side to the other and towering up at least a hundred feet. The temple sat atop a raised platform made from huge blocks of black-grained granite. Leading down into the square and stretching across the whole width of the temple was a broad staircase of alternating black and white steps.

A massive wrought-iron altar shaped in the image of a gigantic serpent, tied in knots and wrapped about itself, rose from the center of the platform near the head of the stairs. Its eyes were huge ruby orbs burning with demonic life. Sandy remembered the demon gates and shivered. This was so like them, made of dead metal but infused with unearthly vitality.

Uskban spoke in a voice smoldering with anger, "The

altar comes from the hell from which Kels Zalkri originated; it was bought and paid for with the blood and souls of his victims. Each year a hundred more are tortured with fire and iron so that the spell which binds it to this world can be renewed: it is the nail which holds the mountain to Zarathandra. Destroy the nail, and this foulness will be wiped away."

Sandy glanced sharply at the little man. The strange calm which had gripped Uskban since his experience at the gates was gone. His eyes bulged, his hands clutched convulsively at nothing, and his breath came in hoarse rasps. He teetered on the edge of madness, ready at any moment to explode into berserk fury—Sandy wished fervently that the madman had enough fear left to keep his rage in check.

"Hold your anger, Uskban," Sandy told him in a sharp voice. "What can three of us do against this many crazed zealots? Let's hurt them the only way we can—by stealing their hoard and rubbing their pride in the dirt."

"Aye, we'll steal their treasures," Uskban agreed. "But afterward those misbegotten bastards will have a reckoning with Pognak and me." The giant banged his hand against the hilt of his sword and vigorously nodded his assent.

Sandy, seeing how close the smoldering hate within them was to bursting into flame, took action. He strode forcefully toward the altar, hoping they would follow him and get too embroiled in the action to explode. Immediately Glupp trundled after him, content to go where Sandy went. After a moment of hesitation the two grim-faced humans followed.

Sandy climbed up into the air until he was level with the platform: he did not want to repeat the experience of walking into the mind of another being.

As Sandy walked above the square, he looked down and watched the Zalkrings at their worship. He almost smiled when he saw a little boy kneeling by his mother and trying to stifle a yawn. It seemed children were the same everywhere, bored by the dry formalities of religion. He was so busy getting to the platform and keeping a wary eye on his companions that he really didn't notice the bloody doings at the altar until he had nearly reached it.

Then he gagged in revulsion. Behind the altar was a deep pit. On the far side five women and four men had been staked down, small pyres built across their loins, and then set on fire. All that remained were the blackened remnants of bodies, their untouched faces contorted in agony. In the pit a monstrous beast slavered over its food. It was an amorphous, white-colored blob with dozens of tentacles sprouting haphazardly from its body. At the base of each tentacle was a mouth filled with thousands of ripping teeth. As these teeth were tearing to shreds the raw red flesh of dismembered human bodies, gastric juices from the mouths were turning the flesh into a pinkish mush.

Around the altar clustered priests of the inner circle. Each wore only the tanned hide of a human being. Four of them were holding a naked young woman spread-eagled atop the altar. She struggled frantically in their grasp, screaming —but no sound came from her lips. At each end of the altar, at her head and at her feet, a priest stood intoning prayers to Kels Zalkri. Behind the altar another priest hovered over her, holding a knife chipped from obsidian in his right hand. He waited as if for some sign.

The gong sounded again, and another of those great droning chants rumbled up from the square below: the priest's signal. He plunged the knife down and then sideways, ripping her open from crotch to breastbone in one great stroke. The terrible wound broke the spell of silence and her tortured death cry mingled with the holy tones of the Zalkrings' chant. The four priests held the quivering body as the priest with the knife quickly and expertly flayed it and carved it into quarters; after that they tossed the remains to their creature in the pit. Two priests brought another victim to the fore.

Uskban went berserk. With a howl of agony and rage, he slammed into Sandy, sending him sprawling and the crystal ball flying into the air. Uskban sprang forward and grabbed it, then charged with headlong fury toward the altar. He skidded to a stop in the air just over the altar and heaved the crystal ball at it with all his force.

The crystal ball struck the altar and exploded, sending millions of crystal shards flying in all directions.

Thousands of cracks zigzagged through the unearthly substance of the altar. It almost exploded as the crystal did, but the supernatural forces which bound it to Zarathandra held it together—just barely. Most of the priests surrounding the altar and their next victim were cut to ribbons by the flying slivers of broken crystal. Uskban's action, whether the result of insane cunning or blind luck, had had a terrible effect.

The near destruction of the altar destroyed the uneasy stability of the mountain. Earthquakes, like the shudders of some enormous beast, shook Tham Og Zalkri and the lands surrounding it. Gigantic landslides came hurtling down into the valley below, smashing buildings to dust and Zalkrings to bloody pulp. The ground bucked and heaved, great crevasses opened and fiery lava mixed with smoking brimstone spewed from the depths of the earth. Swirling black clouds lashed the ground below with lightning and hailstones, while hurricane-force winds fought no-quarter battles throughout the valley.

The moment the crystal ball shattered, Sandy and his companions were dumped from their shadowland and into the raging chaos Uskban had unleashed. Uskban and Pognak crashed to the ground on the platform, between the altar and the temple. Too crazy to notice much difference, they immediately began slaughtering any Zalkring priests who still survived.

In moments Uskban disemboweled one priest and chopped off the head of another. Pognak knocked two dazed and bleeding priests into the pit—the beast in it ate them just as readily as it had the tidbits they'd thrown it—and slashed open the belly of another, and skewered his fourth priest through the throat.

By this time more priests had come spewing out from the temple. They were led by a wild-eyed fanatic waving a gold-encrusted ceremonial sword. Uskban quickly disposed of him, lopping off his sword arm and then slashing his throat. The rest of the priests quickly surrounded them, but they were not as skilled in dealing with enraged madmen as they were with helpless sacrificial victims. Pognak and Uskban more than held their own, making the haphazardly armed priests pay bloodily every time they got within range of their blades.

Meanwhile, Sandy and Glupp had fallen straight down to land hard on the stairs. Sandy had the wind knocked from him and was out of the fight for the moment. However, Glupp was made of sterner stuff, and the stairs suffered more than he, breaking and splintering under the impact of his weight. Remnants of the Zalkrings worshipping in the square below and struggling up and away from the chaos there saw them and with enraged shouts began scrambling toward them. Glupp gave a thunderous bellow and charged like a runaway express down the stairs, right into the Zalkrings.

Broken and bloody fanatics went flying in all directions—
except for the ones squashed by his ponderous feet.

Sandy picked himself up and immediately fell down again
as the stairs heaved and rolled. He cursed and struggled to
his feet again. He looked around and saw several wild-eyed
Zalkrings picking their way over the broken stairs toward
him.

An ornate sword with an arm attached was lying on the
stairs near Sandy. He kicked the severed arm aside and
snatched up the blade. By this time four Zalkrings had more
or less encircled him. Praying for divine help to any god who
would listen, Sandy prepared to fight—determined to get at
least one before they got him.

Just as the Zalkrings charged, the stairs to Sandy's right
buckled and split open. Steam burst out, scalding alive the
two foes attacking him from that direction. The force of the
blast knocked the two Zalkrings to his left off their feet.
Reeling drunkenly, Sandy managed to lunge forward and
skewer one of them through the guts. Then, given strength
by his fear, Sandy yanked the blade out and turned to face
his remaining enemy. The Zalkring was advancing awkwardly, holding a huge battleaxe in his left hand; his broken
right arm hung uselessly by his side. With a bloodcurdling cry
the Zalkring slashed clumsily at Sandy, who stumbled aside
and then buried his blade in his foe's head.

Hurriedly, Sandy tried to yank his borrowed sword from
the Zalkring's skull. It wouldn't budge. Cursing like a
trooper, Sandy tried again. It still wouldn't come free. He
looked about, saw he wasn't in immediate danger, and gave
up.

The place was a shambles. The stone stairs were crumpled
and rent by crevasses, the temple had partially collapsed,
and the square below was a smashed ruin. Fires and poisonous miasmas were constantly erupting from new fissures.
Dead and dying were strewn everywhere: crushed, scalded,
torn to shreds, choked by poisonous fumes, and some few
slain by Sandy and his companions.

On the platform, Uskban and Pognak, fighting back to
back, were hemmed in by a dozen or more armed priests.
"Destroy the altar, you damned fool!" screamed Uskban.
"Destroy it and you destroy them," he added as he nodded
toward the Zalkrings surrounding him.

Sandy snatched up the dead Zalkring's battleaxe. It was

just as well, he thought. He wasn't a trained swordsman and he probably could do more damage with the axe than any other weapon. Besides, the battleaxe had some kind of edge —it had deeply scored the stone when it had fallen from the Zalkring's hand.

He worked his way up the damaged stairs toward the altar, making good time despite the debris and the deep fissures in the stone. He heard an angry shout to his right and turned to see several Zalkrings rushing to intercept him. A large crevasse kept him from going left and they had the angle on him. He damned his bad luck and prepared to fight.

Again angry nature intervened. There was a roar and something plunged from the skies and exploded as it hit the stairs. Sandy was blown over by the force of the blast. Pieces of hot rock pelted him, but none more than glancingly. Somehow, he staggered back to his feet and reeled up through a stinking cloud of brimstone-laced steam. He made it to a patch of clear air and inhaled it in great gasps, trying to ease the pain in his poisoned lungs.

His stomach turned over and he started to heave as the poisons in his system began to get to him. At that instant, two coughing and gagging Zalkrings staggered out of the cloud. An adrenaline rush of fear gave Sandy control of his nausea and he attacked, slashing out twice at his partially disabled foes. Two heads went flying. Then the weaknesses of his body caught up with him and he bent over and heaved up his guts. Moments later, green and shaking, Sandy was able to move toward cleaner air. A short pause and fresh air calmed his nausea and he began climbing toward the altar.

Uskban and Pognak were still fighting off their attackers, but they looked tired and battered. Sandy started to charge over to aid them, then thought better of it and continued on toward the altar: it seemed more his line than vicious swordplay.

He paused at the altar, wondering what to do. His axe, big as it was, seemed too puny to damage that massive thing. While he hesitated, a bloody and wild-eyed priest rushed at him from behind the altar. Splinters of flying crystal had ripped his skin to shreds, but Sandy recognized him. It was the tall, gaunt, and withered-looking priest who had so joyously disemboweled the young woman—in his hand was the bloodstained obsidian knife.

Raving madly, he shrieked and slashed at Sandy. Sandy

stumbled backward barely dodging the knife. Like a striking snake, the priest whipped around and slashed again. Sandy jumped aside and slashed back with the heavy battleaxe, taking off the priest's right arm at the elbow. The blow didn't even slow the priest. He wheeled about and charged madly into Sandy, closing his left hand around Sandy's throat with a grip of forged iron.

Sandy tried to recover from his previous stroke, but with supernatural strength the priest forced him backward and he tripped over a dead Zalkring and fell, the insane Zalkring on top of him. His right elbow hit the stone pavement and the battleaxe flew from his grasp. He struggled to break the fanatic's grip, but the gaunt priest had muscles like steel cords and a rabid intransigence only death would still. The priest pushed him down against the pavement and tightened his grip. Sandy's lungs burned and there was a roaring in his ears.

Sandy shook the priest's blood from his eyes and smashed a stiff arm to the Zalkring's head. It had as much effect as hitting a stone wall. He brought a knee up and rammed it into the madman's balls; the priest didn't even grunt. Horror chilled Sandy to the core and he wondered if he were fighting a dead man. Any normal being would have collapsed from his wounds by now.

Desperately Sandy lunged sideways, managing to roll over. However, the priest never relaxed his grip and rolled with him—ending back on top again. Sandy's flailing left hand touched the axe he had dropped and he grabbed hold of it just below the head. He slashed it across the bottom of the Zalkring's wrist; the supernaturally sharp edge slit tendons and muscles to the bone. The deadly fingers went limp.

Sandy pushed the maimed priest from him and staggered back to his feet, gulping air by the barrelful and still not seeming to get enough. The priest, his mad eyes filled with savage despair, hurled himself at Sandy—trying to batter him to death now that it no longer had arms to use. Sandy cursed the thing's unnatural vitality, leaped aside, and slashed downward with the battleaxe.

The priest's head went flying off and rolled against the base of the altar. The eyes glared madly at Sandy for a moment and then a look of savage determination appeared on the face. The maimed and headless body got to its feet and staggered around trying to find Sandy, the severed head somehow controlling it. Sandy stepped behind the clumsy thing and gave it a shove, and the body flew into the pit behind the altar. A tentacle grabbed it in midair.

A hissing, bubbling scream came from behind Sandy. He whirled and saw the severed head contorted in unholy agony and shrieking as if its flesh too was being dissolved by the fierce gastric juices of the monstrous thing in the pit. Wildly Sandy charged it and slashed down with the battleaxe, splitting the head in two.

Sandy looked down and shuddered. Then he noticed how the axe had buried itself in the pavement as if the stone were soft as butter. He wrenched it out and looked at it in wonder.

It did not have the look or feel of Zalkring work; indeed he had a fancy it enjoyed drinking Zalkring blood. His sixth sense kicked in and he knew it had belonged to a dwarf king slain a thousand years ago by Kels Zalkri. The fell weapon remembered the hate its master had had for the dark one and his toadies and thirsted for revenge.

A shout from Uskban roused Sandy from his reverie and he looked up. Three Zalkrings were coming this way. The broken and crumpled pavement atop the platform slowed them down, but wasn't stopping them. Sandy wiped the sweat from his eyes, flexed aching muscles, and wished he were someplace else. If this was an adventure, he didn't care for it.

Knowing he didn't have much time, Sandy turned his back to the Zalkrings and hobbled to the altar. Up close he could see it was ready to disintegrate. The crystal had shattered it into millions of fragments and only its soul—a flickering black-red flame—held it together. The altar would quiver and shake, ready to explode, and then the flame would flex its vaporous sinews and draw the pieces back together.

He looked into the snake altar's ruby eyes and was nearly transfixed, his mind seeing the altar come to writhing life and slithering over to swallow him whole.

Angrily he threw the unwelcome image from his mind and swung the axe at the left eye. The battleaxe made a weird singing sound and quivered with joy in his hands as it smashed into the snake altar.

The axe blade bit into the eye and crimson splinters flew in all directions. The altar shuddered as the axe rebounded from the bone-jolting blow. The axe almost flew from Sandy's hand, but somehow he hung onto it.

The altar of iron started to writhe slowly, and it let loose a creaking hiss which curdled Sandy's blood. Savagely he lashed out again, smashing the right eye. Like a wild thing in agony, the axe rebounded and tore itself from his hands. Sandy staggered and fell.

Stubbornly he got up and grabbed the axe again. Its edge was now scored, but still usable. The axe stirred in his hands and Sandy intuitively knew the weapon was ready to do battle again—like some mortally wounded warrior determined to die in a blaze of glory. He heard steps to his right, remembered the Zalkrings, and looked. Dimly, through air murky with smoke, he saw a small figure advancing, a blue-white light gleaming in its hand. Behind him on the crumpled pavement lay three bodies.

"I didn't save your neck just now so you could scratch your butt," Uskban yelled. "Smash the damned altar."

Sandy nodded and together they grimly stalked toward the snake altar. A Zalkring priest, mortally wounded and crawling on his hands and knees, tried to grab Sandy's ankle. Sandy kicked him aside and kept going: past the pit behind the altar. A tentacle groped its way out of the pit and tried to get him. The glowing thing in Uskban's hand, the key talisman he had recovered from Idman's tomb, flared to a brilliant blue. The blue flame touched the tentacle, charred the unearthly flesh, and set it on fire. With a hideous scream, the monster yanked back its flaming tentacle. Soon the pit was filled with shooting blue flame, black smoke, and the shrill death cries of the creature.

Finally, Sandy reached the altar again. With all his strength he smashed the axe into the enchanted metal. Blood-red fire sizzled and smoked about the weapon for a long moment. The axe handle grew intensely hot and Sandy cursed and let go. The next moment the weapon disappeared in a flash of fire and black smoke, leaving behind only a few drops of molten metal.

The snake altar still held together. Sandy cursed it and gave it a kick, doing no damage except to his foot.

A sudden terrible blackness in his soul sent icy needles of fear through Sandy. He knew that Kels Zalkri had broken some restraining barrier and was coming through from hell.

They were doomed.

Uskban roughly pushed him aside and yelled, "Go!" He was clenching the iron key tightly in his fist and it glowed like a blue supernova, almost blinding Sandy. The amulet's cleansing rays touched the red-black flame that held the altar together and burnt it away, penetrating deep within to destroy the last foul vestige of the altar's soul.

The snake altar exploded; the almost manifest Kels Zalkri screamed his rage as the unholy bond he had forged between his corner of hell and Zarathandra disappeared in the cataclysm.

Sandy, caught in the destruction of the altar, was torn asunder and hurled from mortal realms. Dead and yet alive, he found himself engulfed in a writhing maelstrom. Lightning, nothingness, torn bits of men and demons, mixed pieces of hell and earth, ice and fire, hatred, love, screams—more fragments of experience than he could possibly remember exploded into the dark which lies beyond the universe. Sandy, body and soul, was mixed, merged, and annihilated as the universe reacted to this event which threatened to rip its fabric apart.

In his last moment, Sandy saw Uskban and Pognak standing in an island of calm amid the chaos. Uskban was holding his talisman high; blue-white rays curved from it, wrapping about them to form a redoubt against the cataclysm that was trying to engulf them. Sandy marveled, screamed in agony, laughed, cried, and explored the far corners of the universe as atom by atom he was torn asunder.

Until he was no more and knew no more.

26

THE Goddess looked into the darkness lying between the worlds and smiled, tired but triumphant. The struggle had been exhausting, although she had stayed in the background and not directly fought against the dark one and his minions. She had for a moment manipulated the threads on the loom of destiny. The effort had drained energy she dearly needed, but it had been worth it: The axe given so long ago to Dromdroghogar the Dwarf by Vuth-Mazal the Bear God had found its way into Sandy's hands—and it had made a critical difference.

Kels Zalkri had for the moment been thrown from Zarathandra, and his foothold destroyed. He had gotten used to sitting in his corner of hell, nibbling on the tortured souls his followers sent him, and gleefully planning how one day he would make all of Zarathandra his. Now he howled at the wounds he had received and hungered for the human dainties which were no longer his to slaver over.

She had had a great victory, but not a complete one— Kels Zalkri yet lived, and still had not paid the terrible price his befouling of her world demanded. A crack had been left, one Kels Zalkri would find and would burst through to seek revenge. She'd be waiting—and then he would see who was the more merciless.

She gave thought to the future and gave a grim smile. If she won, those gods and near-gods who had allied with Kels Zalkri would feel her wrath. They had made their choice: now they would regret it.

27

SOMETHING wet and slimy crawled over Sandy's face. He shuddered and feebly tried to brush it away, but it evaded his aimless pawings. With a faint curse he sat up—to discover that he was staring up into the huge toothy maw of a beast.

Sandy was frozen with shock for a moment, until he recognized the fearsome teeth: they belonged to Glupp. His heart dropped out of his throat to where it belonged. Just then the grundzar gave him another affectionate swipe with its tongue.

"Damn you." Sandy tried to push him away. Halfheartedly, Glupp tried to sneak in another sloppy lick, but at Sandy's hard look he let himself be browbeaten into giving up, a woebegone look in his eyes.

Sandy tried to get up, but his legs felt as though they were made of loose rubber. Glupp nuzzled him concernedly and Sandy took the hint and grabbed the beast's loose hide, letting Glupp help him to his feet. Leaning against the beast for support, he looked around.

The mountain was gone.

He had trouble believing his eyes: something that gigantic doesn't just disappear. He closed them, shook his head, and looked again. The view didn't change: that enormous chunk of rock had vanished as though it had never been. Remaining were scattered heaps of rubble; and a thick layer of dust covered everything. All in all it was an enormous amount of debris, but not even a tiny fraction of what it should have been, if the mountain exploded. Uskban had been right. Kels Zalkri's citadel had come from hell, and to hell it must have returned.

He looked again at the devastation, then at Glupp, and said, "How did you survive? That explosion should have de-

stroyed you and everything else." The grundzar listened
quietly, unconcerned with Sandy's worries. *I'm here and
that's all I care about,* his manner seemed to say. A thought
struck Sandy and he asked in a troubled voice, "For that
matter, how did I survive?" He looked around at the destruction for a third time and shook his head in puzzlement.

For a moment he wondered whether he was still on Zarathandra—but in the distance he caught sight of the hills
called Admith's Knuckles. The sight of those barren knobs of
rock made him none too happy. He was beginning to suspect
that magic could be a lot more dangerous than any atom
bomb.

Feeling his strength returning, Sandy released his hold on
Glupp and tried a few wobbly steps. He felt as weak as a
new-born baby, but otherwise seemed all right. He stepped
on a sharp stone, swore, and for the first time noticed he was
stark naked. He turned toward Glupp, intending to see what
he could find in his packs, when he suddenly switched his
eyes back to his body. He looked, and his stomach did a
flip-flop.

Sandy's mind whirled. His body was now perfect, without
a nick or bruise on it—not even the scar he'd had on his
right knee since his seventh birthday. Considering what he
had been through, he should have been a well-battered
wreck. A sudden shiver brought on by the cool morning
breeze interrupted his train of thought. He shivered again
and decided he had better find something to cover himself
with. His questions he pushed to the back of his mind,
though they still nagged at him.

He looked around for Glupp, who had wandered off, and
saw him rooting through the dust and debris looking for
munchables. Walking gingerly, he managed to catch up with
the slow-moving browser. He rummaged through the gear on
the grundzar's back, noticing it was as undamaged as the
beast and himself.

As he looked for some usable clothes, he tried to recall
what had happened after the altar exploded. His bits of
memory didn't make sense, and they faded away as he tried
to bring them into focus. He shrugged and decided to save
his thinking for later, when he had food in his belly and was
better able to face this new terror.

In the packs Sandy found a pair of rope-soled sandals that
with a bit of adjustment fit him rather well. He donned an

old robe, threadbare and patched-up but still wearable, and found that having some clothes did wonders for his confidence. It was hard to be daring and self-confident without a stitch on.

The jerked meat and water that Glupp carried were most welcome. Until he saw them, Sandy hadn't realized how hungry and thirsty he was—as though he had been on short rations for an eternity instead of just a day. The thought made him turn and look at the sun so low in the east. *Where has the night gone?* he wondered.

As he was wolfing down his food, he thought he heard a voice. It spoke again, and he recognized it. There was no mistaking Zhadnoboth's querulous tones.

The sound drifted over from behind an enormous heap of rubble which lay to his left. Sandy sprang to his feet and beelined toward it. He had a few bones to pick with that old conniver.

Sandy was too impatient to find a way around the rubble, and he started climbing up and over the loose and sliding stuff. Glupp, who had followed him, gave a disgusted snort and then ambled off to find the easy way to the other side.

From the top, Sandy could see a large rocky depression. It looked like a treasure cave with its top ripped off. The shattered remains of large chests were scattered among the glint of gold, silver, and gems.

In the middle of the former treasure cave sat Uskban, staring morosely at the ground from his perch atop a small boulder. Pognak stood at his shoulder, protecting him and glowering at the sorcerer, who was yelling at the top of his voice and shaking an angry fist at them.

Sandy shivered involuntarily. He'd expected to find Zhadnoboth, but not the other two. It was eerie enough that he himself escaped unhurt, but for his companions to do it also was stretching luck too far.

A sudden warmth banished his misgivings. Here were his companions, alive and as cross-grained as ever. It was good to be among friends again, especially with all that treasure to share.

"You crack-brained numbskulls," ranted Zhadnoboth. "What did you think you were doing? I spent years scheming how to steal the Zalkring treasures! I rooted out information we needed, and nearly killed myself bringing a demon to

Zarathandra! And what do I get? This!" He swung his arm at the desolation surrounding them.

"We came for treasure, not to be heroes nor to destroy Zalkrings and scatter their treasure from high heaven to the far hells. Am I supposed to be satisfied with the paltry scraps that remain? A couple of drunken scum from the gutters of Darzan Og Rith could have done better than you two."

Uskban looked at the sorcerer with tired, tormented eyes. "*You* came for treasure, old man, not I. I came for vengeance, to exact blood for blood, pain for pain. You don't understand that—your soul is small and your heart is stone. I could squeeze you dry and only get vinegar! *Take* your damned treasure—it's small use to me. It can't quench the fire in my gut or return to me what I have lost."

The madman gazed with despairing eyes at the desolation and said bitterly, "I've had my revenge and it was sweet— but it wasn't enough. It blots no memories and soothes no pain." He gave a half sob and added, "Still, it is something." Agonizing memories welled up from where he had buried them and he shrieked, "May they know the torments of hell forever! They tortured my sisters and made me watch—and they laughed as if it were a jest."

Uskban shook his fist at the sky. "Why must I live and still suffer? Damn me, but give me more revenge to ease my agony." His head sank down to his chest in a kind of defeat and he stared hopelessly at the ground.

Zhadnoboth looked at him with openmouthed disbelief for a moment, and then stalked off, muttering under his breath. Soon the disgruntled sorcerer was poking through the rubbish littering the ground. He quickly found gold and other valuables and began gibbering happily and hopping here and there, picking choice baubles out of the rubble.

Sandy was just about to clamber down from his perch when he saw the sorcerer stiffen. Like a bird dog, Zhadnoboth pointed his nose toward a black abyss that plunged into the earth. Excitedly he scampered over and bent to pick something up.

A fiery cloud exploded from the abyss and knocked him over. As Zhadnoboth staggered to his feet, a magnificent and terrible figure stepped from the dispersing cloud: a Zalkring priest of the first circle, robed in all his finery. His red silk caftan was embroidered with cabalistic signs in black thread which detailed all the names and appellations of Kels

Zalkri. His waist was belted with a wide girdle of braided human hair, lustrously black and interwoven with filaments of gold and dotted with myriad tiny rubies. Around his neck was a wide collar of small gold links, meshed together in the manner of mail armor—every third link in each direction was threaded through a ruby bead.

Here was one of the greats among the Zalkrings—maybe the greatest. His eyes were filled with a holy rage that bordered on madness and his voice as he spoke had the sound of doom in it.

"Cringe, blasphemers, for now you shall pay for your crimes. When my most holy lord returns, I will offer your souls to him. Then you shall know what it is to be damned."

The priest raised his staff, carved from the night-black wood of the dragonclaw tree and shaped in the semblance of a serpent, and pointed it at the sorcerer. The dumbfounded Zhadnoboth hastily tried to counter with a protective spell— but was too late. A shadow flowed from the end of the priest's staff and enveloped the sorcerer. To Sandy it looked like a giant leech had wrapped itself around him and was trying to suck out his life. The shadow grew tighter and the sorcerer disappeared from view.

A flash of lightning—then an explosion forced away the shadow. Zhadnoboth was just too cantankerous an old bastard to succumb so easily. The shadow kept flowing from the priest's staff and again surrounded the sorcerer, but couldn't quite touch him as Zhadnoboth by sheer stubbornness held it at bay . . . but gradually the shadow crept closer.

It was clear that, in time, the Zalkring's relentless attack would destroy Zhadnoboth.

Uskban yelled a bloodcurdling challenge, full of hate and renewed purpose, and charged the Zalkring, sword in one hand and his talisman in the other. As he fell upon the priest, the iron key burst into life, burning with its terrible blue light. Its rays struck the amorphous cloud surrounding Zhadnoboth and shriveled it to nothingness.

The sorcerer, freed from the onslaught, staggered backward and fell to his knees.

Uskban slashed with his sword at the priest who deftly batted it away with his staff. The madman kept on attacking. While the Zalkring was busy countering the sword, the blue light streaming from the talisman wore down his magical defenses. Soon the staff was smoking hot, and each parry made the heat and smoke wax greater, until the priest's hand began to blister where it touched wood.

In desperation, the Zalkring clawed left-handed at a snakeskin pouch hanging from his belt. He plunged his hand inside and withdrew a fistful of dull yellow powder—Telemarek's famous dust of oblivion—which he threw at Uskban. An evil-looking cloud enveloped the madman as the powder got into his lungs and eyes. Retching violently and staring sightlessly, Uskban staggered back. The blue light from his talisman faded to a pale glow.

Like a snake, the priest attacked. Uskban was in a bad way, but he was too stubborn to give up. Still retching, he struck out blindly with his sword.

Unnerved—never before had the dust of oblivion failed to completely disable an opponent—the priest risked all and threw his staff like a spear at Uskban, hoping to blast him to smithereens with the energy trapped in it.

At that moment Pognak charged forward to save his friend. Moving with the speed and power of a striking hawk, the giant's sword lashed out and through the priest's staff. There was a blinding flash of light and a thunderous explosion as all the magical energy stored within the staff was released in a split second of time.

The mute's sword fell to the ground as hissing white-hot drops of molten metal. A firestorm engulfed Pognak and moments later a black and smoking cinder fell to the earth.

The explosion blew Uskban backward, blistered his hands and face, and charred his clothes. By sheer willpower the madman staggered to his feet and returned to his attack. He reeled toward the priest, still blinded by the powder, but with the talisman drawing him toward the Zalkring. He stumbled against the smoking corpse of his friend and fell down. The stench of burned flesh filled his nostrils and blindly he reached over and felt the object he had tripped over. Suddenly he realized what it was he touched and he screamed as if his heart had been torn from him.

His grief poured power into the talisman and its blue light blazed again. The energy radiating from the talisman purged the poison from his body and he could see again the charred thing which had been his friend. With an agonized howl he charged the priest.

The priest had been badly injured when the explosion smashed him against a boulder, but displaying an uncanny vitality, he managed to get back on his feet to face Uskban. The madman was too fast for him, and his sword caught the Zalkring in the gut and then through the lungs. The priest collapsed, but this was not enough for Uskban who in a frenzy kept hacking and slashing, spilling the priest's entrails on the dusty ground.

Finally, his fury spent, an exhausted Uskban stepped back and glared hatefully at his fallen foe. Triumphantly he raised his sword and gave a howl of victory. Then he hung his head and wept bitterly.

At his feet, the Zalkring refused to die. Slowly, moving with painful, jerky motions, the priest's left hand crawled toward the belt of human hairs which had been severed by one of Uskban's wild strokes. When the hand touched the belt and grabbed hold of it, a shudder went through the priest's body. He forced himself to his knees as he tapped some hidden store of energy through the human hair belt.

The Zalkring pointed his free hand at Uskban and began to invoke a spell. His dying lips and tongue fought him and he stumbled over a word. Stubbornly the priest started over.

Finally, the painfully spoken words penetrated Uskban's grief. He stopped his wailing and looked down at the unnaturally alive thing. The sight of the creature—entrails spilling from its belly but still spouting words—roused Uskban to a new killing frenzy. His sword impaled the Zalkring, splitting his heart and coming to stand a handbreadth out of his back.

The priest groaned, losing the thread of his spell, then he began it again, refusing to die. The little madman screamed his hate and spat in the priest's face, but the words of doom kept coming. Spying the top half of the priest's staff on the ground, Uskban snatched it up and rammed it down the Zalkring's throat. This stopped the spellcasting, but not the priest, who tried to crawl toward Uskban.

Suddenly Uskban opened his left hand as if it pained him. A brilliant flash of blue light shot from his amulet, struck the priest's human hair belt, and clung to it. The power in the belt resisted for a moment as the blue light sizzled on its surface; then the belt disintegrated, leaving only bits of gray ash and small blobs of gold behind. The blue flame from the iron key now swept across the priest's body, making it shrivel to almost nothing.

Silently Uskban stared with empty eyes at the mummylike thing at his feet. A much shaken Zhadnoboth tottered over to his side. "The books said their arch priest was old," the sorcerer said, "but they never said he had died a long time ago." His eye caught sight of the key which had dropped from Uskban's hand. He reached down to pick it up, but a grip of steel about his wrist stopped him.

"That is mine," Uskban said in a cold and forceful voice.

Zhadnoboth quickly backed off, frightened by the madman's tone. Evidently he recognized the talisman for what it was and just as evidently realized to grab for it would only buy him death.

Uskban reached down, picked up the talisman by its silver chain, and put it back around his neck. For a moment his chest was exposed and showed a key-shaped burn where Sandy had pressed against the talisman when he'd been trying to revive Uskban. The madman walked over to the body of his friend. Bleak and silent, he stared for a moment at it. Two tears welled up from the corners of his eyes and dribbled down his cheeks.

The sorcerer watched and then gave an angry shake of his head. "Bah," he muttered, "why cry over death? The dead are dead and the living must go on about the business of life."

Dismissing Uskban from his mind, Zhadnoboth looked about to see if there was anything nearby worth scavenging. Something caught his eye and he scurried over to where the Zalkring had jumped him. He scrabbled around in the rubble and came up with a ring. He blew the dust off, rubbed it against his robe, and then looked at it with gloating eyes— until it was snatched from his hand.

Zhadnoboth spun about angrily—to face Sandy. The shock turned the sorcerer dead white; he looked as if he were seeing a ghost, and a particularly nasty one at that.

"What's biting you?" Sandy snapped. "Your conscience? Are you worried I'll treat you fairly—by wringing your scrawny neck?" He pointed angrily to Pognak's body and the wreckage surrounding them. "Damn you," he said bitterly. "If you were halfway decent either as a sorcerer or a human being, none of this would have happened." His words were much more than unfair, but he was in no mood to be charitable. As far as Sandy was concerned, the sorcerer got them into this and therefore everything was his fault.

Zhadnoboth stared at Sandy in bug-eyed silence, too shocked to defend himself, though he was making a rapid recovery from his initial terror at Sandy's reappearance. He had seen too many uncanny things in his life for even this to scare him for long.

Sandy twirled the ring about and then slid it onto the little finger of his left hand. It was just a plain silver band set with an emerald hardly the size of a grape seed. It didn't seem much of a prize, but he meant to keep it just to irritate the sorcerer.

Zhadnoboth screamed, "Give it here!" Jumping forward, he tried to yank the ring off Sandy's finger, but it wouldn't budge. It was stuck to the finger as though it were welded on.

With a great show of patience, Sandy peeled the clutching hand away and gave the sorcerer a push backward. "I am keeping the ring as part of my share of the treasure," he said emphatically. "If that doesn't sit well with you, I'll break your neck and you can happily count your treasures on your way to hell."

"It's the Ring of Uncertainty! It's priceless," Zhadnoboth protested. He saw Sandy get even more steely-eyed and he quickly backed down. "Keep it. I'll find other things of even greater value," he said hastily, but his tone was not happy. He looked like the man who was forced to drink gall and vinegar and say he liked it. A glint in his eye hinted at trouble in the future.

"When do I get back home?" Sandy said suddenly.

Zhadnoboth gave a guilty jerk and began to hem and haw. "I don't know. Later, of course—after I have looked at my spellbooks." He cleared his throat and said, rather unconvincingly, "It should be easy."

Sandy gave him a disgusted look. "By God, you don't know. Talk about incompetents." He did a slow burn and then said, "We had a bargain and you better keep it—or else!"

The "or else" shook Zhadnoboth up, knowing what he now knew about Sandy, and he replied unsteadily, "I got you here, so I should be able to get you back."

Sandy shook his head slowly and disgustedly. He'd believe it when it happened—it was beginning to look like this self-important nincompoop had stranded him in this back end of nowhere forever.

Sandy pointed to the desolation surrounding them and asked, "What caused this?"

"Who knows?" the sorcerer replied peevishly. "You idiots destroyed the altar, and that was the link which tied the mountain to this world. With it gone, the mountain returned to hell where it belonged. As to what happened between the destruction of the altar and when I got here, I doubt even the Goddess knows all that occurred—the return of the mountain to hell unleashed forces which rearranged the balances between mortal worlds and the nether world." He paused and added sourly, "There is no justice in this world. You idiots destroyed the mountain and most of the treasure, yet Pognak and Uskban came through the holocaust almost unscathed. You should have robbed the Zalkrings first and then thought about destroying them."

"And so much the better if we destroyed ourselves as well," replied Sandy, saying aloud what he thought the sorcerer left unsaid. Zhadnoboth sputtered a protest but Sandy ignored him. Jerking his thumb toward Pognak's body, he continued, "Still, you lucked out, sorcerer. Now there is one less to share the booty with."

"His death was not my fault," Zhadnoboth protested. "If the Zalkrings' chief priest had been less of a sinner he'd have been destroyed with the rest of them. Instead he must have skulked somewhere when he should have been at the altar. It's a fine thing when dead men are as untrustworthy as the living." Zhadnoboth paused to regain wind and continued, "Besides, Pognak was a fool. One does not pit steel against magic."

"If he had been wise, you would not be here now," retorted Sandy. "Only fools achieve the impossible, because they can dream." He stopped and looked at the sorcerer as though seeing him in a new light. He added in a thoughtful voice, "And aren't you the same kind of fool, old man? Nobody ever robbed the Zalkrings and got away with it. Yet you dreamed of doing it, and so you did what should have been impossible."

Zhadnoboth, insulted, retorted, "I was in this for gold, not some stupid dream. Dreams are for addle-headed romantics and children. I didn't moon about wishing I had the Zalkrings' treasure! Instead I spent years learning all there was to know about them. I went to many strange and far places, some of which would have made this hellhole seem like paradise, in order to gain the knowledge needed to triumph over them. And it was all for something solid and real: their treasure, and the power it would give."

Sandy gave a wry smile and shook his head in disagreement. "As I said, old man, you had a dream and made it come true."

Zhadnoboth refused to reply. Instead he peevishly turned his back and stomped off to resume his treasure hunting through the rubble. "I should have thrown that demon back the moment I hooked him," the sorcerer muttered to himself. "I knew he was a bad catch—though never *how* bad until this morning. There are magics and there are magics, and a wise sorcerer backs off when he finds he is dealing with a major demon." He paused to pick up a jeweled pin dating back to the Carthanic Hegemony. "The dead should stay dead."

Sandy watched Zhadnoboth go and then turned and headed in Uskban's direction. He was feeling good—there had been something really enjoyable about getting the sorcerer's goat—but sobered as he approached Uskban. The madman was standing by his friend's body, silently grieving, his suffering so intense that it made the day seem sunless. Sandy touched him gently on the shoulder and said, "It's time to go."

Uskban shook off his hand and looked up. "Go," he croaked. "Leave me to my grief."

Sandy tried to reason with him. "The dead are dead; let's get on with life."

Uskban snarled, "What do you know of life and death? You haven't lived hard enough or fierce enough to understand either one. Nor can you really know friendship." He pointed down to Pognak's charred remains and continued more quietly, "Friendship isn't liking a person, it's something more. He was sullen and unlovable, but no less a man or friend for all of that. He stood by me when I needed him. What more could one ask of a friend? Now he is dead and I must sorrow alone." A blackness welled up within him and he fell silent.

Sandy thought over Uskban's words for a moment. "I thought I hated that big bastard's guts, but now that he is gone I miss his orneriness. Somehow, despite the bad blood between us, we had a kind of understanding. It's like I've lost part of myself. He was not a friend I would have chosen, but does anyone ever choose a true friend?"

Uskban gave a half nod as though he comprehended Sandy's confused feelings.

For a minute or so Sandy joined the madman in his silence. Then he shook off the black mood and looked around, taking stock of their situation. After a moment's thought he realized he would have to take charge: Neither a conniving and impractical sorcerer nor a grief-stricken madman was fit for the job. He grimaced, then set out to do what was necessary.

"Let's take care of Pognak's body before the vultures do." Sandy pointed to a couple of black shapes circling overhead. Uskban glanced at the sky, then nodded.

They built a funeral pyre from various odds and ends of wood lying about—there were plenty of broken beams, smashed furniture, and the splintered remains of treasure chests to choose from. When the pyre was chest high, they picked up the mute's charred body and placed it atop. Uskban carefully crossed Pognak's arms across his chest, then he trussed up the mummylike body of the Zalkring priest and put it at the dead giant's feet. "Now he will have a dog to accompany him as he walks the paths of the dead," Uskban said with black humor.

Sandy stood back and watched while the madman went through the simple funeral ceremonies. First, Uskban placed himself to the east of the funeral pyre, the same direction Pognak's head was pointing. Then he lit a torch and slowly marched to the pyre and set it in place by his friend's head. In a low mournful voice he chanted an ancient funeral dirge of his people. Sandy did not know the religious convictions or the traditions behind the ceremony, but Uskban's deep-felt passion gave it a sublime beauty.

When he was finished, Uskban stepped forward and reverently picked up the torch. Holding it level in front of him, he chanted, "Of earth, wind, rain, and fire are we made, and to them we return."

As he was about to light the pyre, a roar exploded from the desert behind him: a bone-chilling sound, like that which chases you across the dark wastes in your nightmares. Uskban and Sandy whirled to face it. Outlined against the black gloom covering the eastern sky was a gigantic swirling pillar of darkness, blacker than night and yet throbbing with flame. It was retribution come straight from hell to get them.

It was Kels Zalkri.

Sandy stared in openmouthed horror, his feet frozen in their tracks.

Uskban's nerve broke. He dropped his torch, fell to his knees, and began to shriek. The sight of the god unleashed the horrors which had haunted his soul for years, overcoming even his hatred. Now fear had seemingly destroyed the last shreds of humanity within him.

"Over here, you fool demon!" screamed the sorcerer. Roused from his terrified stupor, Sandy turned and looked at Zhadnoboth who, white and shaking, was frantically motioning for Sandy to join him. "Hurry, you damned lamebrain! We must be gone before that thing fully materializes in this world or we are doomed."

Not waiting to see whether Sandy obeyed, the sorcerer, began rummaging through the packs strapped to Glupp, who had earlier been appropriated by Zhadnoboth to help carry treasure. Zhadnoboth went through the gear piled high on the grundzar's back like a cyclone, tossing unwanted equipment right and left until he found what he was looking for, an oiled rope made from braided rawhide. He threw the rope into the air, rapidly mouthing a levitation spell. The rope started to fall, but suddenly stiffened and hung stationary in midair. As more words of enchantment were uttered it formed itself into a great circle, a man and a half high.

Zhadnoboth stopped his spellwork long enough to wipe the sweat off his brow with the back of his hand. Then he snapped his fingers and a white spark leaped off them and bit into the rope. The oily rawhide sputtered and smoked briefly but the flame went out. Zhadnoboth swore and tried again.

This time the spark took hold. Soon a line of crackling orange fire was working its way rapidly around the circumference of the rawhide circle. When the flame touched its beginning, the orange-red fire became blindingly intense. Fiery streamers jumped across the center of the circle in confused and sinuous patterns that formed a kaleidoscope of orange flame and greasy white smoke.

Sandy was entranced by the weirdly beautiful sight until a stray breeze blew some of the smoke at him. Coughing, he backed away. The burning rope's stench smelled like the worst possible combination of sulfur and rancid skunk.

Sandy's reddened eyes opened wide in surprise: the area inside the burning rope had in a split instant become a portal to another place. Through it he could see a land nothing like the desert and devastation which surrounded them, a land filled with tall, feathery trees and buildings of white marble. He could hear the soft, sweet calls of birds and the gently murmuring of brooks as they traveled down from low hills. The air which wafted from the portal was redolent with the spicy perfume of flowers and the aroma of new-mown hay. Sandy yearned for it as he had never yearned for anything in his life.

Zhadnoboth saw him standing back and gawking. "Come!" he snapped. "We have little time." The sorcerer tugged on Glupp's halter, trying to get him to the magical gateway. But the huge beast ambled along at his own pace: not even the sight of Kels Zalkri looming monstrously against the eastern horizon could make him quicken his gait.

The wall between Zarathandra and the outer bounds of hell split apart for one brief instant with a thunderous blast that shook Zarathandra to its foundations—

In that instant Kels Zalkri came through.

Galvanized by a wave of terror, Sandy pelted toward the sorcerer and safety. He did not need to look to know that the vengeful god was now in this world. He was almost to the portal when he skidded to a stop and looked back. Uskban was still on his knees, staring in horror at the doom fast approaching him. "Come here, you stupid bastard!" Sandy screamed.

Uskban didn't move.

Sandy turned to the sorcerer and yelled, "Wait! I have to get him."

"Leave that crack-brained dunce!" the sorcerer screeched. "You have no time. The rope is almost burnt through."

Sandy hesitated for a moment, cursed, and started racing toward the madman.

Zhadnoboth watched, startled, aghast at such utter foolhardiness. Grumbling in disgust he headed for the portal, stopped, and turned to yell back at Sandy, "Remember your name—it has power." To himself he muttered, "And may the Goddess be with you." He yanked on Glupp's halter, trying to hurry the grundzar toward the gateway, but Glupp looked at Sandy's retreating figure and balked.

After a moment of thought, the great beast laid down to wait for Sandy's return. Cursing, Zhadnoboth tried to drag him back to his feet, but neither words nor force could budge him.

The earth shuddered, knocking Zhadnoboth down. Hurriedly the sorcerer scrambled up and began digging through the packs on the grundzar's back at a furious rate—stuffing as many treasures as he could into the extra-dimensional pockets of his robe. His sharp ears heard a change in the sizzling noise the burning rope was making, and he dropped everything and sprinted for the gateway. An instant after he had plunged through the portal, what was left of the rope burned away and the gateway disappeared with a sudden intense flare of light. All that remained was a few specks of gray ash slowly drifting to the ground.

Sandy was trying to drag Uskban away by brute force. It was as much use as trying to move a solid block of granite. "Damn you!" swore Sandy. "Get moving or you're dead."

"Death," Uskban murmured dully. Then something— maybe his madness or maybe an unquenchable spark in him —burned away the terror which had paralyzed him. With a laugh he shook his fist at the god. "Aye, black one, it's death: your death and my peace."

He gave a wiggle and slipped from Sandy's grasp, snatched up the guttering torch at his feet, and ran eagerly toward the indistinct and fearsome shape which now blacked out the whole east.

Sandy screamed at Uskban to come back, but his words were drowned by the roar coming from the swirling vortex surrounding Kels Zalkri. Muttering a few choice obscenities, Sandy plunged after the little madman. He didn't stop to think that he might be throwing away his life for a man he didn't particularly approve of. He just knew a friend, crazy and cross-grained as they come, was in trouble and needed to be rescued.

28

THE Goddess gave a fierce smile. The hour had come for her final showdown with Kels Zalkri. This throw of the dice would determine whether she or he would rule Zarathandra.

Kels Zalkri had been lured into leaving the safety of his corner of hell and was coming to fight her on her home ground. This time the dark one would not be able to freely draw minions and power from his hell. The destruction of the altar had closed the portal he had forged between Zarathandra and the lands of hell a thousand years ago.

Now Kels Zalkri would pay dearly for his overweening pride and for his crimes. He was weaker than he had been a thousand years ago and she was stronger, with weapons to hand she had not had at their first encounter.

The Goddess meditated for a moment, called her full power to her, and went to battle.

29

Running full tilt, Sandy stumbled over some rubble and went sprawling. Cursing, he scrambled back to his feet and looked for the harebrained madman. He saw Kels Zalkri in all his horrifying majesty and knew fear as he had never know it before.

The dark god was immense, blocking out the entire sky in front of him and all the ground beneath. Though Sandy could see the god, he could not quite glimpse his true shape, only a series of shifting images.

What he *could* see was soul-shattering enough: Kels Zalkri loomed against the sky like an enormous black pillar, swirling with hurricane force and sending out stormy tentacles to claw the world apart. His blackness was an intense darkness shot through with streaks of unearthly colors and at the same time a great unseeable emptiness. The immense strands of uncolor seemed like great talons inset with myriad eyes flickering with hellfire.

Sandy was terrified, but he doggedly searched for Uskban. Finally he spotted him perched atop a small hillock, defiantly facing the angry god. Holding the torch in one hand and his sword in the other, Uskban howled like a rabid wolf and shook his puny weapons. All his fear had been burned away, and only hate and courage remained.

A roar exploded from Kels Zalkri. Uskban's amulet flamed into life, surrounding him in a halo of blue-white light. Kels Zalkri retaliated with a crescendo of lightning bolts, huge jagged things which screamed through the air. On and on the barrage continued, bouncing off the shield protecting Uskban to scour and flay the ground about him. Soon the whole area was a blackened, bubbling mess of tortured earth—but Uskban stood unscathed.

227

Apparently galled beyond any bearing, the god shook the world with his anger. Probably never, in a lifetime so long it was beyond the comprehension of mortal beings, had Kels Zalkri been made such a fool of by such a puny being.

Gigantic masses of the god swirled like a tidal wave toward Uskban. They smashed into the madman with titanic force, reducing the hillock to fine rubble. But Uskban was unharmed—the sphere of blue fire protecting him grew bright as a sun. Streamers of azure light reached out and sundered the black and stormlike limbs hammering at Uskban. Smoking and shredded pieces of the god fell to the ground, each fragment eating craters into the earth. Uskban laughed and shook his weapons tauntingly.

The immense evil which was Kels Zalkri swirled about Uskban in maddened frustration, its black masses pressing him close but not assaulting him. Uskban stopped laughing with a great howl and attacked the god. He lashed out with his torch, trying to burn the unearthly substance of Kels Zalkri, but it guttered and went out. Uskban gave an obscene curse and tossed the dead torch away, resuming his attack with his sword. Slashing savagely at the dark masses around him, he tried to sever the demonic sinews. His blade bit into the swirling chaos of Kels Zalkri, but it was like trying to slice water.

The sword turned white with hoarfrost as it slid through the unearthly body of the god. With supernatural swiftness the cold traveled down the sword and froze the hand holding it. Uskban screamed, yet still faced the fearsome god in unreasoning defiance.

Kels Zalkri drew back and for that instant the area about Uskban became absolutely calm. The god pulled his substance together until he resembled a gigantic writhing snake, miles wide and stretching to the heavens. Then he struck, his immense head and body roaring down from the sky with such a speed that he seemed only an immense dark blur.

In that moment Uskban disappeared in a tremendous explosion. Rock, dust, and debris went flying in all directions; mixed in were black swirling gobbets torn from the vortex which was Kels Zalkri.

By instinct more than reason Sandy dove for cover behind a large boulder. All hell and earth ripped through the air about him, but left him unscathed except for minor scratches. After the storm had passed he sprang to his feet and looked around for what was left of the madman.

Amazingly, Uskban still lived. The field of force protecting him had crumpled under the god's savage onslaught, but had held together long enough to save his life. The iron key had been torn from around his neck, his frozen right hand had shattered into icy fragments, and he himself was knocked flat; but his spirit hadn't even been dented.

Stubbornly Uskban picked himself up and looked for his talisman. The stump he had left as a right hand didn't seem to bother him. The intense cold had sealed off the arteries so it didn't bleed, and either because of the cold or because of his madness he seemed to feel no pain.

The key lay a few yards from him, its glow flickering and dimming now that physical contact with his life force had been broken. Uskban reeled toward it.

Just as he grabbed for the talisman, Kels Zalkri pounced. Sinuous tentacles of unearthly flesh picked him up and shook him the way a terrier does a rat, then tossed him aside. Stubbornly Uskban got up and staggered back toward the talisman.

With infinite cruelty, the god played with him, attacking just as Uskban tried for his talisman; each time the god savaged him and threw him aside. Battered, bleeding, the madman persisted.

Sandy watched the drama in horrified fascination. Uskban's struggle was senseless and crazy, but at the same time grand: he had been transfigured from a sullen madman to a doomed hero, from mortal flesh to the stuff of myth. The more the little bastard refused to bend to the black god's will, the more Sandy felt a pride in his humanity.

Finally, Kels Zalkri tired of this game and started a new one. He snatched Uskban up and tossed him into the sky, grabbed him again and dashed him to the ground. Uskban hit hard, but not hard enough to die or even to lose consciousness—Kels Zalkri was never that careless with those he wished to torment.

Like an enormous leech smelling blood, the swirling darkness hovered over Uskban. For a moment the god seemed to gloat. Writhing tentacles formed and came down to envelop Uskban. The little man screamed in agony and horror as a ripple went through the darkness surrounding him.

Sandy's sixth sense at that moment waxed strong. He felt the god's infinite and abominable delight in slowly savoring and absorbing an atom of Uskban's life force.

Sandy shuddered, feeling desecrated and befouled by the thoughts he had inadvertently picked up. He screamed an obscenity at Kels Zalkri and charged for the talisman. A cold fire ate into his hand as he picked it up—and for the first time the god seemed aware of him, as though until now he had been invisible to it.

The black winds spun faster, and the god roared with world-shaking anger, made all the greater by a germ of doubt. Floods of malevolence poured from him, and Sandy went cold with fear. He clutched convulsively at the talisman, instinctively seeking its protection. It bit at his fingers and he threw it to Uskban, knowing only the madman could use it rightly.

The talisman flew like a live thing to Uskban's good left hand. As it touched his flesh, the fierce blue light sprang from it and tore into Kels Zalkri's substance. The winds roared louder, but with a high-pitched keening that spoke of inhuman agony.

Simultaneously a beam of white flame shot from behind Sandy and into the god's turbulent substance. It set fire to Kels Zalkri's hellborn flesh, burning out great swathes as it slashed into him.

The dark god fought back, even as his hurricane winds howled their anguish. Tremendous bolts struck at Uskban and whatever was behind Sandy.

The earth bucked and heaved: Sandy was knocked down and clung desperately to it through the convulsions. Something came flying and hit him a glancing blow on the head—he lost consciousness for a moment. By the time he got his wits back together, things had settled down a little.

Kels Zalkri was making the fight of his life, his black substance a maelstrom which lashed at his enemies. To one side Uskban was on his knees, holding the iron key aloft with his only hand. The talisman, powered by Uskban's defiance, was radiating an unceasing stream of blue fire, visibly eroding the god's substance and making his winds howl louder.

Off to one side, veiled by a shimmering field of energy, was a slim, menacing figure—an opponent even more fell than the enraged madman. This foe savaged Kels Zalkri with lashing streams of white energy, each searing bolt annihilating great masses of his intangible flesh.

But Kels Zalkri was far from defeated. Against his enormous size, the damage from his enemies seemed mere scratches. Given time they might be able to reduce him to nothingness, but they didn't have the time. The flame from the talisman was weakening noticeably, as Uskban's unnatural vitality was sapped by approaching death—a death which should have taken him long before. And the energy field around the veiled figure was being squeezed smaller and smaller by the black god's onslaught. It could only be minutes before Uskban would breathe his last and Kels Zalkri turn his full fury on his remaining foe.

Sandy had a sudden vision, a scene out of Hieronymus Bosch. He saw a hellish landscape: a place of twisted earth, of leprous vegetation which rotted as it grew, and of dim red light from a dying sun. Across this landscape men and demons fought, tortured, raped, maimed, and abased one another during gluttonous orgies of sex and food.

Humans danced on a red-hot grill as a demon, with one head and upper body, two lower bodies, and three arms to a side, kept the fire hot with a bellows and simultaneously raped two women and assaulted another with a barbed tongue. Elsewhere a group of ragged humans had pinned an eagle-headed demon to the ground with skewers and diverted a stream of fiery lava over him as they laughed hysterically. In a roofless and ruined building scuttling crab-shaped demons stuffed screaming humans twelve to the barrel and pickled them in brine. On a bed of spikes a many-breasted demon ripped a man's lungs out with her talons while she copulated with him. Through this nightmare landscape strode Kels Zalkri, clothed in darkness, with his head touching the sky and each of his thousand legs greater than a mountain. As he walked his feet stomped into jelly friend, foe, henchman, and victim indiscriminately; while mile-long tentacles lashed out in every direction to seize living food. This world was his and all worshipped him, all feared him, and all fed him.

The vision vanished as abruptly as it had come and Sandy shuddered violently. He didn't know whether it was real or imaginary, what was or would be, a stray thought of the black god or a sending from one who hated him; but whatever it was, he wanted no more of it.

Sandy looked at the merciless battle taking place in front of him and with a start realized he could flee and save his life if he so chose. It might be hours before the dark god overcame his final opponent; by that time Sandy could be long gone from this hellish place. He almost obeyed the thought —until with a fierce rage, he realized there was a cold alien *feel* to the thought. Instead, filled with revulsion at this invasion, he lifted his head and yelled his defiance.

Sandy seethed with angry frustration, knowing his only weapons—teeth and hands—were worse than useless. Zhadnoboth's parting words came to him and unlocked a door in his mind. He remembered something from the chaos which followed the destruction of the black mountain.

He was in an immense room and in front of him was a stand holding a large book bound in reddish brown, pebbled leather. As he watched, the book opened itself to a page written in gold runes. In his mind he heard a voice reading aloud the passage written there—Zhadnoboth's voice.

Once and only once is a name of power first said and made real. Beware when such names are spoken, for even a lesser name can unleash forces capable of destroying the mightiest of sorcerers. When a great name of power is spoken, there will be unleashed power which can shake worlds and universes. Never again will the name have such immense and uncontrollable power. Once established and made real a name is limited and bound by cosmic law; each name has its province and only that. But for that first brief moment, it can make anything happen—it can destroy worlds and create them, or reshape destiny into new forms.

The vision faded, but Sandy knew what he had to do. He stood tall and hurled his only weapon: his name.

Sandy bellowed it out at the top of his lungs, every last syllable of it—and there was a lot to say. *Alexander* (for the conqueror, who had been idealized by his father) *Archibald* (for an ancestor who had died fighting at Killiecrankie) *Llewellyn* (in honor of his mother's mother) *Warwick* (for the charming scoundrel who had been his maternal grandfather) *Thorvaldsen* (in remembrance of his other grandmother) and finally *MacGregor* (the proud surname inherited from a brother of Rob Roy).

Sandy spoke his name as he understood it on Earth, but in the speaking now knew its different and deeper meaning to Zarathandra—a meaning which spoke of the mysteries of this world and their intimate connection to who and what the

Goddess was. The fabric of space and time trembled in reso-
nance to the syllables he spoke. The last syllable left his lips
and there was a cosmic stillness.

Then the name, given reality by being spoken, exploded
like a sun going supernova. It ripped apart the fabric of Zarathandra, remaking its connections with the universe over
and over again as it continually rewove the iron threads of
destiny. The area around Sandy was engulfed in a holocaust
where a million million destinies were, and then were not.
Elsewhere subtle tremors shook the reality that was Zarathandra, but only a few beings knew enough to understand,
and fear. Rivers ran uphill, rain turned to wine, people disappeared and others found themselves twinned, trees
marched, and cheese soup changed to brandy punch. Most
people marveled, scratched their heads, and went on with
the business of living.

At the eye of this world-storm everything was slopped
into the pot of possibilities, split asunder, recombined—over
and over again. There was music which tasted like butter-
scotch; howling screeches of color smelling of mint and sas-
safras; light which tasted like salted herring; and a blackness
with the feel of sandpaper. Strange textures, tastes, smells,
sounds, and sights were sensed in odd and mysterious ways.
All that was became jumbled together in a weird mishmash
of what could have been—a dazzling experience.

What was became what wasn't. The next instant it was
again—or maybe something—or many things—else. *Here*
and *there* were at the same time opposite, identical, and totally unrelated to each other. In the narrow precincts close to
Sandy, eternity was turned inside out and constantly resorted
and reshaped.

One thing asserted itself against the maddening chaos:
Kels Zalkri. By the power of his immense will he held his
dark substance together. He raged, screamed, and lashed at
the interdimensional storm that tried to tear him apart. But
the dark god, enormous and terrible as he was, was no match
for the power unleashed by Sandy's name. Kels Zalkri fought
like a being possessed, contesting every change and obstinately trying to make the storm of destiny bow to his will. For a
time, he seemed to succeed; then the chaos ripped him to
shreds. For an instant he saw what awaited him beyond his
annihilation and knew despair—

And then there was no Kels Zalkri.

Sandy rode the storm like a feather in the wind, going with every eddy and riptide and thus enduring as himself. Then he was caught between the backlash from the destruction of Kels Zalkri and the raging currents of destiny. He felt fire, utter cold, the distinctness of every atom from any other atom, a total oneness with the universe, what was, and what would be. The maelstrom ripped him to fragments and then to less than atoms—he screamed though he had no voice. His body, his essence, his being, were annihilated and the residue flung to the far corners of the universe. For timeless moments nothing; and then he was whole again, though now much more than human.

30

FOR a thousand years the Goddess had awaited this moment. Yet even for her it was a time of travail. She did not fight the universe's raw power as had Kels Zalkri, but waited and endured. She was the Seven Times Seven: the goddess with seven natures and seven aspects to each nature. She became that part of her which was most fitted to survive—Kels Romakil, she who waits and conquers.

Eventually a balance was struck and Zarathandra settled back into normalcy, not much different than it had been before. She emerged with it, transformed yet unscathed, exultant that her full primacy had been restored. The malignant intruder from the lower darkness would never again try to wrest her heritage from her. The Goddess smiled grimly, remembering Kels Zalkri's despair when he realized his last moment was upon him.

She stretched her shapely limbs and rejoiced in the ecstasy of warm blood once again surging through her veins. It had been a very long time since she had been both goddess and living flesh. Now she could be mother, wench, and bawd as she had not been in centuries—and there was a lot of loving to savor and revel in. Zarathandra and its people would have such a year of passion and fecundity as would be remembered for generations.

The Goddess thought of Zarathandra and her heart grew large. It was a fine world, and would get better as she helped to heal its wounds. How she loved its inhabitants despite their faults and foibles—not that they didn't need to feel her anger on occasion. Let them have their wars and squabbles so they could grow wise in their own way and at their own pace—there was time and more for all their follies.

The Goddess had to but seal the final bond with Sandy to

achieve the fullness of her new power. However, her supremacy was flawed. This new power was a product of a secret bond between them and by rights as much his as hers. As a man she approved of him, but as an equal—never. He must know his place and know hers; even then it would be irksome that she would not have total and unchallengeable control.

Still, there were compensations. She smiled. Since she had him, she was going to use him to the full and then some. The road ahead would be hard, but interesting and enjoyable between the rough spots.

31

ONE instant Sandy was struggling against unknown demons in a nightmare and the next he was fully conscious. He found himself standing amid a scene of utter devastation: the land had been torn, twisted, and turned inside out. Here and there he could see the ruddy glare of cooling lava, mixed with wisps of colored steams and the fumes of burning brimstone. Jets of burning gases, the flames weirdly hued in greens and purples, shot from scattered fumaroles and rents in the ground. Off to his left the earth gave a cough and spit out hot cinders and molten drops of glass. Covering the entire landscape like a death shroud was a blanket of fine dust the color of old concrete.

Only the sky was pure and undefiled. It had become wonderfully clear, yet tinged with that rich blue-black it sometimes gets just before sundown.

Sandy rubbed his temples. In a tumbling rush his memories came back—up to and including the destruction of Kels Zalkri. He frowned, dissatisfied, feeling that other and important memories lurked just beyond his grasp—something he must know but which his subconscious had thoroughly repressed.

Sandy shivered, then realized he was naked again. Peevishly he wondered why his clothes kept getting destroyed when he came through without a scratch. Then he shivered again, in fear: by all rights he should be dead, or at least looking like something the dog dragged home. Instead he was alive and, except for a slight headache, felt in as fine a fettle as he had ever been. It was more than strange.

Thoughtfully he picked up some dirt and let it slowly sift through his fingers. Dirt it had been and dirt it was still. Men and maybe even gods would die, but no doubt the dirt would still be around when the last star was a burned-out cinder.

He spotted a bluish flicker out of the corner of his eye. He turned and for a moment the breath caught in his throat. A short distance away lay Uskban's broken body. Painfully Sandy limped over the broken ground toward him, muttering curses at the sharp rocks biting into the soles of his feet.

The body lay on its back, the iron key glowing softly in the outstretched left hand. He stared in anguish at what was left of Uskban. He would miss the crazy bastard. He'd had real grit in his craw and had been honorable in a bloodthirsty way—and was as close to a friend as Sandy had made in this world. No! He *was* a friend. Sandy had liked him in spite of his madness and in spite of not wanting to. There would not be another like him.

Sandy reached down to pick up the key but recoiled when he touched it and felt a weird, agonizing shock go through him.

The madman's eyes slowly opened. Apparently the talisman in some mysterious way kept a spark of life glowing within him, for Uskban should have been long dead.

There was a pleading look, almost a demand, in Uskban's eyes. After a moment that seemed forever, he painfully looked at the iron key in his outstretched hand.

Sandy, his sixth sense stronger than it had ever been, knew what was being asked. He reached down and touched the talisman again. A voice traveled from the key, through his arm, and into his mind.

Take the key and keep it safe. When the time comes, and you will know it, give the talisman to my son. Until that time I name you the key's guardian. For a moment the voice in his mind failed. Then, very faintly, it said, *Let me die now, friend.*

With a heavy heart, Sandy nodded. Gently he tried to ease the key out of Uskban's hand. It stuck to Uskban's hand as though reluctant to change masters. Sandy pried, staggering backward when the key came loose all of a sudden. A shuddering sigh escaped from Uskban's body and he was finally at peace in death.

Sandy saw the fine chain that had held the key lying beside Uskban. He picked it up, put the key on it, repaired the silver links as best he could, and placed it around his neck. There was a faint burning sensation where it touched his skin.

Reverently Sandy stooped and picked up the madman's small body. He looked around for a likely place to bury it and saw with some surprise that the pyre bearing Pognak's body was still standing, undamaged amid all the destruction. It was strange, especially since Sandy had a nagging suspicion it hadn't been there a few minutes before. Nevertheless he carried Uskban's body over and placed it by his friend. What was one more unexplainable event compared to what had already gone on.

A huge pile of rocky debris near him exploded with a cloud of gray dust and a clatter of stone as the creature buried beneath surged forward to get to Sandy. His heart left his throat when he saw the fearsome, grinning maw of Glupp emerge from the dust cloud—the grundzar seemed no worse for wear. Gurgling and woofing happily, he waddled over to Sandy and caught him with a loving *whoosh* of the tongue.

"Damn you," Sandy whispered as he threw his arms around Glupp's head and gave it a hug.

Sandy quickly routed through the packs still on the big beast's back. He found a lot of treasure and not much in the way of clothing. The sorcerer must have struck it rich in his scavenging and discarded supplies whose space could be better utilized by gold. He did find an old robe of Zhadnoboth's and some blankets. The robe was too small, but was a lot better than nothing. Out of one of the blankets he improvised some crude footwear.

Practical matters taken care of, Sandy returned to the pyre and prepared it for the cremation rites. After heaping it with as much wood as he could find, he said a short informal prayer. "Go now, friends, and may your goddess give you the happiness that was never yours as mortals." He set the pyre aflame and stepped back to watch. It made a magnificent spectacle, framed against the black of the desert night and the white glory of the stars.

For a moment Sandy yearned for the familiar comforts of his own world and wondered if he had much of a future. Now he was probably stuck in this damned world forever. Not that it was that bad, it just wasn't home. Still, Zarathandra wasn't all that different from Earth, physically. A lot of the plants and animals looked to be closely related to Earth stock. Somewhere in the past there had been a tie of some sort, he was sure. This desert could be deadly, but with Glupp's help and the supplies he carried, Sandy should survive.

He lifted a leather flask of wine—another useful item found in Glupp's packs—and took a healthy slug. For an hour or more Sandy solemnly watched the burning pyre, polishing off the wine and silently mourning his comrades. The wine chased away the chill of the night, but did little for the ache in his heart.

When Sandy finished the flask he dug out another one. He turned to the huge pile of glowing embers, all that remained of the pyre and his friends, and raised the flask in salute. Ceremoniously he poured two generous libations on the ground. "Have a drink, you bastards," he croaked. "You two were worth a dozen ordinary men, even if there be few as foul-tempered as either of you. The world of Zarathandra will remember your courage and your deeds—for I will tell them—and forget your flaws. That's as it should be, because a hero is no less a hero for being human." Sandy raised his flask high and drank deeply in honor of his friends.

"Well spoken, man." It was a woman's voice, rich and haunting like the call of a loon. A cold shiver ran up Sandy's spine. The shock he felt at being surprised was compounded by the primal dread that the voice raised within him.

Sandy turned slowly to face her. She was an awesome and eerie figure, tall and lean as a willow, and wrapped in a hooded robe the deep blue of midnight, but with a shimmering of moonlight threaded in. Of her features, he saw nothing but the dark shadows which cloaked them.

Tall, aloof, entrancing, mysterious, and above all powerful—she was also the coldness in the pit of his stomach and the way his skin prickled. Sandy had an idea who she was, and that suspicion caused him great discomfort.

She spoke again. "Your words had a fine ring to them, maybe better than those two deserved. They were, after all, only a bully and a madman." The implied scorn in her words broke the spell which held him in thrall.

"They were worth my words and more," he said passionately, anger and too much wine smothering his fear. "Bastards bleed the same as everybody else. And rough men can have as much worth as their softer kin. Even bullies and madmen can love and suffer. *You* should know that."

For a moment there was an ominous silence and Sandy could physically feel her icy stare raking him. "Yes, I know that," she said finally in a quiet voice which showed her displeasure toward what she considered insolence, but which had undertones of deeper and more subtle emotions. "They were hard men and bent, yet they had quality." The tone of her voice became less forgiving. "In some ways you are like them, flawed and yet of some worth. Therefore, I accept your allegiance to me."

Sandy had been getting less drunk by the second. Now she shocked him into sobriety. "Allegiance? Who said anything about that?"

"I did." There was a finality to her tone which said she would accept no refusal.

Sandy, deaf to what she left unsaid, retorted, "I'll be damned before I knuckle under to a high-handed bitch."

"Then be damned!" She raised her hand and pointed at him.

Sandy burst into white-hot flames and in an instant was nothing but pieces of floating ash.

The Veiled Goddess smiled triumphantly and held out her hand, this time with the palm up. An eddy formed, drawing ash to it until a pile two inches high formed on her palm. She blew on the ash and flung it away.

The ash swirled about in the air until it formed into the semblance of a man. The figure rapidly thickened, drawing substance from air and earth. First the stark outline of the bones could be seen, and in seconds muscle and sinews wrapped themselves about the skeleton. Finally, skin and hair appeared. It was Sandy. Uskban's talisman was around his neck, the silver chain now undamaged, and the Ring of Uncertainty was on his little finger. She blew air into his nostrils and the body began to breathe. Then she reached into the realms beyond, found his soul, and, touching him, returned it. Quickened to life, Sandy's eyes snapped open.

"Now, mortal, you know some of my power. You can be destroyed a million times, and a million times I can raise you from the dead. Four times already have you died and four times have I clothed you with new flesh. Your name binds you to me: it says who you are, who I am, and what we are together—it gives me power over you as I have over no other being. Serve me, and you shall have gifts as no mortal has ever had. Defy me, and I shall send you to eternal damnation."

Sandy now knew her power and knew fear as he never had before. He remembered the terrible pain as he burned like a torch and the horror of the death beyond. Terror made his heart pound like a jackhammer, but it didn't matter. He had known death and yet lived again. Anything else from now on would be an anticlimax—even death itself.

His death had changed him in a way the Goddess never intended. He was stronger because the threat of death could no longer cow him—it terrified him because of the agony of dying and bone-chilling horror of the beyond, but it was no longer unknown or permanent. He might not laugh at death, but he could laugh at those who threatened it.

Sandy smiled and thought wryly, *Now I can be the obstinate and bloody-minded bastard I've always wanted to be.* He was tired of being pushed around; now he had a chance to do some pushing of his own. He might even try to do what was right, if he could figure out what *right* was. The Goddess had to be a hell of a lot better then Kels Zalkri, but that did not make her an angel either—she might just be the lesser of two evils. Maybe, if he played his cards right, he might be able to finagle his way back to Earth and be able to forget about Zarathandra and its hair-raising problems. But, whatever, he was not going to be her yes-man—not when he didn't have to be.

"Worship me as your goddess, and become my servant," she commanded.

Her high-handed attitude raised Sandy's ire. He retorted, "Damn me if you will, but you still won't get me to bend my knee to you. You're a goddess, maybe, but not mine."

For long seconds they faced each other like two silent and unyielding stones. "You're a stiff-necked fool," she said. "I am supreme in Zarathandra—the last who could have challenged me is damned as only a god can be. Where can you flee to escape my wrath? Who can you seek refuge with?"

Sandy refused to be daunted. "If you are the supreme and omnipotent goddess you say you are, then justice must be one of your attributes. I demand justice. I was shanghaied to this world, and I did you a great service. Would it not be just to return me to my own world? And with some gain for my troubles besides experience."

"You demand?" she raged, nearly choking. "Nobody demands *anything* from me!"

Sandy backed down. "Okay, I *plead* with you to give me justice."

A black silence fell between them. Though Sandy

couldn't see her face, his sixth sense could feel her glowering at him. Finally, she spoke. "Now hear me, mortal. Your fate will be as you have chosen it. You shall have justice, even if what is just for you is not just for me or Zarathandra. Render me one service and you shall have your reward. I will send you from this world to where you belong."

Sandy looked at her suspiciously. He had a nasty hunch she was going to double-cross him. "It sounds fair," he replied. "But how do I know you'll send me back once I have done what you wanted?"

"I always speak the truth." Her enraged tone gave the impression he had mortally insulted her. "I am the goddess of truth and wisdom. I cannot lie."

Sandy reluctantly nodded, still not quite trusting her. Vaguely he sensed that he had some hold over her, though he had no idea how or what. He also had a shrewd idea that hold made his safety less certain. She was not a being who took kindly to having her will curbed.

"Then it is agreed." And the Goddess began to scrutinize him carefully, as if he were a stud bull or prize porker. Involuntarily Sandy reddened from toes to the tips of his ears as he realized he was once again naked, except for the ring and the key amulet. The Goddess gave no outward sign she noticed the blush. Sandy cursed her inwardly, gritted his teeth, and tried to appear nonchalantly nude.

Having seen what she wanted, the Goddess turned and walked over to Glupp. She seemed another woman with the big beast, kinder and warmly loving, as she stroked the grundzar's head. Pure bliss on his ugly face, Glupp rubbed affectionately against her. "He is a good beast," she said dotingly, "wiser than many men. It was through his eyes that I kept watch over you and your companions."

Sandy gave the spy an accusing look. Glupp hung his head as if he were abashed. But looking at the beast brought back painful memories. "What of Uskban and Pognak?" he asked. "They deserved the most and got the least."

"They would tell you death was a cheap price to pay. They helped destroy an evil which blighted their lives and their world. There was nothing for them in life. In death they will have peace."

"It was still a poor reward, not that either wanted to do a grand deed or save Zarathandra—they wanted revenge." He paused and added, "Maybe fame will do, though I doubt they wanted that either."

She said in a sure voice, "They have their rewards. And it doesn't matter how petty their reasons for doing what they did—and there were other, nobler, reasons mixed in with the petty—what matters is they did a great thing."

Sandy nodded grudgingly, then smiled wryly and asked, "Whatever happened to that old scoundrel Zhadnoboth? I owe him something—either a good swift kick or my thanks. I'm not quite sure which. I miss that testy old codger."

"He's surviving quite well," she said in an impassive voice that somehow managed to give a smile to her words. "Though, as usual, he has already managed to bring trouble down on his head."

The Goddess pointed to Sandy's left and a beam of soft white light came from her fingertip and drew a circle ten feet in diameter—its bottom edge just touching the ground. Inside the circle the air shimmered; then a picture appeared within. It showed Zhadnoboth scuttling down the back alleys of some far city, nervously looking back over his shoulder every few seconds. His scraggly gray beard was singed, and his robe was torn and stained.

Sandy grinned. Knowing Zhadnoboth, he figured the old scoundrel must have been caught trying to hornswoggle someone.

The Goddess snapped her fingers, and the circle disappeared. In its place was a large gray tent striped in black. "There is food, drink, and a bed inside," she said abruptly. Then she faded from view, becoming first a shadow, then a shimmering array of motes, until finally she was not there at all.

Sandy wasted only a few minutes in wondering what was up with her before he shrugged and started walking toward the tent. Who could ever comprehend the ways of goddesses?

Glupp came waddling after him. Sandy turned and gave him a halfhearted glare but the big beast ignored it and rubbed against him affectionately, almost knocking him over.

"Don't butter me up," growled Sandy. Such a heartbroken expression appeared on the creature's face that, in spite of himself, Sandy had to smile. "All right, secret agent, I forgive you."

Glupp rumbled happily and flopped down in front of the

tent, refusing to let Sandy enter until he had paid the toll: a good scratching on the back and behind the ears.

Finally Sandy lifted the entrance flap of the tent. The Goddess had done very well by him. The small room off the entry was luxurious, in a rough-and-ready way: the walls were covered with rugs in rich tones showing scenes from an enchanted forest with wondrous beasts hiding in feathery grass or peering from behind jeweled trees. The floor was thick with rugs patterned in geometric designs and with ankle-deep piles. A brazier of hammered brass was filled with glowing embers which warmed the room and colored the air with a pleasant rosiness. Sitting off to one side was a large copper tub with steaming water, surrounded by a tumbled heap of clean towels. Sandy headed right for it, and sighed with pleasure as he got into the tub. He'd almost forgotten what a pleasure a good soaking could be.

Half an hour later, feeling like a new man, Sandy went into the next room. This was the main part of the tent, as large as two ordinary living rooms. Silver lanterns hung from hooks near the tops of the tent poles, illuminating the room with a moon-silver glow. Again the floor was covered with several layers of richly woven carpets. Scattered along the walls of the tent were chests of tooled leather.

Curious, Sandy began snooping into the contents of these chests. The first two contained pewter dishes and various pieces of riding gear. The third was more rewarding: it contained items of clothing. Sandy found a robe which took his fancy. Woven of blue-gray silk, it had a fire-breathing dragon embroidered on the back and two griffins challenging each other on the front. He put it on and felt rich; the touch of silk against his skin was sensuous and oddly calming. This feeling alone was almost reward enough for what he had gone through. Maybe serving the Goddess wouldn't be such a bad idea after all.

At the far end of the tent was a large, low bed, big enough to hold ten people. Seeing it, he realized how tired he was. Right now he felt he could dive into it and sleep for days. As he got closer he saw it was made from alternating layers of silk pillows and deep-piled rugs—first a rug then a layer of pillows, and so on. On top was a feather-down mattress covered by silk sheets and quilted silk blankets. It was like no bed he'd ever seen before, but it looked inviting.

Beside the bed was a low table made from a yellow-orange wood which glowed like a summer sunset. Atop it was a tray of engraved silver holding a decanter of rose-colored alabaster and ten matching cups. He pulled the stopper from the decanter and a deliciously spicy aroma drifted out. It brought back memories of summers spent at his grandparent's farm, of summer evenings spent in meadows redolent of honeysuckle and sun-dried hay.

"The wine is sacred to me in my aspect as goddess of love and passion. It is a rare vintage, well worth the trying. Few who drink it forget its savor."

The Goddess's reappearance startled Sandy, and he wondered what she wanted now.

She still wore a hooded robe, but this one was of form-fitting silk the color of wild roses. For the first time Sandy realized how tall and slim she was. He was a good six feet tall and yet she towered over him by nearly two inches. Her waist was as narrow as a schoolgirl's yet her breasts and hips were those of a full-figured woman, if the silk covering them didn't lie—and there wasn't much to lie with. Almost he could catch a glimpse of her features, but the shadow inside her hood veiled her face.

The force of her presence was enormous—a potent mixture of physical size, power, self-assurance, and an unearthly allure intermingled with raw sensuality. Sandy was nearly overwhelmed, simultaneously wanting to shake in his boots and go into high rut. He cursed inwardly, knowing she was deliberately tantalizing him, and deeply suspicious of this change in behavior. He wished she'd revert to being bitchy; it would be a lot easier to stand up to her.

"Do I meet your approval?"

Sandy reddened like a schoolboy caught peeking and then said irately, "Yes, you do." As soon as the words left his mouth Sandy knew he'd said the wrong thing.

She shrugged gracefully and her robe opened and began sliding down her body, slowly and tantalizingly. The breath caught in his throat and his eyes couldn't tear themselves away from what was being unveiled.

Her well-rounded body and features were divinely perfect, at least to Sandy's shamelessly appreciative eyes: silky hair as black as a moonless night flowed against skin like new ivory but as soft as thistledown; breasts like young mountains, the brownish pink nipples jutting high with excitement.

Sandy blushed deeply when his eyes became fixed on her

loins, reacting more like a bashful teenager than a somewhat experienced lecher. She opened her legs slightly, glorying in her nakedness and her womanhood. She managed to be both wanton and regal.

"Do you think me desirable, man?" she asked softly. Then, with the lanquid grace of a tiger, she sidled close to him. She took his unresisting right hand and placed it on the warm flesh of her breast, gently using his fingers to caress herself; then she moved his hand down her soft flesh toward the inside of her thighs.

Sandy pulled his hand away and backed off, highly aroused but suddenly skittish. He didn't know what bothered him more—being intimate with a stranger, or her so unashamedly spoiling for action. He'd always preferred to know and be comfortable with a woman before taking her to bed—and a little dawdling tenderness as they both joyfully worked themselves up to it was better.

The Goddess was stalking him with a sensuous rolling walk that showed off her sexual charms to full advantage. She rubbed her breasts up against him and stroked the hair on the back of his head. Nervously Sandy tried to back away, but she held him with gentle firm hands and nudged him tenderly with slight thrusts of the pelvis.

By a supreme effort of will, Sandy broke her hold. "Stop the vamping! Damn you!" Sweat was heavy on his brow as he barely held his raging passion in check.

The Goddess looked witheringly at him. "Are you a man," she demanded, "or a man-child afraid to know a woman?"

Lust was burning like volcanic fire inside Sandy. "No!" His voice was shaky. She was pushing too hard. If she had gone a little more slowly, as was more congenial to him, she'd have swept him off his feet and onto her. Now, even through his arousal, he knew there was something unnatural about her sudden passion.

But the Goddess was insulted by his resistance. "Am I not comely enough for you, man? Don't you want a woman to lust for your embrace? Or are you one of those who prefer their woman cold as ice . . . or are men your choice . . . ? More likely, you fear love."

Her anger was like a cold wind, chilling the passion she had aroused and letting him start to think rationally again.

"Call it by its right name, slut," he said. "And I am as

lecherous as the next man, but I don't want to be steamrollered into it."

"For one who is no better than he should be, you are awfully finicky," she retorted.

"Why me?" Sandy asked. "What have I got that is special?"

When the Goddess spoke there was an angry undertone in her voice. "Let us talk, mortal." She pointed to the alabaster decanter. "Pour us each a cupful; it will make us forget our anger."

Sandy carefully poured them each a generous portion of the wine. He did it with a certain ceremony, glad of the time it gave him to mull things over. Something about this situation was not quite right. He was certain only that her power over him had limits.

The Goddess raised her alabaster cup, sipped the wine, and smiled. "Try some," she suggested good-naturedly.

Encouraged, Sandy took a small sip, and then a large swallow as he found he liked it—a very enjoyable wine, slightly sweet but with an indefinable tang to it. It warmed him pleasantly, from his stomach to his veins and then into every cell in his being. He felt alive and vibrant, yet deliciously relaxed.

"When you spoke your name," the Goddess said, "it did many things and the destruction of Kels Zalkri was only one of these. Your name, in the most ancient and sacred language of Zarathandra, tells both who you are and the nature of the intimate relationship between you and me."

Sandy desperately wanted to know again what he had known the moment he had spoken his name. For an instant he was sure he'd known what his name meant and who the Goddess was, or so it seemed to him—somewhere or somehow he had lost that knowledge. "What is the connection?"

"Now is not the time for that," the Goddess replied, and went on with what she wanted him to know. "Because of this connection, a great magic was worked the moment you said your name aloud. It reknit sinews which the dark one had destroyed long ago, and I was reborn in the flesh. Now I am both flesh and spirit, with the full powers and appetites of both." She paused, smiled enigmatically, and added, "With your help, I can gain an even greater level of power. There is a magic which only a man and a woman can work together. With it, I can mingle the power which is inherent in your name with the power that is in me. This magic I will work whether you will or no." These last words were spoken in a quiet but very emphatic voice.

Sandy listened, but in a mellow and unsuspicious mood, lulled by her pleasantness and the insidious intoxication produced by the wine. He refilled his cup while eyeing her. Her quiet sexuality was doing a lot more to raise his lust than her hard-sell brazenness had.

"One thing is needed to seal the bond between us." The Goddess gave a slight emphasis to these last words, but Sandy was too entranced to notice. Her fingers caressed him, sending sensuous vibrations through every fiber of his being. One of her fingers brushed lightly against his robe and it became a live thing which slithered off him and to the ground. Dreamily Sandy realized that the warmth from the wine, enhanced by her overwhelming sensuality, had settled in his loins.

Gently the Goddess drew him to her, warming his flesh with her inner fire. "There is magic in sex," she murmured. "A magic which makes both lovers become a part of something greater."

She rubbed her nipples gently against him. Sandy responded in kind, raging passion burying his doubts. He put his lips to hers, and they kissed long and deeply, before sinking to the bed. Their lovemaking was a joyous war of many hard-fought engagements.

Sandy awoke in the small hours of the morning, pleasantly exhausted and rather confused. For a moment he didn't know where he was or what he was doing here. Then foggy memories started to return. He sat up with a start and looked at the bed beside him. There was nobody there. Had it been some wild imagining?

"So you are finally awake." Her words had a steel-edged sharpness. Sandy looked up and saw she was robed again, this time in the black of doom and damnation.

"No mortal may see me and live: So was it pronounced in the time of the ancients. You have seen my face; you must suffer the consequence—even if you are now more than merely mortal."

The Goddess paused to let her words sink in before she went on. "You knew me as a woman and not as the Goddess

I am. This is sacrilege, punishable as rape under the ancient laws of Zarathandra."

She paused again in order to give greater emphasis to her words. "Thirdly, you abrogated power which is mine and which you still hold. This I cannot permit. I do not share my power. And I can only regain full control of my power when you are dead."

She paused. This time the silence was long and full of menace. Finally she said, in a voice full of her power and pride, "I pronounce this doom on you: You shall wander the netherworlds until such time as I have need of you and you have learned respect for my godhead—the time will be long or short depending on how quickly you learn my place and yours."

Sandy jumped out of bed, steaming. "Do your worst, bitch!" he yelled. "But by God there'll be a reckoning— even if I have to fight my way through a thousand hells to get to you. Sin, my foot! You're damning me for being inconvenient."

Provoked by his unbending stubbornness, the Goddess smote him with her anger. In an instant his mortal body was torn to atoms and his soul flung into the netherworlds.

32

SANDY ran and he ran, knowing not what he was fleeing. Slowly fragments of memory came back; soon he could remember who he was. The recollection stopped him dead in his tracks. Determinedly he faced back toward the direction he had come from, holy anger in his heart.

He was in the middle of an immense marshy plain, not his idea of hell though it was scary enough. The reeds and grasses covering the boggy ground were livid light green; but they wriggled and rippled more like rooted worms than any kind of plant. Here and there haggard trees—their wood half rotted and black with fungus—dotted the plain like ghouls who had been rooted in place.

A thick mist shrouded the land, making more horrific the creatures in this land he did catch a glimpse of. He saw a herd of beasts, looking like long gray sausages mounted on thin rubbery legs, grazing on vegetation which either sought to flee or fought back with barbs and thorny teeth. But the sausage-beasts fled as an immense slime-green worm plowed through the muck, gobbling up truckloads of mud and vegetation—as well as any creature unwary enough not to get out of its way. A thing with a tubular red body the size of an elephant, its head just a large toothy maw surrounded by eight clawed arms, erupted from the ground and tore great strips of flesh from the worm. As the predator gorged itself, its victim went on with its own feeding, unaware it had even been attacked.

With an eerie howl, a whitish monster that looked like a furry haystack burst out of the mist. It rushed by Sandy, gibbering manically and bleeding a green ichor from many savage wounds. There was another howl, and a pack of black hounds the size of bulls raced by. These misshapen beasts

251

glowed with a faint phosphorescence, their huge saber-teeth covered with yellow slaver and the green blood of their prey. They raced by Sandy, dead eyes glaring.

A powerful, echoing howl, drowning out the cries of lesser beasts like thunder does the moan of the wind, reverberated through the mist-shrouded landscape—the howl of a wolf. The howl turned Sandy's blood cold and he shuddered violently. The shadowy image of a slavering nightmare-sized beast flashed through his mind, and he remembered fleeing for an eternity—gibbering in terror—from the wolf. Fear clutched at his heart with icy talons, but he forced himself to turn and await the thing. He would flee no more.

A deathly hush surrounded Sandy. Over the musty stench of decaying vegetation, he could smell a bestial fetor which made him want to gag. He peered apprehensively through the dark fog and could almost glimpse the huge beast cautiously circling him, its low growl like the roll of distant thunder.

Sandy kept turning to face the hunting wolf—fear kept him alert to its changing position. Eventually it stopped its circling and stalked cautiously out of the mists. At first all Sandy could see was its enormous eyes: larger across than the breadth of his hand and burning like the heart of fire. Next he noticed bone-white fangs, as long as his forearm and dagger-sharp. At last he saw the whole beast: eight feet tall at the shoulder and as burly as two bulls. Green hellfire danced and flickered through its black coat. It was a creature out of myth, a nightmare from the dark wastes which lurk in the human soul.

A vague memory stirred in his mind and he heard a demonic voice chanting in glee. "Fornvorak the Devourer is he. Through the netherworlds he stalks, hunting the souls of dreamers. Upon them he shall feed until he has grown mighty enough to break through the barriers separating the underworlds from mortal realms. Then he shall ravage the worlds and devour their suns, and so shall come the end of time." There was a fiendish snicker and the voice added, "For now he shall harry and savage you to the ends of hell."

The immense eyes of the wolf glared balefully at Sandy. There was no fear or pity in them, only bloodlust. Still, the beast was wary, seemingly unsettled by prey which faced him instead of fleeing.

With no warning, the huge creature flung itself at Sandy.

His teeth shredded Sandy's fragile soul, but as fast as it was torn apart it reknit itself. Sandy howled in both pain and a kind of exultation—knowing he was truly in hell, and no longer mortal flesh. The bitch had damned him, but—either because of the power in his name or because all souls are immortal—he could not be destroyed. Sandy flung himself at the great wolf in a blood-mad rage and tried to strangle it with his bare hands.

For hours they fought, neither able to do permanent damage to the other. Fornvorak had much the better of it, his spirit-body larger and better armed, though Sandy got in his licks. The wolf disemboweled Sandy a thousand times and more, tore him limb for limb almost as often, and ripped his ghostly flesh to bloody ribbons innumerable times. Still Sandy fought on. He had his small victories, once tearing out Fornvorak's left eye and several times breaking bones, but only his will and his indestructibility kept him in the fight.

As time went on, the frustration of being able to rend his foes to pieces and yet unable to destroy him drove Fornvorak into a frenzy. He foamed at the mouth as he frantically began to rip apart the battleground as well as Sandy.

Sandy was as frustrated as the wolf. His spirit-flesh didn't have the iron thews which would allow him to strangle his foe by main force. All he could do was annoy the beast, and once in a while grab a leg and break it—but the wolf's flesh reknit as fast as his own. Stubbornly Sandy refused to admit defeat.

Fornvorak ripped Sandy's throat open for the thousandth or more time and for the thousandth or more time Sandy's flesh made itself whole. Sandy felt a fire burning into his chest and looked down. There, around his neck, still on its silver chain was Uskban's talisman—somehow the thing was as real in hell as in the mortal world; it had come here with him when the Goddess had destroyed his earthly flesh.

With sudden inspiration, Sandy grabbed the key and once again sprang at the great wolf. It ripped open his face, blinding Sandy for an instant, but though Fornvorak tore his flesh, Sandy persisted, and finally managed to loop the silver chain around the beast's neck. The chain had seemed too small to encircle the wolf's neck, but the amulet's power and Sandy's will had enlarged each link until the chain was large enough to garrote the creature.

Slowly and mercilessly Sandy tightened the chain until it

cut a deep bloody line into the flesh of the beast. Fornvorak fought on tearing savage wounds into Sandy's arm and neck with his fangs, and time and again ripping out his entrails with the claws of his hind feet. Sandy screamed and sobbed his agony, but refused to let up. After what seemed hours, he became aware the wolf was starting to weaken. The great beast was not alive as mortals know life, but the talisman was slowly sapping its enormous strength. To Sandy's aroused sixth sense it felt like a white-hot flood being drawn into a bottomless pit.

The wolf's great eyes bulged and the fire within them grew dim. Its black coat became dull gray, and fiery blood now flowed from a wound which would not heal. Fornvorak tried one last convulsive attack before he collapsed with a shudder to the ground. Because Sandy refused to let go of the chain he was thrown down also. But his triumph quickly faded, for the body was rapidly dissolving into a gray mist. Sandy prepared to fight again, but the gray mist did not re-form itself into the bizarre wolf. Instead it turned and fled.

Sandy held the talisman high. "I'm coming for you, Goddess," he yelled. "Somehow—some way—I'll find my way from this hell and back to you."

He found her even sooner than he had hoped. It seemed his victory over the wolf had broken the power of the divine curse which had sent him to the netherworlds; and a few moments later he was back in mortal realms with the flesh re-forming on his bones. It was hard to say who was more surprised, the Goddess or Sandy.

The look of consternation on her face quickly changed to rage. In a blink of the eye, she snatched the talisman from his hand. "Now, man, you shall truly be damned," she said triumphantly. "Let's see you escape hell without this bauble. Go to your fellow demons." She raised a finger and pointed.

A torrent of coruscating energy poured out to engulf him —and missed. Sandy had leaped aside, determined to make her victory as tough as possible. Briefly he succeeded in evading her attack, then she caught him. For an instant the energy bit unsuccessfully at him, as though by sheer obstinacy he fought it off, then his new flesh was ash and he was hurled back into the netherworlds.

Sandy found himself afloat in a great ocean, its water as gray and greasy as the leaden sky. A mighty wave, seventy or more feet high, came from behind and crashed over him. He was buffeted, beaten, spun head over heels, and forced fathoms deep into the water. Desperately Sandy fought his way back to the surface. He broke through, coughing and gagging on the bitter seawater he'd swallowed—it tasted of sulfur and metal as well as salt. If he was dead, Sandy thought, why did he still have to feel agony. Hell, he was better off alive if this kept up.

Without warning, a monstrous worm-white tentacle, covered profusely with suckers and razor-sharp bone hooks, erupted from beneath the surface of the water and grabbed him. Tearing his flesh and cracking his ribs, it yanked him under. Deeper and deeper it pulled him, through the clear waters near the surface into the blue-green depths, down to where was the blue-black of ink, and then into the realm of utter darkness. Still he kept on going down. The water burned his lungs, but he still kept breathing despite the pain. Even while fear raged within him, a part of his mind tried to figure out why he had to breathe at all.

He came to rest in the muck that floored the deepest part of the ocean. Despite the utter blackness, he could see—not with his eyes, but with some alien sense which perceived in all directions at once. It was as if each cell of his spirit-body felt the form and texture of the world surrounding him, instead of sight with its colors. His perception saw the same forms, but such things as *grittiness* and *smoothness* now hued them instead of color.

In front of him, he perceived a large cave in the side of an underwater canyon. The two-foot-thick tentacle which was holding him came from the cave, but he couldn't see to what it was attached. All he could sense were four shiny, squishy eyes staring unfeelingly at him.

A hint of motion to his right caught Sandy's attention. A large school of oddly shaped fish was swimming rapidly in his direction. Their bodies were ordinary enough, four feet long and formed like that of a flattened moray eel. However, their heads were something else—two feet from top of head to bottom of jaw, most of it widely gaping mouth with saberlike teeth. A line of spots, the luminous green of graveyard mold, ran the length of their bodies.

The huge tentacle held him fast while the fish attacked, ripping away his spirit-flesh. His body tried to regenerate as fast as it was torn apart, but the fish in their frenzy ate his flesh faster than it could renew itself.

Sandy fought to break free from the tentacle's grip, but it was like trying to snap an iron cable. He could only move his head and hands a little. In desperation he tried to bite through the tentacle. It was like biting into stone—all his struggles were useless.

Until the little finger of his left hand touched the tentacle and the unnatural flesh quivered in pain. He looked and saw that the silver Ring of Uncertainty had come with him to this hell. The small emerald was gleaming with an angry glow. Sandy moved the ring until it touched the tentacle again: the creature's flesh blackened. Sandy wished he knew what the powers of the Ring of Uncertainty were.

Whatever else the ring might do, it was deadly to this creature. Grinning, Sandy attacked with gusto. Soon great patches of charred flesh were falling away as the ring's glow became a living fire. The monstrous section of tentacle wrapped around Sandy sizzled like a sparkler on the Fourth of July as the green fire attacked it, turning to ash and burning down to its core in seconds. Four more times the tentacle stubbornly rewrapped itself about Sandy and four more times he burned it away. Finally, the pain penetrated to its dull brain and the creature knew fear. Sandy heard a hideous scream—no less loud for being heard only in his mind.

What was left of the tentacle was whipped back into the cave. There, the creature in a frenzy of pain and insane terror attacked the stone walls sheltering it. The side of the canyon rumbled and shook, then collapsed in a catastrophic landslide which buried the cave and its occupant under thousands of tons of rock.

Yet the thing still *lived*. Sandy could hear its whimperings in his mind.

Sandy had been flung free and now was slowly floating upward. The predator fish still surrounded him, but the ring's blazing green light kept them at bay. They circled him warily, seeking an opening for attack. He felt weak; over half his spirit-flesh was in the bellies of the fishes.

As if something called them, the fish turned tail and fled in all directions. Sandy felt himself growing weaker as the parts of his soul they had devoured got farther away from him. He had to do something—he was so enfeebled by lack of soul that if he didn't regain what he had lost he might just fade into oblivion.

Anger at his fate blazed inside Sandy—and fueled the ring's sphere of radiant power. With his mind he called—willed—his spirit-flesh back. Soon every fish which had tasted of his soul was being dragged back to him as if by a magnet. They struggled and fought against the pull, but they came. As each fish touched the emerald radiance enclosing Sandy they were incinerated, and a precious bit of his substance returned to him.

When the last piece of his spiritual body rejoined him, Sandy was instantaneously transported back to mortal realms: to find himself facing the Goddess once again. She was just lowering the finger which had destroyed him. For a bare instant something like fear crossed her face, quickly replaced by unholy rage, and bafflement.

Sandy felt mightily aggrieved and was determined to let her know it. "What are you trying to do, you damned bitch? If anyone was sinned against, it was me."

The Goddess paid him no heed. She was determined to have her way and obliterate this obstinate blasphemer from the face of the universe. She raised her hand and a fiery sword appeared in it. Her stroke was like lightning, lopping off his little finger and the Ring of Uncertainty with it. "Now let's see you come back," she said maliciously, then smote him on the hip and the thigh with the fiery sword.

Again Sandy was hurled into a netherworld. He came flying out of the sky toward an immense forest which seemed to stretch forever in all directions. Like a meteor he smashed into the forest and then into the ground. The force of his landing splattered him over the landscape and he blacked out from the intense agony.

Moments later his spirit-flesh had reknit itself and he was looking around at his surroundings—feeling shaky, but more from mental shock than any harm done him by the impact. He could hardly see as the only light in the dark green surrounding him was what could filter through layer after layer of branches and leaves.

He was standing at the base of an immense tree which seemed at least a block wide. It shot up to gigantic heights, or at least it seemed to—he couldn't see far enough through the mass of leaves and branches overhead to be sure. On every side were other trees just as large or larger. They all had the same dull brown bark, knotted and furrowed with cracks as deep as his forearm. The leaves were leprous brown-green things, looking like hands with seven snaky fingers. Covering everything were massive strands of gray moss, scrubby entwined stuff which looked like hair of long dead corpses. Sandy gave an involuntary shiver. The trees seemed to be staring at him with hostile, hungry eyes.

The forest floor was a rotting mess of leaves and broken branches, with not a spot of color to show where some small flower had usurped a tiny domain for itself. Even worse was the almost utter silence: no sound of birds, no croaking of tree frogs, no chirping of crickets, no chattering of squirrels. Aside from the trees and their ghastly mantle of moss, the forest appeared empty.

Sandy stood and waited for something to happen. Nothing did. He waited for more interminable minutes; then, impatient, he shouted, "God damn it, do your worst." Still nothing—not even the quiver of a leaf. Disgusted, Sandy started walking, picking his direction at random.

He walked for an hour or more. There was so little difference from one part of the forest to another that it seemed he'd never moved. He was a city boy; all trees looked alike —and right now he never wanted to see another one. He could feel the trees glowering at him in their slow way. His sixth sense could feel their resentment at this intrusion into their world and anger at his freedom of motion. The air was oppressive, thick with moisture and the trees' hate.

He stopped, feeling weak and utterly washed out. He looked about dully, and that spark of obstinacy which was at his core flared into anger. He realized, then, that a very slow and insidious nibbling had worn away his soul: the trees had sucked away his essence little by little.

"Damn you," Sandy yelled at the trees. "You'll not get me." The trees ignored his protest and kept on with their slow, ghoulish feeding. Despite his stubborn determination, Sandy could feel himself getting weaker. And all he had to fight with was his obstinacy, no talisman or ring. But there was one thing she couldn't take from him, no matter how great her power.

Sandy raised his head and tried to shout his name. It came out as a weak and almost soundless whisper, but it sufficed. "Alexander Archibald Llewellyn Warwick Thorvaldsen Mac-Gregor!" With each name his voice grew stronger.

This time there were no spectacular effects, because now his name was broken-in and accounted for. In fact, nothing seemed to happen at first, except that Sandy's confidence in himself was renewed. But gradually the air beside him grew hazy and a figure began to appear: scattered motes coalesced into a body.

It was a very angry and disgruntled Goddess. Evidently the saying of his name had called her to him. Both were taken aback: the Goddess had not until now realized the power of the link between them, and Sandy had expected his name to deliver some devastating blow to destroy the forest and set him free.

"You fool!" she screamed in righteous anger. "What have you done?"

Sandy was wondering the same thing. There was a powerful, almost magnetic attraction between their two bodies. Their spirit-flesh drifted together and began to intermix, despite stubborn efforts by both of them to stop the process. His atoms drifted into the spaces between hers until they were one and yet separate. They were in intimate contact, but refused to know the other—though stray thoughts and feelings constantly drifted between them.

The Goddess, enraged, made titanic efforts to pull her soul free from his, but couldn't. Their connection was too strong to be broken by her efforts alone. A backwash from her power gave Sandy renewed strength. At the same time, he could feel his soul and substance being drained from him in an ever-increasing flood. He realized that the vampire strength of the trees had become enormous and their appetite ravenous now that they had fed on the Goddess and gained a portion of her power. When the Goddess noticed, she refused to endure it.

Her anger was like a fiery hurricane as she fought against the forest. She hurled bolts of power and curses which should have withered every demon-tree to its root. Sandy fought too, but not with her—his only weapons were a fierce defiance and sheer stubbornness.

The forest gloated at this rich food and never ceased its voracious feeding. Through his sixth sense, Sandy could catch glimpses of strange grandiose dreams: of unlimited and unstoppable gorging on the souls of demons and gods, of growing to fill all the worlds of hell and then the mortal worlds beyond, and of becoming the grandest and mightiest god of all and worshipping itself in sublime wonder.

At about the same time Sandy and the Goddess realized their efforts were in vain. If this kept up much longer they'd both be nothing but minute fragments of soul scattered through the immense substance of the demon-forest—they'd both cease to exist as separate individuals. Despite their mutual animosity, both now knew they must either fight together, or perish.

Tentatively they touched minds, struck a truce, and agreed to work in harness together—all done in an instant and without anything more than understanding being exchanged. Tentatively they meshed their minds together, both galled by the enforced intimacy, but they swiftly accommodated and began working as one. The Goddess was the head and sword arm; Sandy threw in his fierce obstinacy and maverick temperament. Together they were mighty, much more than the sum of two parts, a force which could fight the demon-forest.

The Goddess ravaged the forest with their combined might, searing it with bolts of energy, battering it with blows of divine anger, and ripping its soul force to tatters with talons of thought. While she fought, Sandy husbanded their strength and called back by sheer will that part of their souls which had been sucked from them by the forest.

The struggle was tooth and nail, with the foes in a virtual standoff. The demon-forest had grown powerful with its feeding—the same feeding that had weakened Sandy and the Goddess. The Goddess burned huge swatches in the forest, turning tree after tree into charred cinders. But the demon-forest was immense; the trees stubbornly endured the punishment and kept drinking in their energy and soul-matter.

The Goddess tried every tactic she could think of. She burned the forest in a thousand different ways, hit it with whirlwinds and hurricanes, froze it with the cold of deep space, released horde after horde of ravenous insects to devour it, and tore the ground with enormous earthquakes. The trees endured it all and kept on with their plodding but persistent attack.

For a day, a year, an eon it was a stalemate. Then the Goddess changed her ploy. From the beginning of time she called the fire of life, the primal stuff that first was and from which the universe and everything living was formed. She grabbed handfuls of this chaotic, turbulent energy and formed it into mighty javelins of blue-white fire. These she hurled in a monstrous and continuous cannonade at the demon-forest.

The barrage made from the essence of life struck the trees, which were made from the stuff of death, and annihilated the wood with a raging, all-consuming fire—a fire which would not go out. An incandescent firestorm roared at light speed from tree to tree: touching in one moment and moving on the next, leaving behind white ash and a rising pall of fiery smoke. The fire exploded outward until it soon engulfed the immense forest. The demon-trees fought to the last, stubbornly and stupidly ignoring their own destruction as they tried to drain all soul force from Sandy and the Goddess.

At last the trees were no more, and with nothing to feed its hunger the fire died. All that was left was a vast and desolate plain, covered several feet deep with ash and glowing embers—the air and the sky dirty with smoke, soot, and floating cinders: a lifeless hell.

The destruction of the demon-forest had sent a torrent of energy flowing into their spirit-bodies, as they regained the soul they had lost, plus the soul-energy which had been the forest's. It was too much for their unwillingly combined bodies to contain. All that extra energy now exploded: sundering the oneness Sandy's name had forced on them, blasting them back into mortal realms, and annihilating the netherworld they had been expelled from.

Sandy hit the soil of Zarathandra with a jolt, as new-formed flesh went skidding over the rough surface. He sat for a while and then gingerly picked himself up, elated. What the hell did he care about scrapes and bruises? He was mortal again, with warm blood in his veins.

Glancing around, he saw the Goddess. She too was naked, and for the first time she looked disheveled. Sandy drank in her innocent and lusty nakedness with an appreciative eye. She seemed nearly human. Sandy felt a warmth toward her until she gave him a steely glare.

With an annoyed gesture she conjured a new robe for herself. It was of somber blue and gray, matching her mood.

His good humor gone, Sandy stomped over to her and looked angrily into the shadowed hood which hid her face. "When do I get sent back to Earth, as you promised?"

"Never."

"What do you mean, *never*? You promised to send me to where I belonged."

The Goddess held up a hand and said ruefully, "I sent you where I thought you belonged. I was wrong. I misjudged the strength of the bond between us. By uttering your name, you forever bound your fate to me and to my world. We are in a sense one. Since I belong to Zarathandra, so too must you belong."

Sandy was furious. "You mean I am stuck with you forever? Now I know I am damned—tied to an ungrateful bitch who'll stomp on me every chance she gets."

The Goddess retorted, "What do you know of damnation, my demon friend? You have a small soul, a small mind, and a small heart."

"I am not a demon. And so what if I'm small in every way? You don't have to be big in order to get done dirty. I do the best I can. If that doesn't satisfy you, *too bad.*"

With a grudging smile she replied, "You are right, but that is neither here nor there. I am the supreme and unchallenged mistress of Zarathandra and it irks me to share even a bit of my power. Your name says you share this power—so it must be so. In my rage I banished you to hell. But I am just; in time I would have righted the wrong done you. Besides, you can be useful."

"*Great.*"

"You have touched me and made me human as well as goddess, while I have touched you and made you demon."

"I am as human as ever."

"Are you? You go to hell and return, you die and come back to life, and you know things you were never taught. You cannot be human, yet you are not a god, so demon you are."

Sandy thought her words over for a moment and reluctantly decided she had to be at least partially right—he was more than human, but he knew damned well he wasn't a demon. "All right, I'm not human, but what magical powers do I have?"

"Witches work magic by main force and mischance, magicians by trickery and illusion, sorcerers by knowing how to manipulate the laws of magic, and then there are those who work magic because it is inborn in them or they draw power from some deity. You are like to one of these, since in a way my power is your power. What I can do, you can do, if you but put your mind to it. Since I am immortal, so are you, though because of the humanity you still retain you also can die—and this you will do many times."

Sandy grimaced wryly, shrugged, and decided to be practical. "What about me? Can I go my own way now or are you going to tie me to your apron strings?"

Sandy's rueful tone shook the Goddess out of her blue mood and she gave a quiet laugh. "I learned my lesson well, my demon: to hurt you is to hurt myself. I'll not try to damn you again, but neither can I ignore you. Our fates are forever intertwined. We both must accept that. And we will be useful to each other—I need an agent among mortals and you will find you have gained many things beside immortality—things which will make you my deadly right hand."

The situation did not sit too well with Sandy. She seemed to be gaining the lion's share and he did not relish having to put up with her capricious and willful behavior forever, though he supposed he could have got stuck with somebody a lot worse. Grudgingly he said, "All right, I'll do your dirty work. I'm not qualified at sword-fighting or slinking around with cloak and dagger, but I'll do the best I can." He paused. "This doesn't mean I want to live cheek by jowl with you. If you just show up when you need me that will be enough; more than that will ruin my digestion—you make life too exciting."

"So be it," the Goddess said in a tone that was simultaneously eerie, sad, and smiling. "Here, these are yours," she added. The silver ring and the iron key on its silver chain were in her outstretched hand. "The ring is yours forever. The Ring of Uncertainty was forged long ago in the fires of eternity by Hudzevan the Smith. It changes realities, giving its wearer the ability to do the impossible. The talisman you may keep until it is time for you to pass it on. It is not yours to wield, but to hold until the rightful heir has need of it. I made it in the days when I was young to this world; it commands the power which is native to Zarathandra. I gave it three times: once to Arimithos, then to she who betrayed me, and finally to Idman and heirs of his flesh."

Sandy took the objects from her. The ring slid onto the little finger of his left hand as if it were glad to be back. The amulet he hung around his neck reluctantly. There was an uneasy feel to it, as if it just barely could stand his touch.

"The nearest outpost of the Rithian Empire is three days journey to the north," the Goddess said. "Follow Glupp—he will lead you there. Now let us have peace from each other for a while." As she said these last words, she swiftly faded from view and was gone—leaving not even a ripple in the air.

For a long while Sandy stared at where she had been, wondering about the odd tone in her last words. He had an idea it boded no good. He swore softly to himself when he had identified the tone in her voice that bothered him. She had sounded as if she were enjoying some private joke.

Sandy headed for the tent she'd created for him. First he would have some breakfast, which was a couple hours late if the sun and his belly were any indication, and mull things over in his mind. He was in no hurry to head north and needed to figure her out—she might not lie, but that didn't mean she told all the truth—not by a long shot.

Later, as he drank hot tea and nibbled on cold flat bread, he weighed things over in his mind. It was inescapable that he'd have to make the best of this world and the Goddess. He didn't have much choice. He trusted her as far as he could throw Glupp, but she was no Kels Zalkri and that was a big plus. He remembered the wine and resentment smoldered in his heart for a moment—he didn't mind being seduced, he just didn't like it being so underhanded.

Still he'd have a hard time saying *no* if she came to him as a bawd in heat—the musky smell and soft sinuous feel of her was enough to ...

Sandy frowned, thinking back to the episodes in hell. Had he been led on? Or had she really been surprised? He made an obscene comment and thought some more. He was still thinking about it when he and Glupp headed north.

The Goddess sat cloaked in shadow, brooding over her relationship with Sandy. She didn't know whether she hated him for being what he was, or both hated and loved him for the same reason. She deeply resented having to seduce him and having no choice in the matter—full power should have been hers by right and not by conquest. She'd seduced him with her eyes open and had enjoyed it, but she wished it had been just because he brought her to heat.

A long buried memory rose from the depths of her mind and she suddenly smiled and sat up straighter. There *was* a way to break the bond and her dependence on him. It would take time and would be dangerous and difficult to bring about, but it was possible. In the meantime it would be fun dallying with him, both to refresh her power and to enjoy fully her rights.

Sandy would prove useful while she waited the opportunity to end their mutual dependence. There were evils which needed cleansing from the face of Zarathandra, lives to be changed and redirected, and enemies who had wronged her and now must feel her wrath. He would be her right hand which would bring these things about. The Rithian army would make him into a great warrior—there was not a better fighting force on her world. A slightly malicious smile brightened her features as she thought about his reaction at being impressed into the Rithian army. The experience would do his soul good.

DONALD AAMODT works for the Social Security Admin-istration, and recently moved back to Minnesota from Maryland. He lives with his wife, two daughters, a cat, and a dog in the far northern outliers of Minneapolis. A NAME TO CONJURE WITH is his first novel.

Mr. Aamodt writes, "I was born in Minnesota on May 17, Norway's equivalent of the Fourth of July, so every year Norwegians around the world make me feel good as they celebrate my birthday. By hook and by crook I graduated from the University of Minnesota in only seven years—tak-ing a forced vacation in the army between entering and graduating. (My military time was very uninteresting except for the plane crash I survived.) I majored in anthropology and history while in college, especially enjoying the hard-digging archaeological summer projects (with especial fond memories of a site located between two breweries)."